the
Robin
on the
Oak
Throne

the
Robin
on the
Oak
Throne

NEW YORK TIMES BESTSELLING AUTHOR

K.A. LINDE

Entangled Publishing, LLC
644 Shrewsbury Commons Ave., STE 181
Shrewsbury, PA 17361
rights@entangledpublishing.com

Red Tower Books is an imprint of Entangled Publishing, LLC.

Visit our website at www.entangledpublishing.com.

Edited by Liz Pelletier and Sylvan Creekmore
Cover design by LJ Anderson and Bree Archer
Edge design by Bree Archer
Case design by Elizabeth Turner Stokes
Case image by Tithi Luadthong/Shutterstock
Endpaper original illustration by Melanie Korte
Interior map design by Amy Acosta
Interior map image by FrankRamspott/Gettyimages
Interior formatting by Britt Marczak
Interior images by Maresam/Gettyimages, steved_np3/Gettyimages,
Andrey_KZ/Gettyimages, ArtDiktator/Gettyimages, Antonel/Gettyimages,
igorr1/Gettyimages, Cattallina/Gettyimages

HC ISBN 978-1-64937-852-1
Ebook ISBN 978-1-64937-463-9

Manufactured in the United States of America
First Edition June 2025

10 9 8 7 6 5 4 3 2 1

To the girls who fell for the crown
before the prince.

The Robin on the Oak Throne is a tale of monsters, mystery, and romance. However, the story includes elements that may not be suitable for all readers. Combat, violence, sex, drug and alcohol use, sex work, and gang violence are depicted. Abuse, genocide, colonization, infertility, and assault that is physical and sexual in nature are discussed. Readers who may be sensitive to these elements, please take note, practice your magic, and prepare to take the Oak Throne...

PART I

BELTANE

Chapter One

Tromping through wet pastureland in high heels was a crime against humanity—unlike the crime Kierse was about to commit. She stepped out of the squelchy green grass and onto the ancient, graveled walkway with a sigh of relief. New York City hadn't prepared her for acres of empty farmland on the outskirts of Paris or otherwise.

She lifted her dark eyes to what lay at the end of her trek: the magnificent Versailles gardens. The greenery was bracketed by twin towering fountains boasting statues of the gods mounted on gilded horses. A long grass promenade cut between the fountains with bonfires igniting the night and revealing the entrances that led deeper into the wooded grounds. On the top of the hill, in all its splendor, was the Palace of Versailles.

Kierse could only imagine what it looked like at the height of King Louis XIV's reign. Tonight, it was teeming with both humans *and* monsters for the annual Beltane festival. A party to which Kierse hadn't *exactly* been invited.

Not that that had ever stopped her. There were always entrances and exits for a clever little thief. And having multiple exits was thieving rule number one.

But for now, she was just a girl blending in with the crowd in a pink satin slip dress with a thigh-high slit, her dark hair piled on the top of her head and her makeup light like spring. No one paid her any mind as she snagged a glass of champagne off of a human waiter's tray and navigated the grounds.

Kierse had one mission today—steal a bracelet from the Queen of the Nymphs.

Step one: get an invitation into the palace.

Well, that was the easy part.

She'd already picked her mark as she ascended the stairs to the promenade. A group of female nymphs traipsed around a bonfire in nothing but tiny scraps of dresses, little purses at their hips, and flower crowns. They were almost all shorter than Kierse with a kaleidoscope of hair color and wide, slightly unnatural eyes. The few horned male nymphs lounged on the other side of the fire, shirtless in white linen trousers.

Kierse bumped into a nymph with vibrant magenta hair as she passed, sloshing champagne everywhere.

"Oh! Pardon," Kierse said by way of apology.

The nymph spit rapid French in Kierse's direction, and while the girl was distracted, Kierse slipped the crisp card out of her bag. She discreetly moved the invite to her purse, waving her other hand to indicate she didn't understand.

The nymph laughed at her lack of comprehension and returned to the festivities. A similar interaction back home could have ended in disaster. But the rest of the world hadn't suffered the way that New York had during the Monster War. Back home they were four years past the war and just coming to the other side of things. Here, when the monsters had stepped into the light, the humans had made deals with them before it devolved so drastically.

Tonight, phoenixes controlled the flames of the bonfires that nymphs deftly jumped over, performing their fertility rites. Mer lounged in fountains, and shifters jumped in and out of their animal forms at will over the hedges and into the tree line. Humans drank champagne and mingled with vampires and werewolves and an incubus/succubus pair.

Laughter rang out.

Lips locked.

Revelry ensued.

All excellent cover for Kierse's plan. She ditched her champagne flute on a table, thankful it had helped her with thieving rules three and four: distraction and sleight of hand.

She palmed the heavy cardstock invitation gilded with the sun king's symbol, granting access into the palace proper. Step one complete.

Step two: get inside the palace.

Kierse filed into the line behind a shuffling goblin. He passed off his invitation. The troll bouncer scanned it and then nodded, allowing him access. He repeated the process with Kierse's stolen invite. Then she was breezing through the doors and inside.

Her breath caught at the sheer magnitude of the place. It didn't matter how much time she'd spent memorizing the original blueprints or the hours engaged on a tour earlier in the week. She would never get used to the display of wealth. There was money, and then there was the magnitude of this place in all its extravagance.

Kierse turned off the part of her brain that calculated the cost of everything. The answer was unfathomable. She wasn't here to steal just anything. From here, she needed to get into the queen's chambers. Despite modern adjustments to the over seven-hundred-thousand-square-foot palace, the rooms that the current queen resided in had been the same for hundreds of years.

Thankfully, Kierse had perfect cover. Every attendee had the option of meeting with the queen publicly. She would be in the throne room receiving guests until midnight, when the ball officially began. It was one of the new customs she had instituted when she'd reclaimed her ancestral land. These woods had been home to the dryads long before humans had built on the property. The queen was so beloved that she'd had other monsters rally to her side to reclaim the forest and place her on the throne of Versailles.

And honestly, good for her. Kierse could appreciate a woman who could take back what was rightfully hers. It was a process that Kierse was still working on for herself. Especially considering how her life had been turned upside down last winter.

Five months ago, she had learned she had magic, stolen a spear straight out of Celtic myth, and discovered she was part of a race of ancient Fae—a will-o'-the-wisp. The last wisp in existence. All while falling for the dark warlock who had upended her life—Graves.

The same person who had lied to her, withheld her history, and broken her trust.

So she'd left New York to find answers that didn't come with strings attached. While she missed the city, her family...and even Graves, she wasn't ready for that reunion.

She didn't have time to think about Graves. He was a problem for another day. Right now came step three, the tricky part: sneak into the queen's rooms.

Kierse extricated herself from the flow of people heading toward the receiving room. When she came upon the next enormous staircase, she waited until the pair of goblin guards were distracted by a group of werewolves to slip past and up the stairs. Her feet were feather light as she crept along the deserted upper level, toward the private quarters. Her heart beat a staccato rhythm against her chest, and an old, familiar smile graced her features.

It wasn't a natural smile. It was her *wrong* smile. The one that said she *liked* the thieving. The danger, the suspense, the act of doing something she wasn't supposed to do.

It sure helped that she was damn good at it. She wouldn't go as far as to say the best in the business, but her old mentor, Jason—may he rot in hell—had been the best in New York, and she'd ended up better than him.

Now to get that bracelet and get out of there. Then she could happily return to Dublin, where Gen was safely tucked away, working on their next fruitless mission into the Irish countryside.

Kierse blew out an exasperated breath as she hurried down the crisscrossed hardwood floors. The hallway was white and narrow with arched windows looking out across the grounds to the left opposite a series of closed wooden doorways. The rooms she glimpsed weren't decorated to the same picturesque standard she'd seen on the tour earlier that week. Instead, she found peeling antique wallpaper, furniture covered with white sheets, and even empty rooms with exposed wires. They were in sharp contrast to the magnificent Hall of Mirrors, the carefully restored display of original bedrooms, and thousands of priceless works of art.

It made the palace feel more real than myth. Much like everything else in her life.

Following the blueprint in her mind, she turned down an empty servant hallway. Thankfully, most of the workers were busy with the rest of the party. Then her enhanced Fae hearing picked up the sound of voices up ahead.

Kierse cursed, backtracked a few steps, and slid behind a large, floor-length curtain. She held her breath as two female voices approached and then passed her, speaking in hushed French. She'd learned a few passing words before she'd made the trip, but they certainly weren't sufficient to follow this conversation.

When the coast was clear, Kierse eased back out and hastened down the rest of the hallway, nearly to her destination. She peered around the corner and found two guards standing in front of the queen's chambers. Same as when she'd slipped away from her group on the tour—they'd taken the queen's bedchamber off the official route now that the palace was occupied once more. Lucky for her, she wasn't going in through the front door.

Kierse retrieved her tools, delved into her wisp magic, and manipulated time. From one breath to the next, the world slid into slow motion. The gold of her magic floated around her as she darted to the door adjacent to the queen's rooms and got to work with her lockpicks. An easy click of the lock later, she pushed into the room and closed the door firmly behind her. She released her magic, letting everything come back into focus.

Her wisp magic was something she was still getting used to, but her slow motion had always been part of her. The little edge that she used to get herself in and out of bad situations. It was the newer magic that she was still wrangling. Like wards.

She pressed her hand to the door, closed her eyes, and pushed her intent into the door. A trickle of power rushed into the frame. She shivered at the release. That would act as a trip wire for at least the next hour. If anyone walked through this door, she would know to use another exit.

Praying she wouldn't need to, she hurried to the balcony window and slipped through it into the cool spring air. The party didn't wrap around to this side of the palace, so the grounds were empty of witnesses. Clouds hung heavy on the horizon, promising rain. She needed to be done before it reached her.

She judged the distance to the next balcony with unease. Before the spell that hid her true nature had been removed, revealing her Fae heritage — pointed ears and all — Kierse never would have attempted this. And though she'd gotten over her fear of heights before — thanks to a quick shove from Jason and a swift plummet to the ground below — she didn't particularly want to test a three-story drop. But with her new magic came increased sensory awareness, quicker reflexes, and strength. Not that she was 100 percent confident on using any of these new skills, but tonight she'd have to make it work. Because a human wasn't going to make this jump.

Good thing she was no longer human.

Kierse winced at that. She still identified as human, having spent the last twenty-five years thinking she was one. Thinking otherwise sat wrong with her. At least she'd learned enough magic to glamour her pointed ears back into the rounded ones she'd had most of her life. It was useful on missions where she needed to blend in, but sometimes she liked to wear the glamour just to feel more like herself.

She slipped off her heels, leaving them hidden on the balcony, then hiked up her skirts and scrambled onto the iron balustrade. She hissed as the iron touched her bare skin. It didn't incapacitate her like the faerie tales had made it seem like it would, but it also wasn't comfortable.

"Here goes nothing," she said.

With a spring, she jumped, reaching out for the enormous lantern suspended between the two balconies. She caught it and swung back once, her muscles protesting the strain. Then on her forward swing, when her momentum was at the right angle, she released. She barely held back a scream as she launched, landing in a roll on the next balcony. She heard a rip from her dress. *Fucking great.*

Kierse stood on shaky legs. Well, she'd made it.

She dusted off her dress and inspected the rip. It had only made the already high slit slightly obscene. This was why she wore practical clothing when she broke into places, but there hadn't been another choice for this job. And now there wasn't time to deal with it.

After a quick listen at the door, she pushed into the queen's opulent chambers. Everything was sixteenth-century chic, à la King Louis XIV, with patterned armless chairs and an impressive four-poster bed with gauzy white curtains obscuring it from view. Kierse strode across the antique rugs and to a door at the back of the room. Her contact had told her exactly where the bracelet would be. She felt her thieving smile return as she swung open the door and revealed the safe behind.

Nothing fancy, but it didn't need to be. Kierse inspected the wards written around its edges—fleur-de-lis inside that illusive language she always felt hovered at the edge of her understanding. The magic was old—a warlock had put these wards in place a long time ago. Not that a magic's age affected Kierse's ability to bypass it.

Kierse's main magical ability was absorption. Magic didn't affect her unless she took in *way* too much magic at once. Which meant the wards weren't a problem, and she could crack a lock like this in her sleep.

The safe was older than the warding, which always worked in her favor. She pressed her ear to the safe door, listening to the tumblers as she put together the code. Then she grinned devilishly as she turned the dial one last time and the whole thing popped open.

"Excellent," she breathed.

Inside was an assortment of sparkling jewels all encased in lush gold and silver settings. It was a smaller collection than she'd been anticipating. Probably just what the queen wore on the regular—not the state jewels.

The bracelet she was after was goblin-made with an amethyst at the center of the silver filigreed band. It should have been here amidst the jewelry. While there was every other manner of gemstone, there wasn't a single amethyst bracelet in sight.

"Fuck," she hissed.

A goblin back in Dublin had assured her it was in the queen's vault and that no one else they'd hired had been able to access it. If she could steal it, he'd give her a coin to access the goblin market. A coin she desperately needed. Part of her had known that all of this trouble meant the bracelet was far more valuable than what the goblin was offering in exchange, but

she figured wiping the smug smile off of his face would be worth it. Except…
it wasn't here.

Everything had gone right, and yet there was no bracelet. Where the
hell could the queen be keeping it? She scoured the safe one more time,
testing for a false back or hidden compartments, but no amount of looking
would make the bracelet appear. With another curse, she sealed up the safe
and made a quick sweep of the queen's rooms, but there didn't appear to be
any other safe inside her chambers. There was likely another vault deep in
the heart of the palace hiding the rest of her jewels, but that was an entirely
different sort of mission. The kind Kierse would need a great deal more
planning to attempt.

"Fuck," she repeated as she backtracked to the window.

She made the return jump to the lantern, and her hand caught on the
edge as she moved forward. She withheld a cry as it split open. At least
she'd judged the trajectory better this time and landed on her feet on the
neighboring balcony. Her palm was only bleeding a little, but still, she
scoured the room until she found a handkerchief in a dresser drawer and
wrapped it around her hand to stem the flow. Once that was finished, she
reclaimed her heels, pulled them back on, and went to listen at the door.

It was silent, save for the two guards she had already accounted for. With
a sigh, she pushed into slow motion and hustled back into the hallway. The
guards didn't even turn in her direction as she bypassed them. As soon as
she was out of sight around a corner, she dropped out of slow motion with
a huff. Her thoughts were locked on the bracelet and what she was going to
have to do to acquire it now.

Then a vampire guard strode out of an alcove, fangs extended. A girl in
a low-cut blue dress giggled behind him, trying to pull him back into their
liaison. His nostrils flared before his eyes widened at the sight of Kierse.

The cut on her hand. Shit.

He barked at her in French.

"I…" she said in panic. She started to backtrack, but there were guards
in the other direction as well.

"Wait, stop," the man said, switching to English.

This would have been a good time for the rest of her new wisp powers
to kick in. The powers she currently *didn't* have but research said wisps were
capable of. While she had time manipulation, absorption, glamours, and an
affinity for finding treasure—which amounted to the ne'er-do-well thief
variety of wisp magic—she was still missing magical intuition, pixy lights,

portaling, and persuasion. Her ancestors had definitely been using the latter to lure people off their paths and manipulate them to a different course in all those old folktales. But she had spent all spring fighting with her powers and had come to the conclusion that either she couldn't access them...or she didn't have them. Since she was in dire straits with this vampire and they still didn't manifest, she was going to go with the latter.

Which meant Plan B. Kierse could either play the stupid party guest or go for thieving rule number two: run. Running usually felt like the better option, but she didn't have enough safe exits.

As the guard approached her, she made her choice. She put her hand to her chest and released a sniffle. "Thank God, I found you."

Confusion flickered across his face. "You're not supposed to be in here. You need to return to the party."

"I got turned around," she lied. "I'm not even sure how I got through here. And then I fell and cut myself." She held her bleeding hand toward the vampire with a little tremble. "I would be so grateful if you could help me."

She batted her eyelashes and tried to lay it on thick. She could act so long as she didn't have to hold onto it for long. Stealth had always been a better option.

His eyes darted down to her hand, and then he hastily retracted his fangs. After clearing his throat, he said, "This way."

He grasped her arm and propelled her down the hall.

"Wait, I — " she began.

Then a man rounded the corner ahead of them and said in a smooth voice, "I've been looking everywhere for you."

A chill ran up her back as she promptly froze. The guard stuttered in shock at the sight of the man dressed in a pitch-black suit. His midnight-blue hair was artfully pushed off of his angular face, and his gray eyes held the power of thunderstorms. He was easily the most beautiful nightmare Kierse had ever seen.

"Graves," she whispered.

"Unhand my wife."

Chapter Two

*W**ife.*
Had he just said wife?

Graves held a gloved hand out to her. "Shall we?" The tilt of his lips said he knew exactly what she thought of the title he'd bestowed upon her. But she was smart enough to take the out he was offering.

"Husband," she spat back as she dropped her hand into his.

His dangerous smile sent her stomach tumbling.

It was unfortunate that she was still furious with him for his deceptions, because when those stormy eyes trained their full attention on her, passion and longing and anger mingled together in her core. Heat like a furnace came off of him in waves. Her brain told her that was just the force of his magic, but it was hard not to feel the embers spark to life between them.

"Miss me?" he teased in his crisp British accent.

She tipped her chin up, refusing to let him think he rattled her. "Ever so much."

He lifted her hand to his mouth and placed a kiss full of possession on her knuckles. Sparks turned to flames, licking up her wrist, elbow, shoulder, until her chest was flushed and warm. His eyes dipped briefly to her low neckline and then dragged up her neck to her equally warm cheeks. The fire in his gaze made her swallow.

"Monsieur," the vampire said with a practiced bow. "I'm required to take her to security for trespassing."

Graves's attention snapped to the guard. His expression turned on a dime to severe and merciless. He twisted into the monster she'd met all those months earlier when she'd been tasked to break into his library and steal a ring. A job that should have been impossible, but thanks to her absorption magic, she had succeeded in bypassing his wards where others had failed, putting a target on her back. Instead of killing her, Graves had offered Kierse a job, propelling her life on a whole new trajectory.

Looking at him now, she couldn't see anything other than this cruel monster who radiated sinister energy. Except that wasn't who Graves had been to her. For a time, she'd even thought that she could read him when no one else could. How wrong she had been.

"Did I ask for you to speak?" Graves demanded.

The vampire took a step backward, realizing his error. The girl in the alcove melted into the shadows. Just another day with volatile monsters.

Graves dismissed them both. He drew Kierse against him, slipping an arm around her waist and pulling them nearly flush. Her head felt dizzy, and her heart raced at the contact.

She wanted to pull away.

She wanted to stay there forever.

Then all thought fled as he dipped his head down and nipped at her neck, leaving a mark that said *mine, mine, mine.*

The hold he had on her felt like a vise. She breathed in the scent of his magic—leather and fresh parchment. The first time she'd ever been able to access her magic and scent his, she'd thought he smelled like the books from his holly library, but now she could distinguish the two. It was distinctly and specifically Graves in every way.

"Play nice," he teased as his nose brushed her earlobe.

She nearly jerked back at those words. Her anger flaring at his fucking audacity. "Graves," she snarled.

"I love my name on your lips."

She retreated from his hold to see his mocking smile. "I bet you do."

"Monsieur," the vampire tried one more time, a note of desperation in his voice.

Graves's magic heated the air. "Don't bother us again."

He shifted his weight and directed her down the hall. She seethed as he extricated her out of the situation. She was about to open her mouth when Graves wrenched open a door and all but shoved her through it. The door banged shut behind him. He flicked on a light to reveal a storage closet and then fixed his hard gaze on her.

Air hung heavy between them. His mask of fury still clung to his features as if he had unlearned how to soften for her. For a span of a moment, she wasn't sure if he was going to knock her out or slam her back into the door and kiss her.

She broke free of his trance. "What the fuck are you doing here?"

Graves straightened to his considerable height. He looked ready to spit vitriol, but he was as poised as ever. "I could ask you the same question, Miss McKenna."

Kierse forced herself steady at that name. He hadn't called her by her last name in ages, and she wasn't prepared to have gone from the nickname *Wren*—his partner, a name that meant she belonged to him, the source of his own destruction—to this. Let alone from *wife* back to acquaintances... business partners.

"Don't *Miss McKenna* me."

"What would you prefer me to call you, then?"

She narrowed her eyes. "Nothing."

"I don't believe you." He brushed a lock of her dark hair out of her face, and she nearly groaned as her body betrayed her.

She wanted Graves. She had wanted him almost as soon as she had met him. Known he was beautiful and dangerous, and fallen into him like a drop of water in the ocean. But wanting him didn't mean she trusted him, and she didn't know how to move forward without that.

So she pulled back and said, "You shouldn't be here."

He waved a hand around the closet. "No. I certainly had other plans tonight than to be stuck in a broom cupboard."

"You're the one who stuffed me in here."

"You were *caught*," he snarled like it was an offense.

And it was. After all, she prided herself on her stealth.

"I was doing fine before you interfered."

He leaned back against the doorframe with that damn smirk on his lips. "You could simply say thank you."

"I can handle myself."

"Of that I'm certain," he said with bite.

"What are you even doing here?" she asked again in exasperation.

"I was invited."

"Invited," Kierse scoffed. "There's no way in hell that you would *accept* an invitation to a party like this without reason."

She reassessed him. Graves was a master warlock with the ability to read the immediate thoughts of anyone he touched—except Kierse. He used that magic to make his business a network of secrets and blackmail to shape the world around him. If he was in Versailles on business, then he was here to get information.

"Who exactly do you want answers from?"

"Currently? You," he purred, stepping into her orbit and tilting her off axis. "If your assessment of me is that I'm here on business, then should I expect that you are here to steal something?"

Her eyes locked onto his, and she knew. In his five-month absence, she'd tried to imagine that Graves wasn't trailing her every move. That she was really on her own as she had asked to be. But no, of course not. She knew exactly how he worked. It shouldn't have surprised her. And yet…

"You knew I'd be here."

He slid gloved hands into his pockets as if he had not a care in the world. Answer enough. She wanted to swear at him, but arguing was futile. He would always think he was in the right. Wasn't that part of the problem?

"Whatever you're planning, it isn't going to work."

"Why do you think I'm planning something?" Kierse asked.

"Because you're *always* planning something." His words were sharp, but his eyes were amused. As if she was unaware that he understood her as well as she had believed she understood him.

"Pot meet kettle." She pushed against him, reaching for the doorknob.

"Your skirt is ripped," he said. "There's dirt under your nails. One knee is red. Your hair is askew."

"So?" she countered.

He reached up and moved a piece of her hair back into order. His finger lingered on the visibly round ear as if he was trying to see through the glamour to the pointed Fae ear.

"You've already stolen what you were here for, haven't you?"

She released a harsh sigh. "It wasn't there," she finally admitted.

"And what was it?"

She ground her teeth together. "As if you don't already know."

"Does it please you to think I am omniscient?"

"I bet it pleases you."

His smile was feral. "I never know what *you* are thinking."

"Lucky me." Kierse glanced away. What was the point of hiding it from Graves anyway? Maybe he knew of another place where the bracelet might be kept. His magic *was* knowledge, after all. If only every bit of it didn't come with a price.

But she needed that bracelet. She'd been working all spring on a way to get into the market. This was the only opening.

"A goblin-made bracelet," she finally said. "Silver with an amethyst at the center."

Graves's eyes lit on her. After a beat of silence, he began to laugh.

Kierse put her back up. "What's so fucking funny?"

"Even you could not have succeeded."

"Why?"

"Because, little thief, Queen Aveline is *wearing* that bracelet tonight."

Chapter Three

Graves made it seem like a problem that the queen was wearing the bracelet. But it wasn't a problem.

It fixed everything.

"Even better," she said.

Then she jerked the door open and strode out.

Graves was hot on her heels as she navigated the never-ending corridors. "You cannot think you'll take it from her."

Kierse smirked at him. "And why not?"

"She's one of the oldest living dryads, and you are in her domain. She is queen of this domicile."

"And tonight is the night where every person at the party can have an audience with her. Which includes me."

Graves shot her an exasperated look. "An audience is not a private matter. It is in front of the entire court."

"Are you questioning my skills?"

"Not at all," he assured her. "But you'll never get close enough."

Kierse ignored him as she trotted down the last set of stairs that led to the receiving room. Midnight was approaching and with it, the end of the public audiences and the beginning of the ball. She had to get to the queen before that happened.

A pair of guards stepped toward her with menacing glares but backed off at the sight of Graves. Well, at least his threatening energy worked in her favor.

She moved into the dwindling line that led to the throne room. But Graves grasped her elbow and jerked her out of it.

"This is reckless even for you," he argued.

She sighed. "Look, you aren't even supposed to *be* here. I told you that I'd come back to New York when I was ready. I don't know what part of that you don't understand. I don't need your help."

"As flattered as I am that you think that I came all the way to Paris just for you," he said with a pointed look, "you needed my help to extract you from that guard."

She snorted. "Like I couldn't have handled that on my own."

"Without leaving a trail of bodies…"

"What were you even doing in that hallway anyway?"

"Lurking."

She rolled her eyes. "Can you ever give a straight answer?"

"Can you?"

"I don't have time for this…for *you*," she said, pulling away from him. "Contrary to what you think, I'm not acting reckless. I'm going to go scope out the room and the queen and form a plan from there. You can stay here—out of my way."

But he grasped her elbow again before she could leave. "I am trying to keep you from getting thrown into jail."

She laughed. "Like a jail could hold me."

She'd broken out of a number of them long before she'd known she had magic. Growing up as a prodigy to a New York thieving master sometimes came in handy. As long as she didn't think too long about the abuse she'd endured from Jason.

Graves looked her up and down as if reassessing her. She knew that look. He sized people up the way she evaluated objects. He was determining how much he could get out of her if he helped keep her out of a jail cell.

She jabbed her finger into his chest. "Don't look at me like that."

His gloved hand slid from her elbow to her wrist, tugging her palm flat against his chest. "Like what?"

She swallowed at the nearness. "Like you're trying to determine my value."

"We both already know what your value is." His other hand slipped around her waist, drawing her nearer. Her breath hitched as his head dipped to her ear again. "Priceless."

"Graves," she warned.

"I can help you."

Her eyes lifted to his mercurial gray orbs. "How?"

"I am…acquainted with the queen. Once she is in the ballroom, I can get you close enough."

"For what price?"

"Must there be a price between us?" he asked almost gently.

For a second, he seemed earnest. As if he wanted to help her out of the goodness of his own heart. A magnanimous gesture for the man—monster—who had never done anything magnanimous.

Somehow that made her more suspicious.

There was an angle here that she wasn't seeing. That was how it always was with Graves. She didn't miss the fact that he hadn't answered what he was doing here in the first place. Obviously he'd known she was going to be here, but he'd known she was in Dublin, too. He could have flown across the pond at any point to interfere in her life. What was different about Paris? Why accept this invitation?

And yet she couldn't deny that she and Graves worked well together. The weeks leading up to the winter solstice had proven that. She recalled hours spent locked away in the Holly Library going over blueprints and vault sequences. The feel of his body pressed against her whether in training or sex. All of it had been exquisite.

She cleared the image that conjured of her pinned against the stacks. Not helpful.

"Just spit it out," she said instead.

"You're going to dislike this enough for that to be the cost anyway," he said as he drew her out of their nook.

She blinked at him. "What does that mean?"

"Smile," he commanded. She bared her teeth at him, and he chuckled. "There you are."

A clock chimed midnight as one wall of the throne room opened to a magnificent ballroom straight out of a faerie tale. Everything was gilded and marble and towering chandeliers. It was almost too beautiful to look at let alone hold hundreds of people while they drank, danced, and celebrated.

Graves led Kierse into the ballroom, and her first look at Queen Aveline took her breath away. She was solid as the tree she derived her name from, with ample cleavage spilling out of her ornate golden gown. Her skin was as brown as tree bark, and her eyes were the vivid blue of a spring. She had a defined dimple when she smiled at her adoring subjects. The layers of her dress accented the curve of her waist but didn't hide her full figure and round stomach. And there on her wrist was the goblin bracelet.

"We should—"

"Not yet," Graves interrupted.

"But—"

"Dance with me."

Her eyes widened as she watched couples join the dance floor. "I don't know how to dance."

"I'm good enough for the both of us."

She shot him a look. "So modest."

He smirked. "If you keep complimenting me, I'll think that you like me."

She clenched her jaw to keep from sputtering in indignation. He took her hand and twirled her in place. At the end of the turn, Graves drew her into him, positioning their arms properly—his against her waist, hers on his shoulder. Then their hands met and she swallowed, looking up into his eyes.

"Ready?"

And before she could even think to say "*no,*" he drew her out onto the dance floor. They merged with the crowd already moving in time to the classical music played by the musicians against one wall. Her back was stiff through the first few steps. She was thinking too much, and she knew she was thinking too much. She was a thief. Her footwork was impeccable, but this was completely out of her repertoire.

"Relax," he said.

Easy for him to say. He clearly *was* incredible at this. It shouldn't have surprised her, considering he was several hundred years old and had grown up in a time when this was standard for the upper classes.

"Relinquish control," he coaxed. "Let me lead."

That was the problem. She didn't do well giving up control. And doing that around Graves had only ended in disaster.

But as he guided her around the sparkling ballroom, she could feel herself melt into him. He made the steps feel effortless. One dance turned into a second, slower number. He drew her in closer until she could breathe in the scent of him. Practically taste him on her tongue. It was too close, too much all at once. Being like this with him addled her senses.

She needed to regain the upper hand or she'd never survive him.

"The plan?" She forced the words out through her teeth.

He gave her a knowing look. "I'll make the introduction. You steal the bracelet."

"That simple? What part of it am I going to hate?"

"Can't ruin the fun," he promised.

They stepped off the floor, and as soon as they were separated, she inhaled sharply. There was still an inferno raging in her body at the feel of her hand clasped in his. Her cheeks flushed as she followed him through the crowd. She was irritated with herself for letting Graves steal that reaction from her body. He was the liar. He'd betrayed her. He shouldn't be able to elicit this response.

The queen sat on a gilded throne, watching the crowd with a smile on her round face. Guards stood on either side, and a group of simpering nymphs were seated around her, laughing and pointing out dancers.

When the queen's eyes found Graves, she tilted her head back and laughed. "Well, if this isn't a surprise."

She came to her feet, and all the other nymphs jumped up as well. She fluttered her fingers, dismissing them, and then gestured for the pair to come forward. Graves tucked Kierse into his side, and together, they approached the queen.

Kierse hadn't factored in that she was literally meeting a royal monster sitting on an actual throne. She wasn't usually dazzled by pretty much anything, but the queen was gorgeous and regal and daunting. When Graves drew her to a stop, Kierse forced herself back into her body and dipped into some sort of curtsy. Graves grinned at her before inclining his head at Queen Aveline.

"It's always a good day when I get to see you, Avie," Graves said with a charming smile.

"'Avie,'" the queen said with a laugh. "You haven't changed in all your years, you devil."

Graves took another step in. "I have, actually."

Queen Aveline looked between Kierse and Graves with a question in her blue eyes. "And who is this?"

"My wife," he said evenly.

Oh.

Well, no wonder he'd thought she wouldn't like this plan. The wife bit had gotten her out of one situation, but she hadn't intended to let him continue to use the incorrect moniker.

Still, the queen took her in at the word. Kierse had never felt so underdressed in her life. Her slip dress had been perfect for the outdoor Beltane festival but hardly felt fitting to meet a queen. There was no derision in her expression, though. Only appreciation.

"A wife," Queen Aveline whispered. "I am so rarely shocked at my age." Her eyes cut to Graves. "You? Married?"

"Allow me to introduce you to Kierse McKenna."

"My dear," the queen said.

"Your Majesty," Kierse said with another little bob.

"Oh, you must be something spectacular to have caught such a man."

Kierse met her gaze. "I generally find him to be the lucky one."

Queen Aveline smiled in amusement. "As you should." She gestured for

Kierse to come closer. "We're always the catch, aren't we?"

"I can hear you," Graves said with a laugh.

"I sure hope so," the queen said, turning to Graves and pointing a finger at him. "I don't have the time right now, but I must have the whole story. You cannot leave a single detail out. For instance, why does she not have a ring? I know you have many jewels in that old house of yours."

Graves flashed his teeth. "If only I could get her to wear one."

Kierse snapped her eyes to him. "I would wear one. You keep choosing incorrectly."

The queen laughed. "There you have it, Graves."

"Tell me what you would wear, my dear, and it shall be yours," he promised with an earnest expression on his sharp features.

"If I have to tell you, then you've lost the game."

"Noted," he said with a knowing smirk.

"Personally, I'm a fan of something understated," the queen said, enjoying the spectacle. She put her hand on Kierse's and winked. "Or a family heirloom."

Kierse looked at Graves and gestured to the queen as if to suggest he take her advice. She was purposely keeping the queen's attention on the scene they were making. Because while she and Graves were a good distraction, the sleight of hand she had to perform was next level. She'd already admired the bracelet while they'd been speaking, and once she got the clasp undone, the rest was easy.

Her heart was pounding so hard she was sure someone would discover her deception by its racing beat. She tucked the bracelet into her small bag with her pickpocketed invitation. Time to get out of there as fast as they could.

"Another day," Graves assured her. "Tonight you have your ball."

"Yes, yes," the queen said. "Are you in Paris long?"

"I have business tonight and then back to the city, I'm afraid."

"The city. As if there's only one."

"There's only one for me," Graves said with a shrug.

"Next time, then."

Graves kissed her hand and made their excuses. But Kierse didn't release her breath until they disappeared into the anonymity of the crowd.

"Nicely done," he said as he escorted her out of the ballroom, heading swiftly toward the nearest exit. His hand rested on the small of her back, directing her down another hallway away from a set of guards.

"How many exits do you know?"

His smile dropped her stomach. "All of them."

"Let me guess—you were here when it was built?"

He shot her a look that she interpreted to mean *yes*. Of course he had been.

They were nearly out of the palace when Kierse asked, "How long before she realizes?"

A cry went up behind them.

"Keep going," Graves said at the same time she hissed, "Don't look back."

Their eyes met, and they both smiled. Finally, they were on the same page.

Kierse forced her steps to stay even despite the fact that all she wanted to do was dash out of the palace. But no one knew that they'd stolen from the queen yet, and running would certainly give them away.

Footsteps pounded behind them, and a man yelled out a word in French.

Graves cursed under his breath and said, "Run."

Chapter Four

Kierse took off after Graves. She tapped into one of her new preternatural abilities—speed. Which, at that precise moment, she was grateful for.

Graves crashed through the palace side door that led back onto the grounds, startling a group of partygoers. Kierse followed as they dashed onto the wide gravel pathway deeper into the gardens.

"This way," he said.

She glanced over her shoulder. A few guards were chasing them. Many of them were monsters and certainly not slowing. She was glad for the head start, because she wasn't sure if she could outrun a vampire. She'd never exactly wanted to run the race to find out.

"We're never going to make it."

"We'll make it," Graves snarled.

They cascaded down a hill, hitting a speed she could hardly fathom. A few months ago, she would have killed for this ability.

Monsters had ruled her life ever since they'd come out of hiding fourteen years ago. She'd spent her young life abandoned to the streets by her father and then swept up into the thieving guild, when the monsters appeared. The vampire visionary Coraline LeMort was killed by a werewolf from an opposing faction, and her death sparked a decade-long Monster War. Millions of monsters and humans alike had been caught in the crossfire as they carved up New York City as their battleground. Those dark years had only ended with the signing of the Monster Treaty—a new set of laws that governed how monsters and humans would coexist.

And she had just broken the treaty...again.

She knew that she wasn't human this time when she broke it. It didn't make it any less likely that they'd kill her for stealing from their queen.

They barreled around the tree line and came upon a group of mer singing in the dragon fountain. Kierse clapped her hands over her ears to avoid the siren song. Graves jerked her the opposite direction, down a straight path toward a closed gate. A troll guard stood at attention as they approached. Trolls were generally unintelligent monsters, but what they lacked in brains they made up for in brawn. This one was enormous, with giant muscular arms and tree trunk legs. Her head was smaller than average and rested squarely on her shoulders. Between her beady, narrowed eyes and the sneer on her lips, she was terrifying.

Back in New York, trolls were allied with the gangs that crisscrossed Manhattan. The trolls controlled access to the subway stations, and you had to pay the toll to enter. She didn't think that was going to work here. Nor did she think she could take down a full-grown troll.

Graves seemed utterly unconcerned, which was so fucking Graves. The troll blinked down at him as he approached and pulled her hand back like she was going to swipe him aside. But Graves retrieved a slip of paper from his jacket pocket and offered it to the troll, speaking in French. The troll frowned in confusion at the paper Graves had handed her. It was always a moment of confusion when the subway trolls were paid off to let travelers through, as if unsure if the toll had been sufficiently paid.

After a pregnant pause, the troll frowned and said, "Expired."

"What?" Graves asked in confusion.

But the troll gave no response. She let the paper flutter to the ground and swung her mighty fist. It landed in Graves's stomach, sending him flying a half-dozen feet into the air.

"Fuck!" Kierse yelled as she hurtled toward the troll. "What did you give her?"

"A troll pass," Graves grunted from the ground.

"That didn't seem to work."

"Well aware," he said as he rolled over to his knees. "Goddamn it, I liked this suit."

The guards crested the hill behind them. They were running out of time. Kierse needed a strategy to deal with the massive mountain troll. She had been certain that she couldn't take her down, but with her new Fae abilities, was that true? Seemed like now was the time to test it. Her eyes darted up, up, up the enormous troll's back to the flag fluttering above her head, then down to the blocked gate behind her. She only had a few seconds. Time to improvise.

She took a running start and vaulted up the back of the troll, using her legs and meaty muscles as footholds and her shirt to climb. The disoriented and now infuriated troll leaned forward, making the hike up her back easier, especially in these stupid high heels. Just as the troll reached back to try to swipe her off, she grasped at the flapping banner, yanking with all her might and ripping the thing clear off of the pole. She dodged another swing and whipped the banner around the troll's neck. Digging her heels into the troll's shoulders, she pulled with all of her might, choking the giant beast.

"A little...help here," Kierse grunted.

Graves finally stood, dusting off his suit. "Looks like you have it."

The troll wobbled as air left her lungs. She began to topple forward, and Kierse jerked sideways so the monster fell into the giant gate, ripping it from its hinges and sending it screeching to the ground.

Kierse rode the troll to the ground, executing another dive roll to escape the worst of the fallout. Graves was there a second later with his hand extended to help her up.

"Nice work."

"You could have been useful," she said as they dashed out the now-open gate just as the guards approached.

"I thought you had it under control," he said with a smirk on his too-pretty lips.

Should she be upset that he'd left her to deal with it alone? Or happy that he trusted her enough to get it done without interfering? Why did *both* feel like the right answer?

They hit the main road, and a limousine screeched to a stop. Graves ripped the back door open, and Kierse tumbled into it. He followed, slamming the door and yelling, "Move!"

George, Graves's private driver, took off, leaving the guards in the dust. Kierse turned in her seat with a laugh to see the guards disappear into the night.

"They're going to follow the limo," she said. "We should ditch it and lay low."

"It's warded," Graves said.

"So...no one can get in?" she asked, jerking her eyes back to his face.

"It can't be tracked."

"You can do that?"

"So can you," he told her as he popped the button on his suit coat and peeled his gloves off, tossing them onto the seat between them. Her eyes went to his fingers. Long and slender, they had always made her think of a pianist's fingers, even though she knew he didn't grace the keys but turned the pages of books. With the gloves gone, she caught a glimpse of the holly vine tattoo snaking around his wrist. She'd seen the vines that wrapped his forearm, bicep, over his shoulder. Thorns digging into his skin like hands into the flesh of Proserpina in the famous Roman sculpture.

She cleared her throat. "I thought warding kept things out."

"Magic is about intent," he told her as he slipped out of his jacket. The tie went next, and he undid two buttons at his throat. "Wards work by pushing your magic and intent into an object. My intent could be to keep people from entering my home." He ripped out the cuff links and rolled the sleeves of his white button-up to his elbows before lifting his eyes to her. "Most of them."

She swallowed at the sight of his powerful forearms. Not to mention him so…undressed. On most men, it wouldn't be much to write home about, but Graves wasn't most *anything*.

She averted her gaze. "If your intent is to keep people from finding you…"

"Then people won't find me." He ran a hand through his midnight-blue hair. "At least, they won't find the car. It doesn't work on animate beings."

She'd learned much about her magic and lineage since leaving his home five months ago, in the wake of his betrayal. Still, five minutes alone in his presence and she was learning all new things. She wished the knowledge had all been as easy to acquire as this.

Graves had lied about who and what she was. And while he might have laid clues for who and what *he* was, she had still learned he was the Holly King, a primordial Celtic winter god, too late. Or that Lorcan, his enemy and the head of the Brooklyn gang, the Druids, was the Oak King.

The night it had all fallen apart, Lorcan had kidnapped her two best friends and forever family—Gen and Ethan—intending to force Graves to give up the spear and the sword, both powerful Celtic magical objects. An ancient battle between Oak and Holly had reignited, and in the end, the gods' magic had hit Kierse, nearly killing her.

Graves had valiantly attempted to save her life, but it hadn't worked. At the last second, Gen and Ethan had combined their fledgling magic into a triskel—a powerful bond between a wisp, High Priestess, and Druid. They'd healed her and together been forever changed.

When it was over, Lorcan won the sword, and Ethan had gone with him to study as a Druid. While Kierse left with the spear and fled to Dublin with Gen and the spear to get answers that didn't come with strings.

And now…the strings had followed her to Europe. Here she was with Graves, on *his* terms, all over again.

"Well, I guess you can drop me off at my hotel, then," Kierse said.

Graves didn't even look at her. He'd pulled a book out and was scanning the pages to recharge his powers. Each magical user renewed their powers differently—for Graves, reading, and for Kierse, it had always been stealing. While Graves seemed blue from their encounter, Kierse was revved up.

The goblin bracelet was in her possession, and she was one step closer to the market.

His lips pursed before he said, "You're not staying at a hotel with that in your possession."

She slid her eyes to him. "Where are we going then? Your place?"

"It's being renovated."

"Could you give me a straight answer?"

He flipped a page. "We're going to stay with a friend."

"You don't *have* friends."

He smirked at his book. "A longtime acquaintance."

"Why?"

"Why did you need to steal the bracelet?" he countered.

She narrowed her eyes in frustration. Around and around and around again. The same as it always was with Graves. He didn't give unless she did, and even then, only half as much. At first she'd liked the challenge, but now she saw it for the defense mechanism that it was.

"Never mind. You can let me out *here*," she said. "I can find my own way to the hotel."

Graves finally lifted his gaze to meet hers. She could still see the cruel warlock master in his expression. She hadn't been wrong that he'd had too long to get used to being closed off again. He didn't know how to soften on his own. And maybe it was for the better. He didn't need to soften for her, because she wasn't playing his games any longer.

"Her name is Estelle. She's the warlock of Paris."

Warlocks were territorial, so each major city only had one master. Graves was the one in New York City. Kierse had also met Kingston, who ruled London, and Imani in Chicago.

"They call her the Game Master. Her magic is primarily illusions, but it also shows up in other, more nefarious ways."

Kierse shivered at that. "And you want to go to her house?"

"Aveline won't cross her."

"And..."

"And I want you to steal something from her."

"You could have led with that back at the palace," Kierse said with an eye roll. "I knew there was a price for the audience with the queen."

Graves was silent a moment. "This isn't the price."

"No?" Kierse asked with derision. "So what would you call it? A favor?"

"A job."

She turned away from him and smoothed her dress. "Nothing is that simple with you."

"It's for the cauldron."

Kierse froze. The cauldron was one of the four magical objects of the gods—the Sword of Truth, the Spear of Lugh, the Cauldron of Dagda, and the Stone of Fal. Graves had spent a lifetime trying to acquire them all. At one point he'd had half of them in his possession, and now he had none. Getting the cauldron would be huge.

She met his gaze again. "She has the cauldron?"

"Yes."

She knew what this meant to him. He'd paid her ten million dollars to get the spear. He'd do *anything* for this. She didn't need the money this time, but the thrill of stealing something this powerful was too much for this thief to say no to.

"You could have just called."

He raised an eyebrow. "And you would have answered?"

"No." She smirked. "But I'll do this."

Chapter Five

The limo rolled to a stop in front of a distinctly Parisian apartment building with the quintessential white stone facing, flat roof, and black wrought-iron balconies. A designer wedding dress shop took up the windows for the shop on the first floor. Streetlamps dotted the expansive avenue, illuminating the empty sidewalk.

George hastened to open their door, knocking open a large black umbrella. Kierse took his hand as she stepped out onto the wet pavement with the umbrella open high above her. The sky had unleashed on their drive, but the rain was now a misty drizzle. Graves took the umbrella from George on his way out and held his arm out for her.

"Ready?"

Kierse lifted her chin, determined not to show an ounce of fear. She grasped his arm and let him guide her toward the awaiting door, where Graves punched in an entry code. When the door popped open, she entered a small black-and-white tiled stairwell with an antique wooden banister. Graves stepped in after her, dropping the wet umbrella into a basket.

"When Hausmann renovated Paris," Graves explained as they took the stairs, "he standardized the design of the new buildings so that the ground floor boasted shops, the second floor was lavish flats with the highest ceilings for the elite, the next two floors were smaller apartments, and the top floor was servants' quarters. Of course, now, the top floors are highly coveted for their views, but they're still more closets than apartments."

"So, Estelle is on the second floor."

"Well, she bought the entire building sometime in the early 1900s and renovated it to her liking."

Kierse shot him a look. "Like someone else I know."

"Who do you think she learned it from?"

Graves's brownstone on the Upper West Side was massive. He'd scooped up as much of the surrounding real estate as he could and connected the buildings. It was the only way he could have a personal library of its size in the middle of Manhattan.

At the second-floor landing, they stopped before massive double doors.

Kierse could immediately sense the door was warded against entry and great swaths of magic were being used within. Symbols had been etched into the doorframe in that same language that always hovered at the periphery of Kierse's mind. Permanent markings helped to hold the ward in place with less continued magic, which meant that these wards were strong. At the center of each of the wardings was a fleur-de-lis. The same symbol that she had seen guarding Queen Aveline's jewels in Versailles.

"She's allied with the queen," Kierse said.

"Indeed," Graves said as he reached forward and knocked.

"Won't she be upset that we stole from her majesty?"

"I believe she'll find it a very fun game."

The door swung inward, revealing a pale young woman in a white silk gown and elbow-length formal gloves. "My mistress has been expecting you."

"Of course she has," Graves said.

The woman's gaze shifted to Kierse. Her eyes were wide and piercing blue, and she had a prominent mole above her top lip. "She isn't sure about you."

"Well, I am," Graves said as he drew Kierse across the threshold.

Estelle's magic melted over her skin. For the briefest moment, she smelled fresh-baked bread and a hint of dry champagne before it let her pass into an incredible foyer complete with towering, coffered walls and decorative ceilings with ornamental molding. The herringbone-style hardwood floors crossed into a luxurious sitting area full of antique furniture. A gold mirror rested on the mantel over an original fireplace. The room was bedecked with a glittering crystal chandelier, and heavy embroidered drapery covered the array of French doors leading onto terraced balconies she had glimpsed from outside.

Kierse's entire job had been to steal from and for billionaires. She had thought nothing could be as ornate as Graves's brownstone, but compared to Estelle, Graves favored simplicity.

"Please have a seat and enjoy the refreshments. My mistress will be with you momentarily," the woman said before dipping into a curtsy and departing.

Kierse and Graves exchanged a look.

"The game begins when you enter," was all Graves said.

Of course. It always did.

Graves moved to the fireplace, seemingly inspecting the craftsmanship. Kierse circled the room and took up a spot by the farthest balcony. She pushed gently against the French door and found it opened on a breeze. If something went sideways with Estelle, this would be the easiest exit.

On a sideboard against one wall, tiered silver trays held little French delicacies. Gold-rimmed flutes of champagne sat on a matching silver platter. Kierse's stomach grumbled. She'd gotten so invested in her work that she'd forgotten to eat today, and with the adrenaline wearing off, she wished that she'd thought better of it. Not that she would indulge from an unknown warlock.

A few moments later, a slight woman entered wearing a sumptuous red gown that looked like it had walked straight off the runway. Her hips swayed as she moved, one foot in front of the other, on mile-high heels. Her cheeks were painted with rouge, lips a glossy cherry red, button nose highlighted, and her liner, lashes, and shadow only enhanced her arresting violet eyes.

"Welcome," she said with a melodic voice. "It's been too long, mon chéri."

She strode across the room and embraced Graves like long-lost friends. Graves's eyes rose to Kierse's over the top of Estelle's head. Kierse had to stifle a laugh.

"Whatever are you wearing?" Estelle asked.

Graves pulled back and adjusted his collar. "It's been a night."

"And you showed up without even a suit coat?"

"Do you want to hear about what happened in the limo?"

Estelle laughed. "You scoundrel."

Kierse gritted her teeth at the implication. She had been wondering why he'd disrobed in the car. But now his disheveled appearance made more sense with her own torn dress and his rumpled suit pants. They both looked like they'd been having a wild night.

"And you brought your…friend?" Estelle said.

Graves's answering smile made Kierse's knees weak. Fuck, he could be charming when he wanted to be.

"My wife," he corrected.

Kierse's stomach dropped. No matter how many times he told that lie, she would never get used to it coming out of his mouth.

"Wife," Estelle repeated, though there was no surprise in her voice.

"As I'm sure you have already heard."

"Good news travels fast," she said with a knowing smirk. "Now, you're being rude. Introduce me."

Graves took Estelle by the arm and brought her over to Kierse.

"Madame Estelle, might I introduce you to Kierse McKenna." His eyes lifted to meet Kierse's. "Kierse, my longtime friend, Estelle Beaumont."

"Pleasure to meet you."

"The pleasure is all mine," Estelle said. She leaned forward and kissed Kierse once on each cheek. "Anyone who can lock down the most formidable bachelor on either side of the Atlantic has my appreciation and condolences."

"'Condolences,'" Graves grumbled.

Estelle shot him a wry smile. "She has to put up with you."

Kierse snorted. "She knows the right of it."

"Will I get to hear the story of how you brought his heart back from the dead?"

"Is that what I did?" Kierse asked. She directed the question at Estelle but knew Graves would pick up that it was clearly intended for him. Kierse arched an eyebrow.

"Another time," Graves said. "That's not why we're here."

"No?" Estelle said with a soft laugh. "You didn't come to tell me the good news? I'm shocked." She put a hand to her chest. "Truly."

"You know why I'm here."

"You want to play a game," Estelle said with a smile.

"I'm already in one."

"If you brought your wife, then you're foolish indeed." She patted Graves's cheek once. "It doesn't suit you."

Kierse glanced between them. "How does that make him foolish?"

Estelle's smile turned deadly. For the first time, Kierse could see the power behind her Game Master title in her violet irises.

"Graves has played games with me across a century. He knows how the rules work. He knows how my magic works," she told Kierse. "Playing with him used to be more interesting."

"You mean when I won?" Graves teased.

Estelle shrugged. "It's not about winning or losing. It's about what you're willing to lose to play."

Kierse's head snapped to Graves. "What does she mean by that?"

"Graves has sacrificed many others to the game. You may be his wife, but for what he wants, I believe he'd sacrifice you, too. Am I right, mon chéri?"

"It depends on the price," he said, unconcerned.

"Graves," Kierse snarled.

Estelle smiled. "Are you going to tell me what you're here for, then?"

"We both know the answer to that."

"Yes, but we can only begin when you ask for what you want. You know the rules."

Graves's eyes cut to Kierse. "The cauldron."

Estelle grinned devilishly. "Ah, so it has reached your ears that it was found."

"That it's in your possession."

"And you want to play for it?"

He nodded. "Let's play an old familiar game, Estelle."

"Not you." Estelle's eyes cut to Kierse. "Her."

"Me?" Kierse asked, uncomprehending. "I am not here to play a game. I'm actually over games in general."

"She's not part of this, Estelle," Graves growled.

"She's very much a part of this. If she's here in my house…with you, then you knew it was a possibility. What would it hurt to have her play?"

Graves ground his teeth together. "I'm not willing to harm her."

"My games don't harm anyone."

His laugh was sardonic. "We've known each other too long for that."

"Surely you want to play," Estelle said, turning on Kierse. "You could win your beau his greatest prize."

"*I'm* the prize," Kierse argued.

"She is off-limits," Graves said. He moved between Kierse and Estelle. "I am not sacrificing Kierse to your machinations. She is much too precious for that. I will play the game, and I will win my reward."

"No," Estelle said with another cruel twist to her lips. "It's her or nothing."

"Then it's nothing," Graves said.

Estelle reared back in surprise. Kierse could see that she'd been certain that Graves would fold. That he would love nothing as much as his own pride and prize. But he'd gone against her script, proving to her that Kierse mattered to him and he wouldn't use her as a bargaining chip.

"This is your answer?"

"Yes," Graves said defiantly. "We will go if that is yours."

"Ah, you think me devoid of hospitality. You will stay the night." Estelle glanced between them in confusion. "If you would like."

Graves turned to Kierse and held his hand out. "Come along."

Kierse swallowed and then put her hand in his, letting him pull her against him. Her heart hammered in her chest, wondering if this had really been the right play.

"You will change your mind," Estelle said.

"Don't count on it," Graves told her.

Chapter Six

They remained silent as Estelle's servant escorted them to a small, grated elevator that whisked them to a higher floor, then led them down the hall to a wooden door.

"Your usual room," the woman said.

"Merci," Graves said. He pushed the door open for Kierse. "After you."

She stepped inside and found a grand guest suite overlooking the Eiffel Tower, complete with an adjoining bath and a four-poster bed.

Kierse hastily turned away from the bed as Graves shut the door and pressed his hand against it. A second later, the crush of magic around them diminished. Kierse gasped in a breath. She hadn't realized quite how oppressive it was until it was gone. The house was *dripping* in magic. Pervasive and all-consuming.

"Holy shit," Kierse said as she sank into a chair. "How much magic is she using?"

"Too much," Graves said. He shot her a wry look. "She's showing off."

"For you?"

"Me. You. It's all a bluster."

"She must be incredibly powerful," Kierse said.

"She would like you to think so." He swept his hand out, and for a second she could feel his magic wash over her and then disappear.

"Now who is showing off?"

"I don't want her to be able to listen in."

While Graves's main magic was knowledge, his secondary magic was noise distortion. Even another master warlock wasn't going to get through his magic to hear their conversation. Which was for the better. Since they were lying.

"That was quite a performance," Kierse said.

His expression remained hard as he looked at her, but she could see a question in those swirling irises. As if he wasn't quite sure whether she was complimenting him. "It went as planned."

"Stirring," she praised drily. "The way she was shocked that you'd risk your precious objects for a lover." Kierse almost laughed. Instead, she bit the inside of her cheek and glanced away, inspecting the room. "When we both know you wouldn't."

"Hmm," was all he said.

She flicked a glance at him and found him watching her. "What? Are you so surprised everyone knows you? I'm shocked you got away with a marriage ruse yet again. Perhaps it was just shocking enough to get her to believe it."

"Perhaps it was," he said stiffly. No expression change.

Kierse turned away again. No reaction from him shouldn't matter. She wanted to get the cauldron for the thrill of it. If it cancelled out her debt for his help with the bracelet, then all the better. In fact, maybe he'd be in *her* debt. Wouldn't that be a welcome change of pace?

"What did you see when you looked at her?" Graves asked.

"A woman no older than me. Mid-twenties at most, with dark hair down in waves around her shoulders, and violet eyes. She was wearing a red gown and gloves. Did she not look the same to you?"

"She's talented in hiding her appearance when she wants to. She usually has the violet eyes, but the gown was different. An expensive tiered pink thing that she used to wear back in the day, and fancy heeled shoes I'd recognize anywhere. Her hair was coiffed into this big elaborate…" He trailed off as he held his hands above his head for emphasis. "I wasn't sure how much of it was fake."

"I thought you could see through her illusions?"

Graves shrugged. "I can parse the truth from her magic when I touch it. For instance, I knew that the room wasn't a full falsity from the authentic fireplace. And I could tell her dress was false when she hugged me." His gaze swept over her. "But you couldn't see the shape of her illusions?"

"No. I could feel her magic, though."

"Interesting."

He said it like it was something she should be able to do. But she'd never been able to discern the nature of someone else's magic, just that they were using it. She was pretty sure that was part of the magical intuition that was on the other side of her wisp abilities.

"What game do you think she would have made me play if I had been willing or able?"

He shrugged. "Nothing you would have enjoyed. She uses her illusions to put people into difficult situations. She's very perceptive. Her secondary magic is reading emotions between people, and then she uses what she sees there to her advantage. Generally entangling them or making them face hard truths through some kind of trickery."

"If she can read emotions, then she would know we are not married," Kierse guessed.

Graves arched an eyebrow. "Are we not entangled?"

Kierse swallowed at the heat in those words. "That's a word for it."

He bridged the distance between them. The entire world suddenly seemed to drop away in his presence. His bare hand came up to brush aside a lock of her hair. His magic breezed through the glamour as he tucked the hair behind her faintly pointed ears with a smirk on his perfect lips.

His fingers dipped down her jaw and to the pulse in her neck. His hand wrapped gently around her throat as he had done that first night they had met. When he had been testing his powers to find out her ill intentions and found silence instead. He still couldn't discover what she was thinking with a touch of his hand, but that did not mean there were no clues.

"This heart beats for me."

Kierse wrenched herself free. A heavy breath escaped her. She had been trapped in those stormy eyes and felt adrift at sea, his touch a lifeline in an endless ocean. But it was a ruse. This wasn't real. Whatever he was doing was part of his games, and she didn't want to play.

"If all she needs is a beating heart, then we're fine."

Graves dropped his hand. "It's a secondary power," he said, unperturbed. "Powerful emotions swing in either direction, and she cannot tell the difference between contrived emotions and reality. Though she is better at it with people that she knows."

"Then I am safe," Kierse said.

"Indeed." Graves checked his phone for the time. "We'll begin shortly. I would like her to believe us sufficiently out of her hair."

"What are we going to do until then?"

Graves shot her a devious look. "We do have a bed. It would be a shame to waste it."

"Then go to sleep," she said.

"Not exactly what I had in mind," he said under his breath.

"Graves, could you be serious?"

"Who said I wasn't?"

In another life, she would have been able to read him and know what all this teasing meant. But it couldn't be genuine. Graves was lots of things—dangerous, secretive, charming, mysterious, disarming. What he wasn't was sincere or forthright or honest or, god help her, seductive. He'd never had to use wiles to get her to fall for him. In fact, the asshole that he was had done the trick.

They were so alike in so many ways. Both closed off and ruined from abandonment—her by her father when she was a child, him by basically every person who had ever trampled through his life. They'd had to claw their way through the dirt from their buried coffins to notoriety.

Maybe they'd been *too* alike, and that had been the problem.

"Let's review the plan," she said instead, turning her back on the rather inviting bed.

"Excellent suggestion," Graves said. He put his back against a wall, hands in his pockets. "Break out of our luxury suite."

"Easy enough."

"Locate the hidden room where Estelle keeps her prized possessions."

"One floor above us cloaked by illusion magic and warded. All of which I can absorb easily."

He grinned. "Collect the cauldron."

"You don't know if there's a vault or extra security?"

"The vault I'm not sure of, but security is handled," he said, checking his phone again. "Almost set on that front. I assume you can handle a vault by yourself."

"Obviously," Kierse said. "And my exit is…"

"Through the window onto the roof."

"And what will *you* be doing in all of this?" Kierse asked.

He crossed his arms over his chest. "Might take a nap."

"You're joking." Then she narrowed her eyes. "Since when do you joke?"

"When I know that someone is going to understand my wit."

She scoffed. "If you say so."

"I will be covering your exit." He stared down at his phone once more. "Now, get ready."

"For what?"

"George almost has the security system down."

"George can hack security systems?" she asked with wide eyes. "Your driver?"

"Like I would choose anyone in my employ for a single skill set."

Kierse eyed him appreciatively. He certainly hadn't chosen her for just one talent.

"He's good. Here we go. The cameras are going down in…" Graves held his fingers up.

Kierse cursed under her breath and rushed to the door. "How long will I have before they come back up?"

"If we're lucky, a half hour, but could be closer to fifteen minutes."

"Fifteen minutes," she hissed.

"And three, two, one…go."

He pointed at her, but she was already darting out of the room. Fifteen minutes. *Fifteen minutes.* Fucking hell.

That was absurd. She couldn't do this in fifteen minutes. There was no possible way. And yet she had no other option.

She raced barefoot down the hall, yanking open a door to the stairwell. Without stopping to think, she dashed upward on the tight stairs that led to what were once servant quarters. Kierse heaved a deep breath in as she reached the landing in record time. She listened at the door before pulling it cautiously open and looking within.

Okay. Maybe these were still servant quarters. The simple interior was night and day compared to over-the-top decor below. Everything was drab and gray and bare. Not a rug or painting or gilded anything in sight.

Also no people, thankfully.

Kierse hastened down the hallway. The door should be overwhelmingly obvious, guarded by wards and surrounded by magic. There was no need to hide the warding, because it was very difficult to break another master's wards, sometimes impossible. Graves had insinuated that very few people could break *his* wards—though she'd seen a Druid spell on the winter solstice take them down last year.

None of the doors she passed felt right. She was beginning to wonder if this was a fool's errand when the weight of Estelle's magic suddenly hit her like a wave. She retreated a step in revulsion. It was *a lot* of magic. Maybe enough to overpower Kierse's absorption.

The first time that had happened, she and Graves had been stealing letters from Imani and her husband, Montrell. Kierse had been sick for days afterward, even after taking an antidote to Imani's powers. She couldn't overdose on magic tonight. Not when her escape was a climb onto the Parisian rooftops.

But fuck, this was her best shot at the cauldron.

"Goddamn it, Graves," she hissed under her breath.

Then she stepped into the wave of Estelle's magic. She coughed around the heat that was like stepping into an inferno. She wondered what it would be like to see and feel Estelle's illusions right now. Was it a fear tactic? Did it show her death or a person's worst nightmares? What would others see in this scenario?

Kierse didn't know, and she was glad for it, as her hand closed over the doorknob and opened the door.

She choked through a gasp as the sight of Graves lying dead on the floor hit her like a freight train. His head snapped at an unnatural angle. Those storm-cloud eyes devoid of emotion. His tattoo black against his bleached-white skin. It was so real. Too real.

Her heart constricted as she crawled forward. Her hand reached out for his body as if there was possibly a way to put it all back together. Tears fell from her cheeks as sobs wracked her body.

"Graves," she whispered in horror. "It's not supposed to end like this. You promised…"

But what had he promised? Nothing.

Graves had never promised her anything. And now he was dead. Dead and gone, when he was supposed to be covering her retreat. How could Estelle have gotten to him this fast? How could he have let this happen?

Graves? Her Graves? He was the most powerful being on the planet. One of his old apprentices could never have gotten the drop on him. His eyes were lifeless. His body empty of all that fire and magic he always exuded.

She rebuked this. It could not be Graves. Would not be Graves.

Estelle couldn't have done this, not in this short of time. Still, the image remained. He didn't waver. It wasn't until her magic began to drain away as if through a sieve that she realized something about this was really wrong. She wanted to keel over and die from the intensity. Like she'd never breathe again, seeing Graves like this. But it was wrong. This was Estelle's doing, and she could see through the vision if she…just…

She threw herself forward over the threshold and through to the other side.

The magic snapped off. Graves's dead body vanished. The world was once more whole.

Kierse dry heaved onto the hardwood flooring, now thankful that she hadn't eaten anything all day. Her body shook from the loss of magic. Her absorption was used up. Her glamours were down. She had only scraps left.

A throat cleared, and Kierse slowly lifted her head in dawning horror to find Estelle seated on a chair at the other end of the room.

She clapped her hands. "Not bad. Not bad at all."

Chapter Seven

"Farther than I thought you'd get," Estelle said from her perch. She'd changed out of her fancy gown and was dressed in black cigarette pants and a cream blouse. Her hair was tied up into a French twist.

Kierse narrowed her eyes, and the image of Estelle flickered at the edges. She could see the red dress underneath, the hair down and loose.

She quickly covered her own ears with her hair, knowing the points were visible. Estelle's magic had blasted through her defenses like a freight train. Now she was stuck with the master warlock and didn't have enough magic left to know what was real and what wasn't.

Which meant Estelle had the advantage. Kierse would have to face her, in this room, alone. No Graves. No absorption. No defenses. Just Kierse.

Which had always been enough before. And it would have to be enough now.

She pushed up to all fours and then forced herself upright. She had survived her mother's death and her father's abandonment. She had survived Jason's relentless abuse. She had survived on the streets of New York during the Monster War. She was a *survivor*.

This would not stop her. No matter what Estelle had planned for her.

Now that her initial shock had worn off, Kierse turned her attention to the treasure trove around her. The room had no vault. Why use a vault when wards were this powerful? Illusions of the people you cared about dying were a sufficient deterrent. But now Kierse was inside, and she could see there were innumerable priceless paintings, jewels, and artifacts. All pieces she would have killed to steal in another life.

Which was good, because Kierse knew how to replenish her magic—stealing. Easy enough in a room full of treasures.

Kierse swallowed. "You underestimated me."

"Graves," Estelle said on a sigh. Her illusions flickered between the gown and the pants. "He always collects such interesting people."

"Such as?"

Estelle waved a hand. "You, obviously."

"Obviously," Kierse bit out.

"His wife," Estelle said with a bland smile.

Kierse kept her gaze purposely off of Estelle as she made a slow circuit of the room. "Impressive collection."

"Dusty trinkets. You and I both know that's not what I'm interested in collecting."

Kierse slipped a coin in her hand, rolling it between her fingers. She felt Estelle's pull on her lessen slightly. "What are you interested in collecting? Because as far as I know, you have the cauldron."

Estelle *tsk*ed. "Give me more stimulating conversation."

Kierse laughed. For some reason, she kind of liked Estelle. She was likely unhinged, but at least she admitted to her games. "As you wish."

She slipped on a diamond bracelet, and the next time she looked at Estelle, she could barely see the outline of the woman she was pretending to be. Kierse only wanted to deal with the real thing.

"Tell me about the bracelet," Estelle said.

"This one?" Kierse held up the diamonds she'd just slid on her wrist.

Estelle shot her a look, and Kierse grinned. Obviously not this one.

"Why did you steal it?"

Kierse shrugged. "Seemed fun at the time."

Estelle's laugh was a bell. "Fun. You stole from the queen of the nymphs for fun. Perhaps you are correct and I did underestimate you. You are much too like Graves."

She was uncertain what she thought of that assessment from someone else. She'd already thought it too many times herself. "Is that how you knew we were married already? You're in consort with the queen?"

"Do you believe Graves unaware of that?"

Kierse slipped a ring on her finger. She remembered him saying that Aveline wouldn't cross Estelle. Had he meant something more than that? It would be like him to leave out the important details.

"Graves keeps his own counsel."

"You *do* know him," Estelle said with a bitter laugh.

Kierse slipped a ruby pin into her hair before turning back to Estelle. "I do know him, but you already knew that," Kierse intuited. "You were aware of us long before I stole that bracelet."

Estelle inclined her head. "It may have reached my ears that Graves's new apprentice was immune to magic. I thought he might make a play for the cauldron with you."

Immune to magic. That was what Graves had originally believed, and it was the lie they'd peddled around when he'd discovered her absorption abilities. She was glad that at least that truth hadn't reached anyone's ears.

But that wasn't all that Estelle had told her. She had known Graves was going to come after the cauldron, and he was going to do it with someone who could break into this room. She had planned to test Kierse's immunity. Hence the wave of magic. Which meant...

"The cauldron isn't here," Kierse said.

Estelle pointed a lacquered nail at her. "Correct."

"This was a test for me. Not Graves."

"I've lived a long time," Estelle said as she stood. She stepped up to Kierse and dragged a nail down her cheek. "I like new things."

"I'm not for sale."

"Everything is for sale," Estelle said sweetly. She pursed her lips and tilted her head. "He has done quite a number on you, hasn't he?"

Kierse refused to step back. She met Estelle's unending violet eyes with her own dark, narrowed ones. She didn't particularly like being made a pawn in someone else's game, by Estelle or otherwise. And if the cauldron wasn't here, then she didn't need to spend another minute here.

"If the game is over, then I'll be going."

Kierse turned from her, flipping the coin across her knuckles again as she headed for the door. Turning her back on her opponent wasn't her best bet, but she had a feeling Estelle found her more valuable alive.

"I have one more game," Estelle said. "If you don't want to leave empty-handed."

She sighed heavily and stilled her feet. "What game?"

"A riddle. Simple thing. You guess the answer and I'll provide information to what you're after."

A riddle. Kierse didn't know if this was a trap or not. If she felt like she was in one, it was usually too late.

"And what happens if I answer incorrectly?"

"You lose the game," Estelle said with a smile.

"What comes with a loss?"

"A truth."

Truth. Kierse frowned. The truth hadn't been kind, and she doubted Estelle's would be, either. But what could Estelle know about her that would be a truth Kierse did not already know? Was it worth it to try?

"Tell me the riddle."

Estelle's smile sharpened at Kierse's agreement. "I thought you might change your mind."

Kierse hated that Estelle was right—she didn't want to leave here empty-handed. Her magic was recharging, and she could just barely see the film of Estelle's illusions. She wasn't strong enough by a long shot, but it was better than nothing.

"You'll have five minutes to complete the riddle, otherwise you lose. Are you ready?"

Kierse nodded with her heart in her throat. "Ready."

I'm not given, I'm taken away,
A choice that leaves a debt to pay.
For love or honor, or for a cause,
I'm offered willingly, despite the loss.
In games of strategy, I'm a mere pawn.
Moves planned out, a piece withdrawn.
What am I?"

Kierse stared at Estelle as if she had grown a second head. It sounded like gibberish. Wouldn't it have been great to have the master of knowledge at her command to put the pieces together for her? But wasn't that why Estelle didn't play with Graves anymore? He figured out her games too easily. He always won. And Estelle wanted to win, despite whatever she said about not caring about winning or losing.

She needed to look at this section by section. She wished that she'd written it down. Fuck.

Okay. She remembered "not given but taken away," which seemed obvious. Something that "leaves a debt." That could be something like a promise or obligation. Hmm...that didn't feel right. How would a promise be "taken away"?

She needed the next lines. Something about love and loss.

"Can I have the second pair of lines again?"

Estelle sighed but repeated them.

Kierse bit her lip and considered what love, honor, and a cause had to do with offering something up willingly but with a loss. She had no idea. Possibly forgiving someone. You have to give something of yourself to forgive in any of those scenarios. But for a cause...how did that fit?

"And the final lines?"

Estelle finished out the couplet that spoke about strategy, a pawn, and losing pieces. So chess. She knew that much. She'd played chess with Jason to hone her strategic capabilities when on a job. What game could be played here that related to a promise or forgiveness?

None.

She didn't think any of it fit.

"Do you have an answer?" Estelle asked.

"My five minutes aren't up," Kierse said, working through the problem.

All three sections talked about giving something up—taken away, loss, and withdrawn. What could be forfeited in each of these situations?

"The clock is ticking," Estelle said, pointing at an ornate clock on the wall and watching Kierse intently.

Kierse glanced at the clock and winced. She was down to her last minute.

She went back to the last couplet, which made the most sense to her. What happened in chess when she withdrew a piece? A loss. A strategic move. A capture by an opponent.

Was Estelle trying to show Kierse she was on a chess board? That her next move was wrong somehow? Or that her opponent had outwitted her? No, riddles were more veiled than that. What was something offered willing, but at a loss, not given, but taken away, and used in chess?

"Time," Estelle said. "I will have your answer."

Kierse wracked her brain. She needed this answer. A creeping awareness came over her. A tactic that Jason had always been better at than Kierse. When they'd played chess, he'd usually won, because he was willing to let her take his pieces so that he could get ahead. And in his mind, people were as disposable as the chess pieces. She had never been able to think like that—to think that someone was worth throwing away. But it was the answer that she needed here.

"Sacrifice," Kierse said.

Estelle's face froze in surprise. "Correct." Then she smiled dangerously. She gestured to Kierse. "The sacrificial lamb."

Kierse ground her teeth. "You've made your point."

"Have I?" Estelle asked as she retrieved an envelope. "Do you truly believe that Graves thought the cauldron was here? That he could take down my security system so easily, clearing the way for you to come up here and enter this room? He was using you to get information."

Kierse felt the sting of Estelle's words. She had assumed that if she lost, the truth would hurt, but even in winning the truth Estelle imparted was painful.

She had thought that she was in on the game this time. That they'd planned it together. Only now was it obvious that he'd kept part of the strategy to himself. Once again she had fallen right into his trap. The whole thing was exhausting.

Estelle held out the envelope. "Your prize."

Kierse snatched it out of her hand. "This better be worth it."

"And what would be worth it, to you?"

Kierse didn't have an answer for that. But either way, she was done here.

"My jewelry." Estelle held her hand out.

Kierse sighed and then dropped the ring and diamond bracelet in her palm. "If you insist."

"And the coin."

"You said jewelry," Kierse said with a dangerous smile.

"I should have been more specific."

Kierse flipped the coin to Estelle. She waited for Estelle to say something about the pin, but when she didn't mention it, Kierse said over her shoulder, "Enjoy your games."

"Before you go," Estelle said, stopping Kierse at the door. "Are you actually married?"

Kierse put on a matching smile as she turned and said, "That would ruin the game, wouldn't it?"

Chapter Eight

The wet terracotta roof was slick as Kierse hauled herself up onto it, barefoot. She took off at a quick clip as the rain settled into her hair and into the silk of her slip dress. She could not have selected a more inopportune outfit for the occasion. The promise of summer was destroyed by the chilly rain that sank into her skin. All she wanted were her warm black shirt and pants, some sturdy rubber-soled boots, and a waterproof jacket. Or perhaps just a warm fire and no more thieving for the night. Something she so rarely desired.

With no Graves in sight—so much for covering her exit—she hopped from one roof to the next, angling to get a few buildings away before finding her way back to street level. But the next tile she landed on slipped from her under foot, and she careened forward.

Before she crashed into the roof and slid off, an arm snaked out from behind her and caught her around the middle.

"Fuck," she gasped.

"I've got you," Graves said, low and commanding.

She shivered at the sound. Hated and loved how it affected her all the same. She lifted her gaze and found his dark eyes. He was back in his suit jacket and gloves. His midnight hair was soaked from the rain, and it dripped forward against her lips as he held her.

She coughed and scrambled unsteadily back to her feet. "There you are."

"I was on my way to the room. You didn't make the rendezvous."

"As if you didn't already know what happened," she said, slapping the envelope on his chest.

He pulled back. "What's this?"

"The information you wanted."

"I wanted the cauldron." He stuffed the envelope into an inside jacket pocket.

"Well, she didn't have it. Which you already knew."

"Why would I send you in there if the cauldron wasn't there?" he demanded.

"Save me from trying to figure out your schemes, Graves."

He straightened at her tone. "We were in this one together."

"I thought so, too," she said, exhausted. "Can we just get out of the cold? My magic is fucked."

Graves's jaw tightened. "Of course."

Then he removed his jacket and slipped it around her shoulders. She didn't even have it in her to reject it. She wanted to get off of this roof.

They scaled the next gable, and then Graves opened a latched window, which led to another stairwell. He led them down a set of stairs and out onto the street, where the limo waited. She ducked inside with Graves close behind her, and George pulled away a moment later. She stared out the window as the rain picked up, relentlessly beating on the roof.

Kierse gave him the rundown of what had happened with Estelle on the drive. He was quiet throughout her story, but when she got to the riddle, he snarled out the word, "Sacrifice," almost before she'd finished.

"Sacrificial lamb," Kierse said.

"That's not what you are."

She waved him off. It wasn't even worth debating.

He appeared irritated by her dismissal. What Estelle had said made perfect sense. She'd thought they were in this one together, but just like last time, he'd been after something else and had used her to get it. Classic Graves.

Not ten minutes later, the limo came to a stop again on a darkened street.

"Where are we?" Kierse asked.

"My place."

Kierse stared up at the dark facade. "I thought it was being renovated."

"We'll have to make do."

Kierse wanted to argue, but she was starting to feel the strain from the magic loss. Yeah, she'd stolen a few items while in that room—still had the ruby hair pin, in fact—but it hadn't been enough to counteract all of Estelle's magic. She needed to sleep for a good twelve hours, and if she was going to pass out, she needed to do it somewhere safe. She was mad about being Graves's sacrificial lamb, but she didn't think he'd let his prized thief come to further harm.

She followed him through the rain into another entryway and took the elevator to the top floor. When he'd said that his place was being renovated, she'd thought he'd been making it up, but the place was in disarray. White sheets on all the furniture. Nothing on any of the walls. No curtains framing the French doors. A giant ladder stood sentinel in the center of the room along with paint supplies and construction equipment.

"Through here," Graves said.

She tiptoed over the wreckage into a bedroom off of the main living area. Graves tugged a sheet off of a lamp and plugged it in, illuminating the space, which consisted of a king-size bed, set of dressers, and little else. The walls looked freshly painted, as if the bedroom reno had already been completed but they hadn't bothered putting anything back into its rightful place.

The curtains had been cast open, revealing the most spectacular view of the Eiffel Tower sparkling in all its glory. Rain splattered against the windowpane as Kierse stepped up to the double French doors.

"What a view."

"That is why I kept this one," Graves said.

He removed the cloth covering the four-poster. She glanced at the bed. Was there another? This couldn't be the only bed in his whole apartment...could it? The place wasn't large by Graves's standards, but surely there wasn't *only* one bed.

"I probably have a change of clothes for you." Graves disappeared and came back a minute later with a wool sweater. "Everything else is in storage. The bathing chamber is through there."

"Thanks."

She took the sweater and followed where he'd pointed, finding a bathroom with a clawfoot tub and giant double vanity. She dropped her ruined dress to the floor and changed into the sweater, which reached to the tops of her thighs. She removed Estelle's ruby pin before wringing the rainwater out of her hair. She braided it and used the pin to secure the end.

When she returned, Graves had opened the envelope that Estelle had given her and was reading a small card.

"What is it?"

He glanced up and did a full double take as she stepped into the room. His eyes roamed up her bare legs, stopping at the point where the sweater hit her thighs, then up across the oversize thing to her face. He sucked in a sharp breath before returning to the paper.

He cleared his throat. "There's to be an auction for the cauldron."

"Where?" she asked, fighting a satisfied smile at his reaction to her.

He held it out for her. "New York."

"Of course," she whispered as she read through the letter she'd rightfully won. "'Join me at the New Amsterdam Theatre Aerial Gardens for a production of *A Midsummer Night's Dream*. Dress to theme.'"

Graves waved his hand dismissively. "That's all fine, but I've never even heard of the company who is hosting."

"That doesn't sound like you."

"I'll investigate before the auction."

"Sounds like fun," she said as she tossed the invitation back to him. "Who doesn't love a costume party?"

Her magic drain was hitting her hard. She felt like she was going to pass out at any moment.

"You should sleep," Graves said.

She dropped onto the bed. "Probably."

Graves began to unbutton his shirt, and her eyes landed on the strip of bare skin.

"What are you doing?" she asked.

He gestured to the bed. "There's only the one."

"Yeah, but…"

"You're exhausted, and you need to sleep."

"Together?"

Graves shot her a look as he stripped out of his shirt, giving her a spectacular view of his muscled chest and the tattoo that crept up to his shoulder. She swallowed and tried to stop staring but found it difficult. The last time she and Graves had shared a bed, things had been *very* heated.

"What? You can't sleep next to me?"

"I mean…I *can*," she said.

His hands moved to his trousers, popping the button and pulling down the zipper. Kierse swallowed hard at the peek of black boxers underneath. The pants hung loose on his hips, and he smirked as she forced her gaze upward.

"Excellent. Then we'll share."

He let the pants fall to the ground, and she gulped.

"But…"

"Are you so affected by me?" he challenged.

Kierse set her jaw. "You know what?" she told him. "Fine."

She lay back in the bed, letting the sweater ride up high on her thighs. It wasn't as if she were the only one affected. He had absolutely responded to the sight of her in his sweater. And even if he *hadn't*, she wasn't about to let him win this one, too.

She glanced his way only for her eyes to get caught on the bulge in his boxers. He absolutely was not unaffected by her. Not with the length of him on display as it strained against the material. Fucking hell. She jerked her gaze away as he slid under the covers.

Graves pulled the string for the lamp, casting them into darkness except for the dim glow from the window. She could reach out at any moment and touch him, and it suddenly felt intimate.

And fuck, she wanted that. She didn't know if she was his sacrifice or if there was some other game that *Estelle* was playing. She was too tangled up in him—had been, for far too long. She'd crossed an ocean to escape him, and it still hadn't been far enough.

"The world looked different when I first purchased this flat," Graves said into the darkness.

Kierse turned on her side to face him. She could only see the outline of his beautiful face. A visage cut from stone. She knew how it would feel to give in. To say fuck it, like she had that first time. If only things were so easy.

"Less noise. Less people. Less chaos," he mused.

"When was that?"

"Before the World's Fair. I was here with Imani as my apprentice," he told her. "We met Montrell when he came from Nigeria for the Fair."

"And you loved him?"

Graves's lips quirked up. "An obsession," he said instead. "For me and Imani both before he chose her."

"Because you let him go," she corrected.

"Perhaps," he admitted.

She blinked in surprise. "You think you made a mistake? *You?*"

"I have been reevaluating my past since you left." He turned to look at her, and her heart stopped at the heat in that gaze. The way he seemed to reel her in, tugging bit by bit. "And perhaps some things were my fault."

"Like what?"

Graves leaned forward and settled his hand on her hip. She inhaled sharply as he said, "You."

"Me?"

"Everything that happened with you." His fingertips circled on her naked hip. "I wish I could rewrite my life with you in it."

She swallowed. She didn't know what to do with this information as her body hummed to life. She leaned toward him until their bodies were mere inches apart, her heart rate ratcheted up, and she glanced at his perfectly kissable lips and then back into his eyes. His gaze settled on her, fingers sliding down her thigh.

The dark was where they both existed the best. It was easier to be here with him like this when she didn't have to consider consequences or what came next.

"Kierse," he breathed her name in the darkness, his fingers digging into her thigh as if he could barely hold himself back.

She shivered, wanting nothing more than his lips on hers. He drew her leg up, settling one leg between hers. His fingers drifted up the back of her thigh. Sensation rushed through her body as if awakening from a cold winter.

"Graves," she said, and it came out more like a plea.

"Have you not missed me?" he asked. Their breath mingled as he brushed his nose along her jaw. "Have you not thought about this moment all these cold months without me?"

"I..."

She had. Could he read her? Was her magic that low? Or was it that obvious that despite her anger, she still wanted him with a fiery, obsessive desire?

He nipped at her earlobe. "Tell me what I can do to correct your estimation of me."

"Stop lying," she ground out.

"There will be no lies between us, then," he agreed. He dipped his head into her neck. "I can smell your arousal."

She tilted forward and into his embrace. Damn him. Damn her.

Her hands splayed across his solid chest. The heat of his fire, an inferno, was the only thing that could quench the ache building between her legs. His fingers shifted upward, brushing against the soft silk of her panties. They groaned together at the feel, and she nearly came right then and there. She was already soaked through from his teasing.

"Do not lie to yourself either," he said as he brushed his lips against her throat. "We both know you want this."

"Graves," she panted.

His finger began to swirl around her most sensitive bud. "All those long months with just your hand."

"I...could have had a lover," she gasped.

His chuckle was rough against her throat as his fingers swished through the slick material, feeling all of her. "My wren, my little thief, who else could satisfy you?"

She wanted to argue with him. Arguing with him had been the foreplay that led to this moment. But as his fingers were currently occupied with her clit, she could do nothing but hold on for the ride. She couldn't even fathom how turned on she was. He was still working her over her panties, and she felt close to bursting.

"Let the monster off the leash," he commanded, using the words she had said to him all those months ago. "Come for me."

And she did, shuddering, panting, and feral, her moans a chorus in the silent French apartment.

When she finished, he gave her pussy a little slap and rolled away from her with a satisfied smirk on his face. "At least that is still mine." His eyes sparkled as he said, "Bonne nuit."

Kierse glared at him through waves of pleasure as he closed his eyes. As if he could pass out after *that*. He'd proven his point. The bastard. No matter how far she ran, her body betrayed her with him at every turn. Something she very clearly could no longer lie to herself about.

Chapter Nine

A red light was blinking in their house. She knew that was wrong. Daddy had said to find a hiding spot when the red light blinked.

"Daddy!" she cried. "The warding."

Her father strode into the house, grizzly and hardened. "They found us and pulled down the warding."

He was all hard edges. She'd seen the hardness take him more and more each day. Tears streaked down her cheeks. She knew what this meant, and still she ran into her father's leg and held onto him tight. "Daddy, I don't want to."

"You must," he said in his thick Scottish accent.

"I'm strong. I'll stay here with you."

His hand settled into her hair, and then he bent down to pick her up in his arms. "Shh, now, my darling, you know what we have to do."

She rubbed her face in his jacket, drying her eyes. "Hide."

"That's right. I'll take care of everything."

"Daddy…"

"Come now." He set her on her feet. "We don't have much time."

She ran ahead to the back room where Daddy had installed a false drop through the floorboards. He pushed aside the rug, pulled up the flooring, and revealed a space just big enough for a young girl to settle into.

He kissed her temple. "I love you so much, my wee darling." He slid his fingers under her cheeks, brushing away her tears. He pressed a kiss there and eased her down into the hollow.

She heard the front door crash open.

"No," she gasped.

Daddy put a finger to his lips. "Not a peep."

She nodded even as her tears began anew. The flooring settled back into place. She could see from the light filtering in from between the boards. Then the rug was thrown back on top of her hiding spot, and she was cast into darkness. All she heard now was yelling and pleading and screaming.

"Kierse," a voice broke through the screaming.

Kierse thrashed against the hand on her. A second hand gripped her shoulder and shook her, repeating her name over and over again.

"Fuck, what is that?" the voice said.

"No," she moaned. "No, no, no, no, no."

"Kierse, it isn't real. Whatever you're seeing is a dream. Wake up." The shaking grew more frantic. "Come back to me."

She was still there. Locked in that floorboard. The screaming all around her. Tears running down her face. And there was nothing she could do. No way to escape, except to give away her position, and then it would be all for nothing.

"Kierse!"

And then she was ripped free.

Everything was gone. No screaming, no floorboards, no locked rooms. The tears were real, though. They had soaked the collar of her sweater and into the pillowcase. She scrubbed at her cheeks to erase the evidence of her pain.

A dream. It was just a dream.

Her breath came out in heaving pants as her vision cleared to reveal Graves. She was okay. She was with Graves. He had an arm around her shoulders, and she was cocooned against his bare chest.

"What…what happened?" she whispered.

Already the edges of the dream were fuzzy. Like she'd been clinging to something important that only slipped through her fingers the tighter she held on.

She couldn't remember what had happened. A woman's screams. No, had it been a man yelling? Something about hiding or being chased down. It had been terrible. As had most of her dreams in the last couple months.

"You started screaming," Graves said. "Like someone was harming you and I couldn't wake you."

"Oh." Kierse shuffled upright. She didn't want to move away from him. In fact, his arms had been one of the few things to silence the terror in her mind. "Sorry I woke you."

"I don't care if you wake the entire block. That's hardly my concern. Has that happened before?"

She bit her lip and nodded. "Most nights."

At his displeasure, she wanted to take it back. She shouldn't have confided in him, but having someone there to wake her in the middle of it made her feel safe. Gen had helped her through it in Dublin. In fact, she'd been studying her healing magic to make Kierse sleeping concoctions. And while the brews had dimmed the dreams, they'd only resumed in a murkier and more hypnotic form, as if she were swimming under water. Sometimes she preferred sheer terror to being trapped in a potion-induced sleep.

"Do you dream of the hole under the floor every night?"

Kierse jerked backward. "What do you mean?"

He furrowed his brow. "That is what you were dreaming, correct? Your magic was drained enough that I got a read on it when I touched you."

"You *read* me?" she accused.

"You were *screaming*," he shot back. "It wasn't intentional. I thought you would absorb it, and when you did not, you practically threw the images into my mind."

Kierse pursed her lips. "I did not."

"How it happened is irrelevant. Answer the question. The same dream?"

"I don't…I don't usually remember." She blinked. Graves could *see* her dream. He could remember it. "You remember it, though?"

"Yes," he said with a sigh. "I remember. How much do you recall?"

"Mostly the sense of being chased and hiding. I was under the floor?"

Graves sighed. "I came in when you'd already been in the dream. You were young. You called a man Daddy while he put you in a hole under floorboards. He told you to stay quiet as he covered you up. Then there was screaming."

"The screaming I remember." She shivered. "The screaming is always there. I hate these nightmares."

"I don't think it was just a nightmare. It had the feel of a memory. It's different than the quality of dreams."

"But my…dad," Kierse whispered. "I don't have any memories of him. Except that I was only six when he left."

"And that never struck you as odd?"

"What?"

"That you remember nothing else?"

"I assumed the trauma…" She trailed off. "Wait, do you think it was the spell?"

He nodded. "It must have wiped away all knowledge of your parents. And if I had to guess, you're starting to remember."

"Oh," she whispered.

A part of her wanted to believe her parents were still out there, but that was just a dream, too. Her mom had died in childbirth, and in her head, she knew that if her dad was still alive, he would have come back to New York at any time in the last twenty years and found her. But he hadn't. Which meant that her parents were dead. And she would never find them again.

"Why is it like this?" she asked. "Why can't I remember?"

"A spell like that is incredibly powerful. The amount of magic needed to hide your identity as well as erase parts of your memory had to have been outrageous."

"Beyond you?"

"*No* my kind of magic," Graves said—though he didn't deny that he was powerful enough. "What matters is that you *are* remembering."

"Well, fuck," she said, standing from the bed and pacing away from him. "What I don't understand is why the memories were taken in the first place. Why would someone do that? Why bother to put this spell on me? Why didn't they kill me?"

Graves wavered at that. "My guess is as good as yours. But I do know that the best way to get answers is to retrieve your memories."

She huffed. "Yeah."

"What? Do you not wish to remember?"

"I do," she said on a sigh. "But the bracelet—the one I stole from the queen..."

"Yes?"

"I've been trying to find a way into the goblin market in Dublin. I stole the bracelet to trade for a way inside."

Graves frowned. The sheets fell from his bare torso as he rose to his feet. "The *actual* market and not the bookshop?"

"Yes, Nying Market," Kierse said, waving him off.

"Nying Market is *no* place for you."

Kierse narrowed her eyes at him. "You don't get to decide what is and isn't good for me." She held her hand up to keep him from saying more. "I wanted to get rid of my nightmares."

"Nightmares you now realize are memories."

Kierse nodded, hugging her arms around her waist. "So now I can get a gift from Nying to remember them."

"That is not a good idea."

"It's perfect."

"Nying does not require fair value for trades, Kierse," Graves told her. "There's no guarantee you'll get exactly what you want, and it always takes more than it gives."

"So I should forget it altogether?" she demanded. "Whoever did this to me took my first *six years*. I can't sit back and do nothing, and this is the best plan."

"I didn't say you should do nothing. There are other ways to retrieve memories."

Kierse glanced down at his hands as she realized what he was suggesting. Graves could read people. But not her—not unless she was drained of magic, like she was tonight. She couldn't just turn off her absorption powers, and frankly, she didn't want to. He might be able to get back those memories, but who knew if it was even possible to let him into her mind without leaving herself utterly vulnerable? This felt like the easier of the two options.

"No," Kierse said flatly.

"You'd rather go into the market than let me help you?"

"I'd rather at least try," Kierse said.

"You're being obstinate."

"And *you* made me that way." She wrenched away and turned to face the window. The tower was illuminated in all its glory. "There's a reason I don't trust you in my mind. You were the one that hid my identity from me. You were the one who burned this bridge. You don't get to choose the terms for when to mend it."

"Fine," Graves said through clenched teeth. "Then you're not going into the market alone."

"What?" She looked at him over her shoulder. "Don't you have to run home to New York? Prepare for the auction to get your precious cauldron?"

"If you're going to be at risk, then I'll be at your back." He took a step into her space. "Every time."

Interlude

E stelle should have realized the girl had her pin. Damn her. She'd had that handmade in the early 1900s from a local jeweler. That the thief had pocketed it without Estelle realizing irked her. She had even known of her prowess as well as her powers. The fact that she'd won the game at all still surprised Estelle. That she'd stolen from her as well was beyond the pale.

"Mistress, your guest has pulled up to the curb," Celine said with a demure bob of her head.

Ah, Celine, her most dedicated attendant. There were a full dozen at present, all over the city, but only Celine was allowed in her home. She wasn't the most spectacular with any kind of magic, but she was certainly... dedicated.

"Thank you, Celine." Estelle walked to the front windows to peer down at the black limousine in the rain. The streetlamps barely illuminated the row of cars. She remembered when they were gas lamps, lit at dusk and extinguished at dawn. Oh, how much had changed.

What *hadn't* changed was Graves. Estelle clenched her jaw. That man. Insufferable.

She remembered the first time that she'd met him. She'd been born and raised in the country on a vineyard in Bourdeaux. Her father had brought her into the city to take up art lessons on a visit with her aunt, a much-accomplished fashion designer. The boutique under her home had been in the family that long. Though the name had changed once or twice. Her aunt was dressing all the most eligible ladies for the big galas happening during the Fair. While Estelle herself, a nobody from the countryside, wouldn't have been afforded an invitation on her own, her aunt had sent Estelle in her stead all summer.

She danced with dozens, hundreds of men, finding them all lacking. None wanted to have a serious conversation with a woman. They commented on her beauty and then spoke of their business, as if she had no thoughts or dreams of her own. It was only with the women that she found real conversation, and the women were much more attractive, anyway. Oh, the afternoons she'd spent...working on her art with many a grand heiress. What a delightful time that had been.

Until Graves had shown up and realized that all the social weaving she had been doing naturally, playing games with the wealthy socialites, had been *actual* magic.

Then he'd wanted to train her. Undo all her hard work. And generally annoy her.

So she'd started to play games with *him*. Games he won more often than not. Her magic was strong enough that she started to stake claim over areas of the city. She learned warlocks were territorial, and there were too many of them in Paris at that time. She thrust Montrell into Graves's path and watched his world implode around him. Estelle won that game, but Graves got his revenge after all.

She still remembered the moment the telegram had come in, informing her that her longtime lover had just accepted a proposal. No one had known she was courting the queen of the nymphs—that Aveline was her heart, body, mind, and soul. That she was the one Estelle had always wanted. Now Aveline would have a consort, engineered by Graves, and that consort was not Estelle.

A power play that she never forgot.

A knock came at the door. Celine opened it and bowed low. "Your Majesty."

Aveline strode into Estelle's home as if it were her own, even though it hadn't been in nearly a hundred years.

"Hello, Avie," Estelle said with her chin held high.

"My star," Aveline said, kissing both of her cheeks. "Did you get my bracelet back?"

"She left with it."

"I see." Aveline's expression didn't change, but Estelle could read her displeasure.

"She was a formidable opponent."

"And did you give her the invitation?" Aveline asked.

Estelle nodded. "I assume they'll both be there."

She liked her games. She liked to hold her cards close to her chest and only dole them out when she was most at an advantage.

She hadn't anticipated the convoluted mess of emotions that had stepped into her flat this evening. Graves was usually a closed-off book, his desires only known to her when he wanted them to be known. She had been skeptical at the ferocity of his affections for his apprentice. She'd thought the "wife" bit was just that—a falsehood.

But what swirled between them made her question it. There was desire—oh yes, that much was obvious. However, lust, love, hate, desire were all so connected. And if she didn't know Graves better, she would have thought he was being *sincere* that he wouldn't risk Kierse in his games. Yet he had sent her ahead as his sacrificial lamb anyway.

A conundrum. One she wasn't certain how to parse. Had the villain of the age finally met his match?

Her smile turned lupine as she turned away from her old lover. What a pretty game they were going to play, if that were the case.

"What are you smiling about?" Aveline asked.

Estelle looked at the love of her life, who she would never have again. The woman who had pieced together her world and then crushed it. She wanted to play another game with her. Wanted to have another chance to win her over. But she had chosen her place as the premier warlock of Paris, and Aveline had chosen Versailles. They were two sides of a coin—forever connected, never meeting.

"The Curator will take it from here," she told her. "Let the games begin."

PART II

THE ROBIN

Chapter Ten

Graves was aghast that she'd flown commercial into Paris, let alone that she would *debase* herself in coach. As if she didn't have ten million dollars in her bank account from the job she'd completed for him to steal the spear. That didn't change the fact that she had grown up stealing for her next meal. It didn't matter that the first time she'd ever flown had been on Graves's private jet—she couldn't imagine paying for anything other than coach. But getting on the jet again on their way back to Dublin reminded her that his over-the-top luxury was *maybe* a little better than her quiet suffering.

They touched down at the Dublin Airport two hours later, where a limo was waiting on the tarmac to whisk them away. George stood at the back with the door open.

"Do you fly the plane, too?" she asked him as she stepped off the stairs.

"Maybe," George said with a cheeky smile.

"He can," Graves said. "But I keep a pilot on standby as well."

"A backup pilot," she muttered. "So like you."

"Let's hurry this up, George," Graves said as Kierse ducked into the limo. "I want to get out of this country as soon as we can."

"Yes, sir."

As soon as he was seated, Graves pulled another old brown leather book into his lap. His head was buried in it before they started moving.

"Why don't you want to be in Ireland?"

"I'm not exactly welcome," he said.

"You're not welcome in the entirety of Ireland?"

"Where do you think Druids come from?" Graves grumbled.

Kierse chuckled. "Ah, the age-old Oak and Holly King affair."

Graves glanced up at her, amused. "It is not an affair. It is a battle for the turning of the seasons."

"That you engage in every summer and winter solstice. Yes, I know," Kierse said, waving her hand. "I remember the Oak King magic obliterating me."

Graves frowned. They hadn't discussed how she had felt when the god magic had blasted into her the night she had saved Graves's life. How it had felt like it was eating her from the inside out. Like she was going to implode at any moment. That she wanted it to be over, no matter how much Graves had begged her to keep fighting.

Since her arrival in Dublin, she'd spent time researching the Druids as well as the Oak and Holly Kings. The stories were long but obscure. The Romans had destroyed so much of what was known about the Celtic history. Druids were scholars and priests who ruled and educated the masses. They were known for their spirituality, association with nature, and prophecy. If all the stories were to be believed, they were the forever good guys.

Her own experience differed considerably. In the short time that she had known Druids, they had tried to kill her, kidnapped her, threatened her friends, stalked her, broken into Graves's library, and blasted her with magic. Not the heroes described in the histories. Even if Lorcan had changed his tune when he discovered that she was a wisp.

It made sense to her, based on her knowledge of Druids, that Lorcan, the head of the Druids, would be the eternal Oak King heralding in spring and summer. While Graves, a warlock and Lorcan's eternal foe, would be the Holly King, the winter god incarnate.

The stories said: Druid, good guy. Warlock, bad guy. Reality was that they were all weapons cloaked in gray.

"Anyway, there are Druids elsewhere," Kierse said. "Are you not welcome in Scotland, Wales, or Brittany, either?"

Graves blinked at her. "Someone has been doing some reading. Or have you been acquainted with more Druids since our last meeting?"

"Trust me. I don't want to be involved with Druids any more than you do."

"At last, something we can agree on."

"I can tell when you're avoiding my question."

"The problems with my mother's people originated here."

Graves had admitted to her that his mother, who had died in childbirth, had been a High Priestess from Ireland. After his father had named him a monster and sold him like a cow, he'd managed to escape to Ireland, where he was welcomed by association with his mother. Until it had all gone wrong. Yet another story she had never gotten the end of.

"Well, don't let me stop you," Kierse said. "You have a private plane. You are free to return to New York."

His gaze landed on her again. "I am not going to let you enter the market alone."

He returned to his book with a wave of his hand, letting her know he needed to level up. Something she would also need to do. She'd gotten reliant on always having her powers charged. It had been months since she'd been this drained. She'd eaten half of the food on the plane and was certainly going to need to do some pickpocketing to get back to full strength before she could walk into Nying Market.

"At least you're in a nice part of town," Graves said as they took the turn onto Leeson Street into the city center.

Kierse turned her attention back to the window as they circled St. Stephen's Green. She had made it a part of her morning routine to walk through the historic public park. Bordered by busy streets, it was a refuge similar to what she had back at home in Central Park, albeit a much smaller area. She enjoyed feeding the ducks and watching the mer swim in the lake at its center.

"This used to be for grazing livestock," Graves muttered.

"When was that?" she asked with a laugh. "I can't even imagine it."

He shrugged. "A couple hundred years ago."

She sometimes forgot that he'd been born in the 1500s. It didn't always feel possible to imagine him having been around during the Tudors and the Paris World's Fair and so much of history. That he could remember a time when there was livestock in the center of Dublin proper.

They navigated the remainder of the streets before coming to stop in front of a Georgian-style apartment building. The row of brick buildings along the whole street was dotted with vibrantly colored doors, and the door to Kierse's apartment was the brightest yellow on the block. She hopped out as soon as they stopped, relief rushing over her at the sight of the place. She hurried up the stoop to the elaborate entrance.

Graves cleared his throat behind her, and she glanced back at him with a quick smile. It was surreal to see him in the Dublin daylight. Graves belonged in winter, in darkened libraries, and secret passageways under the subway. He wasn't spring in the, albeit, rare sunshine of the city center. It was like she was seeing two people written on top of one another.

"Be prepared to be amazed," Kierse teased, turning the knob and entering a stairwell. The elevator only worked every fourth trip, and it wasn't worth it to get stuck for the afternoon, so they took the steps.

She had a giddy lift to her step. She hadn't even been gone that long, and she already missed Gen. Those weeks she'd lived in Graves's brownstone had been the longest she had been without her best friend, and she didn't want to repeat the experience.

It was bad enough that there was no Ethan. The only word she'd had was from Nate, letting her know that Ethan had gone underground with the Druids and no one had heard from him. Not even his boyfriend, Corey. Now...ex-boyfriend? She still couldn't fathom it.

Kierse stuck the key in the door and turned the antique brass handle. "Gen! I'm home!" She stepped inside to find the sparse living quarters exactly as she had left them.

"Miss McKenna," Graves said in irritation, stuck on the other side of the door.

"What are you, a vampire? Should I invite you in?"

"Would you like me to take your warding down?" he asked like a threat.

"Can you do that?"

He shot her a look.

"Right." She pressed her hand to the door and adjusted the ward to allow him to pass.

"You know that you can change the wards without touch once they're connected."

"Sure. But I'm low. I didn't want to use the effort."

"Kierse?" Gen called. She rushed out of her bedroom in pink sweatpants, a white tank, and oversize cardigan. Her bright copper hair was piled high on her head in an intricate messy bun. "You're back!" She collided with Kierse, wrapping her up in a hug. Kierse settled into her. Gen was home; she was home.

"I'm back."

"And you brought a...visitor," Gen said, glancing at him out of the corner of her eye.

The one benefit of having money was that Kierse had paid a spectacular amount for a doctor to look at Gen's eyes. She had been diagnosed with early onset macular degeneration when she was just seven. She now saw almost exclusively out of her peripheral vision. Kierse had unfortunately discovered that the doctor who had bailed when Gen was a kid wasn't a quack, and there wasn't anything that could be done for her vision. At least nothing that science had discovered.

"Prophet Genesis," Graves said with a bow. "Always a pleasure."

Gen blushed. "I haven't heard that name in quite a while."

"It's a tragedy not to use a talent such as yours."

Gen had always had a piece of magic buried within her. Just a touch of sight that allowed her to read tarot for truth. Not all the time, but when the cards spoke to her. It turned out that her touch of sight had been a blossom waiting to flower—a flower that meant she was actually a High Priestess.

"I have been cultivating other gifts." Gen glanced at Kierse. "Though I am surprised to see you here. In our apartment. In Dublin."

"It's a long story," Kierse said with an eye roll. "Graves, tell her about how you engineered our meeting so that I could help you steal the cauldron."

Gen squeaked. "What?"

"I'm going to go change." Kierse headed into her bedroom.

"I assure you she was safe the entire time," she heard Graves say from the other room.

Kierse snorted. "Except for the period I was alone with a master warlock who snapped my magic like a twig," she yelled back.

"What?" Gen asked in increasing distress.

Graves's extended sigh was oh so satisfying.

Chapter Eleven

"I'm just going to…" Gen trailed off, and then Kierse heard her scurrying footsteps. "Kierse, Graves is in our *flat.*"

"I know. I know."

"What is he doing here?"

Kierse kicked the bedroom door closed. It probably wasn't enough to keep Graves from listening in if he wanted to, but he might take the hint and afford them some privacy. She knew how important it was to *him.*

"Scheming," Kierse said. She stripped out of her travel clothes, tossing them into an empty hamper.

"Are you involved in his schemes again?"

"Against my will," Kierse assured her as she tugged on black leggings. "I was stealing the bracelet and he just *happened* to be there."

"So he was stalking you."

"What else is new?" She threw on a fitted black crop top and reached for her new favorite red jacket.

"I really didn't think he would leave us alone all this time."

"I don't think he has. At the very least, he's been spying on us," Kierse said as she slid her arms into the cozy material.

Fully clothed, she reached for her most treasured possession—a wren necklace. She stroked a finger over the bird at the center of the silver emblem. It was the only thing that she had left from her parents. And it was the first sign that had made Graves hire her for that job last winter. Wrens and the Holly King were connected. She'd been his little power booster until the winter solstice. While she may have been the one to walk away from him, she could still hear him saying how poetic it was to fall for the source of his own destruction.

She shivered at the words and then looped the necklace around her neck, where it belonged.

"Well, I can't imagine him letting you walk away. Not after…" Gen trailed off again.

Kierse wasn't sure how Gen would have ended that sentence, but maybe she didn't want to know, either.

"Did you sleep together?" Gen asked.

Kierse shot her a look. She never could get anything past her friend. She had been *this* close to doing just that. "Not yet."

"Kierse!" Gen said with a shake of her head.

"I'm kidding. Things got heated, but nothing happened. You know it's complicated."

"So you still have it bad?"

Kierse made a little shrug. "Well, he's very pretty."

"Big trouble, though."

"Tell me something I don't know."

Getting the third degree from Gen was unsurprising. It was what family did when they were concerned, and Gen was family in every sense of the word. After Jason had beaten Kierse to within an inch of her life and left her for dead, Gen had found her, taken her in, and healed her. She'd done the same with Ethan when he'd escaped a similar fate in the church. Gen had been there to pick up the pieces for the both of them.

"I'm not going to tell you not to do it, because I know you better than that," Gen muttered.

"Good. I love you," Kierse said with a laugh. "Anyway, we have more important things to deal with."

Kierse reached under her bed and felt around for the hidden compartment she'd created when she'd first moved in, to store the spear. Gen had thought that they should keep it somewhere more secure, like a bank vault, but Kierse had broken into enough of those to want it near her person.

She reached through her ward and pulled out a gray metal box. The carrying case was bulletproof and hermetically sealed. She'd had a keypad and facial recognition scanner attached and then etched her warding in by hand. No one was breaking into this thing. It didn't keep anyone from stealing the entire case, but still, they'd have to get through her wards or through *her* for that, and the spear inside would remain inaccessible.

And through everything—the wards, the security, the case—she could *feel* the spear there. A humming under her fingers that called to her. It had gotten stronger once the spell on her was broken, like a metal detector vibrating to life as she got near the thing.

"So did you get the bracelet?" Gen asked.

"Yep. In there." Kierse pointed to her purse. "Thanks to Graves."

Gen chuckled as she pulled the bangle from the purse. "Tell me the whole story."

Kierse relayed what had happened last night as she got through her locking system and opened the case to reveal the Spear of Lugh. It wasn't a long-handled spear like she'd first assumed it would be. Instead, it was a handheld spear, for thrusting and parrying and slicing. The thing had an iron blade attached to an ash handle that somehow looked brand new and not hundreds of years old.

She reached a shaky hand into the case and touched the spear.

The spear said, *Hello, old friend.*

And then its normal bullshit, *Who are we killing today?*

Kierse laughed and pushed aside the thought. No killing today.

The first time she had wielded the spear, it had imposed its will upon her. *Kill thy enemies. Use me. Conquer the world.* That sort of refrain. And while it still generally wanted to be used as the weapon it was, it had gotten, dare she say, used to her.

Gen shivered. "You should put that thing away."

"I think I'm going to bring it into the market."

She pulled it out of its case and twirled it expertly. She'd been practicing with it. Partially to get used to its particular weight and partially because she liked the weight of it in her hand.

"What? That's a horrible idea."

"I'll glamour it," Kierse told her. "Don't worry."

Gen snorted. "Worry is my birth right. How can I not worry about you?"

"Well, don't worry about this. My glamours are improving."

"They're not *that* good yet."

Kierse shrugged. "Fine. Fine." She set the spear back into the case. "Maybe it's not the best idea."

"I feel like I should go with you, but that place creeps me out."

"No," Kierse said at once. "I don't want you to go in there."

The thought jostled her out of her reverie. She hid the spear away again. For a second, she felt as if she could still hear the echo of the spear's murderous refrain, but it was there and gone.

"I know. I know. I just wish I could play point like Ethan."

"I miss him," Kierse muttered.

"Same," Gen agreed.

Neither of them commented on his radio silence. Clearly it was Lorcan's doing, and Kierse didn't want to reach out to the head of the Druids to get answers. It was likely part of his plan to get to her, anyway.

"But I wouldn't let Ethan follow me into the market, either," Kierse told her quickly. "And I'd worry about you the whole time. It'd make me reckless."

"As if you aren't already reckless," Gen said with a laugh.

"Fair."

"But Graves is going to go in with you?" Gen guessed.

Kierse smothered a smile. "The bastard insisted."

"Shocking," Gen said with dripping sarcasm.

"I'll be safe," Kierse promised.

"Safe isn't in your vocabulary."

A knock from the front door interrupted their conversation. "You're not wrong," Kierse said as she left her bedroom and headed into the main room. "Think it's Niamh?"

"I thought she was working today," Gen said on her heels.

Graves had his head in a book but looked up when they emerged. Kierse pulled the door open and found a tall, stunning woman with burgundy hair down to her mid-back standing at the door.

"Hey, Niamh," Kierse said.

"Hey! Heard you're back!" Niamh said. She wore an impractically short, pleated mini skirt straight out of a Catholic school uniform with a white polo tucked in and lug sole loafers.

Kierse put her hand on the warding to let her friend inside. "I thought you'd be at the bookstore."

"My shift starts in a few minutes. Heard your door open and…" She gestured to herself as she crossed the threshold.

"You have got to be fucking kidding me," Graves said.

Niamh turned her attention to Graves, who was now standing. "Well hello, handsome."

He immediately moved into a defensive stance. "Get the fuck out."

"Uh…do you know one another?" Kierse asked in confusion.

"This is the *robin*."

Chapter Twelve

"The...robin," Kierse repeated, uncomprehending.

"What's the robin?" Gen asked.

Graves looked between them as if personally affronted by their lack of knowledge. Niamh cocked one hip and flipped her hair, waiting for him to explain.

"You've read the stories," Graves said. "Surely you can piece it together."

"So you haven't changed *at all*," Niamh said with an eye roll. "Can't give a girl a single straight answer."

"Niamh," he snarled.

The way he pronounced her name, *Neev*, with a slight Irish lilt instead of his customary British accent, knocked something loose in Kierse's mind.

"Like a wren?" Kierse guessed.

"But for the Oak King," Graves said with distaste.

Kierse was Graves's wren. A bird that was aligned with the Holly King, able to enhance his power up until the winter solstice. Traditionally, wrens were hunted and killed the day after Christmas to symbolize the return of spring. Kierse had heightened Graves's power during that time before she'd known any of these Celtic myths were real.

After leaving New York, she'd read every story she could get her hands on regarding the Oak and Holly Kings. Tales of Sir Gawain and the Green Knight—a classic tale of the separation of the seasons—but also of the Wild Man, a Dionysian-esque figure, and the most famous Divine Kings who were mortal representations of the seasons, sacrificed to sustain their relentless cycle. Yet, while the stories were fascinating, none of them compared to meeting the actual Oak and Holly Kings.

The tales were incredibly vague about the role of the wren and the robin. They mentioned a wren in relation to the Holly King and a robin aligning with the Oak King, but they made the connections seem metaphorical. Since Kierse knew them to be more fact than fiction, that meant...Niamh was here for Lorcan.

"No," Kierse said, shaking her head. "Niamh is our friend."

Graves scoffed. "I'm sure Lorcan would want you to believe that."

"Niamh?" Gen asked in a small voice. They had been particularly close in the intervening months. It was Gen who had convinced Kierse to get the apartment down the hall from Niamh after befriending the girl in the bookstore. "Is all this true?"

"Okay. He makes it sound bad," Niamh said. "It's not so dramatic."

"Did Lorcan send you?" Kierse demanded.

"Yes, but…"

"Then it *is* that dramatic."

"I am not *reporting* to him," Niamh said with another eye roll. "Fuck Lorcan Flynn and all his drama."

"Then why are you here?" Gen asked.

"Let's see her twist this one up," Graves said. "We all know why she's here. She's here to spy on you for the enemy."

"Drama," Niamh muttered.

"For the record, *you* were spying on me, too," Kierse argued. "You knew that I was going to be in Paris."

"I had someone making sure you were safe. I didn't send an agent in to pretend to be your friend and monitor your actions," he said, as if they were two different things, when it sure felt like two sides of the same coin.

"Hey! I *am* their friend," Niamh argued.

The glare Graves shot her was deadly. She knew that, at any moment, he might actually murder Niamh—it wouldn't have been the first time he'd acted similarly. And as much as she wanted answers for Niamh's behavior, she did like the girl.

"Can we all calm down?" Kierse asked. "You're going to freak Gen out."

"Already there," Gen said. "Just tell us the truth."

Niamh gestured to Graves. "Like he even knows the definition of truth. Can't believe half of what he says."

"Why don't you let us decide for ourselves?" Kierse said.

"All right," Niamh said. "Lorcan did send me as his robin. But I don't *work* for him, and I didn't report on you."

"Are you a Druid, then?"

"She's a High Priestess," Graves said.

Gen gasped, her hand going to her chest. Kierse could see the hurt on her face. All this time they'd connected more closely than Gen had ever known. "You didn't tell me."

Niamh frowned. "Sorry, babe. I hated not telling you."

A light went off in Kierse's head. "You were training her."

"Both of you, as much as I could," Niamh admitted.

Kierse touched her ears, thinking about the little bit of glamour that could magically hide them when she wanted to appear wholly human. Or the healing abilities that Gen had been working on for Kierse's nightmares. Both of which

Niamh had shown them. "All of those books that magically appeared in your hand as if you knew exactly what we were looking for and how to find it."

"I wanted to tell you," Niamh said, momentarily sheepish. "I just liked you and knew you'd probably not take kindly to Druid interference after Lorcan's bullshit."

"As if you weren't *interfering*," Graves said.

Niamh flipped him off. "This doesn't change anything between us. Yes, I'm a High Priestess, and I'm even sort of in charge."

"I thought Lorcan was in charge," Kierse said. "I don't understand how the hierarchy works."

"He's technically the head of the whole thing," Niamh said on a sigh. "But you can't think he can handle everything back home from Brooklyn, can you? Didn't you lot throw tea into the Atlantic because you were upset with the Brits for doing exactly that?" Niamh winked. "Honestly, good for you."

Gen giggled and then carefully forced her mouth back to neutrality.

"Sorry 'bout it, Brit," Niamh said to Graves.

"I assure you that I am as much Irish as I am English, and I was never on the side of the colonizer in history anyway," Graves said stiffly. "Could you get to the point?"

"Lorcan told me to ingratiate myself with you and report back," Niamh said. "Well, then we met at the bookstore and you didn't seem like what Lorcan had suggested."

"And what did he suggest?" Graves asked, deadly low.

Niamh shrugged. "I gathered that he thought you might be controlling her. But you weren't around. There were only two lost girls in my city, and I just couldn't have that. So I offered to help. I haven't been reporting anything to him, and here we are."

"Obviously she's lying," Graves said.

Kierse tilted her head at Niamh. She'd known the girl for the better part of five months and felt an unexpected kindred connection with her. There was no way to discern the truth for certain, but Kierse usually trusted her gut.

"I don't think she is," Kierse said.

Graves clenched his hands into fists, but he said nothing further, though she knew he wanted to. He was in *her* apartment. She could make her own decisions. And despite everything, she liked Niamh. Maybe she was still working for Lorcan. Maybe she wasn't.

"Come on. Oisín will tell you the right of it," Niamh promised. She yanked the door open for everyone. "The man doesn't lie."

"At least someone doesn't," Kierse grumbled. But she followed everyone else out the door, double-checking the warding before taking the stairs.

"He knows how to twist the truth to suit him, though," Graves said.

"Did he learn that from you?" Niamh asked, tilting her head. She might look like a bubbly Catholic school girl, but Kierse knew that there was more to Niamh than met the eye. Maybe that was what had drawn Kierse to her to begin with.

"From the Fae." Graves turned away from Niamh in exasperation. "I agree that a trip to Oisín will be illuminating. He can convince you to leave this foolish task you are set on, as well," he said, glancing at Kierse.

"What task?" Niamh asked as they reached the landing.

Kierse rolled her eyes. "I am not changing my mind about going into the market."

"Wait, you're going *into* the market?" Niamh asked in alarm. "What could you possibly want in Nying Market?"

"She's been having nightmares," Gen explained.

Graves pushed past Niamh and opened the building's front door. "The market is the nightmare."

"He's not wrong," Niamh said.

"It's unnerving to agree with her this much," Graves told Kierse.

"Is that what the potions have been for?" Niamh asked. "The nightmares?"

Kierse nodded. She hadn't had a chance to tell Gen the nightmares were possibly real memories when they had been alone together. She was going to have to figure out how to tell her that things had changed.

Graves gave her a knowing look as the limo pulled up to the curb.

"Uh...the bookstore is around the corner," Niamh interrupted. "We don't need a *limo*."

"It's for safety," Graves said, opening the door for them.

"It looks like convenience. Don't you want to walk the Dublin streets while you still can?" Niamh asked with an antagonizing smile.

"'While I still can'?" he all but growled.

"Seriously, Graves, it's fine," Kierse said. "I've walked this route a hundred times. But if you need the limo..."

Gen sealed her lips shut as if she could barely suppress a laugh.

Graves shut the door and tapped the top twice in some signal to George. "A walk sounds lovely."

"I'm sure," Niamh said with fluttering eyelashes. "Well, come on, handsome. I bet you still remember the way."

"I certainly do."

"Oisín will set this all right," Niamh promised.

Chapter Thirteen

The entrance to the bookstore was so small that if you blinked you might miss it. Tucked into a corner in the shopping center on Grafton Street, the front entrance was only the width of a single doorway that read THE BOOKSTORE in crumbling gold lettering with THE GOBLIN MARKET written underneath it in red paint. There was a single exterior window crowded with moldering books that looked out onto the cobbled stone street where tourists flocked. It was flanked on one side by a noisy pub and on the other by a jeweler that proudly noted they had been established in the 1800s.

Niamh tugged the door open. A bell jangled overhead. "Here we are."

Kierse stepped through to the darkened interior with a single Edison bulb swinging over the entrance before disappearing into the maze of bookshelves. She inhaled the scent of paper and ink and leather. It settled her.

"Just as I remember," Graves said, stepping to her side. His sleeve brushed against her jacket. For a second, she could smell his magic, and she realized that what had settled her in this place the whole time was…him.

She cleared her throat and put more distance between them.

Gen and Niamh followed next, the door swinging shut noisily behind them.

Niamh called into the bookstore, "Oisín?"

No response.

She waved her hand at the lot of them. "Just stay put. I'm sure he's around here somewhere."

Niamh tramped off into the stacks, disappearing almost instantly as if a cloud of black shadow had swallowed her whole.

"How classically Oisín," Gen said, taking a seat in one of the threadbare, sagging armchairs in front of the antique cash register. "He probably got lost in the biographies again."

"He does love to live in other people's lives," Kierse agreed.

Graves moved to the nearest bookshelf, looking a bit like a kid in a candy store. He removed a book and thumbed through it before grabbing another one. His stack almost instantly became ten high. He brought them over to the counter by Gen and went back to the shelves. Kierse focused her magic on him and could actually see the wisps of gold magic sliding around his body as he recharged.

Kierse had pickpocketed a few unsuspecting tourists on their way here. Nothing of note—a pack of gum, a gel pen, and a handful of euros that she'd passed off to a local busker. Stealing from Oisín was too easy, since the old man was always distracted and never quite cared what she carried off. It didn't energize her the way other tricks did.

Graves *tsk*ed. "Someone should really categorize some of this. This entire stack is almost unreadable from the mold. And the dust." He wrinkled his nose. "Whose job is it to tidy this?"

"Who cleans *your* library?" Gen asked him.

"Magic," Graves said with a smirk.

"Of course," Kierse muttered. "Well, use some magic to clean this place up."

"There's a difference between keeping something clean and cleaning it to begin with." He shook his head in dismay as pages fell out of a large leatherbound book. "Tragedy."

A throat cleared hoarsely. "Sometimes the pages like to find new homes in other volumes."

Graves looked aghast.

Oisín smiled toothily up at him. "Hello, Brannon. It has been many years."

A grimace was all that revealed that Graves detested the use of his first name. He held his hand out to the stooped bookstore owner. "Long enough that I no longer go by that name. It's simply Graves now."

He took Graves's hand in his wrinkled and age-spotted one. "Ah, yes, I believe someone mentioned that." He tapped his forehead. "Some things stick forever and some things..." He waved his hand as if indicating a dark abyss from which it might never return.

"You still remember who I am, though, right?" Niamh asked.

Oisín smiled and reached up to pat her cheek. His long, robe-like clothing puddled on the floor, but when he lifted his arm, you could see he was wearing worn brown leather loafers that looked like they'd been plucked straight out of a medieval tale.

"I'd never forget my Niamh. You or my faerie love that you've named yourself for."

"I love that you chose the name based on the story," Gen told her with a small blush on her pale, freckled cheeks.

"It was always my favorite tale," Niamh said, winking at Oisín. "And when I transitioned, it felt more me than anything ever had."

"You are so like her," Oisín said with that same sad smile.

The first time Kierse had entered Oisín's bookshop, she'd never heard the story of Niamh and Oisín. Kierse had thought Graves and Lorcan had suggested she try the Goblin Market bookstore to get more information, not that the owner himself actually had involvement with the Fae. Oisín had given her a copy of the faerie tale, and it had been the first story she'd read when she began to dig through the spotty history of her people. Graves always said that there was a kernel of truth to every tale that persisted, but until then, she hadn't really believed him.

In the popular Irish faerie tale, a beautiful fae woman, Niamh, came into this world and fell for a human man. Oisín left with Niamh to return to her world of faerie, where they were very happy for many years. But he wanted to say goodbye to his family back in the human world. Niamh agreed under the condition that he never left the horse she gave him, which he readily agreed to. When he returned to his Dublin, he found that instead of a handful of years, hundreds of years had passed and no one he once knew remained. On his return voyage, he fell from his horse and thus lost both his true home in faerie with his love and the human world that had left him far behind.

She'd returned to Oisín the next day, wondering if the story of Niamh and Oisín was one of the ones that held a kernel of truth.

"You are that Oisín?" Kierse had asked.

"I am," he'd agreed.

"But...how? Wasn't that hundreds of years ago?"

"My time in faerie marked me. While I aged to this almost instantly," he'd said, gesturing to himself, "I remain the man I was when I left faerie in here." He'd touched his heart. "I have not aged a single day since. With hopes to return and find my Niamh still waiting."

Since then, Oisín had been helping her and Gen learn more about Fae. She'd trudged through massive tomes, reading everything she could get her hands on. The scant knowledge of wisps was particularly disturbing. In most of the tales, will-o'-the-wisps were nothing more than faerie lights, especially around swamps, which led travelers off of their path. In other iterations, they were jack-o'-lanterns, or a will-of-the-torch that helped luckier travelers through the night. Sometimes wisps judged whether to help a stranger or not based on their actions. So much of it was a mix of urban legend and faerie mischief. For a few centuries, mortal scientists had claimed they were just bioluminescence in the marsh due to decay. Boy, did she have a story for that hypothesis.

It was only with Oisín's help that she had reconstructed an index of all powers the wisps had historically wielded to compare them to her own. Absorption, time manipulation, glamour, and finding treasure—check. Pixie light, persuasion, magic intuition, and possibly portaling—negative. No matter how she worked at the latter powers, they stayed squarely out of her grasp. She was happy enough with what she'd had, but Oisín feared that the spell had horribly altered her magic.

"I feel something has changed," Oisín said, looking between them.

"She's going into Nying, Oisín," Niamh said. "We were hoping you'd talk her out of it."

Oisín sighed. "You've been seduced by Nying as well? There won't be answers about the Fae in there."

"Or if there are, you can't pay for them," Niamh insisted.

Kierse hadn't even considered that, but now that she was…

"Don't even think about it," Graves growled as if reading her mind.

"She's not going for that," Gen said. "It's for her nightmares."

"They're not nightmares. They're memories." She swallowed, deciding that she might as well lay it all out now. "Memories of my past, my father. And they're all jumbled up from the broken spell. So I need something to fix them."

Niamh looked to Graves. "That sounds like your area."

"I've been working on it," he said roughly.

"Can't you just read her mind and…"

"He can't get through my absorption," Kierse clarified.

"And she already turned down my offer. Anything you can do, oh High Priestess?"

Niamh shook her head. "I've been sending Gen all the books I have on nightmares. Memory is even harder to deal with. There might be a spell, but it wouldn't be ready for another full moon, and it requires more energy than I can channel alone. Maybe if we brought in other Druids…"

"No," Graves said at once.

"Well, tell us your great idea then, warlock," Niamh said.

"If she won't work with me," he said carefully, "and it isn't safe for her to work with Druids…then we should take her to the Covenant."

"The witch doctors?" Niamh said, her eyes wide.

Kierse's jaw fell open. "You'd work with Dr. Mafi again?"

Dr. Mafi had turned on them and given Kierse's blood to the vampire King Louis. She'd only done it because she was indebted to him, but Kierse didn't think Graves would ever forgive something like that.

"I would do whatever it takes to help you," he told her, his eyes earnest. "Including aiding this asinine quest into the market."

"Science isn't going to fix a magical problem," Niamh said. "Even witch doctor science."

"You can't know that," Gen argued. "We don't even know if what happened to Kierse's memories is entirely because of the spell. That's just one hypothesis. And to be fair, none of your potions were working, either. So why not try the medical side?"

"Because the Covenant is back home," Kierse said. "And I'm going into the market *tonight*."

"Is there any way to talk her out of this?" Oisín inquired.

"Probably not," Gen said. "Not when she's set her mind on it."

"I can't stop. Not when I'm this close to finding out what happened to my parents."

"My dear, my deepest condolences on the loss of your parents and people. I feel the pain acutely," Oisín said. "It does not, however, change the fact that that place is a monstrosity."

"Surely, it can't be that bad. Your shop is the entrance, isn't it?" Gen said softly.

"Indeed, the market has resided in this location far longer than I have had this shop. It is the home to goblins, true. They run their goblin fruit operations out of the market entrance, which is its primary purpose, but it is an illicit den of iniquity, the likes of which I have never seen elsewhere on this earth."

She needed to recover her memories. For her magic, her parents, and for herself, it was worth it, even if she had to walk into a monstrosity to get them back.

"I'm going," she said decisively.

"Kierse..." Gen whispered. "It sounds like this place is really dangerous."

She nearly laughed. "Yeah. What else is new?"

"Stubborn," Graves grumbled.

"It's a bad idea," Niamh said.

"I'm prepared to pay the cost," Kierse said, turning around. "There's a reason the spell was put on me and why my memories were taken from me. My parents are dead. There are no more Fae. I am the last of my entire race. I need answers. If this is how I get them, then so be it."

Everyone fell silent. Even Graves just crossed his arms. He didn't agree, but perhaps he knew her well enough not to argue any further.

Gen put her hand on Kierse's arm. "I want you to have those memories back. Of course we all want you to regain them." She stood and tugged Kierse into a hug, and Kierse was still amazed that she didn't flinch at the intimate touch. "Are you sure this is the only way to get them?"

Kierse glanced at Graves.

"Do you trust me?"

"Yes," Gen said without hesitation.

"Then this is the best option." She steeled her spine. "I'm going in tonight."

"Tonight it is," Graves said with a slight shake of his head.

Chapter Fourteen

Clouds obscured the moonlight on Grafton Street as Kierse and Graves stopped at the back exit to the bookstore where the entrance to Nying Market had been located for hundreds of years. Already there was a line of humans and monsters alike waiting to get inside. Goblins stood sentinel at the entrance, selling goblin fruit.

"So many eating the goblin fruit," Kierse whispered.

"The most addictive substance on the planet," Graves said.

"And one of the deadliest."

Like vampires with blood and wraiths with souls, goblin fruit sustained goblins. Not from specifically eating the fruit, which had no ill effects on them, but by getting others addicted to the fruit. The temptation, the sin, the euphoria, and then the need, which was all-consuming. Goblins lived off of the money, but the trade was for their life.

Goblins were not only completely immune to their effects, but their scholars had learned how to harness the energy and life force to power the doors inside. With that power came an increased vitality for all goblins within the market. That was why so many chose to stay within its bounds and hawk the fruit. Though she knew plenty of goblins who refused to sell it and lived on the outside.

It was the reason Kierse had risked everything to get the bracelet. With it, she could trade for a coin and not have to eat the fruit to get inside.

"I shouldn't bother to ask if you're certain about this, should I?" Graves asked.

"I robbed the Queen of Versailles to get entrance and then spent all day recharging to full power. I don't think I'm going to change my mind now."

"Yes, but you wanted to do that anyway."

She had, that was true. She used to walk around the Upper East Side and steal from the unsuspecting for a good time. Though bigger scores had always gotten her more jazzed.

Like the spear. Which was currently in its case back at her flat. Instead, Kierse stood strong in black, knee-high boots and a black, long-sleeve dress, which concealed the gun strapped to her thigh. She had two others in holsters against her side, hidden by her favorite red jacket—which Graves had tried and failed to talk her out of—and knives tucked into slots under her sleeves. She had the bracelet in a purse at her waist, ready to exchange it for a coin. She was as prepared as she could be.

"Have you considered the cost at least?" Graves asked. "There will be one, and it's better to have a few in mind before you go in there."

"I have a few ideas."

"As do I," he said gruffly.

Like he'd thought of what *he* could possibly pay for her to regain her memories. She couldn't imagine him doing anything of the sort. But when she looked up into his eyes, she could see something swirling there. As if he really might do it.

"Aye," Niamh said, sauntering toward them in the line. "There's still time. We could head up to Temple Bar. Have a pint, music, craic."

"What are you doing here?" Graves asked.

"You thought I'd let you have all the fun?" She twirled in place in her houndstooth mini skirt, black tank, and platform heels that brought her eye to eye with Graves. Her burgundy hair flew out like a fan around the shoulders of her faux-fur coat. "A girl can enjoy the market even when there's nothing to buy."

"You're eating goblin fruit now?"

"Snagged a coin from HQ," she said with a wink at Kierse.

"You just have coins hanging around?" Kierse asked in exasperation.

"I wouldn't say they were lying around, but a girl knows where to look."

Graves released a low breath. "Druids."

Niamh linked her arm with Kierse. "We'll be so inconspicuous."

Kierse couldn't help but laugh. It was hard to dislike Niamh. Though Graves was doing a good job of it.

The trio filed into the back of the line. Two goblins were moving down the line, selling the fruit to each person. In front of them, a teen girl with sallow skin and clothes barely hanging on her thin frame took a little reddish-purple fruit in her hands and immediately bit into the meat. The juice ran down her chin, but her face showed only a look of pure ecstasy.

Graves stood stone-faced, and Niamh could barely contain her disgust, but Kierse felt nothing but pity. She had seen the same thing on the streets during the Monster War. Jason always kicked out any of his thieves in the guild who got addicted. There was no point. Even if there were a cure, no one wanted it.

Luckily, publicly distributing the fruit was made illegal, and most of the crops were destroyed after the Monster Treaty was signed in the city. Goblins raged about the hypocrisy since humans could still be blood donors to vampires and soul patrons to wraiths and the like. But people could survive that; humans didn't survive goblin fruit.

They stepped forward as the girl headed through the gate, munching on her fruit. The goblin at the entrance was roughly Kierse's height with a humanoid appearance save for the greige tint to his skin, long, wide, pointed ears, and deep, inset forehead around unnaturally large eyes.

"Fruit?" he asked, gesturing to a carton filled with the reddish purple fruit. They almost looked like plums the size of apples, with the skin of a peach.

"No," Graves growled.

"Pass," Niamh agreed.

"Hello again. Remember me?" Kierse said.

The goblin glanced at Kierse and then revealed a row of razor-sharp incisors. "Ah, little girl, did you bring me my bracelet?" He laughed uproariously and elbowed another goblin at his side.

Kierse tugged the bracelet out of the small bag and twirled it before him.

The goblin's jaw dropped open in shock. "Blessed ore."

The other goblin punched him in the arm. "Fucking hell, Fraan, is that what I think it is?"

"It is," Fraan said, slack jawed.

"Where'd you get that?" the second goblin demanded.

"Off a queen," Kierse told him. "And it's the price you claimed I needed to pay to get a coin inside."

"It was a joke, Chots," Fraan said. He pushed the other goblin away and held his grubby hand out. His nails were nearly black and razor sharp. "I'll take that off your hands."

"Rio is going to want to see that," Chots said.

"Shut the fuck up," Fraan said, shoving him away irritably. Chots clamped his mouth shut.

Nying Market translated to "gift market," and the motto over the entrance read *A GIFT FOR A GIFT*. And while there was always a cost to get in the market, they made it obscenely high because they wanted more people to get addicted to the goblin fruit. So she was unsurprised that they were trying to dick her around when she could easily become another cog in their machine.

"We can all agree that's *not* a fair price," Graves argued.

"This is clearly worth more than the price of entrance," Kierse agreed.

"Doesn't fucking matter," Fraan snarled. "We agreed. Fair and square."

"You said it was a joke," Niamh countered.

"That's not how the market works," Fraan said.

"We all know you were dicking me around because you thought there was no way for me to get my hands on this bracelet," Kierse said. "But I delivered. So why don't we figure out a good trade?"

"You really took it off a queen?" Chots asked.

"I said shut the fuck up, Chots!" Fraan bellowed. His bulging eyes narrowed, and he plucked a shiny gold coin half the size of her palm out of his pocket. "This is what you asked for, and by rights of the market, you agreed in good faith to the trade. Going back on it now would be against the goblin code."

Chots eyes widened. "Fraangyng!"

Graves sighed as if he had anticipated something like this and stepped up next to her, casually placing his hand on a gun at his waist.

Kierse glanced around and saw that the goblins who had been stationed at the doors had noticed their confrontation and were heading toward them. They had battle axes resting on their shoulders and AK-47s slung into position in their arms, ready to fight.

"Uh," she muttered. "What just happened?"

"He called you a cheat," Niamh said.

"And they take that kind of thing very seriously," Graves added.

Taking a battle axe to the head was not her idea of a good time, but Kierse was confident she could take on a few goblins. With Graves and Niamh at her back, maybe more than a few. Still, they were on goblin turf. This was not a fight she wanted to engage in.

"Fine," Kierse said, holding the bracelet out. "A gift for a gift."

Fraangyng grinned wider and signaled to the approaching goblins. They stopped in their tracks, then retreated to their positions. Fraan snatched the bracelet from her hand and dropped the coin into her palm. "Happy doing business with you."

Kierse fumed. "Sure thing."

His large eyes lifted to Graves and Niamh. "You'll have to pay separate."

Graves revealed his own coin. "I'm good."

"Same," Niamh said cheerfully. "Well, this was lovely. Think we'll move along so you can sell someone else into goblin fruit addiction."

"Niamh," Graves grumbled.

"Right. Right."

Kierse hooked arms with Niamh and hurried toward the large double doors labeled NYING MARKET in large letters across the top.

Graves was at their back. "And look, you didn't even have to kill anyone."

"There's still time," Kierse said as she flipped the coin back and forth across her knuckles.

"There was almost time back there," Niamh said.

"We could have taken them," Kierse said.

Graves shrugged. "Probably."

"Are you two always like this?" Niamh asked. She blew her bangs out of her eyes.

"No," Graves said at the same time Kierse said, "Yes."

"Got it. No wonder Lorcan wanted me to watch you," Niamh said with a shake of her head. "Anyone who can keep Graves on his toes must be valuable."

"That's not the half of it," Kierse told her.

Niamh glanced between them. "I don't know if I even want to know. I've been avoiding Lorcan's bullshit for so long. I was hoping to go a little longer."

"I fear you're out of luck," Graves told her.

"I fear that as well," Niamh said with a sigh. "Well, should we do the thing?"

Kierse nodded. "Let's fucking do it."

Then she pulled the doors open, stepping forward into the goblin market.

Chapter Fifteen

The market was dirty.

Kierse had been imagining a forest grove containing wooden stalls filled with wares and fields beyond growing the coveted fruit. Never had she pictured a darkened city street lined with tall buildings that seemed to lean into each other. The light of the moon vanished into the murky fog that pervaded the area. Puddles of stagnant water and filth littered the cobbled street, bringing with them the scent of sweat and refuse. Despite the inescapable feeling of unease, it teemed with monsters and humans alike.

"Whoa," she whispered.

Niamh sniffed. "God, I hate this place. Can we get in and out quickly?"

"Voicing that aloud seems to be asking for trouble," Graves said.

Kierse pulled her gaze from a group of mer haggling over a display of bones. Niamh looked visibly unwell. Graves, despite his cool exterior, also clearly hated it here. She didn't see how it was much different than Third Floor, the underground monster market, beneath Grand Central Station in Manhattan. Both places were dark and dank and filled with illicit dealings. The real difference was the pervasive dealing of goblin fruit. Humans gorged themselves on the addictive substance on every street corner. It made her stomach twist.

"Let's just hurry," Kierse finally said. "I've researched the market and know that we need to find a bookkeeper."

"Find a bookkeeper," Graves said with a sigh. "As if it's that easy."

Kierse narrowed her eyes. "I know there's one on this floor. Fraan mentioned it the last time I went to try to get access. I was going to find it on my own, but I assume you've both been here before."

Graves shot her a noncommittal look. Yes, he'd been here. No, he wasn't going to talk about it.

Niamh just said, "Sometimes we need very specific ingredients for our spells."

"Excellent. Hopefully you can speed up my search. No stakeouts. Woohoo," she said with an eye roll. "Where should we start?"

"The goblins mentioned Rio at the gate," Graves said.

"Rio's a bookkeeper?" Kierse asked as Graves took the lead navigating the cobblestone streets, Kierse and Niamh on his heels.

From what Kierse had gathered, bookkeepers were sort of a glossary for the market. Most illicit dealings could be done right out in the open. Drugs, sex, and weapons were as easy to come by as goblin fruit. But if you wanted something more interesting, more dangerous, or more unique, then a bookkeeper could find what you were looking for.

"Yes. Likely the one they had mentioned to you before. Though not one I've worked with. Their shop is nearby. Let's try not to draw attention to ourselves."

Niamh threw an arm across Kierse's shoulders. "Just look like we belong."

Kierse leaned into Niamh and forced her face into neutrality. That had basically always been her motto: stealth over muscle. Only recently had she had enough muscle to take on a monster, but she didn't particularly want to do it more often than necessary. Especially not in a place like this, teeming with monsters.

Every storefront and stall on the never-ending street was run by a goblin. Signs on the buildings reinforced that impression. GRAX AND GIRD: MONSTER MATERIALS with bottles labeled for vamp venom, werewolf bites, and wraith souls. CRUIGGIC'S WEAPONS, showcasing every manner of sword, axe, spear, and knife with a violet banner that proudly proclaimed GOBLIN MADE. GAUKUL was full of living creatures—spiders, rats, and snakes—and next to it was its competitor, TRUTIZ, which had all the parts and none of the living creatures. SAFIA AND THAFIA: FORTUNE READING was a tiny stall with two goblin women sitting in front of a crystal ball and a deck of tarot cards. Behind them a goblin man was herding their clients inside to the amulets, talismans, and divination materials.

The rest of the street was taken up with human items: restricted substances, offers for forged documents, and luxury jewelry, as well as the ubiquitous "food"—whatever that meant for monsters or men—and, of course, sex.

In New York, Kierse had lived in the attic of a brothel owned by Gen's mother, Colette, who was the premier madame of Manhattan. Kierse was far from naive and wasn't surprised to see goblin brothels inside the market. After all, it was the oldest profession.

They skirted the brothels and continued past other vendors until they reached their destination. It was a plain door with the word VRIOSA on the front in red letters and a little yellow sign read: BEWARE OF DOG.

"Dogs," Graves said with a sigh.

Niamh grinned. "Not a dog person?"

"Dogs love me," he corrected her and turned the handle.

Niamh and Kierse exchanged a look as they followed him inside. The room was bare and dusty. A row of wooden shelves had been smashed and left in pieces, and whatever had been on them had long ago been looted. Probably by whoever had done this. The floor near the rear of the room was strangely eroded and caving in, the remnants holding together precariously. Beyond the door, deep gouges marred a door that led to another room. Its broken hinges clattered as Graves pushed it open.

"Nothing," he said, standing on the threshold as Niamh and Kierse picked their way to him.

"What do you think happened?" Kierse asked. "A fight, obviously."

"Bookkeepers are notoriously difficult to find because they get a lot of angry customers." He kicked aside a few boards. "And angry customers in the market usually leave people dead."

"I've never had to use a bookkeeper to find spell supplies," Niamh noted. "Is this risk really necessary?"

"Probably," Kierse said. "What I read about them said that they can find anything you want in the market, but the rarer it is, the more difficult to locate."

Niamh waved a hand. "Assuredly that's true, but what I meant was: is what you want worth all this?"

Graves's eyes shot to hers. She stared him down, daring him to say it was not. Thankfully, he didn't voice his opinion on the matter.

"Yes," Kierse said with determination. "Where would the bookkeeper have gone? I didn't see a handy note with their forwarding address."

Niamh snorted. "That would be convenient. Is there another bookkeeper that would be easier to locate?"

Graves shook his head. His gloved hand sifted through a pile of rubble, and he came away with nothing but scraps. "There are other bookkeepers. None close. Plus, since the goblins at the gate mentioned Rio, we're more likely to have some leverage in negotiations with them. I wager it'd make the most sense to follow through with this if we can."

"All right." Kierse would have liked an easier option, but she hadn't thought that going into the market was going to be easy. "So our next move would be to get information about Rio. I'm guessing there are pubs down here?"

"In fact there are," Graves answered. "I know just the one."

"Why do I feel like we're not going to like this?" Niamh asked as she followed him to the door.

"Because it's Graves."

"I have an…acquaintance who frequents a place in New York."

Kierse blinked at his back. "How exactly is that going to help us?"

"You didn't think that Dublin was the only place that opened into the market, did you?"

"Well…no. I know there's one in New York, too, but I didn't think we could reach it." She frowned. "How many are there? Is there one in Paris?"

"No," Graves said. "There are only seven openings—Dublin, New York City, Shanghai, São Paulo, Lagos, Istanbul, and Rome."

Niamh linked arms with Kierse as they followed Graves down the main street. "It's like the spoke of a wheel. Each entrance comes to the same place, and when you enter from other doors, that section is built out to the aesthetic of that location. That's why here on the Dublin side, it has the old-world feel."

Kierse frowned at that analogy. She could picture a giant wheel connecting corners of the earth to this one location. It would be incredibly valuable to have that setup.

"How did the goblins achieve this?" She stepped around a particularly filthy puddle, avoiding a lumbering troll who barreled past.

"They didn't. Goblins don't have magic," Graves said.

"Something great and powerful built the portals. Some long-lost god probably. After the god—or creature—left this realm, they were abandoned," Niamh told her.

Gods. Right. "If everything else is true…"

"It all comes from somewhere," Graves muttered.

"Anyway, the goblins have built everything else you see here. They found the empty doors and figured out that the fruit would power them to stay open. They've been using it for their market for much of recorded history."

"Wow. That's pretty impressive. We're walking through dead god tunnels that have been repurposed as a black market. The world is a strange place." She continued down the cobbled street. "So explain how these portals work. We could jump from Dublin to New York like right now? I could be home just by stepping through their door?"

"Maybe the god could," Niamh said with a shrug.

"That's not how it works." Graves led them down a darkened alley. "The coin that you're using only lets you in and out of the entrance that you came through. You wouldn't be able to find the New York opening if you went looking."

Kierse sighed. "Of course. Nothing can be easy."

"The easier magic makes your life, the more costly," he said.

"Much more costly," Niamh agreed. "I doubt there would even be coins if you could jump between one opening and another. The cost is already the goblin fruit, and since I don't particularly want it to run more rampant, I'm glad for the limitations."

Finally, from the gloom, a set of stone stairs was illuminated by bracketed lanterns.

"Up through here to the next level," Graves said as he pulled out his phone. Kierse was surprised to see that it worked. When she pulled out hers, it had no signal.

A handful of straggling humans stumbled in front of them toward the stairs. A pair of goblins stood on either side, one with another giant axe on his shoulder and the other with a big black club across his chest. A box of goblin fruit rested at their feet and one of them kicked it toward the lumbering group.

"Pay for some fruit and eat to move up the floor," one goblin grunted.

The humans jerked forward, handing off whatever cash they had and grabbing a fruit each out of the basket. They half crawled up the stairs as they brought the fruit to their mouths.

"Eat," the goblin snapped at their group.

Graves flashed his coin. "We have leave of the market."

"Don't fucking care. Eat or leave."

Graves's eyes went from thundercloud gray to nearly black as he straightened to his considerable height. It was easy to find his cool demeanor endearing when they were alone together. Sometimes she forgot that he was actively terrifying. "Say that again," he said in a deep rumble that shook their bones.

The second goblin glanced warily at the first. These seemed like lowly guards compared to the ones at the gate. It was unclear if they were even really guards or just civilian goblins who had enterprised themselves into a side-hustle.

"I said that you have to pay and eat to take the stairs," the first goblin snapped back, too stupid to be afraid.

It happened in an instant. The first guard swung the axe threateningly but inexpertly at their group. He came within an inch of Graves, who jerked out of the way at the last second, only succeeding in pissing Graves off more. The second guard panicked and lunged at Kierse with his club. Kierse deflected it on instinct, but she felt like her forearm was going to shatter.

"Shit," Kierse gasped. "Can't we just pay them?"

Niamh wrestled the second guard to the ground, trying to maneuver the club out of his hand. "We aren't going to eat the fruit."

Graves had the axe now and used it to bash the first guard in the head. He dropped like a sack of potatoes. Footsteps sounded behind them, as if reinforcements were coming.

"Knock him out, Niamh," Graves snapped.

Niamh snarled at him, but it was Kierse who dealt the blow that knocked the final guard unconscious. Niamh stood, breath slightly ragged, and she hauled the goblin away from the stairs.

"Bloody business. This never happens when I need specialty herbs."

"The market always throws some sort of bullshit at us," Graves said. "Let's just take the stairs before more of them show up."

Kierse couldn't agree more. So they started climbing. She couldn't help but admire the stairs, especially as their style changed from an Irish stone to a dark reddish brick. Her arm still ached, and she tried to hide it as they climbed, but Niamh noticed.

"I can fix that for you."

"When we're safer," Kierse said. "I can still hear goblins behind us."

It was true. She'd thought the farther they climbed, the safer they would be, but it seemed the reinforcements had discovered their unconscious brethren and were giving chase. If a horde of goblins caught up to them, they were in for a world of trouble.

The stairs had changed again to a modern concrete. They had climbed high enough to be in the cloud line—or what Kierse had assumed was a foggy cloud, but what turned out to be a barrier of some sort between the Dublin she had left behind and the next city on the wheel.

Kierse stepped off the stairs onto familiar pavement. Her heart stuck in her throat at the sight of the sleek city gleaming before her. A version of Manhattan, with its characteristic brownstones and fire escapes. Humans and monsters bustled through the metropolis at a relentless pace. Their clothes were mostly black and inconspicuous, but some were outrageous and unique. The air somehow even smelled like the city.

Home.

She swallowed back the lump of longing in her throat. She had missed New York more than she could possibly explain. While she had come to love Dublin, it wasn't home, would never be in the way that New York was. Even if the will-o'-the-wisps had come from Ireland, New York would always be hers.

"Beautiful, isn't it?" Graves murmured at her side.

"I didn't realize how much I missed it," she confessed.

"It's waiting for you to come home." Their eyes met across a New York City street as they had so many times before. "As am I."

She had to turn away from the intensity of him. He made so much more sense in this environment. But she was still too tangled up in him to know which way was up or down. Just like being inside this indescribably strange, spoked wheel of a market.

The rumbling of footsteps broke Kierse from her reverie. She could see the goblins coming up the last few stairs.

"Fuck," she hissed.

"That's them!" a goblin roared. "Get 'em."

"This way," Graves said and then took off.

They weren't the only people cutting through the New York streets, but they were the only ones being chased by a horde of goblins. They barreled through monsters and people alike, running through a stand of goblin fruit and pushing aside performers who got in their way. Kierse was thankful that the goblins chasing them were brandishing knives, axes, and clubs, and not heavy machine guns like the ones at the entrance. Yet another indication that these weren't official guards, but some lesser, unsanctioned group.

"How are we going to get out of this?" Kierse gasped.

She was grateful for her Fae strength. She'd been fast before, but now she could outpace the goblins. She didn't know how long she could keep it up.

"I know a place," Graves said.

And he did seem to know these streets better than the ones in Dublin. Which made sense, considering he was the warlock of New York City. He'd probably been to the New York entrance of the market more times than the Dublin one, especially once he'd been banned from Dublin years ago.

"Here. In here," he said, wrenching open a door. They burst through, and Niamh slammed it behind them. Then they were running again. A few seconds later, the door opened, and a cacophony continued to follow them through the twists and turns of the market. Kierse would have been entirely lost without Graves directing them. It might look like her city, but it wasn't her city.

They fled down a narrow alley and through an open, unwatched back entrance into an unlit warehouse—or were they backstage in some underground cabaret? Graves turned sharply, still running confidently in the dark…and then a woman screamed as they burst out onto the stage where she was performing.

"Excuse us," Kierse said with a wave.

They barreled back off stage left between the curtains in the wings. The squawks from the audience as the goblins appeared on stage behind them would almost have been humorous if they weren't still being hotly pursued. However, the crowd and performers had slowed the goblins down enough that their trio finally had a lead. If they could just…get out of sight.

"This way," Graves said. He opened another door into a darkened room and stepped aside for Kierse and Niamh to follow him through, then eased it closed, throwing a heavy bolt.

They all held their breaths as they listened for the goblins. There came the grunts and clanks of the troop careening into the hallway outside, then a pause. For a moment, they could hear snuffling as the goblins tried to figure out where they had gone. But then their pursuers continued on, barreling past in their haste.

Kierse blew out a heavy breath. Niamh doubled over, panting. Graves dusted the dirt off his shoulders from the chase.

"That was fucking close," Niamh grumbled as she straightened. "We could have negotiated before violence."

"Did they look like the kind of goblins who were going to negotiate?"

"You could have tried before bashing their brains in!"

"I'll remember that next time I want to be incapacitated…"

"Enough," Kierse said. "We made it through. That's all that matters."

"I hate the market," Niamh grumbled.

"So say we all," Graves agreed.

"How do we find the bookkeeper from here?" Kierse asked.

"We'll backtrack to the bar. I put out a feeler for a contact I have in the market. He's going to meet us there."

Kierse eyed him skeptically. "Someone you trust?"

"Not exactly."

"Who *does* he trust?" Niamh asked.

Fair point.

"Lead the way."

Chapter Sixteen

From the outside, the pub looked like any seedy bar Kierse had ever been to in the city. It had a wooden sign out front proclaiming it Ye Olde Pilgrim.

Kierse glanced down at the sign and back up to Graves. "Seriously?"

"This place is older than the pilgrims, actually. Puritans rename everything," he said with an exasperated sigh. "The market had settled in the New York space before the Americas were even colonized. It only began to reshape itself around the Manhattan entrance after the area was taken from the indigenous people."

"Know-it-all," Niamh mumbled under her breath.

Graves smirked, taking it as a compliment, before pushing the door open. A little bell jingled overhead announcing their arrival, but inside was loud enough that their entrance was lost in the cacophony.

And while the outside had reminded her of her city, the inside could have been a medieval pub. A dirt floor covered in straw opened up to a hard wooden bar and a bunch of wooden tables and benches. A goblin band was playing a collection of old string instruments and singing a bawdy tavern tune. Mugs of ale were thrust into the air as most of the occupants—a mix of monsters, predominantly goblins—sang along.

"It has a certain je ne sais quoi," Niamh said.

"Feels like old times," Graves agreed.

They grabbed a table with their backs to the wall, and then Graves went off to grab drinks. Kierse didn't trust the ale in this place not to knock her on her ass, but they needed the disguise.

A barmaid in a knee-length brown dress dropped off a plate of crusty bread and cheese. "Drinks are at the bar, babes."

"Thank you," Niamh said properly.

The woman winked at her. "Love your accent."

Niamh beamed. "Thanks, love."

"Find me if you need *anything*." The implication was clear as she bustled off to another table.

"Making friends with the locals, I see," Graves said as he dropped three pints in front of them.

"I can hardly help that I'm irresistible."

Kierse ignored them as she surveyed the room. She'd spent many an evening trapped in a dive bar waiting for an informant or a contact. It felt like a lifetime ago that she'd honed her skills on the backs of billionaires to scrounge enough of a living. Now she had millions in the bank from the spear heist, but she still felt like that same girl who had to be hyper-independent to survive.

"When is your contact showing?"

"He should be here any minute," Graves assured her.

"What do I need to know about him?" She met his gaze. "And don't give me any shit about how it's 'need to know.' I need and I want to know. Dish."

Niamh barely covered a laugh. "She has you there."

"His name's Vale. He's a sort of mercenary around these parts. He knows enough magic to be dangerous, but there's no one who knows the inner workings of the market better than he does."

"So he's a warlock?"

"He's the child of a warlock," Graves corrected. "Managed to get some magic of his own. Otherwise human."

"Okay. And does he hate you?"

Niamh snorted. "I really like her, Graves. You should keep her around."

"I intend to," he said, holding her dark eyes. "We have a complicated relationship."

"You and I? Or you and Vale?"

"He has a complicated relationship with *everyone*," Niamh said.

"Is he your kid?" Kierse asked bluntly.

Niamh went still, either shocked that Kierse would ask or surprised she hadn't considered it herself.

"No," Graves said flatly.

He glanced down to his phone and sent out another message, clearly done with the interrogation. Kierse was tempted to press her luck. He was actually giving her information, and that was so unlike him that she wanted to see how far she could go.

But before she could open her mouth, a man in black leather lumbered over to their table. He had to be at least part troll, because he towered over them. His skin was a green-gray, and he had so many muscles that he looked part rock.

"Graves?" he grunted.

Graves came slowly to his feet. "Can I help you?"

"This you?"

He dropped a tablet down with a fuzzy picture of Graves on the screen. Underneath the image was an identification number of some sort and a price of two million goblin marks.

"Fuck, is that a bounty?" Kierse asked, scrambling to her feet. "A for-real bounty?"

"What did you *do*?" Niamh asked. She rose to stand as the rest of the bar turned to stare at them. Real inconspicuous.

"I didn't *do* anything."

Kierse shot him an exasperated look.

"We can do this nice and easy," the man said, producing particularly ancient-looking metal shackles. "You come with me."

Graves plucked his gloves off one finger at time. The fact that the gesture didn't terrify the bounty hunter meant that the bounty didn't include information on Graves's particular power. The guy saw an easy score, probably assuming he was a human who had done something bad to someone important. Not a magic-wielding warlock.

"This is inconvenient," Graves said. "Does it even say who wants me dead?"

Niamh shot him an exasperated look. "As if it isn't your life mission."

"Don't care who is paying as long as I'm paid," the bounty hunter grunted.

"An entrepreneur," Kierse said. "You have to appreciate the gall."

"Sounds like your kind of business strategy," Graves said.

"Then just *pay* the guy."

Graves arched an eyebrow. "I'm not paying him two million goblin marks to leave me alone."

"Maybe he'll settle for half."

"Cease," the man rumbled. "I'll take you in however you prefer. Don't much care."

All the back and forth between the three of them had been sufficient distraction for Graves to finally have his gloves off. Kierse's hand was on a knife at her belt. Niamh had taken a step behind them, muttering something under her breath.

"Now," Niamh gasped.

She and Graves shot to the sides as the table flew forward with the momentum from Niamh's spell. Kierse kicked the bounty hunter in the knee. It felt like her foot connected with solid rock. He stumbled forward a step, though, colliding with the wreckage of the table and ale that now covered him from head to toe.

The rest of the bar exploded at the commotion. Fights broke out. Ale was sloshed everywhere. Fists were thrown, and goblins tumbled to the ground in a brawl.

Graves was kneeling beside the guy a second later, placing his hand on the first bit of exposed skin. Kierse could see the gold of his magic ignite in the millisecond it took him to infiltrate the man's mind. The bounty hunter lay on the floor stock still and then turned around, looking confused. Graves winced and removed his hand.

"Come on. Let's get out of here."

"What did you do?" she asked with wide eyes.

He didn't get to answer, because the bounty hunter hadn't come alone. A handful of his minions crowded at the front door, blocking them in. Kierse glanced behind her to the other exit she'd clocked when they'd first walked in. She didn't know if they could make it in time, let alone survive *another* chase through the streets of the market.

It seemed as if the market was set out to kill them. As if it were angry she'd refused to give up her secrets so easily the first time she'd entered its embrace. It had teeth, and she was being consumed. But she would not give up—not even with a group of bounty hunter underlings at her front and room full of brawling goblins at her back.

"I got the two in the middle," Graves said before diving into the melee.

Kierse cursed as she followed him, engaging with a female goblin wearing spiked shoulder pads on her leather uniform like something out of a video game. She brandished a curved knife like someone who knew how to use it. Fuck, Kierse missed stealth missions.

Luckily, her Fae sense helped her meet the strike with a thrust of her own knife. Her already injured arm nearly buckled under the force. She really should have taken Niamh up on that healing now that she was thinking about it.

The goblin pressed her advantage, angling her long knife closer to Kierse's face, forcing Kierse to retreat just enough to get leverage to kick her in the stomach. The goblin grunted, falling backward a few steps. Plenty of space for Kierse to grasp one of the overturned chairs and bring it down onto the goblin's head.

She cried out as she collapsed to the ground. Kierse kicked her swiftly under the chin, and she went fully down. One down, one to go.

Graves and Niamh were lost in the rest of the fight, but she trusted that both of them could hold their own. All she had left to handle was a pair of goblins, one wielding another massive club and the other with a knife in each hand. Fuck.

Kierse glanced around her immediate vicinity, using the mere seconds she had to find an advantage.

"Come on, bitch," one said.

Time's up.

She dashed to the left, using a burst of slow motion to freeze her opponents for the moment it took her to jet past them. They gaped at her in shock, but she was already jumping onto a bar stool and careening forward onto the bar itself. From the high ground, she hurled herself forward, grabbing onto the heavy wooden ceiling fan with both hands. The momentum carried her forward into the goblin with the club. She kicked him in the face with both of her feet and let go at the top of her swing. Then she backflipped, landing heavy on her feet to meet her last opponent, who was unfortunately not where he was supposed to be. He'd recovered enough from his shock to reposition, anticipating her trajectory.

A knife slid between her ribs. She gasped in shock as the white-hot pain lanced through her. It was blinding. Everything else evaporated in the wake of that metal sticking out of her side.

She struggled to breathe as her vision went blurry at the edges. Was this it? Was she going to die knifed in a bar fight? After all of this trouble, for her memories? She wanted to know—God, did she want to know what happened to her, who had done it, why it had been done to her. And yes, she deserved to remember her family. To know whether they were dead or not. The world had taken so much. It owed her that, at least. But she didn't want to *die*, either.

A man appeared at her side, slicing casually through the goblin's throat with a sword. His head clattered to the floor next to his body, and she would have gone down with him if the stranger hadn't gotten an arm under her.

"This one yours, Graves?"

"Fuck, Wren," Graves said, assessing the knife still lodged in her side.

"I'm...I'm fine."

"Vale," Graves said with a desperation she'd only heard in his voice once before, when he'd thought she was dying.

"We'll take her to my place," Vale said.

She was hoisted into Graves's warm, comforting arms, and darkness beckoned.

Chapter Seventeen

Kierse awoke to the tangy scent of blood. Her eyes fluttered open to reveal a bare room. Just a twin pallet on the ground and a hanging lightbulb.

"Don't move," Niamh insisted.

"What happened?" she groaned.

"You got a knife to the ribs. I'm currently healing you."

"How?"

Niamh winked at her. "High Priestess, remember?"

"Oh," she said as the groggy memory returned to her. She wasn't in her apartment back in Dublin. Niamh hadn't come to check on her. She was in the goblin market. And it had almost taken her life.

She winced at the pain in her side, but it was already much better than it had been. If Niamh hadn't been here, would she have died?

Then she remembered the sound of Graves's voice when he'd seen her injury. No. No, she was pretty sure he wouldn't have left her for dead. He would have found a way.

"You're awake," Graves said as he entered the bare room. "How are you feeling?"

"Like someone tried to kill me."

"All in a day's work."

She blew out a harsh breath. "Going to try to not die anymore for a while."

"That would be satisfactory."

"What happened while I was out?"

"We're at Vale's...apartment," Graves said, looking around at the four walls as if they offended him.

"He saved me."

Graves nodded. His expression was carefully blank. Was he beating himself up because he'd let her get hurt? Or because he'd almost lost his prized thief?

"Does he have the information we need to find Rio?"

"Maybe we should end this fool's errand."

She glared at him. "I made it this far."

"You almost died," he snapped back. His calm evaporating for a moment. "Is your memory worth all of this?"

She'd asked herself the same question. Wondered if all of it was worth dying for. And no, she didn't want to die.

"Aren't you at all curious what happened to me?" she asked instead.

Niamh glanced back at Graves, then eyed Kierse consideringly. "Who do you know who can take memories?"

Graves's gaze hardened. "It was the spell, which is nothing like my magic. It's more likely a Druid."

"You don't know that!" Niamh fought back.

Kierse winced. "Can we bring the volume down on all of this? I still have internal bleeding. I don't know who did this or why, and I need to know, okay? I don't want to die for it. I just need answers."

Graves sighed. "We'll move out when Niamh gives you a clean bill of health." He disappeared from the room, and Kierse knocked her head back against the pallet.

"He's infuriating," she muttered.

"Tell me about it. I've known him for like five hundred years, and he's *always* been like this."

Kierse turned her face to Niamh. "Even when he was young?"

"Especially so," she said. "Now quiet and let me finish."

It took another hour before Niamh agreed that Kierse could get up and move around. She felt nearly 100 percent better. Still stiff, and she wasn't going to be performing any big swinging motions anytime soon, but much better than she had been. Niamh looked a little worse for wear, as if it had taken a lot out of her. Kierse wanted to ask, but Niamh went into the kitchen to scrounge for something to replenish her.

Kierse found Graves and Vale seated at a card table. Graves was engrossed in a book, clearly recharging his magic. Vale, meanwhile, looked like a medieval cosplayer. He had dark, shoulder-length hair and nearly black eyes in a pale face with a full beard and mustache, and he was wearing dark, fitted pants, a brown jerkin, and leather bracers. A sword hung at his waist, and an actual bow and arrow rested in a corner. In fact, the only decoration in the otherwise empty room was the sheer display of weaponry of every type. A chest full of knives, maces, axes, throwing stars. A wall of samurai swords. A dozen full-length spears. A dented metal shield, two wooden crossbows, and what looked like an actual halberd. The guy clearly had a weapon fetish.

"You look hale," Vale said with a head nod.

"Thank you for your help."

"I was surprised Graves would ask for help," Vale said. His smile lit up his face. "Though I can see why with such a beautiful woman at his side to protect."

Graves glanced up at that. "She doesn't need protection."

"She was injured when I arrived."

"She can take care of herself."

Vale held up his hands in clear amusement. "Ah, she is spoken for, I see."

"*I* am right here, and I'm not spoken for."

"Well, in that case, might I persuade you to stay in the market with me a little longer?" Vale said with a grin, rising to his feet and taking her hand to press a kiss to the back. "This is but my nearest safe house. There are jewels in my possession of which you have never seen the like."

"Vale, cut the shit," Graves said.

Kierse extracted her hand. "I'll take the location of the bookkeeper."

Vale didn't look put out as he straightened. "If you insist. We should get moving, then."

"Finally," Graves said.

Niamh appeared then, looking decidedly more grounded. "I'm ready when you are."

Vale led the way from his safe house and through the warren of buildings. He navigated the streets the way Kierse did the surface. New York was her home, and she knew it front and back. This seemed to be the same for Vale here in the market.

And he appeared well known enough that monsters shuffled out of his way when he approached. A good person to have on her side. She wondered what Graves had offered for his assistance.

It was another hour's hike through the ever-darkening, winding streets before they came upon a door much the same as the first one in the Dublin quarter. This one said RIO, and beneath that, once again, BEWARE OF DOG.

"So the dog survived," Graves said.

Vale held his hand out to Graves, and they clasped forearms. "Until next time, my friend."

"When I return to the city, I'll complete our trade."

"I know you're good for it."

Vale winked at Kierse, tipped his head at Niamh, and then loped off into the distance.

"What did you offer him?" Niamh asked.

"A set of armor," Graves said.

"That tracks," Kierse said. She glanced at the door with apprehension. "Think the bookkeeper is actually inside?"

"Let's fucking hope so," Graves said as he turned the knob and pushed the door open.

Unlike the first shop, this one was new and gleaming with polished hardwood floors. Another damn bell jingled merrily overhead. The shop had the appearance of a jewelry shop with long glass cases along three of the walls, except they were completely empty. Not a single object or bobble in sight apart from an enormous, cracked-leather tome next to the cash register.

At the ring of the bell, a loud bark sounded from the back of the shop, separated from the entrance by swinging double doors. They nearly came off their hinges as the aforementioned dog rushed to meet the visitors.

"What the fuck is that?" Niamh yelled, jumping backward.

"Fuck!" Kierse screeched.

Graves didn't move and sighed another insufferable sigh, as if the thing charging him wasn't some sort of fucking demon. "Calm down. It's a goblin hound," he said.

Dog, or even *hound*, was a generous assessment. The thing looked more lizard than mammal. It had the characteristic green-gray skin tone of the goblins, elongated canines, and both pointed ears and tail. It was roughly the size of a mastiff and could almost be considered cute if she looked at it sideways. It jumped up onto Graves's black suit coat, its tongue lolling out like a rather oversize labrador, panting with excitement.

"That's a good boy," Graves said.

"Daisy, down," a voice called as a tall, thin goblin entered the shop from the back. They were dressed in black, fitted pants and a black vest. This must be the inimitable Rio. A hard goblin to locate.

The hound, *Daisy*, jumped off Graves and headed for Kierse and Niamh.

"Um, hi," Kierse said, holding her hand out.

"I wouldn't do that if I were you," Rio said. "He's still a puppy, and their saliva is acidic until they can control the venom."

Kierse jerked her hand back. "Uh…right." That probably explained the giant, acid-eaten pit in the middle of the last shop.

"Daisy is a boy hound?" Niamh asked incredulously.

"Obviously," they said. "He likes scratches behind his ears."

She slowly reached for the back of his head and gave him a good scratch. Saliva dribbled out of his mouth, dropping with a sizzling hiss to the floor, before the hound collapsed at her feet, rolling around against her shoes.

"He's...friendly," Niamh offered.

"Unfortunately," they said.

"Vriosa, I assume," Graves said.

"Rio will do," they corrected. They ran their long fingers down the front of their black pants. Daisy trotted along past them to merrily flop on a fluffy pink dog bed. Rio settled their hand on the massive brown leather book. "Do you know what it is that I do here in Nying Market?"

"You're the bookkeeper," Graves said. His eyes were fixed on the giant book. "You know where to acquire information."

"You and I are the same in that regard, are we not?" Rio asked with a raised eyebrow.

"You've heard of me?"

"Tales of your time in the market have reached my ear. And what you paid is in here." They patted their book. "Knowledge is power, after all."

Graves clenched his jaw at their words. "I see."

Kierse glanced between them, wondering what exactly was happening. Niamh leaned her hip against the counter and looked down at her nails. "What did he trade and trade for?"

Rio's eyes jumped to Niamh. "I know what you traded for, too."

Niamh shrugged. "So?"

Rio smirked at her before turning to Kierse. "What would *you* like to trade for?"

"I'm trying to regain my memories, and I was told that was something that could be done in here."

Rio shrugged. "Sure. We don't have any magic ourselves." They snapped their fingers. "*Monsters not magic*, and all that."

That was the motto that had been circulated once monsters came out in the open. They were supernatural beings—vampires, werewolves, mer, wraiths, nymphs, goblins, shifters, phoenix, trolls, and incubus/succubus—but they didn't have *magic*. That apparently was not the same as the fact that magic didn't exist. Because it very clearly did.

Kierse laughed softly. "We all know that was a lie peddled to humans at the end of the war."

"It depends on how you look at it. I have no magic myself. The other monsters I regularly work with don't have magic. But there are magic users who have not come into the light, such as your friends here, and they're happy to trade their magic for bits of what we monsters can offer," Rio said with a sharp-toothed smile. "So, for regular people, *monsters not magic* is just fine. For those who see beyond the veil, perhaps not."

"But you have traded with someone who can help a person regain memories."

"Indeed." Rio opened the book and began to flip through the paper-thin pages. "Memories are tricky, though. Not many who specialize in that sort of thing."

"Are you trying to tell me it's expensive?"

Rio flashed her another smile. "Ah, I see why you decided to come here when memory stands at your side." Their eyes flickered to Graves. "Perhaps I'd brave the shadow, too."

Graves crossed his arms. "Do you have someone who can help or not?"

"I do." Rio breezed through more pages before stopping and sliding their long red nail down the list. "Ah. Here we are. Just what you're looking for."

Graves leaned forward against the counter as if he meant to try to steal the information before Rio could shut the book. But it was all gibberish to Kierse, either in another language or in code.

Rio shot Graves a look and then put their hands over the encoded pages. "Now, the fun part. What exactly have you brought me for this information?"

"The bracelet of Queen Aveline of the Dryads," Graves said.

Rio's eyebrows shot up. "Is that so?" Their eyes were greedy as they looked from Graves to Kierse. "Show me this jewel."

"We don't have it on us, but we can give you the location of where to acquire it."

"Would that location be Versailles?" they asked drily.

"I stole it from the queen," Kierse told them.

"Hmm," they said. "That doesn't seem like a fair trade. You give me a location of wherever this most precious artifact *could* be, and I give you exactly what you want when you could never have found it on your own?"

Niamh *tsk*ed from her place at the end of the counter. "You're both trading information."

"The difference is that I'm good for it. This is my job. I don't take I-owe-yous from new customers. Especially with his background," they said, looking Graves up and down.

"Fine. We can add something else to the bargain," Kierse said.

Cost in the market had always been a nebulous thing. It wasn't always money traders were after, or at least not expressly. Kierse had more than expected to have to cut off a lock of her hair or give some tears or a bit of her magic. If the cost was higher, she was prepared to pay.

Rio's expression turned shrewd. They already knew who Graves and Niamh were—the New York City warlock and a Dublin High Priestess were high-end clients. But it was Kierse who made them tilt their head in consideration.

"You're not human," they said.

Kierse forced her hands to stay at her sides, away from her ears. Her glamour was still in place, and Rio had already said they couldn't use magic, so there was no way for them to know.

Still, she nodded. "I'm not."

"In the company of a warlock and Druid who hate each other on a mission for you. Curious."

"All in a day's work," she joked, echoing Graves's words from earlier.

"Very few things could bring together this warlock and the Druids," they said, tilting their head. "Very few things indeed."

"Do you have a price in mind?" Graves growled.

They eyed Kierse up and down. "Perhaps a vial of your blood."

"No," Graves said at the same time Niamh said, "Absolutely not."

Rio's smile was vicious. "That is my request."

Graves shook his head and began to remove items from his pockets. "I've brought fair payment."

Rio looked over his stash. Kierse didn't even know what half of the items were. She thought about what it would mean to give someone part of her blood. It had crossed her mind, but she'd known it was her hard limit. Dr. Mafi had taken her blood and given it to the vampire lord King Louis, who had used it thinking it would give him magical powers. She'd decapitated him with the spear anyway. She wasn't planning on letting someone else try something similar.

"None of this will do," Rio said, waving it away. "I have another bargain if you refused blood."

"What's that?"

Rio showed a row of sharp teeth. "I'll ask you three questions. You answer them truthfully and give me the information for the bracelet, and we'll call it even. If you refuse to answer, then I get the blood."

Kierse glanced at Graves, who was currently returning items to his pockets and looking displeased with the assessment. He didn't like it. Niamh didn't like it. But what other choice was there? Her blood could reveal her Fae heritage, a thing none of them wanted anyone else to know about. Not when most people believed the wisps were extinct.

"Fine," Kierse said. "Three questions."

"Excellent. First question, what is your true name?"

"Kierse McKenna."

Rio's smile widened. "I see. Second question, what is the nature of your magics?"

Graves's hand balled into a fist at that question. Kierse could have said immunity. That was the lie they had peddled to everyone else. But she had a feeling Rio would know if she lied and would void their deal. This was a dangerous line of questioning.

"The nature of my magics is absorption."

Rio nodded as if anticipating that answer. "Final question, what sort of monster are you?"

Kierse froze at those words. Rio knew. The gleam in their eyes said that they had put together what should have been impossible. Fuck. And she couldn't lie to them and say she was a warlock the way she had to everyone else. Somehow, they would know, and then they would require blood. Blood that she absolutely couldn't give. A fact that Rio clearly understood.

Was it worth it to give up this piece of valuable information to someone in the market? Something *this* dangerous? She had no idea how it could be used against her. But if she didn't, she'd never find the person with the memory information. She'd have done all of this for nothing.

Graves leaned forward against the counter before she could say a word. "I would tread *very* carefully."

Rio looked at him with a bland expression. "You and I are curators of knowledge, are we not? If I can guess the nature of who and what she is, do you not think that others soon will as well?"

The threat hung heavy between them.

"She's a warlock," Graves told them flatly.

Rio's gaze shifted to Kierse. "Is that right? With absorption powers? Working with Druids?"

Kierse's tongue stuck to the roof of her mouth. She couldn't say the word. Even though Rio had the answer already.

"I think not," Rio said. "So, will you answer, or will you give me a vial of your blood?"

Graves pushed away from the counter. "This is absurd. Let's just leave."

"After all that we went through?"

"Allow *me* to help you instead."

Kierse turned away from him. Rio already *had* this answer—she just had to confirm it—while she had no idea what more she'd have to give of herself to work with Graves like that. What he'd take. What further trust he'd break.

"Wisp," she whispered.

Niamh tensed next to her. Graves slammed his fist down on the counter. She could see he wanted to choke the bookkeeper for this fact, but it was already done.

Rio slid their fingers over their lips and mimed locking the information away. They ripped out a slip from under the cabinet, scribbled on the paper, and passed it to Kierse. "Go here. Rizz will have what you're looking for."

Kierse took the paper and barely mustered the decency to say, "Thank you."

"Happy hunting," Rio said with a vicious smile that said they were next on the menu.

Chapter Eighteen

Kierse blew out a long, slow breath as they exited back onto the gloomy streets. "Could that have gone worse?"

Niamh winced. "You could have given them some of your blood."

"What are they going to do with that information?" Kierse asked Graves.

He said nothing, just stared resignedly forward.

"What would *you* do with that information?" she countered.

"He'd sell it to the most advantageous buyer," Niamh said.

Graves shot her a look. "I was not part of the genocide. And if Rio uses the information, we'll deal with it."

Kierse shivered at that. Nothing could be done now, but fuck, the market was worse than she had bargained for. Niamh and Graves had tried to warn her, but she hadn't anticipated *this*.

"Where are we going now?" Graves asked.

Kierse waited until a troll and shifter, her skin rippling threateningly, had passed them before pulling out the piece of paper.

Uriosa
1901 Main Street
Dublin Nying Market

Rizz's Oddities
3-1 Xinjiang Rd
Shanghai Nying Market

"I'm guessing that's Rio's old address. And now we head to Shanghai?" Kierse said.

Graves plucked the paper out of her hand and scanned it. "I'm familiar with the area. We have to go up one more floor to get to Shanghai," Graves said. "There's a way nearby."

A group of stooped goblins carrying automatic weapons veered around them. A pair of wraiths were crossing the street ahead of them. This area hadn't been that busy when Vale had dropped them off, and with their luck, it wasn't a good sign. Time to leave.

"Get us there quickly," Niamh said.

"Unfortunately, there's only one reliable way up," Graves said.

They rounded the corner into a busy intersection, full of glaring billboards and rushing crowds. Graves pointed around the commotion to a line leading to a massive glass elevator.

"We just…ride it up?" she asked uncertainly.

"That's the idea," Niamh said.

Nothing at the market had been this easy. From a distance she could see that the line was half full of humans gorging themselves on more goblin fruit as they waited for their turn. But there were just as many monsters of all varieties, halfheartedly grousing about the wait.

"Should we make a plan? Scope it out?"

"We just ride it up," Graves said. "I've never had trouble with it."

"You were the one to convince me that the market is out to get me. And I've learned my lesson," she said as they headed toward the line. "A chase, getting stabbed, the negotiations…I got the message."

Their group got behind a mer, who was talking animatedly to a wraith in swift Mandarin. The line moved at a glacial pace. The elevator was large and jammed full every time, and still somehow it took forever for them to reach the front.

"Fruit?" a goblin asked once they were next in line.

Kierse held up her coin and held her breath. The goblin scoffed and moved on to the group of humans behind them. Kierse released a harsh breath, taking pains to ignore the pornographic sounds of the humans enjoying the fruit at her back.

Finally, the elevator came back to their floor and opened for them, and they followed the mer inside. Kierse ended up against the far wall with Graves and Niamh at her sides as, just like before, more and more people were shoved into the cramped space. Until humans were digging elbows into her stomach, stomping on her feet, and she could smell the fruit's tangy sweetness mingled with body odor. A man in front of her looked half ready to pass out as the heat rose precipitously, but still the juice splashed down his white tank top, all over his hands and mouth, as if he physically couldn't stop himself from devouring the stuff.

When she thought it couldn't get any fuller, the goblins pushed a few more into the knot of bodies, shoving them with all their might and constricting the last vestiges of air out of the place as the doors were closing. A man screamed as the door smashed on his shoulder. The scent of blood filled the already disgusting elevator as the guy was given one more shove and the doors finally snapped shut.

"The fruit," a girl said to Kierse's side. Her teeth were tinged purple and juice dribbled down her chin. "Heaven sent."

"Heaven," Kierse said disbelievingly. "Not what I'd go with."

"Don't engage," Graves told her. He was looking at the ceiling and seemed to be holding his breath.

Niamh looked jovially around as if she might start leading everyone in a rousing chorus of show tunes. Nothing seemed to keep down her good humor.

But the girl was still looking at Kierse, and now her glazed eyes looked mad. "Heaven sent!" she snarled and then shoved the piece of fruit at Kierse's face.

Kierse clamped her mouth shut on a scream as she batted the girl's hand away, but the girl was all bones, and something snapped in her wrist when Kierse hit her. The girl wailed as the fruit went flying into the mass of bodies and several hands grasped for it eagerly.

A smear of it ran down the side of Kierse's face, from temple to jaw.

"Get it off. Get it off!" Kierse cried. Her breaths were coming out fast and quick, and with how little oxygen there was in the elevator, she thought she might hyperventilate.

Graves produced a handkerchief from his pocket. His gloved hand held her jaw and turned her face toward him. "Eyes on me."

She looked deep into those storm eyes. Calm settled around her as he gently wiped away all traces of the juice.

"You're okay," he said. "You didn't get any in your mouth or eyes."

She nodded, but she was still trembling under his touch when the elevator dinged open and the crush of bodies disgorged into the street. Only when she was out of the elevator did she double over and take deep, heaving breaths.

"This place...is trying to kill me," she said.

"Yes," Graves agreed. "Now straighten up. We have business to attend to."

Kierse released the last of her fear. Dying by goblin fruit had been a particularly acute one since her earliest days, but she couldn't show that fear any more than she already had. She let out one more breath and then faced this new section of the market.

Having never left New York until five months ago, it felt as if she had stepped into the future. The Shanghai market streets were loud and busy and tiered with vendors hawking their wares in several dialects of Chinese as well as English. The glowing signs were written all in Chinese characters, with a handful showing the translation in various languages underneath. Everything was fast-paced and exciting, bright and beautiful.

"The streets are named the same as downtown Shanghai," Graves explained. "East-west streets are named after Chinese cities and north-south are named after provinces and regions. Xinjiang will take us north."

He shouldered into the mix, and they pushed through the crowd of onlookers surrounding a phoenix who was demonstrating his fire abilities as he cooked traditional street food. Considering the line he had around the block, he wasn't doing bad for himself. She might even try one of his little dumplings if she didn't suspect that everything in the market was laced with goblin fruit.

Her hackles were raised after the terrible ordeal they'd had on the last two levels, but no one looked their way as they disappeared into ever-darkening and narrower streets. It was eerily silent by the time they found Xinjiang Road. The neon signs disappeared in the background as they entered a dingy street with clotheslines bridging the windows. A sign for RIZZ'S ODDITIES was written under a sign in Mandarin that flickered in once-bright neon green. Inside, a baby was screaming at the top of its lungs. Kierse furrowed her brow, wondering if this could possibly be the right place and what sort of trap Rio had led them into.

They scouted the rest of the street just to be sure nothing was going to come at them from behind, but all seemed ordinary. For some reason, completely unrelated to the events of the evening, that made her nervous. Still, finding the bookkeeper had been the hard part. She had endured the crushing elevator fiasco. It was time for the payoff.

Graves knocked on the door. The shrill cry of a baby intensified, and a moment later, a haggard goblin woman opened it suspiciously, speaking in Mandarin. She was holding the baby in question, and the little thing's mouth was wide open in a prolonged wail. She looked half ready to curse them out—or perhaps she already was. Kierse didn't speak Mandarin.

Of course, Graves did…for the most part. He answered her haltingly as if it had been a while since he'd used the language, or he'd learned a similar but not exactly this dialect.

The woman immediately switched to English. "Here for Rizz?"

Graves nodded. "Yes. For Rizz. We were sent by Rio."

She bounced the baby on her hip, sighed, and called into the shop. "Rizz! Rio sent you more charity." She ushered them inside. "He can't run a shop if his life depended on it. We have a new baby and still he would rather tinker with his clocks than sell the wares he has."

"Congratulations!" Niamh said excitedly. "How adorable."

"She's not adorable when she's shrieking at all hours of the night. *His* mother says we should give her some liquor and put her back down. It explains so much about Rizz now, doesn't it? Even in the market it's frowned upon to let the baby drink. It's not all about how it was done the generation before. You can't even have anything in the crib with her." She cooed down at her wailing child. "At least she's cute."

Niamh stepped up to the distressed mother, looking the baby over. "Oh, she's a delight. You're a wonderful mother. I bet you're doing the best you can and someone is just fussy."

The goblin woman beamed under the praise, and they headed over to a bassinet in the corner together to continue their conversation. Kierse and Graves exchanged an uncomfortable look. Kierse had never seen a baby survive on the streets—not when they stole childhoods from everyone.

A male goblin appeared then, wearing multi-lens glasses, with frazzled brown hair and large greenish lips. The resemblance to Rio was there if Kierse squinted just right.

"What's this about?" Rizz asked.

Kierse stepped forward. "Rio sent us."

He sighed. "What did my sibling get me into this time?"

"They said that you had what we were looking for." Kierse offered him the paper.

The goblin glanced at it with a frown. "Sure. I have this. Memory potions are tricky things."

"Payment!" his partner cried from the other side of the room.

"Yes, qīn'ài de." There was both affection and resignation in his voice. "Sorry—how were you planning to pay for this?"

"We're here for fair value," Graves said as he removed a handful of goblin marks from his pocket. They were dented bronze coins with a notch missing out of the middle.

His partner handed the baby to Niamh and hustled over. She took one of the marks and bit into it, then spoke swiftly to Rizz. He nodded along for a while, until his eyes bugged out of his head. Whatever he said back to her must have made her mad, because she stomped back to the baby, cursing him under her breath.

"My wife believes since the item is so rare, it would cost a quarter million, but I..."

"Done," Graves said.

Rizz gaped at him. Kierse did the same. Since *when* did Graves not negotiate and haggle for price? He sure had with her.

"I'd like to get this over with," he added. But the glint in his eye said something else. She tilted her head and realized what it must mean...the potion was likely worth more than that amount. And what was a quarter million marks to someone like Graves?

"Well," Rizz said, flustered. "All right. Let's uh...get to business, then. Tell me about these memories. How were they lost?"

"A spell was put on me to make me forget."

"Ah," he said, crossing the room to a large cabinet filled to the brim with knickknacks. Kierse didn't recognize a single thing inside that appeared to her to be of value. "So now they're all jumbled up."

"Yes."

"You need a smoother to go with that."

"A...smoother?"

"I don't know the word in English," he confessed. "But it will help put it in order, and then you'll take the memory one after to make you remember." He threw a few boxes aside and then selected a small plastic bottle, dropping it onto the counter. "Smoother." He gestured to it. "Cheap."

"Rizz!" his partner snapped.

Rizz went back to searching through his cabinet. "Memory is harder. Much harder. It's tricky. I can't guarantee you'll get a specific memory back. Are you hoping for one in particular?"

"Well, I wanted something about my parents."

He grimaced. "Doesn't work like that."

"Fine. More specifically, I want to know why my memories of my parents were taken."

"You'll need a direction, too."

"How do we give it direction?" Graves asked.

Rizz looked up at him in surprise as if just remembering he was here. "Intent."

Graves grinned. "Ah, yes. You need to use the magical intent to push it toward what you want."

"I mean, intent." He dropped another bottle on the counter. "Probably can push it in the direction you want."

Kierse frowned. Two bottles and still no memory potion. "Do you have the memory part?"

"Right!" He muttered to himself in Mandarin as he reached deeper into the depths of the cabinet. "Sold one of these already. So I just have the one." He dropped it onto the counter. "Not cheap."

"We're good for it," Graves said.

"Right. Right."

"What's *in* them?" Kierse asked, picking up a bottle and inspecting the little thing.

Rizz shrugged. "I didn't make them. They were payment for something else."

Niamh held the now-quiet baby against her chest and grabbed one of the bottles from the counter. "Do you mind?" She plucked the top off the "smoother" and sniffed. "Rosemary for protection. Mandrake root for healing. Moonstone dust, usually for divination, but I would guess here it's for intuition. And a mix of water and oils. I bet it tastes great." Niamh stoppered the bottle and set it back down. "Probably from a healing witch. Looks real to me."

"There you have it," Rizz said with a shrug.

Niamh inspected the other bottles and proclaimed them all real magic. The market would have a lot to answer for if someone were selling faulty goods.

"All right," Kierse conceded. "So I take it in this order."

Rizz nodded. "Smoother. Intent. Memory. Then find a soft surface and prepare to see what you hope to see. But remember I'm not responsible for what you see. How much or how little or if it's what you want or if you don't like the outcome."

"Got it."

"And no refunds," his partner called out.

"Right."

"Anything else?" Rizz asked with a worried glance to his wife.

"No. This is all we require," Kierse said.

She took the little bottles in her hands and hoped after all she'd gone through to get it that this was the answer she had been looking for.

Chapter Nineteen

A chair clattered over as Gen jumped to her feet anxiously when they entered the apartment. She looked as if this was the first breath she had taken in hours. Her oldest, most-worn tarot deck was laid out in front of her. "You're okay."

"I'm okay," Kierse confirmed.

"The cards…" She shook her head. "They didn't like the market. It was like I was blocked by its magic from scrying you."

Niamh patted her shoulder. "It's a pocket of ancient energy."

"I didn't like it. I don't think you should go back into that place."

"You and me both," Kierse said. The last thing she wanted to think about was what had happened in the depths of that place. She had no strong urge to ever go back inside. Not if she could help it.

"What happened to you? You all look like you've been through hell."

"It was just…" Kierse shook her head. "I could use a shower." She removed the bottles from her pockets. "But first, I got what I was looking for."

Gen chewed on her plump bottom lip. "How does it work?"

Kierse explained how to use the three bottles. "Then I'll lay down and the memories will surface."

"Let me just…" Gen trailed off, hurrying back to her deck. She arranged it back together before bringing it to Kierse. "Cut."

Kierse knew better than to argue when Gen's psychic energy was at its zenith. She split the tarot deck in half, placing the bottom on top. Gen shivered as the weight of her magic bloomed. Kierse had always said she'd had a touch of prophecy while reading the cards. It was the reason she had earned the name Prophet Genesis back in the city.

Gen slowly turned over the top card: The Magician.

They turned as one to look at Graves, silent and sinister, beside the door with his hands in the pockets of his bespoke suit. A lock of midnight-blue hair had fallen forward onto his brow. He was the epitome of dangerous, and utterly delectable. Kierse could have devoured him in that moment if only things weren't so complicated.

"An anchor," he said. "That's what the card suggests."

Niamh snorted. "You think *you* should anchor her?"

"You doubt the prophecy of your own people?" he challenged.

Niamh ground her teeth together at the accusation but shook her head stiffly.

"Yes," Gen said with relief in her voice and set the deck aside. "She needs you."

Kierse didn't know what she thought about that, but Gen was never wrong. Only a fool would ignore divine intervention.

"What does an anchor do?"

"I hold your magic while you drop into your memories," he said evenly. As if he wasn't suggesting something intimate as hell. "I'll pull you out if anything goes wrong."

"I could do it," Niamh said earnestly.

"Graves is stronger," Gen pointed out.

Graves met her gaze. "And I won't let any harm come to you."

Kierse could see the sincerity on his face. He'd had her back in the market. He'd saved her after she had been stabbed. He'd bartered for her. He'd paid the sum for the potions despite disagreeing with the whole endeavor from the start. She didn't trust him, didn't know how to trust him, but he would do this and he would do it right.

"Fine," Kierse said. "You're with me."

Gen relaxed, her magic spent. "Good." She touched Kierse's arm. "Be careful."

"After you," Graves said, gesturing to her bedroom.

"We'll be right here," Niamh said more to Graves as a threat than anything.

They walked into her bedroom, and suddenly it felt like it was too small, not enough air for both of them to breathe at once. Graves somehow took up the entire space.

Kierse turned away from him hastily, but now she was facing the bed and her thoughts drifted back to them entangling at his Paris flat. Gen asking if they'd had sex. *Not yet.* She shook off that thought, too. It was a distraction. *He* was a distraction. That was all.

"Are you ready?" he asked in a low, throaty voice.

She slipped out of her red jacket and tossed it aside before sinking into the bed. "Now I am."

She didn't normally spend time worrying about what could have been, but now Kierse had to wonder what exactly she was going to see in her past. Would she finally have answers? Or would she only find more questions in the recesses of her mind? What if she couldn't sort through the memories? Had the spell turned all of her nightmares against her?

And now she finally held what she hoped was the key.

Graves slid a chair over to the bed and began to remove his gloves. She watched as his fingers worked over the material—every move was somehow both methodical and erotic. "Remember our conversations about intent. Keep your thoughts on exactly what you want to drive the spell to the correct destination."

What she wanted. She glanced up at him and away. She needed to get her head in the game. Graves was *not* what she wanted.

Her parents. This was about her parents. She wanted to know so much. What had happened to them, how they had died, what was in her nightmares, what it had been like growing up. Everything. She wanted everything. But she needed to be specific to guide the intent.

Who her parents were.

It was a small thing, and yet it was what she wanted most of all. She wanted a memory that wasn't destruction that showed who they were.

Graves must have seen her intent settle over her. He dropped his gloves on the side table and said, "Lay back."

Her stomach dipped at those words. So much control.

Slowly she lowered herself onto her back with the bottles in hand. "How does the anchor work? I didn't think you could touch my magic because of the absorption."

"I can't read you or use my magic on you, but I can hold you through this. I will be here the whole time."

Kierse panicked for a second, sitting up. "Oh fuck, what if it doesn't work on me? What if I absorb the spells and can't use them? I'm not empty."

Graves put his hands on my shoulders. "Breathe. This is herbal. Much like what Gen has been giving you for your nightmares. You may absorb some of the magic that binds it together, but much of these spells rely on the user to guide it. You will smooth the direction. You will focus your intent. Then you will make way for the memories."

Kierse nodded, relaxing under his touch as he gently leaned her back on the bed. It was the best she could do. It was worth it to try, whatever it might give her. She could do this. She'd almost paid with her life twice to get it. There was no turning back.

She unstoppered the first potion, meeting Graves's storm-cloud eyes. His magic glowed golden as it wrapped around her like a blanket. When he was done and the anchor was in place, he nodded.

She lifted the bottle to her lips and said, "Bottoms up."

Chapter Twenty

The apartment was a shoebox. A pair of threadbare chairs sat in the open main space connected to a small kitchen. A mattress rested on the floor across the room. The bathroom lay beyond the only door, which was ajar, and the water was running in the shower. A man's voice sang sweetly. Light streamed in from the miniscule window that was half blocked by an air-conditioning unit. Kierse could make out the dirty streets beyond, but she didn't have enough context to place where she was. It was drab and rough and could have been anywhere.

Kierse stared down at her hands in confusion. Was this part of the dream? This tiny apartment with a man singing in the shower? Where was *she*? If this was *her* memory?

"Daddy! Daddy!"

Kierse jerked around as the door to the apartment crashed open. A small girl ran inside as the water shut off. A rough white towel was jerked off of a hanger, and a man strode out of the room with it wrapped around his waist.

"Hello, my wee darling," he crooned in a lilting Scottish accent, picking up the small child and lifting her into his arms. "How was school? Did you learn anything new?"

"Nothing much," she said in what was clearly a lie.

The girl was unmistakably, categorically striking. Long, ashy-blond hair with angelic features and wide, dark eyes that seemed to suck the light out of the room. She had a mischievous glint in those eyes and an impish smile for her father.

In her much younger features, Kierse could see it clearly for herself. *She* was that young girl. She no longer had the dark-blond hair, which had aged to a darker brown. Her features had all been changed under the spell anyway. The ears were there, slightly pointed, the shape of her mouth, and there, the little wren necklace hanging on her much smaller body.

Tears came to her eyes as she watched the interaction. Her father had… loved her. He was looking at her with adoration. A muscular man built like an ox, with the same dark hair Kierse had currently, though with a slight curl to it. A tattoo of a wooded landscape snaked down his arm, a horned stag proud and prominent near his elbow, and the whole thing entwined with a Trinity Knot at the wrist.

"She's a thief is what she is," a woman said, striding inside the apartment door with arms full of groceries.

"Did she get caught?" the dad asked with a similar grin to his daughter's.

"Of course not!" She dropped the groceries onto the only available counter space and swiveled to stare at them. "She was trained too well by her misbehaving father."

"Mummy!" the girl cried.

Kierse's heart stuttered and stopped.

That word alone made her want to sit down on the small mattress in the corner and not get up for a hundred years. Her mother was standing before her. They were roughly the same height. Kierse might have been an inch taller. Their eyes were the same depthless dark brown, but her mom's hair matched Kierse's younger self—an ash blond that had never seen hair dye. Beautiful, stoic, and proud.

Kierse reached out to touch her face, but her hand passed straight through. A memory. Nothing more than a memory. And already it had gotten away from her.

No matter that for her entire life she had believed that her mother had died in childbirth. Here she was—alive and well, locked away in Kierse's memory.

"You need to stop teaching her these things, Adair," her mother said. "It's going to get her in trouble."

"Stop worrying, Shannon," her father said, setting the girl down on her feet. "I'm teaching her life skills. No one is going to find her all the way over here. For now, we are safe."

"For now," Shannon said. A deep resignation settled on her shoulders at the words.

Adair disappeared back into the bathroom and came out in trousers and a fitted shirt. He padded barefoot to his wife and kissed her.

"It will be all right. We're going to fix all of this."

Shannon nodded. "Of course."

Kierse wondered what exactly they were trying to fix. What they were running from—because it was clear in the packed bags and empty apartment and scared hunch of her mother's shoulders that they were running. Was it what had killed the rest of the wisps? Had it caught up to them, too?

The smaller version of Kierse was running around their heels, telling them all about school and the eraser she'd stolen but hadn't gotten caught for. Apparently, her father was the one who had given her that skill. The one that had helped her stay alive when she'd been left to the streets.

"I heard from my contact," Shannon said a time later, when the little girl was pretending to do her homework and was instead listening in on her parents' conversation.

"And?" Adair asked.

"He has an address and a meet time. We can go tonight."

"Tonight?" Adair asked, steel entering his voice. He'd gone from loving father and husband to a hardened soldier in the span of a second. As if the carefree man was the mask he wore over his true identity.

Shannon glanced at her little girl. "We have to do it. She's not safe."

"Are you sure?"

"I am. We can't trust anyone else."

"Can we trust him?"

Shannon met his gaze with a hardened one of her own. "At least we know where his allegiances lie."

"Then tonight it is."

Kierse could have sat in that tiny apartment for all of eternity and watched her family go about their lives. Banal, ordinary, almost boring, and yet it was a spark of a star in her stomach. The life she'd never known. The life she'd kill to have back.

But the memory jumped too quickly and suddenly she was in a town car. Her younger self was tired and yawning, resting her head against her father. But she was still alert in a way that could only be learned from vigilant parents. She knew that she hadn't been woken in the middle of the night and ushered into a car worth more than they made in a year for no reason.

They were in some kind of tunnel, so Kierse still had no context for where they were. As headlights glowed in the distance, they came to stop before an underground elevator.

Her stomach plummeted.

"No," she whispered even though no one could hear her.

The driver opened the back door and ushered them out of the car and into the elevator. Kierse didn't want to believe that she knew where they were until the door opened, revealing a butler dressed in black—Edgar.

There was no denying it.

Her parents—and her younger self—were now inside Graves's house.

"What a pleasure to have you in residence. I am Edgar." He bowed slightly for them. "We shall be going to the library this evening."

Adair nodded gruffly, tucking his daughter into his side. He took Shannon's hand, and together they followed him up the stairs to the most familiar double doors Kierse had ever encountered—the entrance to the Holly Library.

A plaque above the doors announced the name, and wards in a language she could almost read were carved in the doorframe. Graves's symbol—the holly vines—threaded through the pattern. His magic was everywhere. His domain. *His.* Just as *she* was, every time she stepped inside.

Edgar led them into the library. Much the same as Kierse had ever known it. Thousands upon thousands of books covered every square foot of space, towering ever upward toward the ceiling with only a small opening high above them revealing the moon. Holly vines hadn't yet choked the books as they did in present day, but they were beginning to creep in.

The furniture was different as well—still expensive brown leather, made for meetings and not lounging. The table with his infamous book, where he had all of his visitors sign to keep his identity secret, was within reach.

Isolde bustled in then. Graves's chef and old friend was dressed in her usual black-and-white garb. Twenty years younger and Kierse saw the beauty who was now hidden beneath her graying hair and wrinkled skin. "My name is Isolde. It's a pleasure to have you in residence tonight. Tea?"

"No, thank you," Shannon said stiffly.

Isolde smiled kindly at them. Her eyes shifted to the girl, which Kierse still struggled to remember was herself. "No biscuits for the little one?" She held up a thin sugar cookie, and young Kierse's eyes lit up. But Shannon shook her head.

"Of course." Isolde curtsied and disappeared from the room.

No one said anything. Her parents exchanged hardened, worried glances. The girl eyed the cookies and bit her inner cheek, puckering her face as she restrained herself.

They waited a few minutes, and then the doors opened and Graves appeared. Kierse's breath caught at the sight of him. So much the same and somehow more withdrawn, more threatening, more deliciously broody. His sharp cheekbones were cut in the shadows of his library. The perfectly pouty mouth a flat line at the appearance of his guests, those thunderstorm eyes sparking lightning in displeasure. He was pain and pleasure and destruction. Kierse wanted him like this in her memory forever.

"You may call me Graves," he said as he strode across the room in his fancy suit and black leather gloves. He poured himself a drink without offering to anyone else. "Why are you here?"

Just like that. For some reason she'd thought he'd have more finesse in negotiations. This was his job, after all. Knowledge above all else. Perhaps it was just her parents that sent him straight to business. She wouldn't put it past him to already know who and what they were.

"Do you not already know?" Adair asked gruffly.

Graves's eyes slid over Adair and straight to her mother. "I recognize a wisp when they're in my home."

He said the words like a threat, and Kierse realized, in the shape of his shoulders and careful nonchalance, that he saw them as such.

Wisps could kill warlocks. She hadn't found out *how* exactly in her research, but most of the information on her kind had been destroyed. If Graves saw them as a threat, they were.

"I'm not here to kill you," Shannon said bluntly.

Graves arched an eyebrow. "I'm impressed that you think you could inside my own library."

Shannon huffed, but Adair cut in, "We're here about our daughter."

Graves's eyes didn't shift to Kierse's younger self. In fact, he hadn't so much as looked at the child in his inner sanctum. The one who had ignored the cookies for the menacing man before her, watching him like a mouse would a hawk circling overhead.

"She's in danger," Shannon said. "The Fae Killer is onto us. I don't know how he knows where we're going, but we need to hide her."

"How like good parents to have her best interest at heart." The words were bitter, though Kierse could only hear it now that she knew his history.

Shannon bristled as he clearly knew she would. "You may be a monster, warlock, but even you cannot be immune to a child's safety."

"Don't presume to know anything about me," he snarled.

"Enough," Adair said, putting himself between Graves and Shannon before his wife could do something drastic. "We are not here to fight."

"He can do nothing else," Shannon spat.

"Darling," Adair said, low and sweet.

Her shoulders remained tense, but she retreated, sitting back slightly. Kierse's younger self hadn't moved an inch. Just stared up at the threat before her with keen eyes. She took her mom's hand when it was offered, a lifeline in the tension.

"Did you bring something to barter with?" Graves asked.

"Yes," Shannon said stiffly.

Adair grunted and retrieved a handled hunting knife from a sheath. He dropped it onto the table. It wasn't anything special aside from being long and sharp and deadly. The leather was worn in the pattern of Adair's own fingers. The smallest symbol was burned into the edge—a stag's antler inside a Trinity Knot.

"Is this sufficient?" he asked. "It was blessed by the Fae."

Graves took the knife in his hand, and his magic played over the surface of the blade for a moment before he set it aside as if he were bored. "This will do for the information."

Finally, Graves's eyes dropped to the girl. She watched him take in the Fae features: the angelic hair, faintly pointed ears, and unmistakable delicacy. But it was the hardness in her eyes, the straight shoulders, and the fearlessness in the tilt of her jaw, almost a challenge, that made him pause.

"Leave her here with me," Graves said.

"What?" Shannon gasped at the same time Adair proclaimed, "Never!"

Her parents loved her. They loved her more than anything. In the glow of their love, she could stand up to a nightmare incarnate.

"She would be safe here. That is what you wanted," he reminded them.

"There is *no* guarantee of her safety here," Shannon snarled. "She is a child. She is a wisp. We need to keep her safe long enough for her magic to come in so she can protect herself."

Graves shrugged. "As it has protected so much of your kind."

Shannon bristled again. "Her magic will save her."

"Her magic is no different than your magic, or that of any of your kind." His eyes flicked to Adair. "Perhaps even lesser." As if having a human father was an affront. "You'll need to do something more than hide her if you want this one to survive."

He disappeared into the stacks, the darkness enveloping him as he left.

Shannon glanced at Adair in sheer terror, a look she had refused to give to Graves but could barely contain now.

He was only gone a moment before returning with a large, old leather tome. "Ah, here it is. There's a spell. It works on a child before they develop into their powers." His eyes lifted to her mother. "So it wouldn't hide you."

"We're not here about me," Shannon said sternly. "We have a plan for me."

Graves shrugged as if it wasn't his concern how to hide a fully grown wisp. "I don't have the specific spell, but I could retrieve it…for a price."

"More than the knife?" Adair demanded.

"The knife would be worth the spell, if I already had it," he said, his eyes going dark with displeasure. "If I have to go looking for it…then the knife is worth less than my time."

"Fine," Shannon growled. "Who *has* the spell? Can we go get it ourselves?"

He considered again for a second. "Probably a Druid."

"Absolutely not," Shannon barked.

Graves's smile said he knew exactly what can of worms he'd opened, and he couldn't help to prod it open wider. "Aren't your lot friendly with Druids?"

Shannon and Adair exchanged another fleeting look. The answer was clearly no. Not anymore.

"Lorcan Flynn is across the bridge. He could help you at the next full moon," Graves said. The deadly glint in his eye was the only thing that even hinted he was sending these people to his greatest enemy.

"We can't go to Lorcan," Shannon said.

"Obviously," Graves said. "Or else why come to me at all?"

"We heard you would give us information," Adair argued. "Not just jerk us around."

Graves smirked as if that was half the fun.

"Is there anyone else who would have the spell?" Shannon asked. "Surely the knife is enough for a *name*."

"There is another," he said thoughtfully. "You wouldn't like it. He hasn't been much connected with Druids and wisps since he was on the outs."

"If he's not connected, that's what we want," Adair argued.

"I haven't met him personally, but he'd have the spell."

"Who?" Adair asked.

"Cillian Ryan."

"He's a rogue Druid!" Shannon cried.

"Then he won't spill your secrets."

"And a sociopath," she tried next.

"And exactly what you need," Graves argued. "If Lorcan hasn't killed him, then he's doing something right."

Shannon shot her husband a stern look. "We can't go to him."

"We must," Adair said. "We came here for a way to hide our girl. This is what we have to do."

Shannon looked down at her daughter and brushed her blond hair aside. She sighed, resigned. "You're right. Anything for you."

Graves's eyes landed on the little girl. Kierse saw a brief look that was almost *warm*, before he wandered off into his library again. He returned after only a moment. "The knife is worth more than the name." He tossed a palm-size metal piece down on the table. "Take this amulet and trade it for the casting."

Shannon stared down at it uncertainly. "What's the trick?"

Adair grabbed the amulet quickly. "Who cares?"

Shannon glared at Graves a moment. Finally, reluctantly, she stood, thanking him for his help. And it *was* help. Kierse could see that plainly. A mystery she was still grappling with as the memory dissolved.

Interlude

O isín flipped the lock on the bookstore.

Today had made him heartsick. He rubbed the spot under his robe where the Fae curse still sat in stark silver against his heart. On days like this, when the veil was thinnest, so close to a Celtic holiday, he could almost feel his wife's fingers pressing the gift where it now rested. The last thing he had from her.

Now it hurt like a wound predicting the rain, reminding him that faerie was still out of reach. As it had been for so very long.

Sometimes he felt like he was a snap of his fingers away from his faerie bride, Niamh, and sometimes he felt every single year down to his bones. He was an old man and had been since the curse took root. He would remain an old man until the day faerie opened and he could return to his beloved. He hoped she still loved him as the man he was now instead of the wide-eyed youth he'd been when she had claimed his heart.

Ah, but such ruminations were for another day. Nothing to be done now.

He collected books and, despite Niamh's pestering, set them down on top of another stack he hadn't put away, where they would rot for a few years before he needed something in them.

He had been doing the same thing when a young Graves had stepped off a fishing vessel from England. The bookstore hadn't quite been in operation at that time, but he'd been collecting volumes for all the years since his return. Anything to help him find a way back to his Niamh.

Graves should have been unimportant enough to pass notice, but it was impossible *not* to notice him. He didn't act like the rest of the fishermen, who never looked up from the goods they exchanged. The British crown had come over with their army and nominally claimed his Ireland by that time, but they were still largely autonomous. Something that would crumble in the next hundred years.

But Graves didn't look at the country like a conqueror come for battle. Oisín had been heir to a small kingdom in his earlier life, and he knew the look. Instead, Graves was a man on a mission. Young, determined, ambitious. Looking for something...or someone.

When he went in for a pint that night, Oisín made sure he was already at the table. The locals cringed around his British vowels, and he did his best to understand the lilting Irish. He showed complete incomprehension over the Gaelic Irish being spoken, mostly about him.

"What's your name, son?"

"Brannon," he offered freely. "Brannon Graves."

"And are you of Clan Brannon?" Oisín could see very well that he was British with Graves as a surname, but it was worth asking anyway.

"On my mother's side."

"Is that what you are looking for? Your mother's people?"

He considered, clearly a man of few words, who had been taught young to hold his tongue and to speak carefully. "In a way," he said finally. "Do you know of them?"

Oisín confirmed that he did, but he also knew more than he let on. That Clan Brannon had a High Priestess among them. That she had fallen pregnant by a man here on business and he'd taken her with him back across the Irish Sea. That it was possible *this* Brannon may be more than he was letting on as well.

It took many more rounds over a few stubborn days before Brannon confessed to the truth of it. That he was looking for Druids in Ireland even though everyone claimed they had been run off by Rome fifteen hundred years ago.

On their fifth day, Oisín invited a Druid to meet the man and mete his justice, if necessary.

"Who have you brought?" Brannon asked, standing quickly and abandoning the ale before him.

"Brannon, this is Lorcan of Clan Flynn," Oisín told him.

Graves's eyes slid over the man. The judgment was quick and fierce. "Well met."

Lorcan nodded once, as if he could tell in that moment exactly who Graves was. So little did he know, and still he accepted him on sight. "Well met."

Oisín shook himself out of the memory. Uniting those two was one of his greatest victories and deepest regrets. That he hadn't been there when it all fell apart was worse. But there was nothing to be done about the past. As he well knew.

Still, you couldn't blame an old man for meddling.

He reached for the old rotary telephone. A large black thing that he'd never been able to get rid of despite everyone's insistence on cell phones. He pressed his finger to each number, sliding the dial in a circle, including the extra numbers at the front to make an international call.

"Oisín." The rich timbre of Lorcan's voice brought a smile to his face.

"Hello, old friend." There was breathless panting from multiple voices in the distance on the other end of the line. "Am I interrupting?"

"Never. I've taken over lessons for tonight with our youngest Druids. Surely you remember the methods?"

"Of course," Oisín agreed.

"Is this call business or of a more personal nature?"

"A little of both, I'm afraid."

"He's there," Lorcan guessed.

"Yes," Oisín said, unsurprised that Lorcan already knew of Graves's presence.

"Do I need to return to the motherland?"

"I believe they will be joining you shortly."

He could practically see Lorcan's smile. He had been a particularly wild and free youth. Always running around, so confident in his abilities, sure that he would land on his feet. So little could shake him. So little ever had.

Other than Graves.

"Finally," Lorcan said. "Thank you for letting me know, Oisín. And for all you've done in the meantime."

"Anything for the wisps."

And he meant it even as he hung up the old phone and headed back into the depths of his library. He'd do anything to restore the Fae, anything to get back to them. Even betraying the trust of the last one living in the mortal world.

PART III

THE OAK THRONE

Chapter Twenty-One

"A re you hurt?" Graves asked. His voice dripped with concern as he reached across the bed, still holding his magic tight. "Wren?"

"You helped them," was what came out.

Graves pulled back, expression torn between bemusement and amusement. "That doesn't sound like me."

Kierse laughed at his incredulity. "You helped my parents."

"Did I?" He raised an eyebrow.

She sat up in the bed and kicked her feet over the side. "They came to you, asking for your help to hide me. I was young. It was before I was on the streets."

He frowned. "Many people did. Before all the monsters were out, there was always someone trying to hide their existence. The constant string of people begging for a solution that within a few decades worked itself out."

"But not for the wisps," Kierse said.

"No," he agreed slowly. "No, they were hunted and killed."

"They were coming for me and my parents. My mom…" She choked on the word. "My mom was alive. She didn't die in childbirth. It must have been a trick of the spell. She said that the Fae Killer was after them."

At that, Graves entire face shuttered. "She used those words?"

"Yes? Do you know who that is?"

Lines of frustration crinkled his forehead. "I was searching for them. My people kept coming up empty-handed, and as I got closer, the last wisps were killed and they disappeared. I had suspicions, but I never got close enough."

"You think they killed my parents?"

"Yes," he said flatly.

"But because of you, I survived." It was still hard to even believe that was the case. "You sent them to a rogue Druid, Cillian Ryan."

Graves's frown only deepened. "Did you get names? Your parents' names?"

"Shannon and Adair."

"Fuck," he said, coming to his feet and stepping away from her. He fisted his hair before quickly dropping his hand. He was still facing away from her when he said, "They died. *You* died."

"I clearly did not."

"Yes, but…I had Edgar follow up. I wanted to see if your parents made it to the Druid and if you'd been hidden. And he came back and said you were dead. All of you."

Kierse tilted her head. "Do you think he lied?"

"I don't know," he admitted harshly. She could see him wondering if that was false, what else might have been a lie. The working of his empire unwinding before his eyes. "I'll have to ask him."

"Which is why you never went looking for me," she said. "Why you would put the entire interaction out of your mind."

"Yes," he said slowly.

"And why you didn't connect me with what happened," Kierse said, putting the pieces together.

"No, your stories were so different. Your mother died in childbirth. You'd been left to the streets. It never clicked that you could have survived. That my contact would betray me…or had been betrayed." His eyes found hers as he sank back into the chair. "I knew you were a wisp when I found out about your absorption abilities. I thought that you'd been hidden by your lack of magic."

"My *lack* of magic?" Kierse asked.

"Wisps are *powerful*, Wren." His eyes bored into her. He seemed eager to have this conversation. As if he'd been holding this back behind his teeth, waiting to tell Kierse when she was ready. "There are levels of magic. The first is the level that all magical users possess—our ability to ward, enhanced senses like being able to see the glow of magic or scent it, and recharge. That is how I could train you in magic before we knew you were Fae. You have your Fae abilities, which are more on the monster side than magic—enhanced beauty, sight, scent, smell, your pointed ears, typically an aversion to iron." She nodded in agreement. "Then there are your wisp abilities. For all of your prowess in theft, your ability to absorb magic, and your slow motion, you weren't displaying anything consistent with what I knew of their kind."

"Like pixie light or persuasion?"

"Precisely."

"Oisín filled me in on what my powers should be, but I could only ever get half of them to work. Which makes sense," she added, "because I *am* only half wisp."

"Truly, I thought you were more human than Fae. You didn't have the ears or the enhanced senses. You only had a few abilities. When wisps have children with humans, the magic goes all sideways. Sometimes they only get one ability, sometimes none. Sometimes they have all the abilities, but they're so slight they don't even seem to manifest. Your magic didn't conform to my expectations, and thus my expectation was that you weren't a full-blooded wisp."

"And now we know that my father was human."

"I'm amazed you can do as much as you can, to be honest."

She'd never considered that being half human could mean problems for her magic. But she also hadn't ever had enough information about her parents to make that judgment.

His eyes went distant. "When I broke the spell on you, it was the sword that saw the truth of the spell around you. That is its purpose, after all, a truth teller. It told me to break it and reveal what was underneath. I did not once believe you to be the same child that sat in my library. She was long dead in my mind."

As she looked up into his gleaming eyes, she realized that Graves was being frank with her. Earnest even. If that was a word that was possible to describe him.

He had sent her to Dublin for answers. She wanted to make her own decisions and check facts against all he had taught her. She would never regret that she had done so. She needed the ability to discern truth from falsehoods. Graves may have hidden her identity from her, but he had led her to all other answers. And perhaps…there might be a way to even *more* answers. The kind that only a warlock of knowledge could provide her.

Part of her job was knowing the worth of a thing. She had seen her father's knife, and while it was clearly sentimental and of good use, it was not worth a name and a Druid amulet. Graves had given the amulet to her parents as a show of good faith, a way to help. He'd justified it as payment. Sometimes she forgot that he'd also helped the world by initiating the Monster Treaty. He'd put things into place to end the killing and set the world back onto the correct path.

Perhaps both were motivated by selfishness. After all, he was not all good or all bad, just as she was not one or the other. But he had helped a small child when she was in need, for less than the value of the aid. He knew her parents. He helped them. And *now* she had a name.

She had the *who* of her story, if not the *why*.

"So…do you still have contact with Cillian Ryan?"

"Not since the war," Graves said, putting space between them. "But we can find him."

"Oh, it's *we* now?"

He shrugged. "You have the scent. If I know you at all, you're not going to let it go now."

No, she wasn't. She had to have her answers.

"Won't you be busy with the cauldron?"

"Ah, the cauldron," he said as he pecked at his phone. "I have my people on it."

"I can help. That's why you came here, right?"

Graves arched an eyebrow. "I'll admit I wanted your assistance. It wasn't the only reason."

Part of it was because of her. She was beginning to see that he wasn't completely bullshitting her.

"Do you expect me to walk away from a really great score any more than the clues from my memories?"

"Obviously not."

"You need me, anyway. I'm an asset. And I don't think for a second that you're going to go *buy* the cauldron at an auction."

He tipped his chin up, denying nothing. He had the same look in his eye as when he'd entered negotiations with her parents. "And what is the price of your help, little thief?"

She could ask for anything. She knew what he'd offered for her to get the spear—ten million dollars and her freedom. She'd thought then that she would die for obtaining the thing. And instead, it now belonged to her.

This time they were on more even footing. He wanted her help on the cauldron, but she *wanted* to be in on it. So the negotiation should be for something that he also wanted to give her. The thing he'd already offered.

But she hesitated, even knowing the answer scared her.

"I need help with my memories," she said finally.

"I thought you didn't want me in your head."

"I don't, but we did it my way," she said truthfully. "I didn't get half as much as I wanted out of this bargain, and I risked my life more than once to get it. So it's time to do it your way. However, *you're* the sticking point."

"Ah," he said slowly. "Because you still hate me after what happened this winter."

She crossed her arms. "I certainly don't trust you. But I'm resolved to believe that you are part of this journey. After all, with all the memories I could have plucked out of my mind, the one that appeared was about you. Convenient, isn't it?"

Graves's eyebrows rose. "Are you suggesting that I changed the direction of your memories?"

"That's what you do, isn't it?"

He blew out a breath. "I can't touch your mind. Not unless you let me."

She knew that to be the truth, and yet...she couldn't let it go. Not after what he had done to her. She didn't know how to let him in. She didn't know how to need him without giving him everything. But the truth of the matter was that she did need him. How else would she get her answers? She couldn't go back into the market. That much was a fact.

She met his gaze. "How do we do this? How do I get past what happened?"

The question hung in the air between them. Kierse had always been fiercely independent. It was something Jason had loved and hated about her. It was what had kept her alive. But if she was going to work with someone like Graves, who kept his own company and his own secrets as close as she did, then how could they carry on?

"I would earn your trust back," he said finally after a moment, his voice hoarse and full of sincerity, "if you'd let me. I know where I went wrong the last time, and I will do better. Let me prove it to you. I am here for *you*, Wren. For you."

"Not the cauldron?"

"A convenient excuse," he admitted. "While your skills are valuable, I would do everything in my power to prove that it is the woman that I want and not just the little thief."

Kierse tilted her head. There was no way to ensure that he kept his word—no sacred vow that she knew of that would make him do what he said. And would she trust him if he had to vow to be true to her? No, there was a measure of faith here.

Their eyes met. The weight of the tension between them turned warm and inviting.

"Fine. Prove it to me, then." She lifted her chin. "My help with the cauldron for your help with my memories."

"Sounds fair," he said, offering his hand.

She swallowed hard, staring down at his outstretched hand with apprehension. Was she making a mistake? Putting her faith in someone who had already betrayed her? Someone who had kept secrets, hid his motives, and worked against her? She didn't know. But she felt as if she had no other choice.

"Trust me," he said like a death toll.

"Okay," she said and took his hand, hoping she was making the right decision to enter another bargain with her winter god. "Time to go home."

Chapter Twenty-Two

Spring weather in the city was erratic at best. Graves insisted it had been in the fifties when he left, but somehow it was in the high eighties when they landed. Kierse stripped out of her jacket as they exited Graves's jet into the balmy heat, the sun alighting on her dark hair and pale skin.

"Feck," Niamh said, holding her long, burgundy hair off her neck. "It's hot as the devil's tit."

Gen covered her mouth. "It's not normally this hot in May."

"It's usually variable," Kierse said, "but not like this."

"At least you have air con," she grumbled.

Graves said nothing, just glanced at Kierse as if she could discern what his stubborn silence meant. Was what happened on the winter solstice responsible for the unseasonable weather? Was that even possible?

A limo pulled onto the tarmac, and George opened the back door. "Sir."

Niamh held up her patchwork quilted bag in goodbye. "Don't have too much fun without me. And come to Brooklyn if you need a place to stay."

Her eyes flitted to Graves and back to the girls. She'd been adamant that they shouldn't live with Graves again. But Kierse wasn't going to live with the Druids and Gen wanted to stay with Kierse and maybe, just a little bit, wanted to see the inside of Graves's brownstone when not under threat of death. Of course, Gen could be playing protector...as she always had.

"We'll be fine," Kierse said.

"We'll miss you not being right next door," Gen said. "Even if you lied to us."

Niamh laughed. "Yeah. Sorry about that, babe."

Gen's cheeks reddened.

"You don't have to stay there, either," Kierse reminded her. She didn't know the deal with Niamh and Lorcan, but she *did* know Lorcan and his duplicity. He was every bit as frustrating and just as deadly as Graves.

She waved her hand. "I've got it covered. It's you I worry about."

"They'll be taken care of," Graves said sternly.

"I bet they will," Niamh teased.

Then she was off and away, and Graves was shuffling them into the back of the limo where another man was already seated within.

George pulled away from the airport, and Graves gestured to the man. "Kierse, Genesis, allow me to introduce you to an associate of mine, Lazarus Kates."

Laz was everything and nothing like Kierse had imagined him. Graves had briefed her on the long plane ride over that they would be meeting his elusive treasure hunter who had been away for Passover. Somehow she'd envisioned a man in ragtag khaki with a wide-brimmed fedora and a perpetual five o'clock shadow. While he had an actual beard and the khaki wasn't far off, there was no hat in sight. Just deep, dark-brown eyes, a swath of curly brown hair trimmed short on the sides, and tan hands and forearms marked with tiny scars, like he'd seen his way around a few knife fights.

"It's a pleasure." His eyes found Gen, and he nodded once before turning to Kierse. "You must be the wren."

"That's me."

"Yeah, Boss told me about you," he said gruffly. He pulled out a folder from a dark brown leather messenger bag and offered it to Graves. "Good to have you back on board."

"Thanks," she said hesitantly, her eyes flicking to Graves in question. He'd *told* someone about her? That didn't sound like him at all. Graves quirked an eyebrow that said, *See? Things have changed.*

But then his head was buried in the folder Laz had given him and the moment passed. "Is this right?" Graves finally asked.

"Afraid so."

"A Midnight Frolic?"

"Yep," Laz said.

"I saw that they were having it in the Aerial Gardens," he snarled. "I didn't realize it'd be a frolic."

Kierse and Gen looked between the two men. Kierse asked, "What's a midnight frolic?"

She held her breath. How many times had she asked questions like this of him last time and received veiled, half hearted answers? She never expected Graves to trust her with information. Never.

But he began as if oblivious to her whirling thoughts. "One of the theaters on Broadway has a rooftop theater that was closed during the war."

"They destroyed it, you mean," Laz said with distaste. "Fucking vamp-werewolf showdown that nearly toppled the entire theater."

Graves shrugged. "Before it was destroyed, they held a Midnight

Frolic. It was an elite gathering in the aerial gardens with productions that showcased rising talent. If the show did well with the top clientele, they'd move the actors onto Broadway. Sort of a make-or-break moment."

"Okay," Kierse said, trying to figure out how this tied into anything. "And this is why they're putting on *Midsummer*?"

"Yes, the first frolic is going to be the night of the auction," Laz said.

"Is this a problem? Didn't we already know it was going to be a show?"

Graves tapped the papers absentmindedly. "It's not just a show. It's a frolic."

"Think gentleman's club meets nightclub," Laz explained. "Things get rowdy."

"And if the Midnight Frolic is cover for the auction, then it's going to be...messy."

"Oh," Kierse said, seeing how that could spiral out of control.

"We need a list of people in attendance," Graves said. "Entrances, exits, staff."

Laz waved his hand, typing onto a tablet. "Way ahead of you."

"Bring in Schwartz if you need him."

Laz grinned devilishly. "Excellent."

It was the first time that Kierse had been privy to Graves's inner dealings. They'd worked together to get the spear. They'd stared at blueprints and vault codes and ran reconnaissance on Third Floor. But she hadn't been there when he'd gotten the blueprints. There had been no investigation into which vault to open. He'd already had the information, or he'd left the brownstone to "work." It was a completely different process watching him collect it.

He'd said he was going to win back her trust. Still, it was surprising to watch it unfold.

Graves retreated into his phone after that, and Laz deep into his work for the auction. And by the time they came out on the other side of the Battery Tunnel, Kierse was captivated by the sight of her city. Her heart thrummed in time with the pace of buildings dashing by.

Tall skyscrapers, storied brownstones, bodegas, restaurants, and theaters. And most of all, people and monsters alike. More people out and about on the streets than there had been five months earlier. As if they'd all finally put the worst of the war behind them for a new, glittering future. The heart of Manhattan, her home, was alive and well.

Gen put her hand to the window. "It's beautiful."

"It really is," Kierse confirmed, mesmerized by all that she had left behind.

George zipped through the city, and soon enough they were pulling into the underground garage. They exited the vehicle and took the elevator to the first floor. Kierse stepped through and could almost feel the house sigh in welcome. *Home.*

"Kierse," Isolde cried, coming around the corner and throwing her arms around her. "I know you hate hugs, but…"

"I know. I know," Kierse said with a laugh. "God, I missed you."

Isolde swatted a kitchen towel at her. "Just my cooking."

"Always your cooking," Graves agreed.

"I'm glad you brought our girl back," Isolde told him.

Graves's eyes were on Kierse, warm and inviting. "As am I."

"Edgar finished up with the extra bedroom you requested. He should be down any moment," Isolde said. "Oh, there he is."

Edgar moved like water down the stairs, his black suit impeccable, his hair threaded through with silver. "Sir, you're back early."

"We made good time," Graves said.

He bowed slightly at the waist. "I've made up the third bedroom. I can show our guests to their rooms if you like."

"As it pleases you," Graves said.

"Edgar, old man," Laz said, clapping him on the back. "I think I remember the way."

"Yes, of course, Mr. Kates," Edgar said formally. "But as it's my job…"

"Yes, yes, let's do it. We might need a fourth room set up anyway," Laz said as the pair began to climb the stairs together.

Kierse glanced at Gen. "Well, what do you think? Still want to stay here?"

Gen bit her lip, her eyes wide as she surveyed the space.

"I'm sure Colette would have you. Or Nate," Kierse suggested.

Nathaniel O'Connor was a notorious werewolf alpha who ran Five Points, a nightclub in Chelsea, home to the wolf packs. He was also one of Kierse's oldest friends. She'd been thieving for him almost as long as she'd known Gen. She needed to make time to see him, now that she was home.

"I can't go back to the attic," Gen said with finality. "And while I need to stop in at Five Points, I don't know that I'd want to stay there without you or Ethan." Her cheeks were pink again at the mention of Five Points.

"Want to see Ronan?" Kierse teased.

"No!" Gen gasped, then relented. "Maybe."

Gen had confessed that she'd had a short relationship with Nate's second, Ronan, a man of few words and many deadly looks. Kierse had been *shocked* that Gen of all people would be interested in a ruthless killer with a cigarette dangling from his mouth.

"Or just Niamh," Kierse suggested.

"Oh, please, there's nothing there."

"There could be." And Kierse was certain of that. She'd had enough relationships with women to know the difference between friendship and flirting, and Niamh had definitely been flirting. She hoped that Gen explored everything she wanted to explore. Growing up the daughter to a madame had made her wary in a way that Kierse had never been able to penetrate. She hoped that learning these new powers also opened Gen up to all of life's experiences.

Kierse's eyes left her best friend and settled on Graves heading toward the downstairs study. She was exhausted and should absolutely go upstairs, unpack, and pass out for a few hours. But instead...

Gen cleared her throat. "Well, I should catch up with Edgar."

"I can show you," Kierse said quickly.

"I'll make do." Then she was hurrying up the stairs after Edgar and Laz. Kierse would have to check in on her before she went to bed.

Right now, she followed Graves into the study. He was mesmerizing in the dim electric light. She was so used to the fireplace being lit, but it had been winter when she'd last been in this room. What she hadn't expected was to see her case for the spear at his feet. Though he wasn't paying the spear any mind. Instead, he was frowning down at a bouquet of red roses.

"Who are the flowers from?"

Graves plucked the card from the table and passed it to her. He'd clearly already read it.

Heard you were on this side of the pond and didn't stop by.
Bad form, old friend.

—Kingston

Kierse tensed. "Is this a threat?"

"With Kingston, I'm never sure," he admitted.

Kingston was Graves's warlock mentor. They had met when Graves had been bleeding out on the streets of London, and only after Graves had proven he could survive had Kingston brought him on as an apprentice.

They were still friends.

Well, she had thought they were.

He took the card back from her and set it amongst the roses. "Warlocks are never particularly friendly. We take offense easily."

"You don't say," Kierse said sarcastically.

He shot her a look. "Kingston and I have been on steady terms for centuries. He wouldn't challenge me over something this small."

"But you think he might challenge you sometime?"

"Perhaps. But it's not a concern for today," he said easily, turning from the flowers to the case. "This is a problem for today."

"The spear?"

"Yes. It is too powerful to leave out in the open, as I'm sure you're aware."

She glanced at the innocuous case, hating that he was right.

"I wish I could keep it with me," she said, thinking of how much she preferred to have the thing in her hand than in a box.

"It's a powerful tool. And we are not the only ones looking for it," Graves told her. "I'd be wary of its strength. There's a reason there's a trail of bodies in its wake."

"And should I trust *you* with the spear?"

His smile was quick and vicious. "Definitely not." He stepped forward, smoothing a lock of her hair. "Not yet, at least. I haven't proven myself to you."

She swallowed and took a step back. "Where should we keep it, then?"

"I thought I would give you access to my vault."

"Your vault?" she asked in surprise.

His eyes lit on her face. "Since I revealed its existence, I'm sure you could break into it at any point."

"Obviously," she said with no pretext of humility.

"But I want you to have access to it." He wasn't any closer, and somehow she could still feel the heat of him. The pull to him that never quite went away. "You have access to anything you want while you're here. To me."

She nodded. "All right." She picked up the case. "Let's do it, then."

Graves guided her back downstairs and reprogrammed the vault, hidden in the depths of his underground garage, to identify her. It hissed open softly to reveal an empty room where five months earlier the sword had been housed. With trepidation, she set the spear inside and watched it seal shut with finality.

The end of their first bargain.

Tomorrow would begin anew.

Chapter Twenty-Three

Day two without a nightmare. Kierse woke up feeling more refreshed than she had in months. She didn't know if recovering the new memory had kept the rest at bay or if her mental state was more secure now that she had a plan. Either way, she would take the win.

The jet lag was a problem, though. She hastened into a shower in the hopes the hot jets would wake her up. They only did half the job, and she spent some time on her appearance before going in search of coffee.

Voices drifted up to her, and Kierse jogged downstairs to see Gen and Laz sitting at the kitchen island while Isolde filled their plates with heaping portions of eggs, pancakes, bacon, and fresh fruit. Kierse blinked and blinked again. She was used to Graves's house being a somber place. Somewhere he slid in and out of mysteriously in the dead of winter, not a raucous *home* where Laz could regale them with some tale about a pirate ship in a sunken cove.

Isolde slid a cup of coffee to her, and she took it with a muffled, "Thank you."

"I almost had it, too," Laz said. "But then the coast guard showed up and half the crew were arrested." He shook his head. "I barely escaped, watching as they hauled up my score."

Gen's eyes were wide with wonder. "That is quite a tale."

"How much of it is true?" Kierse teased as she reached for a lemon raspberry muffin.

"All of it," Laz said with a twinkle in his eye.

Isolde shook her head. "I've heard many such stories from Mr. Kates over the years," she said. "Embellishment is the name of the game."

He put his hand to his chest. "My dear Isolde, you wound me."

Gen giggled.

"Any word from Graves?" Kierse asked.

"He's in the library," Laz said. "Something business related came in."

"I'm going to let him know we're heading out," Kierse told Gen. "You ready to go?"

"Yeah. Mom is excited to see you."

Kierse grinned. "I highly doubt the grand Madame Colette said she was *excited*."

"Well, I can read between the lines," Gen admitted.

"I bet."

Colette had allowed Kierse to stay in the attic with her daughter. She'd never forced her into sex work. In fact, she was the one who'd introduced Kierse to Nate in the first place, giving her a way to use her thieving for good—sort of. She was the closest thing Kierse had ever had to a mom until her memories had started to return.

"And Ethan?" Gen asked as they left the kitchen.

"Our next stop."

"Niamh is worried about me," Gen muttered.

So was Kierse. The thought of taking Gen into enemy territory made her want to peel her skin off. But to see Ethan, Kierse would consider it. Yes, Gen was a High Priestess, so she would likely be safe, but she didn't trust *any* of them.

"We'll figure it out," Kierse told her.

Kierse followed Gen up the stairs, but as Gen continued to the third floor, Kierse stopped on the second. She stepped up to the double doors entwined with holly warding, THE HOLLY LIBRARY engraved in the same bronze plaque. A warning for what lay beyond and who owned the library within—the Holly King.

At her entrance Graves looked up, his hand on a tablet, a glass of bourbon next to it. His black cat, Anne Boleyn, sat curled up half on top of his work. She lifted her head to peer at Kierse.

"Hey," she said, taking in the splendor before her. "Mind if I interrupt?"

"By all means."

The libraries of the present and past formed layers on top of one another in her mind. The room was now thick with holly ivy, which had taken over as many bookshelves as possible and even begun to crowd into open space. As if this magic, this curse, had grown in her absence, choking out all else.

He seemed to just *fit* here, in this place, like this library was a second skin. In his dark suit, black shirt, tie, and gloves, he was a shadow. The holly encroached on him as much as the library. The midnight blue of his hair blended into the background, and he was twin storm clouds and a perfectly kissable mouth.

Anne hissed as she approached and jumped down from the desk. She slunk around Graves's ankles apprehensively.

"You have been sulking for *months* because you missed her," Graves said in exasperation to the cat. "And now that she's here, you act like this?"

Kierse bent down and reached for the cat. "Is that right? Have you missed me?"

Anne batted at her hand and darted away into the depths. Kierse laughed and straightened, watching her disappearing form.

"Tempestuous," he muttered under his breath.

"What can you expect? She's a cat. I'm a bird." Kierse gestured to the wren necklace dangling between her breasts. "We don't mix."

His eyes flickered down and then back up. "Indeed."

"Laz said you had business." She glanced at the tablet and tensed, anticipating him hiding it away.

But he pushed it in her direction so she could get a better look at the memo titled "Monster Holdings." It had a blue logo at the top, an MH that bled together in a stark, blocky font with a circle around it.

"I'm investigating the company that's hosting the auction," he explained. "Including any paperwork I can find regarding the owner."

"Anything interesting?"

"Frustratingly little. They've apparently been around for at least a decade, so they were founded during the war. The owner is so shrouded that I'm unclear who is even hosting it."

"So a dead end."

"I'll keep looking." He removed his gloves and tossed them onto the desk. "If I've learned anything in my pursuit of knowledge, it's that everything will out if given enough time."

"Ah, the thing we are short on."

The corner of his mouth lifted in the hint of a smile. "We'll get as much as we can and make contingencies for everything else." His eyes moved to her body, running over where her hip leaned against his desk. She tilted toward him like a flower toward the sun. "I spoke to Edgar last night after you retired about the incident with your parents."

Kierse stilled. "What did he say?"

"He showed me the memory where he discovered the scene. There were three bodies, including a young girl."

"What?" she asked. "But that doesn't make any sense."

"I'm aware."

"And you believe him? He couldn't have altered his memory? Maybe someone else did?"

"There weren't any indicators of tampering, and I trust him with my life."

"So...they killed the wrong girl?"

"Or a body was planted on the scene. Or it was an illusion."

Kierse furrowed her brow. "I don't know what to make of any of that."

"We need more information," he agreed. "We'll figure it out, okay?"

She nodded. Her mind was swimming with the information.

"Was there a reason that you came to find me?"

Kierse pulled herself out of her thoughts and met his gaze. "Checking to see if you're actually going to include me in your business."

He spread his arms wide. "I'm a man of my word."

She choked on a laugh. "We'll see."

"And speaking of that," he said, picking up his bourbon and swirling it, "I reached out to the Covenant to see Dr. Mafi."

Kierse's eyes widened. "I thought we were going to do memory work together here?"

"We are," he said smoothly. "But I want to exhaust every avenue."

"Are you saying your knowledge is limited?"

He smirked. "No. We assume that because the spell broke, it triggered your memories. That it is simply a magical problem."

"You don't think it is?"

"That's what I want to find out," he said, taking a sip. "Memory isn't just magic. Yes, the spell likely damaged something. But then I started thinking about that damage and how it could also be physical or mental." His tone softened as he added, "You were very young and encountered a lot of trauma."

"Oh," she said as she realized what he meant. "You think that there's something wrong with my brain."

His gaze was unguarded when he said, "I think we don't know if your brain was injured. After all, you told me yourself that you were thrown off of a building to 'cure' your fear of heights."

Kierse winced at the memory of Jason. "Yes, but…"

"So wouldn't it be better to know? It might be some form of traumatic brain injury, or repression, or just good old fashioned Monster War PTSD. The fact of the matter is that we don't know, and I don't like not knowing things."

"Okay," she said slowly.

He was right. And more than that…he could have told her it was a magical problem and solved it with his own powers. The fact that he was going to involve someone else, different kinds of magic and science, showed that he would leave no stone unturned. He was looking out for *her*.

"When do we go?"

"Next week. I wanted to give you time to settle in."

She tapped her fingers against the desk. "Well, with that, Gen and I are about to leave."

He tensed. "To see Colette."

"Yes and then Ethan," she told him with a shrug.

"And Lorcan?"

She nodded. "We need answers."

Graves replaced his drink on the table and stood to face her. His body was large and domineering, caging her back against the desk. She stilled under the gaze of a predator, lifting her chin just enough to let him know that she would not back down. But the pounding of her heart betrayed her own bravado.

He rested his hands to either side of her on the desk and leaned her back into it, towering over her. She swallowed as her body came alive. Her core pulsed in response to his nearness. His lips so close. His eyes devouring her whole. She existed nowhere except in this moment.

They weren't even touching, and all she wanted to do was rip his clothes off and give in to this temptation. Forget the goblin market with its litany of temptations. Hers was directly before her, body so hot that he was an inferno raging in his precious library. And if she gave in, they'd burn the whole place down.

He brushed a lock of her dark hair off of her face. His fingers ran down her neck, feeling her jumpy pulse, going lower, lower, lower, to the spot between her breasts where her wren pendant rested. She felt him graze the side of her breast as he examined the precious metal with a dangerous smirk.

"My wren," he said like a caress.

He closed his fist around the pendant and slowly but inexorably pulled her forward against him, crushing their lips together. His heat enveloped her. Soft and hard and wanton all at once. A temptation more seductive than the most enticing incubus. A desire more potent than water in the desert. An ache that no touch had been able to satisfy.

His tongue darted into her mouth, commanding and controlling, overwhelming her senses and besieging her mind. She was putty in his hands, and a low moan escaped her, unbidden. Her fingers dug into his sides, dragging them closer, wanting so much more.

And then, he released her, leaving her reeling.

"What was that?" she asked.

He let the metal fall from his fingers. "Just a reminder before you go."

She swallowed, prepared to tell him that she didn't need any such reminder, but she couldn't get the lie past her teeth. She wanted *every* reminder. Damn him.

Chapter Twenty-Four

Gen stared down into the gloom of the subway entrance at Amsterdam and 72nd Street. "Maybe we should take a cab."

"We're New Yorkers. We can brave a troll or two to take the subway."

"Dublin spoiled me."

"That is a fact," Kierse said as they trotted down the stairs.

Dublin proper was in drastic contrast to a post–Monster War New York City. During the war, New York had been sliced up into territories by the monsters and the human gangs. The vampire elite held the Upper East Side, the werewolves Chelsea, and the mer Central Park. There were wraiths doing business in Midtown, and a few disputed territories like Times Square that were just now starting to bring in wide-eyed tourists again. Humans occupied much of downtown with the Roulettes on the Lower East Side and the Jackals in Nolita, while the Italian mafia still ruled in Little Italy.

Traveling around the landscape was like navigating a minefield. Each subway entrance was controlled by a different gang and collected fees beyond what the city already acquired through the tills.

Kierse reached the bottom of the stairs to find a troll blocking the entrance. He wasn't as big as the one she'd met at Versailles, but his head still grazed the ceiling as he glared at them through his small, bulbous eyes. He was shirtless in tattered green pants that flexed around his tree-trunk legs.

"Payment," he grunted.

Gen gulped. While she'd refused to be held back by her chronic eye condition, she hadn't used the subway as much as Kierse and Ethan. The trolls rightfully intimidated her, and she preferred to walk if she could.

Kierse stepped between Gen and the troll. The damn things weren't intelligent, but they could sniff out fear like a bloodhound.

"Here," Kierse said, throwing two twenties at the thing.

It studied the toll and then relented, taking a massive step backward and shaking the entire entrance. Gen glanced worriedly up at the ceiling as dust rained down on them.

Kierse grasped her hand and tugged her forward into the gloom of the subway system. They quickly swiped their MetroCards and pushed through the turnstile, heading to the platform. When they got there, they found a handful of beleaguered people clustered opposite a particularly ferocious-looking panther.

"Panther shifter," Gen whispered.

Kierse grinned. It was so good to be home. She'd almost forgotten what a melting pot New York was.

When the 2 train finally rolled into the station, the panther snarled at the people before pouncing inside. A guy screamed and dashed out, following the rest of the passengers into a separate car.

Gen took an available seat, and Kierse stood over her, holding the overhead rail and watching the rest of the passengers with wary apprehension. Her glamour was carefully in place. Not that any of these people would likely understand what her ears indicated. Her natural suspicion had only intensified with the knowledge that someone had tried to kill off everyone like her. It was good that she trusted so few people.

"We'll change trains at Times Square," Kierse said.

"Yeah," Gen said, sucking on her teeth. "I still hate it there."

"I know. If the theaters are all reopening, though, it can't be as bad."

"Just hard not to think about it like it was during the war," she whispered.

Times Square, for all its capitalistic splendor, had been carved up and taken over by rival monsters during the war. They still killed enough humans, even post-Treaty, that almost everyone avoided it if they could, but before it was known-disputed monster territory, *many* humans had died. The aftereffects of those deaths still made people shudder.

When they got off at Times Square, both girls stopped and stared in surprise. The only word Kierse could think of to describe it was *bustling*. It looked like the pre-war Times Square station, with tourists braving the heat to see the city as summer approached and monsters jostling for space the same as the humans. It was shockingly…normal.

Kierse and Gen exchanged a glance before joining the crowd to change platforms. Kierse followed Gen to the RW line and waited there until the train arrived. The RW train let them off at Prince in the Lower East, where they passed a troll that worked for the Roulettes. When they were out of the subway, they both took a deep breath of relief. It had been nice on the Upper West by Graves's brownstone and confusing around the tourist trap areas, but *this* was home.

There were fewer monsters on the street and more humans hurrying to their jobs. Roulettes manned the corners outside local bodegas. They passed

Bowery and crossed over to Delancey, and Kierse's heart constricted for one beat. Torra, her ex-girlfriend, had lived there. She'd gotten caught up with the vampire, King Louis, and sold to a vampire brothel in Third Floor. Kierse had thought she was dead for a year after their breakup but had discovered her situation while doing reconnaissance on the spear and had made sure Torra walked free at the end of the mission.

"You think she's somewhere thriving?" Kierse asked, still lost in her memories.

Gen squeezed her hand, following her train of thought without missing a beat. "You saved her. I'm sure she got the hell out of the city."

Kierse squeezed back. "You're right. That was all she wanted."

Gen looped arms with her, and Kierse tried to put the past out of her mind. She wanted to live in this moment where anything was possible. Her mouth watered as they passed her favorite bagel and lox place.

"Wish we had time for a detour," Kierse said.

"As if the food isn't free and plentiful at the brownstone," Gen said.

"Free and plentiful it is, but even Isolde can't match New York bagels."

Gen laughed, and they continued forward, just two girls *almost* carefree on the city streets. Neither the gangs nor the crumbling brick buildings nor the hurried steps of the locals could dampen her spirit.

She'd had so little time for carefree growing up. Even when she'd picked pockets on the Upper East Side and indulged in her favorite bakery's black-and-white cookies and cinnamon babka, she'd always had to keep both eyes forward. She'd eat her treats sitting on the steps of the Metropolitan Museum of Art. It wasn't open to the public any longer, but she had gotten to go inside when Kingston had visited Graves. She wondered if it was still closed off now that things seemed to be turning around.

She hadn't realized how much she missed those days, staring up at the statue of Coraline LeMort, the vampire who had sparked a war she never would have agreed to, which they'd installed out front of the museum. She'd asked Graves once if he'd met her, and he'd confessed to hearing her speak—a good orator, but young, with the eyes of an idealist. She had wanted unity and only through so much loss, her own death included, had New York begun to accomplish what she had first set out to do.

They turned the next corner and smiled at the sight of Colette's brothel. Kierse had left the attic behind when she and Gen had moved to Dublin, but it would always be home.

A Roulette was stationed at the door, watching stragglers leave the premises. Early mornings were for walks of shame and for the workers to rest. An all-night establishment meant the girls, guys, and gays worked third shift and slept most of the day.

They nodded at the Roulette as they passed. He gaped at the pair of them. It'd been months since they'd been around, and likely news was going to run rampant that they were home. Gen tugged open the door and stepped inside. The front room was clouded with smoke and led to a long walkway that branched out to various sitting rooms. The silence was comforting as they continued down the hall toward Colette's bedchambers.

Gen raised her hand to knock, but the door opened before she could. Standing there, in all her glory, was Madame Colette. Her curvy figure was on full display in a long, flowing robe made of a dark, rusty-pink velvet with delicate lace trim. Her red hair was piled into a twist at the back of her head, and her makeup was still a vivid mask of her aging features. Yet somehow, she was still the most beautiful woman Kierse had ever seen.

"Girls," she said with a quirk of her lips. "What a surprise."

"Hello, Mother," Gen said with a shake of her head.

"Genesis," Colette said, wrapping her arms around Gen. She extended another arm to Kierse. "You, too."

Kierse laughed and stepped in for a hug. "Such affection. I might think you missed us."

"Just her," Colette said, kissing her daughter's forehead. "We all know you're a brat."

Kierse winked at her. "I missed you, too."

Colette ushered them into a sitting room. "Are you back for good? Or are you going to jet off to another unknown destination?"

"For now," Gen said.

"Will you be working for me again?" she asked, her eyes lingering on her daughter. Gen had worked a tent at the street markets as her alter ego, Prophet Genesis, where she read tarot and used the crystal ball. It brought in steady money.

Gen shook her head. "I think that time is behind me."

"I thought as much." She waved her hand at Kierse. "Pour me a drink."

Kierse went to the cabinet and procured Colette's favorite brandy. This had been a staple of their late-night adventures. She hadn't realized how much she missed it.

She brought over the liquor, and Colette smiled at her approvingly. "And where are you staying in the city?"

Kierse and Gen exchanged a glance.

"Ah," Colette said with another upward tug of her lips. "With *him*."

"Yes," Gen squeaked. "He offered us rooms."

"In exchange for?" Her eyes lifted to Kierse as if she could see straight through her.

"I am not the exchange, if that's what you're suggesting," Kierse countered.

"I know you don't do sex work, girl. I wasn't born yesterday." She pointed her finger at Kierse. "He still wants you."

Gen shot her a look. "It's a mutual feeling."

Kierse raised her hands. "It's complicated. I'm not here for the third degree."

"Well, whatever you're doing there, I want you both to be careful." She smiled in truth. "And happy, if you can be."

Gen burst forth, telling her mother all about Ireland and what it was like. Colette listened, encouraged by her daughter's enthusiasm. Gen was describing their little apartment as the front door banged open again.

They all jumped up to find a man in the black and red of the Roulettes striding into the brothel.

Kierse broke into a smile. "Corey!"

Gen rushed forward, throwing herself into his arms. "We missed you."

He hugged her tight for a long second. His chin rested on her head, reminding Kierse how tall he was. "I'm glad you're home."

"Us, too," Gen told him as he released her.

Corey held his fist out to Kierse, and she bumped it. At least he was one of the few who remembered that she wasn't as accustomed to physical touch. Though her aversion had lessened significantly since she'd faced her fears about Jason and saved Torra. Who knew confronting your trauma could begin the healing process?

"Are you going to see him?" Corey asked without preamble. He brushed his dark hair off of his shoulders. It was parted down the middle, thick and straight as a board, thanks to his Filipino heritage. He'd always had a ready smile, but today it was strained. And Kierse could hardly blame him.

"Manners, my dear," Colette chided him.

"Can I come with you?" he asked.

Gen and Kierse exchanged a look. Corey and Ethan had been endgame for so long. It was still hard to believe the news from Nate that they'd gone separate ways.

"Did he really break up with you?" Kierse asked.

Corey clenched his hands into fists. "I haven't seen him in almost five months. What do you think that means?"

"Not good," Gen agreed.

"And I know you're going to try to get in there. You'll be able to do it, Kierse."

"Hey!" Gen said. "I could do it, too."

"Yeah, but…"

"It's Kierse," Colette finished for him.

"I am going to see him," she told him.

"*We* are going to see him," Gen corrected.

All of them looked down at her, and Gen shrank backward. "What? I want to go, too!"

"I should go alone," Kierse said carefully.

Gen held her hands out. "But Ethan!"

"We don't know exactly what we're walking into. You saw the texts from Nate. It's not like we're the only ones who haven't heard from him." She gestured to Corey. "He hasn't even seen Corey. Whatever this training is, it must be serious."

"I know," she said in a frustrated huff. "It's bullshit."

"It *is* bullshit," Corey agreed.

"And you still want to see him?"

Corey bit his lip, retreating at the question. He was hurt, but he was desperate to have it out with the man he loved. "I always want to see him."

"And you've forgiven him just like that?" Colette snapped.

"I don't know."

"Again, we don't know if everyone can get in," Kierse said.

"But you can," Gen muttered.

Corey looked between them. "Why can she get in where no one else can?"

"Because Lorcan is obsessed with her," Gen said.

Kierse flushed. Lorcan had stalked her for weeks this past winter. When he'd discovered she was a wisp, his behavior had gotten even more intense. He'd called her the pulse of his heart in Irish. He'd asked her to come with him. To uphold the allegiance their people had always had. She'd declined, considering he'd tried to kill her and her friends.

And now that she'd seen a memory where even her parents didn't trust him, she felt more justified in her actions. However, she had a feeling he wouldn't kill her outright the way he might any others who trespassed into his territory.

"That's awfully useful," Colette said.

Kierse rolled her eyes. "It's not like that."

Colette smirked. "It could be. You have wiles. I wouldn't be afraid to use them, darling."

"The day Kierse uses *wiles* to get what she wants instead of subterfuge and stabbing," Corey muttered under his breath.

"Okay. Okay. I get it," Kierse said with a panicked laugh. "But we all agreed that, under the circumstances, I am the one who is best equipped to deal with Lorcan?"

"Equipped is right," Colette said with a wink.

Kierse choked. "That isn't what I meant."

"It worked on Graves," Gen said with a shrug.

She put her head in her hand. "I'm just going to break in and see Ethan. Then I have some questions for Lorcan. None of that means seducing him."

"Or fucking him?" Colette asked. "I've heard from very reliable sources that fucking gets you all the information you want."

"The reliable source being…you?"

Corey barely suppressed a laugh. "I sort of love you."

"If the need arises, use what you have. That's all I'm saying," Colette said.

Kierse sighed. "It'll be fine. It won't come to that."

"All right, you go alone this time." Gen deflated. "But I want to go the next time."

"As soon as I know it's safe."

Kierse hated excluding Gen. They were finally home, finally this close to Ethan and Lorcan and *answers*. But she wouldn't risk Gen any more than she had already been risked. And she would get those answers so that she could bring Gen safely into the fold.

Chapter Twenty-Five

K ierse had to jog to get to the M platform right as the train was about to pull away. She jumped on before the doors closed and settled into an open corner. A group of elementary-aged children in blue-and-white plaid uniforms jostled each other while two teachers tried to cajole them to behave. A pair of goblins were reading a book together in a corner. A man in a suit had earbuds in and was talking unnecessarily loudly. A mer and a vampire were discussing business and laughing.

Humans, monsters. Monsters, humans. All together. The life the Treaty wanted for all of them, one Kierse had been certain was impossible.

If she couldn't still feel the undercurrents of the Third Floor deep beneath their feet, she'd think all was well in her city. But there were always those who didn't agree with the tenuous peace.

The M train took her across the East River and into Brooklyn. She'd so rarely left Manhattan before meeting Graves that it was still strange to step into Druid territory. Back then, she had just thought they were an Irish gang who helped humans on this side of the river during the war. It turned out they were *actual* Druids with magic and a long-held feud with Graves that she'd gotten in the middle of. Now that she'd uncovered that memory, she was starting to think that she'd always been stuck between these two powerful forces. Even as a child.

She got off at the Marcy Ave stop and jogged down the stairs onto Broadway. Brooklyn was much the same as her last visit here, when Lorcan had kidnapped her and brought her to his restaurant, Equinox, for dinner. A delightful interrogation where Kierse thought she'd gotten more out of him than vice versa, but she was never sure with Lorcan.

Kierse had texted Niamh as her train approached and been given a rendezvous location in South Williamsburg. She liked having someone on the inside of the Druids even if the rest of them made her apprehensive. As soon as Kierse entered Druid territory, passing people on the quiet streets lined with large, red-brick buildings, she could tell she was being watched. She ducked her head and tried to look unobtrusive, lingering in the shadows and wishing she'd come at night.

She was two blocks from her meet up with Niamh when a door creaked open next to her, and she felt the barrel of a gun, leveled at her head.

Kierse froze to stone. Out of the corner of her eye, she searched for the face beyond the weapon at her temple. She recognized the bright green eyes and crooked smile—Declan. This was Lorcan's second. He had chased her and her friends through Little Italy at gunpoint. She could see the acorn tattoo confirming his allegiance to the Druids.

"Look what we have here," Declan said. "The boss will want to see our trespasser."

"I'm not trespassing," Kierse snapped.

"Inside," he growled.

"You're making a mistake. Lorcan is going to think you're incompetent."

"I'm the one with the gun," he reminded her.

"I can see that." Kierse snorted. "Not sure how you made second. Niamh probably runs circles around you."

"*Niamh* isn't in charge here," Declan said. "Now get the feck inside."

Kierse shrugged. Perhaps this would get her to where she was going faster, anyway.

She stepped inside the cool interior, which opened into a long hallway. As she walked in front of Declan, gun still at her back, she glanced into the rooms that opened off the hallway. They almost looked like barracks, as if the Druids were sleeping like little soldiers in a sardine tin. Kierse wondered if Ethan was one of them in these little rooms.

She rubbed her hand over her chest at the thought. It was probably just stress. She couldn't endure two heists, magic drain, and the goblin market without some tension. Add Graves and jet lag and it was a recipe for disaster. Yet...

She shook her head, uncertain.

"Through here," Declan growled.

Declan reached around her to open a door connecting this building to another. She walked from barracks to office space. The Druid property must have been larger than even she had envisioned. If all of these buildings connected, one after the other, then it could be the entire block. Or multiple blocks.

They crossed the offices to an elevator bank that was vaguely familiar. Was this the back way to Equinox? Would this take them up to Lorcan?

The elevator dinged open.

Declan took a step forward and then froze. Standing in their path was none other than Niamh in a caramel crop top, high-waisted olive pants, and a gray blazer. Her burgundy hair was up in a high ponytail. She looked almost business professional compared to her femme fatale style in Dublin.

"Declan," she crooned.

"Niamh," he grunted. "Just bringing Lorcan a trespasser."

"Great!" she said cheerfully. "I'll take it from here."

"I…"

"After all, she's really a *guest*. My guest, actually." She pressed a button to stall the elevator. "I don't like when people hold my friends at gunpoint."

"Friends." Declan chewed on that word as if it was a piece of gristle.

"Yeah, Declan. Friends." Niamh shot him a bemused smile. "I've been gone too long and this place has gone to hell."

"You can stay gone," he mumbled.

Niamh straightened at that. "Excuse me?" Niamh was by no means a short person, and as she came to her full height and looked eye to eye with Declan, she seemed twice as formidable. Kierse could make out a golden glow flickering at the edges of her. As if her magic took insult to Declan's defiance.

"Nothing."

"If you're upset by my return because you've been knocked down a peg, Declan," Niamh said threateningly, "then you know how to correct it."

Declan's eyes blazed. "Is that a challenge?"

Niamh crossed her arms. "If you think it is. I'm fine seeing you in the ring."

"Feck off." Declan must have known that Niamh could wipe the floor with him, because he promptly stomped away.

Niamh kept her eyes on him until he disappeared behind a door.

"What just happened?" Kierse asked as she got in the elevator.

"Something that he can't back up." Niamh winked. "That's why he didn't accept. But I should probably tell Lorcan about it anyway."

"If you think that's best."

"I think he's been dying to see you," Niamh admitted. "Let's not insult him."

"No, let's."

Niamh laughed and pressed the elevator button to take them upstairs.

When the doors opened, it was to an immaculate, open-air office that blended together the historic charm of the old brick building and a functional workspace. The hardwood flooring looked original, as did the large, arched windows along one wall with fluttering cream curtains. A light oak desk sat heavy at the center of the space, polished to gleam against the crimson rug. Behind the desk were shelves laden with books. A robin fluttered in a cage next to the desk.

And sitting behind the desk, his dark hair hanging loose in his eyes as he typed away at a computer, was the head Druid himself.

Lorcan glanced up at their entrance. His blue eyes were the cerulean of a clear spring afternoon. They flicked to Niamh and dismissed her as soon as they landed on Kierse. It was like feeling the sun peek out from behind a cloud to alight on her face.

"Little songbird," he purred.

She'd forgotten his magnetism. Even when she had been playing him in a web of her own creation, she hadn't been able to completely pull away from the vortex he'd swirled her into. He'd been charming and genuine. A smile that lit up his eyes like he hadn't known torment. A hero hiding in the cloaks of a villain. Especially dangerous because he didn't care who got in the crossfire and believed the ends justified the means.

She'd seen him for who and what he was, not what he wanted others to believe, but she'd had to work at it. Even when he'd sent people to kill her, kidnapped her, and held her friends at gunpoint, the edges were blurry. And with Colette's words ringing in her ears about using her *wiles* to get information from him...the lines were twice as blurry.

"Lorcan," Kierse said, keeping her voice steady and her head high.

"What a pleasant surprise," he said in his soft Irish accent.

Niamh snorted as she sauntered into the office and went to feed the bird, her namesake. "You knew she was coming a mile off."

Lorcan grinned, a bright blinding thing. "I'm still glad to see you regardless."

"I bet," Kierse said.

"I see you still haven't forgiven me for what happened last year." He swept a hand through his dark hair, brushing it back off of his face. His high cheekbones were accented by the quick movement. His eyes raking over her. "That's understandable."

"So glad to have your approval."

He laughed, leaning back in his chair and resting his arms on the brown leather. His white button-up was crisp, the sleeves rolled to his elbows, muscular forearms on display with just a hint of biceps. He wasn't bulky by any means, but fit. Like he could take down a grown man without even reaching for his magic.

Kierse averted her gaze, taking a few controlled steps into his office. She ran her hand along a hardened oak bookshelf, across a small stack of books. Her fingers closed around a gold letter opener before continuing her perusal.

"And all I want is your approval," he countered.

"Do you think it will be that easy to achieve?" she asked, skimming the titles and avoiding his predatory gaze.

"I'm afraid that I'll have to earn it," he said with a softness to his voice.

"Just tell her you're not going to try to kill her or her friends," Niamh said with a sigh.

"I did tell her that last time."

"And then held them at gunpoint," Niamh reminded him. She swatted at the back of his head, and he shot her a quick glare. "Maybe try to be nice."

Lorcan pushed his chair back against the plush rug and stood. "Thank you for that insight, Niamh," he all but growled. "I will be *very* nice." She finally lifted her eyes to meet his and stilled under his heated gaze.

Niamh cleared her throat. "Declan doesn't like that I'm back."

Lorcan severed the look to draw his attention back to his second. "I'm sure he doesn't."

"He almost offered a challenge, and this is only my *second* day."

The muscles in his jaw twitched. He was clearly annoyed Niamh was still here. "Don't be so infuriating, then."

"Can't help it," she said, swinging up onto his desk and letting her long legs dangle.

"She really can't," Kierse added. "It's why she's so wonderful."

Niamh beamed under the praise. "So glad you sent me to check in on her."

Lorcan's gaze swept between the women in his office. For a second, Kierse almost saw that anger swimming in those bright blue irises, but then it was gone. "How good it is that my girls are friendly."

"Like the good old days," Niamh said. She jumped down and headed toward the door before Lorcan could respond. "I'm going to check in with Maeve. You should take her to Ethan. That's what she wants, after all. She's going to sneak off if you don't do it yourself. So be *nice* and show the girl some Druid hospitality. Not whatever shit you've been getting into since I've been away."

Lorcan growled under his breath, but Niamh blew Kierse a kiss and disappeared. Now she was completely and utterly alone with her enemy. No,

Graves's enemy. They weren't the same thing.

"I am glad that you're home," he said as he walked around the desk.

"I'm glad to be home."

He held his hand out. "Though I forgot your proclivity for stealing my possessions."

She huffed and placed the letter opener in his hand. "How'd you guess this time?"

He flipped it around to point at her chest. "Your heart skipped a beat. Was it joy or fear?"

"Neither," she said. "You can't sense my heartbeat."

He shrugged. "Perhaps not. Perhaps I'm just that good." His smile was swift and heart stopping. "Now, allow me to demonstrate the Druid hospitality that Niamh mistakenly thinks I haven't shown you. We did have a wonderful dinner once before."

"I was kidnapped that night," she reminded him.

He laughed. "You like that sort of thing." She opened her mouth to protest, but he gestured to the door. "Come on. Unless you don't want to see Ethan."

Chapter Twenty-Six

The thought of finally getting to see Ethan overrode all reason. She followed him into an elevator that dropped to a subterranean level, depositing them into a hard concrete passageway. The ceiling was arched as if it might have had some grandiose use before this, but she couldn't discern what.

"It's a bank escape shaft," he explained on their walk.

Her eyes lit up. "An exit." Her favorite.

"It connects to the original Williamsburgh Savings Bank across Broadway. We purchased the bank after it went under and had it restored to its former glory. The tunnel had caved in at two different locations. We dug it out so that we could use the corridor to connect the acolyte training space to their dormitories."

"Acolyte training," Kierse repeated slowly. "Is that what Ethan is doing?"

"Yes. It takes years of rigorous work to become a full Druid." He shot her an easy smile. "Luckily, we are long-lived, as are wisps. So we have the time."

"And that's why no one has heard from him since I left?"

"Ah, most Druids grow up in the Order. We don't get many from outside. But the first line of training is removing attachments to the physical world."

Kierse narrowed her eyes. "You mean brainwashing them into good little soldiers."

"If that is what you want to believe. The Druidic Order is a lifelong commitment. We focus on a large swath of knowledge—nature, the elements, astronomy, philosophy, rituals, spells, justice." His eyes cut to her once before he added, "The changing of the seasons."

"And fighting."

"We strengthen the body through martial arts and weaponry," he agreed. "How can you mete out justice if you cannot enforce it?"

Kierse didn't think he had any right to enforce anything, personally. But he had kept Brooklyn in better shape than Manhattan, so perhaps some of their discipline made sense.

"Where do the High Priestesses fit into this?"

"Thinking of your friend, Genesis?"

Always. A part of her wondered if Gen should have taken the same deal Ethan had, but Kierse hadn't wanted to lose her. Was she now five months behind on her own training? Could she have done more here?

When she said nothing, he continued, "The High Priestesses have their own development. They also train physically and in rituals and spells, but their focus is on the healing arts. It is more a subsect of the Druidic work. There are all genders of Druids, but only female High Priestesses."

"There are no men or nonbinary people with an affinity for healing?"

"There are," Lorcan conceded. "It's just a different alignment. Different training."

Kierse made a noncommittal sound in the back of her throat. They reached the end of the corridor, revealing a massive vault door. It was the width of three people standing shoulder to shoulder with reinforced steel across the sides. If Kierse had to guess, she bet it was several feet thick. A feat of modern ingenuity—not something she would have expected to find in a building built in the 1800s.

"Oh yes, and there's this," Lorcan said, gesturing to the door.

"You let all your acolytes walk past your vault?" Kierse asked. "Isn't it a security risk?"

"It's warded." His eyes slid over her. "Not that that affects you, of course, but I would hope the five feet of solid steel would keep you out."

"You'd be wrong," she said with no bravado. She could break that vault, and she wouldn't even need a drill to do it.

"Well, there's security on it day and night. Just in case you want to try."

She arched an eyebrow. "Is that a challenge?"

"I would so like to watch you work," he teased.

She huffed. It was too easy. He probably didn't even keep the sword in there. Not that she had any reason to steal it from him. That was certainly not part of her deal with Graves. He'd lost it fair and square to Lorcan. He'd have to figure out how to get it back himself.

"This way," Lorcan said with a sly smile.

They came to another bank of elevators and took one up until it opened to a central atrium. Kierse's breath caught at the sight. The interior was massive, with forty-foot arched doorways that looked more like they belonged in Versailles, not Brooklyn. It had a high domed ceiling with a kaleidoscope mural in blues, orchids, and pastel pinks. Much of the original glass windows, chandelier lighting, and antique craftsmanship had been restored. The cashier and clerks' offices shone in gold against one side of the room, in front of the original intercom system and the historic vault Kierse had been expecting for a building of this age. The walls were marble and the floors a reconstructed mosaic in glossy cream, gold, and white.

At the center of the atrium stood a loose circle of acolytes in brown robes, watching a man and a woman face off. An instructor, a Druid in his fifties wearing green robes belted at the waist and loose pants, was giving instruction.

"Begin," he said.

Lorcan nodded at the fight as the pair launched at each other. "This was what you wanted, right?"

Kierse furrowed her brow as she homed in on the pair. The woman was short, at least a head below Kierse, with a cropped blond bob that swung as she moved like liquid. Her opponent was roughly Kierse's height with skin the color of an old sepia photo and close-shorn dark hair. He was built like an ox, with corded arms and broad shoulders. His back was to her, but the second she watched him move, she cried out. "Ethan?"

At the sound of his name, her best friend turned. Their eyes locked, and his widened in shock. His soft face had become angular. His black coils were cut from his head. Where he'd been all lanky knees and elbows, he'd filled out with hardened muscle. The prominent scar that ran down one side of his face was the only thing that didn't seem to have changed. Her soft-hearted friend who wore his heart on his sleeve had been replaced by this huge *man*.

The moment strung taut like a rope between them. All those months ago, they had formed a triskel and used magic that connected her, Ethan, and Gen. It had saved her life. She could feel that the thread hadn't disappeared, just stretched across an ocean. Now she was before him and the ache of missing him threatened to overwhelm her.

But in his moment of distraction, his opponent grasped his arm, executed an intricate spin, and swept his legs out from under him. He grunted as his back hit the practice mat.

Kierse covered her laugh with her hand.

Then Ethan hopped up, vaulting out of the circle and crashing into her arms.

"What are you doing here?" he gasped.

"I came to see you as soon as I could."

Lorcan cleared his throat. "Ethan."

"Sorry, sir," Ethan said, immediately stepping back and bowing to Lorcan.

He turned back to the rest of the class. "Excellent job, Alba. You are an asset to Owen."

"Sir," Owen, the Druid teacher, said with a head bow.

Lorcan tipped his head at Kierse and then moved to the rest of the acolyte circle, directing the next pair to begin.

"Kierse," Ethan gasped, pulling her in for a tight hug once more.

When he held her, she felt like she was finally back in New York. If she had Gen here, too, then everything would be back the way it was always meant to be.

"Look at you," she said. "I almost didn't recognize you. You're huge!"

He laughed and ran a hand across his head. "Yeah. Turns out training day and night does that." His gaze drifted to Lorcan with worry. "He told you about acolytes, right? I'm not breaking any sacred vows?"

"He told me," she said. "But why didn't you?"

"I wanted to. I just…" He shrugged, his eyes pleading. Same Ethan. "I didn't want to hurt anyone."

"Well, I don't think it's me you hurt the most by disappearing."

Ethan chewed on his lip. "Have you…spoken to Corey?"

"I saw him before I came here," she admitted.

"You did? How's he doing?" he gasped.

"Not great," she said, pushing his shoulder. "Gen and I had to hear from Nate that you broke up."

"A break," Ethan said quickly. "Not a breakup."

"And then you disappeared for five months. What's the difference?"

"My isolation ends in a month. I can be out in public again after that. I don't…" he said hesitantly. "Do you think he'll see me?"

Kierse had a feeling that Corey would see him immediately if he could, but she didn't know how that reunion would go. "Probably. I guess you'll know in a month."

"Yeah. I don't know," he said, looking over her shoulder in the direction of Manhattan with distant eyes, as if he could will himself to the Lower East Side to see his maybe-ex-boyfriend. He refocused on her. "Why are you back? Is Gen with you?"

"She's in the city, but I didn't want to risk her in enemy territory."

"The Druids aren't your enemy," he said automatically.

"Like a good little soldier," she teased.

He didn't laugh, though. His eyes went flat. "I'm serious. They're the good guys, Kierse. We were wrong about them."

For the first time, looking around at the Druids, the Order, and their very dangerous leader, she wondered how much she should even *tell* Ethan. Was he compromised? She hated to even consider it. She never would have second-guessed him before.

"Let's put a pin in that conversation for another time. You think the best of everyone."

"And you think the worst."

"Which of us was correct last winter?" she argued.

He frowned. "That's not..." he sputtered. "Graves..."

"Let's not bring him into this."

"Are you working with him again?"

"Yes," she said flatly.

"Kierse," he said warningly. "I've learned some shit about him since I got here."

"Oh, I bet you have."

He grasped her arm and pulled her further from the circle of acolytes. "Don't make a joke about this or try to deflect like you always do. Graves is a monster. He cannot be trusted."

Kierse looked down at where he gripped her arm and then back up at her friend. She had worried about him going to Lorcan. She hadn't expected *this*.

"Are you saying that you don't trust *me*?" she asked carefully.

"If you're working with him again, maybe I can't."

Fire ignited in her stomach. The fucking indoctrination that the Druids had put him through. Five months with nothing but an echo chamber had taken her sweet friend and made him *this*. He had always been a zealot—first for the church, then their friendship, and now the Druids—and it shouldn't have surprised her. But that didn't keep it from hurting.

She jerked her arm back. "You do not want to be my enemy."

Ethan straightened. "Well, I guess I should get back."

"Ethan..."

"I have more training," he said. "Good little soldier shit."

She sighed. "Wait..."

He held his hand up and jogged away, leaving her there on uneven footing.

Chapter Twenty-Seven

Kierse didn't know how it had gone so wrong. One moment they were laughing and hugging and the next ripped apart by a distance she couldn't even explain. Maybe it was a mistake coming here without Gen. She had always been the peacemaker, the healer. Kierse couldn't see a way to bridge the divide.

So she watched him walk back to the very people who had poisoned him against her.

As Ethan rejoined the group, Lorcan returned to her side. "I'm guessing that didn't go as planned."

"You guessed right."

She would have to deal with it later. She couldn't look at it too closely right now or she would get angry. Or worse, upset.

"Whatever he said, he didn't mean it."

"Did you *hear* what he said?"

Lorcan gestured for her to walk ahead of him, away from the acolytes. "Look, I don't have to hear what he had to say. I've seen hundreds of acolytes come through these halls. I've *been* him. I know what it looks like."

She clenched her jaw. "I don't find that comforting."

He stopped before an exit out to the street. "It's boot camp. There's a reason we don't let anyone in or out."

"Because you're indoctrinating them."

"It's boot camp," he repeated. "They eat, shit, and breathe this place. That's how it has been done for thousands of years. They're young and impressionable. They haven't found out who they are yet. They all find their way eventually. Just give him some space." He put a hand on her shoulder. "You haven't lost your friend."

She wanted to tell him not to touch her or try to comfort her, but somehow his words *were* comforting—the touch especially so. Like drinking cool water on a summer's day. She heard Colette's insidious words about using this to her advantage, but she didn't *want* that.

She shrugged his hand off. "You can justify anything, can't you?"

"We have that in common." He pushed the door open to another bright, unseasonably hot spring morning. Brooklyn had come alive in the time she'd been cloistered in with his little army. People and monsters wandered the streets, a little market on the corner full of fruits and vegetables had thrown its doors wide, a fire hydrant had been opened, and kids ran through it like a sprinkler. It was peaceful. A world she might have had with her parents.

"Did you know my parents?" she asked softly.

He tilted his head. "I might have. What were their names?"

"Shannon and Adair."

"Ah," he said softly. "Shannon Cairan."

Kierse stilled. She hadn't known her mother's surname.

"I knew *of* Shannon, though I never met her or her husband, I'm afraid."

"Because they didn't trust you. Because he was human," she accused. "Twenty years ago, they were here in the city trying to hide me. They wouldn't go to you for help."

Lorcan winced. "Walk with me." She followed him out onto the Brooklyn streets. "Shannon was young. Only about fifty when she was killed. Very young for your kind. Wisps can live to be thousands of years old if they hold onto their mind and their magic. Also very young to have a child."

She held her breath as he spoke about wisps in a way that Kierse had never gotten from all of her books and research. Even from Oisín, who discussed them more like faerie tales than reality.

"She was young enough that I didn't know her personally." He swallowed. "My wife was a wisp."

Lorcan took two more steps before stopping and turning back to see she hadn't moved. There was grief in the lines of his face. Something that he managed to hide so well. Because if all the wisps were gone, then so too was his wife. How had he accepted that death and continued on as he was?

"I'm sorry," Kierse found herself saying. She started walking again. "When did it happen?"

"About a century ago," he said, continuing forward. "Her name was Saoirse. We met when we were young and were married shortly after. We had two sons as well—Torin and Gannon. Wisps, the both of them."

"Oh," she said softly.

"So, you see, I am invested in the return of the wisps. But I do not know why your mother feared me. I would have helped her if I could. I would have saved all the wisps if I was able."

She'd thought that she'd seen worship in his eyes when he'd discovered she was a wisp. In reality, he was seeing all that he'd lost in her face. The wife and two sons who had died so long ago.

"I think the wisps didn't like that my dad was a human. They were worried you would judge them for it or refuse to help them."

Lorcan considered. His eyes swept over her. "You believe that *you* are only half wisp?"

"Yes? Once the spell broke, I got a memory that confirmed he was my father."

"Hmm. You don't have magic that acts like any half wisp I've ever seen."

"But I don't have all the wisps' powers, either," she said.

"Not all wisps had the same powers. Some had more or less than others."

"Really?" she asked in surprise. She hadn't known that.

"And your signature…" He cast a hand forward, a soft glow of magic suffusing his palm. He trailed off, shaking his head. His eyes were distant when he said, "I don't know how you could be half and part of a triskel."

"I don't know, either. Until recently, I thought I was fully human. So it doesn't matter to me. But I do want to find the man who put the spell on me."

"Do you know who that was?"

She watched for his reaction as she said, "Cillian Ryan."

"That motherfucker," he growled.

Kierse smirked. So what Graves had said seemed to be true. She didn't know why she kept doubting him. Everything he'd told her so far appeared to be corroborated. "You know him."

Lorcan's hands curled into fists and then relaxed. "*Knew* him. He was a Druid."

"That much I knew. A rogue Druid that you tried to kill."

"That's the least of it," he grumbled. "He destroyed Sansara."

Kierse blinked in confusion. "Who is Sansara?"

"Not who. What. Sansara was a sacred tree. It had roots nearly as old as time." Lorcan looked absolutely stricken. "I don't know how much you know about Druid magic. We have our own secrecy, of course."

"I've done my research. Sacrifice, nature, spells," she said, waving a hand. "A combination of the lot gives you powers."

"That's a very…simplified version." Lorcan sighed like he was suffering. "We say it's the three S: Self, Spirit, and Sacrifice. The self is our inherent magic. The spirit is time, place, celestial involvement. And the sacrifice is what we give to help power the spell."

"Okay," Kierse said. "And what he did went against that?"

"Suffice it to say that drawing on Sansara is generally forbidden except in large ritualistic spells on holy days. And Cillian Ryan drained the tree dry, leaving it crumpled to ash."

"Fuck," Kierse whispered.

Ethan had always had a deep devotion for plants. He'd once been devastated when a single leaf had fallen off of a potted plant he was nurturing. She couldn't imagine the devastation of losing a tree of that magnitude.

"As you can imagine, we moved against him swiftly."

"But he had the tree magic."

Lorcan nodded. "He used it to cloak himself and disappear into Manhattan. No tracking spells worked on him. He was just *gone*. Which probably explains why the force of the spell on you was so powerful."

"Do you think he's still in Manhattan?"

"I heard that someone killed him during the war. I don't know if the magic wore thin or he trusted the wrong person, but good riddance."

Kierse sagged at that knowledge. Another dead end. She'd been hoping that if she met Cillian, he might be able to fill in the blanks—not just how and why he'd put the spell on her, but what happened to her parents after. What their plan had been. How the Fae Killer had caught up to them.

A double strikeout.

"I wish that I had more information for you," he said as they reached the entrance to his headquarters. He pulled the door open and allowed her to enter before him. "I'm sure that you're anxious to know more about your heritage. I may know more about wisps than anyone still alive, and I would share that knowledge with you."

It was tempting. Oh so tempting.

"And what's in it for you?"

His smile widened. "Would you believe me if I said the pleasure of your company?"

"I rarely believe anything you say."

"Fine. Don't believe me, but I speak the truth. Wisps and Druids have been connected since the beginning. I would like us to continue to be." He held out his hand. "Let me show you something."

And despite herself, she put her hand in his and let him guide her.

They walked down a long hallway until it opened to a magnificent set of double doors, threaded through with a Druid signature—acorns and oak leaves—and a brass handle. She could feel the faint buzz of magic and see the soft golden light that suffused it if she squinted just right. The smell of summer and sunshine radiated from the door as if she had left Brooklyn behind and stumbled into the summer god's glen of old. This was a sacred place.

Her breath caught, and Lorcan smiled that bright, brilliant smile as he pushed the door open to reveal a glen, bursting with life. Grass and moss covered the ground. Oak trees sprouted at intervals, their branches reaching toward the glass ceiling. Spring flowers were in bloom in a radiant display of violet, indigo, and marigold.

At the far end of the room sat a throne. It was twice the size of a normal human—made for gods, not mere mortals. Carved into being by some long-dead master woodworker, it was constructed out of an ancient oak tree, filigreed with intricate Celtic knots and symbols that wound up from the roots to reach for the sky. It should have felt cold and dead, but it was still alive. Otherworldly magic radiated from it, as it were the source of all power on this earth.

"The Oak Throne," Lorcan told her reverently.

"Oh," she whispered, overcome with emotion at the sight. She wiped her eyes, unsure why it moved her to tears.

"It was made for the ruler of the Druids since before the doors were closed."

"It's beautiful."

He studied her, those azure eyes earnest. "It could be yours."

She jerked back to reality. "Mine?"

"You could live here," Lorcan said simply. "With me."

"In Brooklyn," she said slowly.

"Yes," he said on a laugh. "Here. You, Gen, and Ethan together again. Your little family. I have plenty of space. Ethan is already learning to be a Druid. Gen could work with Niamh as a High Priestess. You are the last of your kind, and I would give you the information you require about the wisps. You could have access to my library. Access to me."

She hesitated before asking, "Access to you?"

"Me, my throne, my world," he said, his eyes drifting across his kingdom and back to her face. "I'd like to have you here, little songbird."

She flushed under his scrutiny, hating that it wasn't faked. That it wasn't part of some mysterious plot she was weaving against him. In this faerie glen before an ancient throne, it felt like a real offer. What would her life have been like had her mother taken her to Lorcan straight away instead of dealing with Graves and Cillian? Would she have grown up here? Would she have seen his smiles as kind and not duplicitous? Would she have wanted what he was offering?

She mourned the little girl who would have wanted that life. Who could see herself safe in a place like this, instead of the abandoned girl she was, who could think of nothing if it wasn't transactional. As fun as it was to imagine her life here in Brooklyn living with the Druids, it felt more like a faerie tale than most of the ones she had read in the last couple months.

Happy endings like that didn't happen for people like Kierse. She was more likely to be the girl in the tale of the will-o'-the-wisp who was devoured by a bear while straying from her course than the wisp leading people astray.

"And if I say no?" she asked, finally.

"Think on it," he said, pulling her from the room. "Either way, you are welcome on Druid grounds even if you live…elsewhere. I'll still train you. I'll still fight for a triskel."

"Okay," she said uncertainly.

She wanted that information. She wanted to train with her friends. She wanted Ethan even just an inch further from this place. But she didn't know how that would begin to work.

When they reached the lobby, he once again opened the door for her. She stepped outside, her mind reeling from the conversation.

His eyes were full of mischief as he said, "I was part of the last triskel, after all."

"What?" she snapped.

He reached forward, taking her hand in his and placing a soft kiss on the back. "I'll tell you all about it when you come back to me."

Then he let the door slip closed.

"Bastard."

Chapter Twenty-Eight

The brownstone was empty when she trekked back to the Upper West Side. She hadn't heard from Gen, which probably meant she was still with Colette. All the better. Kierse didn't know how to tell her what had happened with Ethan. The disaster that had occurred—with Lorcan, too.

Jet lag pulled at her body, encouraging her to take a quick afternoon nap. She was a thing of midnights. Early mornings irritated her. And Lorcan even more so.

Lorcan had been part of a triskel?

No wonder he'd fucking recognized it when it had happened last year. He'd been so quick to try to scoop them up then, too. As soon as he'd realized, he'd wanted to spirit them all away and hide them forever. He still wanted to do that. And worse, she didn't know if she could stop it all from happening, if she even wanted to. The training, not the getting swept away part. She had shit to do.

She walked through the double doors of the library to find the massive room empty. Anne lounged on a couch, her black body seemingly twice as large as normal, belly exposed. Kierse laughed at the sight. Well, at least some things hadn't changed.

"Where's your person, huh?" Kierse asked her as she walked to the cabinet and poured herself a drink.

"Here," Graves said, appearing out of the stacks like a wraith.

Kierse jerked around. "I didn't know you were home."

"I just got back." He dropped a stack of books onto the table. "I was unboxing what I purchased in Dublin from Oisín."

"Do I want to know why Edgar isn't doing that?"

"Because it is my library," he said simply, stroking a spine. "Books are a singular pleasure. Nothing else in existence can transport you in quite the same way. All you have to do is crack the spine and learn the secrets of the universe."

"I don't think you possibly have the time to read them all."

"Collecting books and reading books are two different hobbies," he told her. "Don't get them mixed up."

"Noted."

She tipped back her drink with a flourish. Graves always had the best liquor. His eyes followed the movement, lingering on the bob of her throat as she swallowed.

"And how was your business?" he asked.

She lifted the drink to him and took another gulp.

"That good?"

"Bombed."

"He wouldn't let you see Ethan?" Graves asked, still as a statue in his crisp black suit. His gloves were on. His eyes ever watchful.

"Oh no. I saw Ethan. He's fully brainwashed by the Druids."

Graves sighed. "You thought he would be otherwise?"

She turned her back on him to refill her drink before saying, "He doesn't trust me because we're working together."

"Ah."

"It's stupid. He thinks they're the *good guys*." She put as much disdain as she could into the words. "I don't know how to disillusion him on that. There are no good guys."

"It's the Druid way," Graves said with a sniff. "It's not even his fault."

She turned back to him. "What do you know of Druid training?"

His eyes met hers as he considered. "I went through it."

"What? When?"

"I was young." He set his book down and reached for the liquor. "It was before I met Kingston, even."

"Really? Forgive me, but I simply cannot picture you as a Druid."

He smirked. "No, I never fit the bill. But I came to Dublin as a teenager, eager to be reunited with my mother's people after my father had sold me." He took a drink. "Oisín introduced me to Lorcan."

"Oisín!" I said in surprise. "You *have* known him a long time."

"Indeed."

"What happened? They let you join?"

"Not exactly," he said bitterly. "They accepted my mother, my blood, my Druidic magic. They rejected...everything else." He waved a gloved hand. "I was an anomaly, and military schools, no matter how progressive, don't like anomalies."

"But you trained with them."

"Yes. I spent many years in Dublin and the Irish countryside learning their ways. Always just a bit of an outsider. Except..."

He broke off and took another drink. She wasn't sure if he was going to finish. She had heard so little of his past, and every bit had been fought for. She was shocked that he was even trusting her with this much information without some huge tug of war. Maybe this was also part of his "prove it."

"Anyway," he said, "I know what Ethan is going through. For someone who wants to belong, the bonding is a high like you've never experienced. It's family. Until it isn't."

Kierse wanted to ask. Did this have something to do with Lorcan's sister, Emilie? Lorcan had claimed that Graves had killed Emilie, and Graves hadn't denied that fact. What had really happened to sever him from the Druids so long ago?

But she knew when he'd hit a subject he wasn't ready to discuss. She saw it in herself as much as him.

"Lorcan said as much," Kierse said.

Graves pursed his lips. "What else did he say?"

"He thinks Cillian Ryan is dead. Sometime in the Monster War."

"Hmm," he responded skeptically.

"I guess he drained a sacred tree and that's how he eluded Lorcan all this time. Sansa-something."

"Sansara?" Graves asked with wide eyes. "Fucking hell."

"That's the one."

"I knew he was pathological, but not that bad. No wonder the spell lasted so long on you, if it was fueled by Sansara."

"Lorcan said that, too."

Graves's face turned dark. He clearly disapproved of the comparison. "Is that all he knew?"

She told him the rest. About his wife and her parents and the triskel. Graves looked unsurprised. He'd known, then, that Lorcan had been part of a triskel. For some reason, that didn't seem to be what he wanted to discuss.

"Did he ask for anything else?" His voice was pitched low, his body leaning toward her like she was the earth and he her moon.

"Well, he asked me to stay. To move me and Gen onto the property."

"Of course he did."

"Which is why you kissed me," she breathed as he loomed over her. She tipped her chin up to meet him.

"Is that so?"

"You knew he'd ask."

"I know what he wants," Graves said with finality. His hands moved to her hips, finding the hem of her black shirt and running it through his fingers.

"He offered me the world," she teased. "Training and magic and a family and a throne."

"How could you deny him?" He toed her feet farther apart, spreading her legs wide and settling between them.

"Who says I denied him?" she breathed. She put her hands on his chest. The heat of him rippled through her. Just a breath away from tipping over the edge.

"Well, if I knew all I had to do was offer you the entire world to get you to accept," he began, his hands slipping to her ass and lifting her effortlessly onto the table, "maybe I would have done so earlier."

"Are you offering me the world?"

"And the stars."

"All of the ones in the night sky?"

"We'll see if I can get you to see them all," he said before pushing her flat on her back.

Her heart thudded noisily in her chest as he loomed over her exposed body, ripe for the taking. His eyes crawled over her chest to the sliver of pale skin exposed at her navel. Down her toned legs in fitted leggings to the black boots. Her wren necklace beat its wings against her breastbone. A thrum calling like to like.

She was the wren to the Holly King. In so many ways—magical and metaphysical and spiritual—wrens belonged to the winter god. A physical manifestation of his power. A hope for spring in a long winter. The source of his own destruction. Because after the winter solstice, their connection ebbed and he lost his power to make way for spring. The changing of the seasons, born in this pair of men and monsters.

Which meant at the summer solstice, their connection would grow once more. A little bird power-booster, destined to destroy him.

Even if they were currently out of season, she could feel the power blossom between them. The temperature in the room dipped, the balmy summer weather responding to the anthropomorphic winter at its heart.

Her breath frosted. Graves smiled. "Hello, my wren."

He methodically pulled his gloves off, finger by finger. Stripping himself bare and revealing the source of his powers all at once. Even though his magic didn't work on her, she never got tired of watching him expose his true nature.

"I've been dreaming about this," he told her as he dropped to one knee.

"What's that?"

He slid off one of her boots. "Being on my knees before you." Her breath hitched. He slipped off the second boot. "Spreading your legs." Her socks were tossed onto the pile. He ran his hands beneath the waistband of her leggings. "Stripping you out of your clothes and tasting every inch of your sweet skin." The leggings came off.

"That's what your dreams are made of?"

"Do you blame me?" He placed a kiss to one inner knee, then the other. "One taste would never be enough."

"You weren't satisfied?"

"Satiated but never satisfied." His bare hands slid up her thighs, dragging her inch by precious inch down the table until her ass nearly hung off. He lifted her knee over his shoulder and kissed a hot trail up her inner thigh. "Never enough of you."

Her breathing was coming in quiet pants. This Graves she hardly knew what to do with. When it had been a game to get him out of her system, she had played it well. Now she heard his words and matched his energy tenfold. She wanted this. Him. Like this. However he'd have her. Laid flat on a table. Bent over. Spread eagle. Bound and teased and high on him.

"Shall I remember the taste of my favorite delicacy?"

"Yes," she gasped as his lips reached the apex of her thighs.

She was already flushed and indecently wet from his coaxing. But the first brush of his tongue against her clit made her moan. He smirked dramatically up at her. Every bit the cat playing with his food before he pounced.

"I have missed that sound. Perhaps you can try to be louder."

"Louder," she whispered.

He slid one of his perfect pianist fingers down the center of her wet pussy.

"Louder, wren."

It was a command, and she could do nothing but follow. All of her clever quips and careful banter lost to his touch.

He pushed one luxurious finger into her core. He gave her body a quick and efficient stroke before adding a second and stretching her wider.

"Oh fuck," she said. Her hands gripped the edge of the table, holding on for dear life. It had been an achingly long five months. That one touch of him in Paris would never be enough. There was nothing like him.

"So wet," he said. "So very wet, this pretty pussy of mine."

"Graves," she moaned louder as he licked up her center.

"I'm going to have you dripping on the floor."

His tongue ran flat along her, dragging out her pleasure as he indulged in her. Then he dug in, burying his face in her pussy. His tongue grew incessant and insistent—hard, quick flicks against her clit that made her jump. She was desperate and turned on, and he was finger-fucking her like it was his job, as his tongue ruined her life in the very best way.

She was not going to last. Not even close.

"I...I..."

"Not yet," he commanded, pulling back but leaving his hand.

"But..."

As his eyes lifted to her face, his strokes turned languid. Two fingers inside her and his thumb stroking ever so gently. Edging her until she thought she'd tip over, but he held her back.

He rose to his feet, spreading her wider.

"Look at yourself." She shook her head. "I want you to watch as I make you come," he said, his voice like velvet across her skin. "Remember that I did it."

She hauled herself up onto her elbows and looked at the space where they were connected. His fingers deep inside of her. His thumb on her swollen nub. The whole thing indecent, with his scattered books on the floor and papers under her ass. A liquor bottle inches away, threatening to topple and shatter into a million pieces. And here she was, nearly dripping onto the antique rug of his precious library. Like *she* was the most important thing in it.

"Perfection, isn't it?"

"Yes," she breathed.

His smile was dangerous when he said, "Now come for me."

He knelt and returned his lips to her clit, sucking it into his mouth before swirling his tongue around the sensitive bud. His fingers worked in and out of her, curling upward to hit the perfect spot. She couldn't have held back a second longer. She released with a roar, her body exploding into a million tiny stars as the cosmos crashed down around her. And as she slowly returned to her body, she saw the entire night sky, as promised.

When her screams subsided, she fell backward, her head striking the wood, and stared up into the depths of the endless library.

"This is how I want to think about you," Graves said as he slid his fingers out of her and wiped them clean with a handkerchief. "Perfectly fucked."

The creak of the door in the now-silent library alerted them with a second to spare that they were no longer alone. Graves blocked the view from the intruder, and Kierse scrambled for her panties—*where the fuck had they gone?*—she snatched them up just as Gen strode into the library.

"Genesis," Graves said.

"I was just seeing if Kierse was ready to go." She was halfway across the room before she seemed to realize what she had stumbled into. Kierse didn't know exactly how much Gen could see of her trying to pull her pants back on, but Gen could read the energy of the room. "Sorry, I..." Gen said, coming to a stop.

Kierse couldn't see Graves's face. She could only imagine what they looked like in that moment, his mouth still covered in the evidence of their indiscretion. That wide, dangerous smile on his lips. Kierse behind him in nothing but her underwear.

"Can we help you?" Graves asked.

"I just...heard voices," Gen said with a note of panic as she retreated a step.

"I'll be right out," Kierse said on a scratchy, used voice.

"Okay. Yep. Yeah. I'll see you later."

Gen turned and fled the room, and Kierse released a breath. She tugged her leggings back on and glared up at him as he turned toward her.

"You have noise distortion," she reminded him. "You could have made it so no one else heard."

"Oh, I know." He leaned in with a smirk on his lips. Close enough she thought he might kiss her again. "I didn't want to."

Chapter Twenty-Nine

Even Gen seemed perplexed by the problem of how to salvage what had happened with Ethan. It likely would have gone better had she been in attendance, but it only made Kierse doubly sure that taking Gen there was a bad idea. Lorcan wanted all three of them, desperately, the way Graves wanted to collect the magic objects. Neither of them thought it was a good idea to be collected.

Though they had a feeling they would have to return to Lorcan eventually to further their training. There was only so much they could do alone, and unfortunately, Graves had no experience with a triskel.

When Gen had asked about what she'd walked in on in the library, Kierse had just given her best bluff. She didn't know how it had happened, only that it had, she'd enjoyed it, and she wanted to do it again. Not only because of the sex, but also because Graves was opening up in ways she had thought impossible last winter. In fact, she hadn't really thought it was possible even when she had bargained with him. But he had said he would prove she could trust him, and at least this was a step in the right direction.

Kierse returned to the scene of the crime, toeing the library door open while she held an oversize mug of tea. She wanted something to fortify her before she began memory work. It still terrified her to think of Graves digging around in her mind. If he even could. Why had she agreed to this again?

Edgar was in the library, fluffing pillows on a dark blue chaise. "Miss McKenna," he said at her entrance. "I set up your arrangements for today. If you require anything else, do let me know. I can send Isolde up with some refreshments as well, if you like."

"Thank you," she said sincerely. "Tea should be fine for now. Unless Graves wants something."

"I do not," Graves said, striding into the room behind her.

"Excellent, sir." Edgar bowed and departed.

Kierse set her tea on the coffee table, carefully avoiding looking at the table they'd had indecent relations on. "This is for me?"

"I thought it'd be more comfortable than the couch."

"We could have used a bed."

His eyes flashed when he looked at her. "I'm more powerful in the library."

Mmm. As if that was all it was.

She took a seat. He dragged a chair over before her, and her body trembled. She was nervous. She had *every* reason to be nervous. Graves, no matter how much she was attempting to put her trust in him, could destroy her mind. She was certain of that. It was what he was good at. If she let him in, he could hurt her...like he had before. But she couldn't afford Nying Market every time she needed information. Graves was right here.

"Your absorption is a problem," he said flatly. All business.

Good. Business made sense.

"It serves me well."

"Generally, people have to learn to keep others out of their heads. There's an entire discipline devoted to strengthening the mind to deflect anyone seeking to get their claws in."

"To stop you, you mean."

Graves shrugged. "They're not usually good enough for that, but sure."

"Modest."

"It doesn't suit me." He passed her a book. "If you want to work on mental fortification, then this would be of use to you. In the event that your absorption fails you, you want to make sure you still have teeth."

She cradled the book in her hands uncertainly. He was giving her information to deflect against *him*? That was...strange.

He must have read that in her eyes. "We're building trust," he reminded her. "I'd be remiss not to teach you self-defense."

"Right," she agreed.

"So training today will focus on lowering your absorption. And if I can get you to do that, then we can look for your memories." He tapped the book. "If not, I'll start you reading the theoretical side of that mental work, and we can work on mental fortitude. There are some easy exercises that you should start doing on your own either way."

Kierse leafed through the book. "More homework."

"You thought you'd escape it?"

She laughed. "With knowledge incarnate before me? Not really."

"Seems you did plenty of research back in Dublin. You should be used to it." He reached for another book and tipped it open. "As far as tackling your absorption, I needed a different plan."

"Have wisps ever done this kind of work before?"

Graves glanced up at her thoughtfully. "Most wisps wouldn't let me close enough to find out."

Kierse laughed. "Yeah, I bet not. That has something to do with me being able to kill you?"

"Something like that."

"And how do I do that exactly?"

Graves grinned, all teeth. "Another lesson, perhaps."

"Oh, how I look forward to it." She set the book aside. "You did call me the source of your destruction."

"And I meant it literally, in every sense of the word," he said, his voice pitched low. Suddenly, they were talking about something else entirely. She flushed, and his smile only grew. "Lay back."

Kierse did as instructed. The chaise was a soft, midnight-blue velvet with enough cushion to cocoon Kierse's body. She swallowed and waited for more instruction.

"Absorption, as you're currently using it, is passive. Just in the way we believed that immunity was. But absorption *can* be active. I've seen wisps siphon magic, store it, and redirect it. You aren't a warlock, but you still follow the rules of magic. You can recharge as I can, but you can also be charged through your absorption. Just as you burn it off when going into your slow motion."

So far all of that made sense. "I need to make it active. Like when I pulled the wish powder magic out of Ethan?"

"In theory, what we're trying to do is the opposite of that. Drawing magic out is one half of the equation and *not* absorbing at all is the other side."

"Is it the opposite?" she asked, scrunching her nose. "Is absorbing the opposite of turning the powers off?"

"Think of active absorption like turning your powers *on*. Right now, they're on standby. When you drew the magic from Ethan, they were on. We need to recreate that. Once you can pull energy, then we'll think of shutting it *off* instead of letting it slide back into standby."

"Okay," she said uncertainly. She'd been in deep, desperate shit when she'd done that for Ethan. She hoped that she could do it again here.

"One step at a time," he encouraged. "I am going to use my magic to try to read your thoughts and just feel the absorption that stops me from doing it."

Graves touched a bare hand to her wrist. She concentrated on his hand against her skin. When they had first attempted anything like this, she hadn't even been able to see or sense the magic, but now it came to her easily.

The soft gold of his magic swam into her vision. Just the lightest touch against her skin and she could smell the leather and books and feel his internal heat, the inferno that was always raging from his constant magic use. When she focused even harder, she could see the golden glow flow away from her, out into the library, out the door, out into the world. It was everywhere. His magic was everywhere.

"Focus," he said gently. "Just here, Wren."

She swallowed and reined it all back in. She could do this.

The magic was part of her. She could control it if she wanted. That was what she had been doing with her slow motion her entire life. She could walk in and out of that like breathing. This was the same, just a different ability.

Her own magic rose to the surface as she felt around for her absorption and the space where it was drawing in Graves's magic.

"Good," he said. "Whatever you're working on, I can see it."

She narrowed her eyes. There was a key turn here. When she went into slow motion, she pushed forward into it like flipping a switch. She needed to find the switch here.

She grappled with it like reaching for slippery soap until she felt her absorption magic settle over her. She gasped. It covered her entire body, like a blanket across her senses. It hugged her tightly, skin to skin, until there was no place where she started and it ended.

With reaching tendrils of magic, she tried to extend that blanket outward. Her hands shook as she fought with herself to stretch her power as easily as she slipped into slow motion, but she couldn't do it. This felt like it was glued to her skin.

"Wren," he murmured, his eyes warm on hers. "Steady. Just drag in a little bit. Don't reach out with your entire body. Just where I'm touching you."

"Okay," she said, her voice trembling.

She focused on his hand. His magic. A tiny trickle in a giant river. All she needed to do was drag the river toward her. Just an inch.

She tugged and there it was. Graves's magic open and waiting for her. Not a trickle—a *torrent*. A giant, unwavering, magnificent tidal wave of power. She could see past the stream he was offering her to the intense flood within him. So much magic it was blinding. He went from her dark winter god to a diaphanous sheen of golden light. Magic beyond measure.

Except…something was missing.

She didn't know how she knew, only that there was a piece of that overwhelming abundance that felt...injured. As if someone had cut a piece out of it and it had never grown back. Which felt impossible. All magic could be rechargeable.

"Enough," Graves grunted.

The connection abruptly severed. Kierse's absorption switched back into neutral. The light suffusing his body disappeared. She felt suddenly bereft.

"I..."

"That was more than sufficient," Graves said, rubbing his hands together.

"Did I take too much?"

"No. You didn't take anything," he said. "You..." For a moment, he said nothing. But he was looking at her with something like concern in his features. "You touched my magic."

"Was that bad?"

"It was...invasive."

"A taste of your own medicine?" she quipped.

He stilled at the thought. "Perhaps. I wasn't sure how much more powerful you would be now that the spell is gone. You did that faster than I anticipated."

"That's good, right?"

"It's good. But..." He wavered a moment as if he wasn't going to finish his thought.

"But?"

"That is how wisps have killed warlocks in the past," he said slowly, as if he didn't want to give her this information.

"By touching your magic?"

"And then draining it."

She blanched. "I'd never survive absorbing all that magic."

"Let's hope we never have to test that," he said, brushing his hands down his suit pants.

He looked...uncomfortable. And how could she blame him? When he had offered to teach her magic, she had panicked about lowering her guard and letting him into her mind. But this was something else altogether. He had taught her how to...hurt him.

He could have skipped this step. He could have not told her what the end result would be, but he had. A light switched on in her mind. He'd handed her a truth that could hurt him. And he'd done it willingly.

She needed to trust him to do the same when she switched her powers the other direction and let him in. A vulnerability for a vulnerability.

"Now turn the powers off."

"Okay," she agreed.

She closed her eyes this time. She didn't want to dive back into that rush of magic. To get lost in the currents of the enormity of him. All she wanted to do was feel…nothing. No absorption at all.

She wanted to let him in. Graves could come in. She would allow that.

The magic appeared to her like something she'd always known how to find. The off button slid into place like breathing. Graves's hand on her wrist was fire hot. She opened her eyes to see the gold of his magic sliding past her defenses and into her skin.

She lifted her chin to meet his eyes, and suddenly the memory of them in this room rose to the surface. Him on his knees before her. Her looking down at where his fingers invaded her core and brought her to ever-higher peaks. The look on his face as she came. The torture of not going further. The want. The need. The…

The memory switched off, and with it her absorption came back online. Her cheeks were flushed. His eyes blazed with an intensity she almost couldn't handle.

"Well, well, well, that was a pleasant memory."

"You weren't supposed to see that," she snapped.

"That isn't how memory works."

She felt in over her head. "I don't want you to see memories like that."

"Then concentrate on what you *do* want me to see," he said. "Think of your parents this time. Guide my powers to where you want them to be."

"Is it that easy?"

He flashed her a dirty smirk. "Never."

"Reassuring."

"Most people think of what they don't want someone to see, and then when I'm in there, that's what I see. That's how minds work. You need to concentrate on the memory you're looking for. What are you looking for?"

Kierse tried to clear her mind. "My parents."

"Be specific."

"The room with the hole under the floorboards."

He nodded encouragingly. "We'll go back to the floorboards and we'll try to see what comes after your nightmare. It might take a few tries."

"I'm ready," she told him, fear creeping through her at the thought of going to that dark place.

This time she kept the floorboards in her mind as she lifted her absorption again. This time her magic felt a little less like glue and more like peeling back layers. It was still sluggish, but it came more easily.

Graves's magic touched her, and suddenly she could see darkness. There were screams in the background. She was under the floorboards. Now that she looked around, Kierse could see dim light coming from the room above her. It was cold. Winter. She wasn't wearing a jacket.

The memory shifted to last winter. Lorcan's magic rushing into her body, and Graves's haunted face begging her to give him the magic.

Kierse gasped and released her powers. She was panting, bent over the couch as that memory sliced through her. The pain was visceral.

"What triggered the shift?" he asked.

"Winter. It was cold in the dream."

"Ah," he said easily. "You think of me with winter."

"How could I not?"

A small smile crept onto his face. "We were there. Try to stay in the moment. See what happens next."

Kierse nodded and pulled her absorption up again. It was even easier than the last time. Easier every time.

She was back under the floorboards. This time she kept her focus on what was happening. The yelling continued. A body thumped nearby. She couldn't see who it was from her hide out. She couldn't see anything. And yet something was happening. Her parents were gone and she was here.

"We know she's here, Adair," a smooth female voice said as heeled boots clicked on the hardwood.

"She's long gone. We sent her away."

The woman laughed, high and disbelieving. "You put up a valiant fight, but even I know you wouldn't send away your precious daughter."

"Maureen," a female voice pleaded. Kierse's mother. "Just let us go. We aren't harming anyone."

"Not you. But the child," Maureen said. Kierse could hear the sneer in her voice. "The relationship is doomed anyway. He will wither and die, and you will stay young forever. Not much of a life."

"It is *our* life," Adair snarled.

Kierse shook under the floorboards, wanting to come out and be brave like her parents. Suddenly she was trapped in another room. In a jail cell after the bank robbery had gone all wrong. Jason's face staring down at her through the bars, his sweet scent wafting toward her.

"Guess you'll have to get out of this one yourself, kid," he taunted.

Kierse shut it off, and reality rushed back in. "Fuck him."

"I agree. It was the trapped feeling?" he guessed. She nodded. "I felt the thread pull you through. Memories are like dreams in that way."

"We were almost there. Do you know who Maureen is?"

"She was a wisp council member," Graves said solemnly. "A powerful one."

"And she wants to…kill me? For existing?"

"I would suspect so, but I don't have enough information to speculate. Why don't we continue and see?"

She shivered, not wanting to go back in there and at the same time wanting answers to this nightmare.

Her absorption popped free seamlessly this time. She dropped back into the memory. Maureen was chiding them for their arrogance, believing they could get away with it.

"The Fae Killer is out there. You won't be able to keep her safe." Her heels stopped over the place where Kierse was hiding. "You should come back with us, Shannon."

"It's all of us or none of us," Shannon told her.

"I'm afraid that's the wrong answer."

And then there was a loud bang. Fear ripped through her, and she bit her lip to stop from crying. She wanted to call for her parents. To beg them to let her out of this hole. To know what was happening up there. If they were all right. But she wouldn't jeopardize them.

Time moved slow as glue and fast as a rapid river all at the same time. The floorboards were pulled up, and her father's face was there.

"Come here, my wee darling."

He hoisted her small form out, and she buried her face into his shoulder and sobbed. "Dada, I was so scared."

"I know, but you don't have to be scared any longer. No one is going to come after you now."

"Hurry, Adair," Shannon cried. "I already got ahold of Bram to fly us to New York."

"I've got her," he told his wife.

Kierse shouldn't have looked back as he carried her out of the room, but she did. It was the first dead body she'd ever seen. Maureen was blank-faced and prone. She'd been rolled out of the way. Her unseeing eyes accusing

Kierse of this murder. What her parents had done to protect her.

The memory vanished a moment later.

Kierse had tears in her eyes. They'd killed another wisp, a powerful council woman. They'd done it to protect her, and all this time she'd had it in the back of her mind as a nightmare. And it was. But it was also a blessing. They'd done this to save her.

Graves cleared his throat. "We'll stop there," he told her, rising to his feet easily.

"Graves," she said, looking up at him with tears in her lashes. "Thank you."

He nodded once. "You were very lucky that your parents loved you so much."

And she felt lucky when she had never felt lucky before. She still had so many questions—all the why and how and who of the situation—but she couldn't deny that this felt like a gift, and it was still worthwhile.

"You got through what I planned for today. Faster than I thought," he admitted.

She picked up the book. "Good. I guess I should proceed to the homework portion of the evening."

"I had something else in mind." And for a second, she couldn't breathe, wondering if she would be able to resist him. He smirked as if he could read her mind in the gutter. "Are you up for a road trip?"

Chapter Thirty

K ierse's head was buried in the memory fortification book. "This stuff is going to give me a headache."

"Probably," he agreed.

She glanced out the window as they crossed over into the Bronx. "I still can't believe we're going to Covenant. The last time we were there, you sent Edgar to smash up their equipment."

"I made a donation to the center afterward," he said dismissively. "I agree with what they're doing. We need a hospital for monsters as much as the ones we have for humans. We have ailments that only magic can help or only monster doctors can assess."

"And Dr. Mafi?" Kierse asked.

"The same."

"Not pleased to see you. Helping you for…reasons?"

He shrugged. "We'll ask her when we get there."

The last time that she had seen Dr. Mafi, they'd been in Third Floor and she'd held them at gunpoint. She was surprised that Graves would ever forgive Mafi, let alone trust her. But perhaps she had proven herself in the end.

They pulled into a back lot behind the hospital. A sliding glass door directed them into a brightly lit lobby, and Graves bypassed the woman at the front in peach scrubs. The Covenant was not just a monster hospital— it was also a coven of witches, who used their powers for healing. Kierse had been appalled when she had first learned that anyone would want to help monsters, but she had come around to the idea that everyone needed assistance.

They passed through a long corridor, stopping in front of a closed office door. He knocked twice, and the door swung open to reveal a beautiful woman in teal scrubs, a matching hijab, and a white coat.

"Hello, Emmaline," Graves said.

Dr. Mafi blew out a heavy sigh. "I got your message." Her eyes flicked to Kierse. "In trouble again, I see."

"And you?" Kierse asked. "Staying out of it yourself?"

Dr. Mafi pointed across the hall. They stepped into an empty patient room, and Mafi closed the door before answering, "I'm only doing this because you killed Louis. My debt was cleared, and now I'm free again."

"I was glad to do it," Kierse said.

"Of course, now I owe you one, instead," Mafi said with a shake of her head. "Not how I wanted that to happen. Well, nothing to be done for it. Why don't you tell me why you're here?"

Kierse glanced at Graves. "How much did he tell you?"

"I'd rather hear it in your own words." Dr. Mafi shot Graves a pointed look. "You can wait in the lobby if you'd prefer."

He crossed his arms and stared at her. Dr. Mafi's relationship with Graves was fraught at best. They had been close before the Monster War while she was getting her medical degree. When things hadn't worked out, he'd paid for her to finish, and she'd owed him for that ever since.

Kierse cleared her throat. "I learned recently that I had a spell put on me that made me forget my past. Since the spell…came down, my memories have been jumbled. I've tried several magical ways to recover them, but we're—I'm—concerned that there might be something else wrong."

Mafi's gaze slipped to Graves. "There's something that you can't figure out?"

"We're in your capable hands," Graves said.

She narrowed her eyes at him as if he'd insulted her. "Tell me what you've tried so far."

So Kierse took her through the magical treatment she'd tried from the market and her work with Graves. Mafi listened intently, asking questions and jotting down notes on a clipboard as Kierse explained. "So, Graves suggested that the issue might not be simply magical."

Mafi nodded. "As much as I hate agreeing with him, it does sound possible. There are some tests we can run to see if there's any damage to your brain, since you mentioned previous falls," Mafi began. "I'll set you up for an MRI first to rule out that possibility. Then we can discuss other options once we have the results in."

Mafi went for the door, but Graves put his hand on it. "You're going to keep your findings to yourself this time, right?"

She bristled under his scrutiny. "I'm a professional."

"You were last time, too."

"Then find someone else," she challenged him. Graves stared her down, but it was Mafi who looked away first. "I won't share it."

"Good," he said and released the door.

They ran a series of tests on her brain, all of which sucked in some way. The idea that her brain was somehow permanently damaged, either from Jason's abuse or the spell, had never occurred to her. She had been worried about magical interference, not normal human stuff. It unsettled her to think that could be the problem.

Afterward, Kierse and Graves returned to the patient room to wait for the results. Almost an hour later, Mafi knocked and then entered. "Sorry about the wait. There was an emergency."

"That's all right," Kierse said.

"I want to say first that the testing came back fine. Your MRI shows a very healthy brain."

Kierse released a breath. "That's good."

"Yes. It's very good, considering the potential brain trauma you discussed with me in your past. I don't know if that spell helped you, or if your magic shielded you from worse pain, but whatever the case, that isn't an issue here."

"So…it's just the spell, then?"

Mafi leaned back against the wall and considered. "I'm not sure that's *all* it is. It's not a brain injury. There's no damage, that's very clear. But I would think that, after everything you went through, you're dealing with a significant amount of trauma."

"Oh."

Kierse glanced up at Graves, but he was as unreadable as ever. As if he didn't want his opinion of the topic to influence however she was feeling. Not that she knew exactly what that was.

"The loss of your parents, your life on the streets, the subsequent Monster War." Mafi glanced at Graves. "Working with a certain warlock. All of it has left its mark on you. If not physically, then mentally. The Monster War alone is enough trauma for any one lifetime. The fact that you went through it all." She splayed her hands out. "Do you understand what I'm saying?"

"I had a tough life."

"Yes," Mafi said with a short laugh, "but not just that. Trauma can cause all sorts of changes in your brain and how it responds to stimuli. While common responses are anxiety and depression, it can shape who you are in other ways, like hyper-independence."

Kierse blinked at her. "Okay? What does that have to do with my memories?"

"The spell *might* have taken your memory, but it's possible that you repressed those memories all on your own as well. That what happened to you was so traumatic, your brain shut itself off from the pain."

"Oh," she said with wide eyes. "That sounds…possible."

"You might find that as you work through these memories, whether with Graves," she gestured to the walking memory machine in the room, "or alone, you might need to process them afterward, separately. Possibly with a professional."

"Wait. Are you suggesting therapy?" Kierse asked with a stilted laugh.

"What's wrong with therapy?"

"I don't see how talking about my problems is going to fix them."

"You're the only one who can fix your problems." Her pointed glance at Graves was telling. "But therapy gives you an outside perspective from a third party who isn't involved in your life. They might help you see it from another angle. We have a psychiatrist on staff…"

"A psychiatrist?" Kierse asked. "And that's different than a therapist?"

"A psychiatrist can do everything a licensed therapist can do and also prescribe medicine."

"Medicine," she said skeptically. "You think I need medicine?"

Mafi arched an eyebrow. "At this time, no, but I want to recommend the best specialist for you. And luckily, we have the best in the business for monster-human psychiatry."

"Are you sure I'd need that?"

"I plan to treat your brain the same way I would any other organ. Your mental state is as important as your physical state. If you broke your leg, you wouldn't shrug off seeing a specialist for the injury."

"If we could afford it."

"Money doesn't seem to be a problem anymore," she quipped. "So let's keep our mind open, shall we? We can get a lot farther together if we all look at this as a combination of magic and science. You came to me for my specialty. If I need to steal something, I'll come to you. Got it?"

"Sure," Kierse said.

Mental health just wasn't talked about on the street. When your entire life was centered around survival, dealing with your trauma any way other than finding your next meal and keeping a roof over your head wasn't possible. She'd never looked into her past even when it seemed to have gaps. She hadn't wanted to know what she'd find.

"So what's your suggestion, Emmaline?" Graves asked finally.

Mafi met his gaze warily. "Our most distinguished psychiatrist, Dr.

Carrión, is back home in Peru at the moment. Her specialty is monster mental health in a post-Monster War New York City. I would suggest Kierse come to see her when she returns. I can let you know when that is."

Graves looked at Kierse. She blew out a breath and nodded. "Done," he said.

Mafi handed Kierse a bunch of paperwork about the benefits of therapy and told her to read through it.

"More homework," she mused. Her eyes found Graves as they headed to the car. "Why do I always have homework when I see you?"

"Always trying to make you a brain and not just a little thief."

She rolled her eyes. "I can be both."

"You can," he agreed. "But you usually think *what's the most trouble I can barrel straight into* first, and the stop-and-think part comes second."

"Fair," she conceded as she slid into the backseat. "You were quiet in there. I know you have thoughts about what Mafi said."

"I want what's best for you." He tapped the book in his hands. "Which means mental fortifications and memory work and yes, even therapy, if that's what you want."

"Yeah," she said, biting down on her lip. "I don't know how I feel about therapy."

"Color me shocked."

She laughed. "What? That doesn't surprise you?"

"Very few things surprise me. You almost always do," he conceded. "But not in this. You've been on your own your entire life. You thought your mother died and your father abandoned you. The only person you've ever let in is Gen."

"I let you in," she said, lifting her chin. "And learned why I shouldn't have."

He stilled at her comment. "As I said, I'm here to prove you wrong about that."

"It's a work in progress."

He *was* working on it. She could see that he was changing. She just didn't know if it was a forever change. She'd been fooled once. She didn't want to make the same mistake again.

"I'll take it."

Chapter Thirty-One

Kierse completed her homework.

She read the mental fortification book, and she considered therapy. Something she never in a million years would have thought about before this point. Maybe she'd do it if Graves got the promised follow-up call. In the meantime, mental work.

The practice seemed simple: create a little mind block to separate her consciousness from an attacker. But it was not simple. Not in the slightest. And it made her head hurt ferociously.

Still, she practiced until her temples throbbed all day and night. Then she practiced some more. Day after day, working on muscles she'd never used before, until she felt a scream building in her throat. Until she thought she'd tear the house down in frustration. From her need to do something physical.

So, one morning, she hoofed it out of Graves's brownstone, paid off a particularly obnoxious troll, and took the 2 to Penn Station. She exited onto 31st Street just as dawn was breaching the horizon and headed at a quick clip toward Chelsea Park.

Only this winter, she'd seen drug deals on the corner here, but the place had been cleaned up. Fresh grass, trees in bloom, flowers around a small fountain, the playground filled with children's laughter, even signs advertising a weekend farmer's market. Her city had changed so much in her absence.

She loved and hated it all at once.

She wasn't even sure that Nate would be up when she'd texted him on her way over, but by the time she'd soldiered past an unknown guard, who had clearly drawn the short stick for such an early shift, she'd received a text back.

Fucking finally.

Kierse laughed and trotted up the stairs. Five Points was a nightclub run by the Dreadlords, but it was also their werewolf headquarters. The three nights surrounding the full moon, which had ended last night, the wolves went underground and locked the place down to keep it safe for the city, in accordance with the Monster Treaty.

"Kierse McKenna," a voice said as she approached Nate's office. "I'd heard you were back in town."

Kierse smirked at the sight of Nate's second, Ronan. He was tall and slim with black hair parted down the middle and severe black circles under his dark eyes. His family had emigrated from Korea, and he'd joined up with Nate's pack for their protection. He'd moved up the ranks like he was born to it. And she supposed he was.

"Hey, Ronan. Who did you hear that from? Gen?" she teased.

Ronan shrugged. "I'm glad she's home. She's not trouble like you."

"Oh, she's certainly trouble," Kierse said.

"She's the kind of trouble I like, though." He slid a cigarette behind his ear and lifted a shoulder. "She doesn't drag the whole pack into her schemes."

"Fair," Kierse conceded. "And if you're asking, I think she'd see you."

Ronan grinned as he melted into the shadows. "Oh, I know she will."

Kierse laughed. Of course she'd run into Ronan and not Finn, his partner in crime. Finn was a burly Black man who was all golden retriever to Ronan's edge, and the best friends made the most unlikely of pairs.

Kierse turned her attention from the shadows, knocked once on the office door, and pushed her way inside to find Nathaniel O'Connor seated at his desk, head bowed, curly chestnut hair falling into his eyes. His tawny-brown complexion was waxen from the early hour. A giant thermos of coffee rested on the desk before him, wrapped in his large hands.

"You've looked better," Kierse said.

Nate's chin jerked up, and those hazel eyes met hers. "It was a rough moon." He got to his feet and held his arms wide. "Kierse McKenna, in my house. Didn't think I'd have to go so long. At least it wasn't a whole year."

"It might have been if not for the situation."

"Graves?"

She shrugged. "As you can imagine."

"Colette sent a runner over after you left. You two are *living* with him?"

"Yes."

"And working together."

"Yes."

He leaned back against his desk. "So what's the plan? Where's the double cross?"

Kierse hesitated. She was always the girl with the plan. With an exit. That was her favorite rule in thieving. She needed ways out of every situation—

physical and otherwise. But she didn't *have* one here. The deeper she got into this with Graves, the more she felt like there were no exits.

"Fuck," Nate said, standing again. "What's going on?"

"It's fine. I'm working on it."

"And you trust him?"

She gasped out a laugh. "No. That's a big no."

He blew out a breath. "Well, that's good. He royally fucked you over last year. I thought you had better brains than that."

"He's…trying to regain my trust," she told him.

"By fucking you?"

She laughed again. "No. Well, maybe," she said with a shrug. "But no, he's bringing me in on his business operations and introducing me to the people he works with and trying to help me with a magic problem."

"Hmm," Nate grunted. "I still don't trust him."

"I know. I told him that I'd let him prove himself, but it's not easy for me."

"With good reason."

"Am I being foolish?"

Nate crossed his arms and looked to the ceiling. "I don't know. Maybe. The fact that you'd even consider letting him back in after what he did says that you've come a long way. If anyone else had hurt you like that, you'd be gone." He slapped his hands together. "That fast."

"Yeah."

"Graves, though…he's got his claws in you."

She bristled. "I don't know…"

"Not with me," he said. "You can't lie about him with me."

"Fine. Yes, I want to trust him again."

"Then just let him show his cards and make an informed decision the best you can with your heart in his hands."

Kierse hated that plan, and Nate must have seen it on her face, because he just laughed and pulled her in for a hug.

"A little discomfort is good for you. And I'm still here if you need a good double cross."

She shook her head with a laugh. The last time they'd worked together against Graves, they'd decided she would feed him information to help the pro-human cause. There were monsters out there trying to destroy the hard work that had been put into the treaty. The last thing they wanted was another monster war. "What's the monster situation been?"

Nate took the out. "Quiet."

"Third Floor?"

"Quiet," he repeated. "The whole city has been suspiciously quiet since you left. Like killing King Louis destroyed the monster rebellion."

Kierse frowned. "That's optimistic."

"It's deceptive. They've gone underground. Burrowed in deeper."

"Any evidence of that?"

He shook his head. "No, there's nothing, but we know they're not gone."

"Rats," she grumbled. "Well, keep me informed."

"Always. But that's not the real reason you're here, right? My midnight girl is never up at such an early hour."

She shot him a self-deprecating look. "You know me too well. It's Ethan," she confessed. "I went to see him earlier this week."

His eyebrows rose. "You got inside?"

"The head Druid owes me a favor or two."

"The head Druid wants to bang you," he quipped with a wink.

She snorted. God, she had missed Nate's easy humor. "That's beside the point. Ethan has been brainwashed. I sort of worry about what happens when his isolation is up."

"For him, or you…or Corey?"

"Yes," she said honestly.

Nate sighed. "Would he leave of his own accord if we broke into the place?"

Kierse thought about it for a second, the mischievous smile tugging on her lips. Then she lost the thread of it all. "No. No, he wants to be there."

"Well, fuck."

"Yeah. Everyone else is like 'give him space.' I'm glad you went straight to 'kidnap.'"

Nate chuckled. "Fuck everyone else being reasonable. We have chains down below the club. We could chain him up and run a deprogramming."

Another laugh bubbled out of her. "He'd hate us."

Nate mimed holding up a picture. "This is a Druid. They are bad guys."

Full laughter hit her in her belly. "You're ridiculous."

"I know. But it helped, didn't it?"

"Yeah. It did."

"I know you hate hugs, but you look like you could use another one."

And the hug was worth it. Worth the early morning and the trek to Chelsea and all of it. Nate was her family. He'd reminded her that he always had her back. Which was exactly what she needed.

A knock at the door pulled them both out of it, and in strode a tall Desi girl in sky-blue nursing scrubs. Nate's girlfriend, Maura, was a nurse at a local not-for-profit hospital. Her long brown hair was up in a messy bun, and she had circles under her eyes that mirrored Nate's and Ronan's. She must have been out all night during the full moon.

"Kierse!" she gasped. She strode forward, knocking her boyfriend out of the way and wrapping Kierse in her arms.

"Hi, Maura."

"You need to stop this disappearing act."

"Working on it," Kierse told her.

"And perfect timing." Maura released Kierse and thrust her left hand out. Kierse stared down at the glittering diamond ring on her finger in incomprehension before she realized what it meant.

"Oh my God! You're engaged?"

"Yes!"

"Who's the lucky guy?" Kierse joked.

Nate glared at her, but Maura just snorted. "Nate did say he wasn't marriage material," she agreed.

"I didn't say those exact words."

Maura laughed. "'Perpetual bachelor' was probably your exact phrasing."

"Aye, baby," Nate said, wrapping arms around his fiancé. "You changed my mind. I'm a changed man."

Maura snorted again and pushed her hand into his face as he tried to kiss her. "I bet."

Kierse laughed. "I'm so happy for the both of you."

"Actually," Nate said as he went back to his desk, "Maura would kill me if I didn't give you this." He handed her an envelope of starch white paper with her name across it. "Wedding invite."

Kierse tore into the letter. Inside the card was all white with swirling gold font:

Please join us for the wedding of

Maura Vendashi Bhardwaj

&

Nathaniel Gabriel O'Connor

Saturday, June 29th

6:30 p.m.

Five Points, Chelsea

Reception to follow.

"This is in only a few weeks," Kierse gasped.

"Yeah. Just decided to do it if we're doing it."

"Damn straight," Maura said.

"I can't wait," Kierse said truthfully. She wanted the best for them. She'd known longer than Nate that Maura was the real deal, and if he didn't settle down, he'd lose her. She was glad that he'd figured it out, too. "Were you on the night shift?"

"I…yes," Maura said. Her gaze shifted to her fiancé. He nodded. "But I got off at midnight. I was looking into something else. Something I thought maybe you could…bring up with Graves."

Kierse's eyebrows shot up. "With Graves?"

"Tell her, baby," Nate said.

Maura took a breath and let it out. "I can't have kids."

"Oh, Maura, I'm so sorry. I didn't know."

"No one else knows really. When I was younger, before the Monster War, I was seduced by an incubus."

Kierse gasped, covering her mouth with her hand. "Maura, no!"

Tears glinted in Maura's eyes. "Yeah. I didn't know about monsters then and just thought I was falling in love and rebelling against my parents. But as you know, once you're…intimate with an incubus…"

"They put the curse on you."

She nodded. "Yes. They feed on your sexual energy."

Kierse's gaze shifted to Nate. "I can't believe this. I'm so sorry. But how do you think Graves would help?"

"He might know a cure," Nate said. "Maura jokes, but she didn't want to get married because she thought I deserved to have children. I told her she was out of her mind, but I have been looking for a way to help her. The pack even tracked the incubus and killed him. It didn't change anything."

Maura choked on that, as if it still hurt to think about.

"I know Graves isn't forthright with information, and he might tell us to fuck off, but we're down to our last resort…"

"I can ask him," Kierse agreed easily.

But she had never heard of a cure for an incubus curse. It was like a vampire draining your blood or a wraith feeding off your soul. An incubus and succubus worked in a pair to drain energy through sex. Once they drained you, the only children you could have were theirs…if you survived. And most didn't. They were monsters for a reason.

"Thanks," Maura said with a sigh. "I hate to bring the mood down."

"No, of course not, Maura. I'm happy to help, if I can."

"Okay," she said, wiping at her eyes. "I'm going to go pass out. Night shifts suck."

She kissed Nate's cheek and pulled Kierse in for another hug. "The invite goes for Gen and Ethan, too," Maura said. "And a plus-one. In case you want to bring a certain hot, dangerous warlock."

Kierse held her tighter. "I love you, Maura."

"Love you, too, baby girl."

Then Maura was gone, and when Kierse turned around, Nate's face fell.

"Do you think he'll help us? I know that's not his MO."

"I don't know what he'll do, but it won't do any harm to ask."

"Thanks. Yeah. We've gone through so many dead ends. What's one more?"

"I hate this for you. I know that you'd make great parents."

He shook his head, still clearly wrung out from the full moon. "At least she's finally agreed to a wedding. If we can't have kids, then we can't have kids. I still love that amazing woman and want her in my life forever."

"I know you do. I'll be there."

"There's an engagement party, too. We're figuring out the details. I'll send more when I know." Nate's smile was full of affection. "It's good to see you. You know that you're family and always will be."

"Yeah. Of course," she said easily and meant it.

Chapter Thirty-Two

Kierse hightailed it back across town, making it back into Graves's brownstone before she was even missed. She found Laz seated at the breakfast table with Gen. His plate was full of some sort of bread pudding delicacy—Kierse didn't know the name, but it was one of Isolde's specialties—and enough fruit to feed a small nation. He was speaking on his phone as Kierse popped a few raspberries in her mouth before taking a scoop of the bread pudding and a glass of fresh-squeezed orange juice.

"Yes. Sure. Got it. I'll let him know." Laz mouthed a silent *good morning* at Kierse as she took a seat. "When do you think that'll be?" A cleared throat. "Sure. I'll tell the boss. See you then." He hung up and flung the phone down. His smile was all teeth. "Bastard is finally fucking here."

Gen's eyebrows rose. "Who?"

"Schwartz," Laz said.

"Oh, good," Kierse said.

Graves had said that they were waiting to make their move until Schwartz was in place. She didn't know exactly what that meant yet, but she also knew that Graves divulged just enough information before he had all the facts. She'd know the whole picture once he also had it. Probably.

"You were up early," Gen said.

"I got up to see Nate. Last night was the last full moon of this cycle."

"Eesh," she muttered. "How was he?"

"Rough. I saw Ronan, too," she said with a wink. "Think he'd be interested in seeing you."

Gen flushed. "Well, yeah, I mean…"

Kierse let her flounder for a second before giving her an out. "Nate gave me this, though." She tossed the wedding invitation across the kitchen island.

"Oh my God!" Gen cried. "A wedding! And so soon!"

"So it seems."

"Is Maura pregnant?"

"He said no," Kierse said with a pang of worry for them. She wanted to tell Gen what they'd confided, but it wasn't her secret to tell. "Also they're having an engagement party and will get details out soon."

Gen was beaming with delight. "I'm so happy for them."

Graves stepped into the room at that moment. "Got your text. Schwartz messaged me as well. Meeting in the library in twenty."

"Sir," Laz said with a little salute.

Kierse nodded. His eyes slid over her, catching on her lips. She centered herself around the way that one look made her feel.

"I need to talk to you," Kierse told him.

He arched an eyebrow. "Should I be concerned?"

"It's a favor."

That made his entire expression shift to intrigued. "Color me interested."

Gen looked between them. "Um...am I invited to the meeting?"

Graves spared her a glance. "Sure."

And that was that. Gen headed upstairs while Kierse and Graves waited to be alone.

"A favor now, Wren? Don't you have to trust someone for that?"

She rolled her eyes. "It's not for me."

"I'm all ears."

"Do you know a cure for the incubus curse?"

Graves's eyes widened. "I'm glad that you started by clarifying it wasn't a favor for you. Who *is* this favor for?"

"Maura," Kierse confessed with a wince.

"Ah," he said as if all the pieces slipped together in his brilliant mind. "She and Nate are getting married. They want to have kids."

"Yes. They've exhausted all the options they have. I think you're their hail mary."

"No," Graves said slowly. "There is no known cure."

Kierse deflated. "I thought not."

"But..."

Her eyes jumped back to his. "But?"

"There may be one, if we get the cauldron."

Kierse's mind whirled at the implication. "You think the cauldron could cure the curse?"

"A curse is a magical ailment. A magical healing might be possible," he conceded. "We'd have to get our hands on it first."

And now Kierse was more determined than ever to succeed at this heist.

Twenty minutes later, they were back in the library. Anne was perched on Gen's lap, purring. Legitimately purring with contentment as Gen stroked her back. As if that cat let *anyone* pet her.

"You're a witch," Kierse said as she sank into a seat across from them.

Graves blinked at the sight. "Have you bespelled her?"

"Animals like me," Gen said with a smile for Anne. "She knows who to trust."

Graves and Kierse looked up at each other, and Kierse bit her lip to contain a laugh. Perhaps that was a fair assessment.

Laz yawned as he stretched out all of his khaki onto the blue chaise that had been brought in for Kierse's training sessions. "He's late."

"He usually is," Graves said in irritation.

At that moment, the library door flew open, and in walked a massive man with the gait of a sailor. His stride was a sway more than a prowl, as if he was still on the deck of a boat out to sea. He was built like a tank, all broad shoulders and thick waist, and he had russet-brown skin with black hair in long locs down his back.

It wasn't until he was closer that she could see the webbing between his fingers and spattering of iridescent blue scales that glittered along his wrists and neck. He was a mer.

She was surprised. As far as she knew, Graves didn't normally work with monsters. She hadn't known what to expect from Schwartz, but she had assumed he was human like Laz.

"Ah, Schwartzy!" Laz said, jumping to his feet. He clapped hands with the man, and they bumped chests.

"Lazarus," Schwartz said in a deep voice with the hint of a Caribbean accent she couldn't place more precisely. "My brother."

"Find the shipwreck I told you about off the coast of Trinidad and Tobago?" Laz asked with a grin.

"If I did, I certainly wouldn't tell you," he rumbled with a chuckle. He pushed past Laz and held his hand out to Graves. "Boss."

Graves shook his hand. "Good to have you on board."

"Good to be back in the city. The weather is more to my liking."

"Hot," Graves grumbled.

"I come from warm waters and clear currents," he said simply. "Your Central Park is far from that."

"I converted the swimming pool to salt," Graves said.

Schwartz grinned, revealing stark-white teeth. "That will do."

"Swimming pool?" Kierse demanded. "You have a swimming pool?"

"Of course I do," Graves said.

Gen raised her eyebrows. "Of course he does."

Kierse was baffled. She had cased this place, covering every inch of the townhouse the last time she lived here. Where was the fucking pool?

"Allow me to introduce you to Augustin Saint-Fleur Schwartz."

Schwartz screwed up his face. "My full name, Boss? Should we start calling you Brannon?"

"Not if you want to keep your head," Graves said mildly.

Schwartz laughed and leaned back against the table. "My mother is a Haitian mer, and my father was a missionary. She wanted me to have both names," he said by way of explanation. "Schwartz just stuck. As did Graves."

Graves continued, "Schwartz here is in security. He's gotten a job in the company in charge of protecting the auction items." Graves nodded at Schwartz. "Why don't you report?"

Schwartz handed Graves a sheaf of paper. "The list of attendees. No one outside of the expected list."

Graves looked it over and sighed. "Indeed. Lorcan is going to be there."

"Is that a problem?" Kierse asked.

"He's always a problem." His eyes continued down the names. "A few billionaires you've probably stolen for or from, some monsters—I can guess what they're after—Amberdash."

Kierse jolted. "What's he doing there?"

Gregory Amberdash was a wraith businessman. He'd been a middleman for Kierse's thievery jobs after she'd dispatched Jason. He'd warned her that something was coming for her after the job to steal from Graves, but she hadn't known where his allegiances lay. She still didn't.

"Same thing he always is," Graves said, "meddling and trying to look important." He tossed the paper aside. "No one who should interfere. How do we get the cauldron?"

Schwartz gestured with one hand. "No way that I can discern. I wrote up the system in place, and no one is stealing this thing."

"Can I see?" Kierse asked. Schwartz passed her a paper, and her eyes widened in shock and appreciation.

The security around the cauldron was like nothing she'd ever seen. Top-of-the-line vault with a card reader, user-specific codes, and multiple biometric sensors needed to deactivate. If she managed to get through all of that, then she'd have to deal with the anti-tampering technology—cutting-edge equipment intended to deter brute-force attacks by destroying internal components before the thief could get inside. Not to mention an entire team of mercenary monsters, Schwartz included, to guard the thing. Their best bet would be to get it when it was being transported, but it would be shipped in essentially a bulletproof tank with yet more armed guards. It even made her pause.

"Fuck," she said, passing it back. "Exactly how big is the thing?"

"Dimensions are here," Schwartz pointed out to her.

Kierse held her hand out to measure the estimated size of the box that would hold the cauldron. It wasn't that big. A two-foot cube with all that security wasn't holding a very large item.

"I don't know why I thought it would be bigger."

Gen snorted. "You've said that before."

Kierse laughed. "I almost *always* say that."

Laz guffawed, and Schwartz shook his head. Kierse glanced up at Graves and arched an eyebrow. He was definitely the reason she said *almost* always.

"But seriously, isn't some ancient cauldron supposed to be large and impressive? To like, hold ingredients and shit?"

"Apparently not," Graves said. "There are legends that suggest it isn't a cauldron at all, but a chalice."

"Like a cup?" Kierse asked.

"Indeed. In some iterations the sword is a 'torch,' as well. It lights the way for the truth," Graves said. "We'll see what iteration of the cauldron we get when we steal it."

Gen raised her hand. Graves's expression filled with amusement. "You don't have to raise your hand."

"Oh," she said with a shrug. "Sorry. That is a lot of security for one item. What exactly does the cauldron do?"

Kierse would have laughed at her directness, but she appreciated it. Gen had a way of cutting through all the bullshit to the point.

"The cauldron is an ancient Celtic artifact created by the Tuatha de Danann," he told her simply. "There are four, and each was created as a means to help an advancing army. The spear that could never be defeated. The sword that revealed the truth to help any strategy. The cauldron to feed an army and heal their injured. And the stone to proclaim the true king."

Kierse had read all the tales of the objects back in Ireland. She knew this much, and she wondered if Graves was going to expound on his hypothesis. The spear had been more than a spear, after all.

When he didn't immediately, she decided to test him. "And what happens if you bring them all together?" she asked with a lift of her chin.

Graves's eyes went dark. "Together they can do great magic."

"Like a spell?" she pushed. The last time she'd asked him why he was trying to collect all four objects, he'd said that he was preparing to perform a very powerful spell but hadn't elaborated.

"The legends may be hyperbolic, but they suggest you could do great, *great* magics, the like we haven't seen since the gods left this plane."

"Shit," Laz hissed.

"Don't get them all together," Gen said. "Check that off my list."

Kierse snorted. She wondered which of those "great" magics Graves could ever want to do. "And you just want them ceremonially."

"Something like that," he said before glancing away.

"Okay, now that we know to not bring them all together, what exactly does the cauldron do?" Gen asked again.

Graves lifted one shoulder. "I've never touched it, Prophet Genesis. Read the cards and tell me."

"You have theories," she argued.

"He always has theories," Kierse agreed.

"Is 'feed an army and heal the injured' not enough to go after it?" Laz asked. "That's treasure to most."

"It is," Gen agreed. "But we have food, and we have healers, doctors, nurses. I just thought it would be more…magical."

"It is," Kierse said at once. "Isn't it?"

"There are rumors, legends," Graves began slowly.

"All legends have a kernel of truth," Kierse whispered.

Graves inspected one of his gloved hands. "It is a grail, of sorts, but it was around before the more notable one. There are stories that say if you drink of its power, it can give magic where there is none, heal magic that has been broken"—His eyes lifted to Kierse's—"even change the makeup of your blood so that a half blood becomes a pure blood."

Kierse's breath caught. Was he suggesting that the cauldron could turn her fully Fae? That would solve many problems if her magic truly was broken, as Graves and Lorcan had both suggested. At the same time, she didn't know if she could ever give up the humanity her father had given her. She had just gotten used to the idea that she was half Fae. She wasn't sure she was ready to be *fully* Fae.

"Oh," Gen said softly. "Well, that would be valuable, wouldn't it?"

"Yes," Graves said. "And it's what I offer all of you. When we steal the cauldron, you'll each get a chance to use it."

A stillness filled the space at that proclamation. Kierse had already made her bargain with Graves, but she could see each member of his team shift in place as they weighed what exactly they could get from something so powerful.

"Whoa," Gen whispered, nudging Kierse. "That's a lot."

She nodded.

"Think carefully what you'd like to get out of this, but keep your eye on the prize." Graves turned his attention to each of them in turn, ending on Schwartz. "Tell me you have better news about the owner."

"Never met the guy. Was hired by an underling who I don't think has met him, either. None of the other guys have. They call him the Curator."

"Like he lives in a museum," Graves mused.

"That doesn't inspire confidence that he'd sell the cauldron to you," Laz noted.

She could see on Graves's face that he'd already had the thought.

"You don't think they're here to sell it," Kierse guessed.

"No, I don't."

"If we're not going to buy it and we're not going to steal it, how are we going to get it?" Kierse asked.

Graves said nothing. She could see the wheels turning in his head. He didn't like being without all the information.

"We're going to steal it," Graves finally said.

"What? But I just said..."

He smirked. "Oh, I know. But the gameboard has been set. He's expecting us to steal it. So we'll do exactly what he expects."

"And play a game of our own?" Kierse surmised.

"If all goes well and people are as...magnanimous as we hope, I'll buy it," Graves conceded.

"When they're not?" Gen asked softly.

"Then we're going to use the opportunity against them. We need more information on the owner, the business, where the cauldron is being taken, when it is being transported," Graves said. "That way we can do a proper heist for it without everyone we know standing in our way."

"Is this where I come in?" Laz asked with a grin.

"Yes. While Kierse is the distraction," Graves agreed.

"Wait, distraction?" Kierse asked.

Graves's eyes traveled down the length of her. "Do you remember that lovely dress you wore to Imani's party?"

Kierse flushed at a memory of being nearly nude in sheer black with nothing but diamond pasties for modesty. "Yes," she said, hoping she didn't sound as breathless as she felt.

"We'll need something similar," he said with dark bedroom eyes. "We need to make an entrance."

Chapter Thirty-Three

One glance in the mirror and Kierse saw a Fae in truth and not the girl who hid behind the glamour. Since the costume theme was *A Midsummer Night's Dream*, Graves had insisted that she lean into her faerie heritage. Her pointed ears were on display in an elaborate updo. Her skin was highlighted in a shimmery gold that made her almost glow. And her eyes accented until the deep depths of brown looked like liquid pools surrounded by smoke. Her lips were dyed a deep, dark maroon, the color of spilled wine and heartbreak. A gold circlet of vines crowned her head.

Isolde had hung her dress up in the walk-in closet for display. A pair of sky-high heels with red soles were set out next to it.

"Subtle."

"Subtlety isn't his style," Gen observed.

"It's going to look stunning," Isolde promised.

"I can't *wait* for him to see it." Gen bit her lip. "Especially considering what I walked in on the other day…"

Kierse elbowed her. "Are you suggesting he'd prefer it on the floor?"

Isolde laughed. "Every man is going to prefer that on the floor."

"And woman," Kierse added. She winked at them. "If I'm lucky."

She slid the fabric over her body and shivered as it graced her skin. She stepped into the fabulous gold strappy heels to complete the look. "Let's see what he thinks."

Butterflies fluttered through her stomach as she descended the stairs toward the first floor. At the bottom of the staircase stood Graves. She had been so concerned with what he would think of her dress, she hadn't considered that he would also be out of his customary suit and tie.

Instead, he was dressed in fitted black pants in a hue that seemed to suck up the shadows and dark riding boots. His chest was covered in a supple black leather with matte black dragon scales etched into the fabric. Thick, crisscrossed gold metalwork had been added to the chest plate and extended out across his shoulders as if golden metal branches were reaching out from his chest. His sleeves were made of the same black leather with hints of the gold underpinning the scale effect. A gold crown that mirrored the branches on his chest adorned his brow, threading through his midnight-blue hair. He looked every inch the dark faerie king, and she his queen.

"I didn't think you'd dress up," she teased to keep from falling to her knees at his feet.

His head lifted at her voice, and he stilled as if all the air had been sucked out of the room.

His eyes dragged down her frame, from the crown atop her head to her bare neck to the scandalous dress, which suddenly made so much more sense. The sheer material molded to her body, revealing every inch of her from collarbone to high-heel-clad feet. Handsewn onto the plunging neckline were branches made from a gold overlay that shimmered as it discreetly climbed its way from the long, trailing skirt up her center and across her chest. The branches came together at the top of the garment to make one strap that looped around her neck, leaving her entire back open. And every inch of her exposed skin had a soft, golden shine.

"Come here," he said, holding a hand out.

She took the remaining steps down and set her hand in his. She was still a head shorter than him even in the heels. Her head tipped back as he drew her to him.

"My wren." His eyes dipped to her mouth. "You are a vision."

She swallowed, running a finger down the gold branch that led to his chest. "You look like you're ready for mischief."

"With you? Yes," he said, slipping an arm around her waist and drawing her closer. "With the party? It's the wrong M-word."

She laughed despite herself. "Now, now, no murdering anyone. We don't want to break the Monster Treaty."

"Don't we?" he teased.

"Stealing is okay. Murder only under duress."

His lips quirked in appreciation. "Your morals are astounding."

"At least I have some."

He tipped his head to the side. "Morals get in the way of a good time."

Kierse couldn't help but laugh. She knew who she worked for—Graves was the villain of everyone else's story. The monster prowling through nightmares. At some point he'd embraced that fact. And while she knew him to be so much more, she wondered what exactly had gone so wrong that had convinced him of it.

"We shouldn't keep George waiting," Graves said, pressing the button for the elevator. They were swept down to his basement garage. Kierse's eyes lingered briefly on the closed and sealed door that held the spear, wishing for a moment that she could bring it with her.

George had the back door to the limo open and waiting. Graves got in first because there was no way to slide across the seat in this dress. She gathered her train and took a careful seat. Graves's eyes were fastened on her as they came out of the tunnel and into the city beyond.

During the war, there hadn't been any traffic at all after the sun went down. It wasn't safe to be out, even in a car. Now, they merged into a row of cars. Kierse could see lights still on in office buildings as they passed through the city. A few people were even walking together down well-lit streets.

"What do you think of all of this?" she asked, gesturing beyond the safety of the limo.

"It's returning to normal."

"Is that what it feels like to you?"

"No," he said simply. "It feels like a calm before the storm."

Same as what Nate had said.

She so desperately wanted it to be the first option. That monsters and humans were getting along. The city was renewed. The world made sense again. But how did a world heal from a scar that deep?

Graves's hand touched her bare wrist. "How go your mental barriers?"

She wrinkled her nose. "Fine. But I don't like them."

"You should try to keep them up tonight. May I test them?"

She nodded and then reached for the black wall she put up in her mind that was supposed to keep anyone from accessing her thoughts. With a breath, she pulled her absorption back.

Graves's magic came up against that black wall, and like smoke it blew away at the smallest prodding. The vision she saw was him, exactly as he had looked as she descended the stairs. The way he had been stunning and dangerous and how she had never been more captivated.

She shut it off. "I failed *instantly.*"

"I did warn you that you would likely never be strong enough to keep me out," he said with no bravado. "Let's try a different approach. You can work on a wall, or you can stick to a single memory. That way, when someone gets into your mind, instead of nothing they see only what you want them to see. Sometimes it's easier to focus on that than on shielding."

"Okay," she said. She'd read that in the book. She tried reaching for a mundane memory. "Ready."

Graves touched her, and he stepped into the memory. It showed Kierse breaking into a small bank vault. She used to do it methodically, like taking apart and reassembling a gun. Break the vault, put it back together, break it again. Until her fingers could do it with her eyes closed.

Then she felt a physical *push* against the memory. It shifted from one vault to the next. A vault that she'd broken into when she was much younger and been caught by the police and thrown in jail. She had been so small then, so stupid, so arrogant. The pain of it all flooded back.

She shut it off again.

"That wasn't any better," she gasped.

He pursed his lips. "It was. I'd keep thinking about the vault. It was more solid than the wall. Try again."

He still pushed against her memory like it was tissue paper. She was quicker to cut him off this time, but he nodded his approval.

"Good. Good. That's stronger. Keep that close," he assured her.

"You think I'll need it? Are there that many other people who can get in my mind?"

"You don't want to find out when it's too late," he said. "Again."

Kierse tried to keep her barriers up against him. For a second, she felt resistance, like she might actually be able to keep him out. Excited relief flooded through her for a single moment before Graves obliterated her defenses. They came crashing down so fast that she was instantly swept back into his gray gaze.

She was on his staircase, staring down at the king of faerie. Her body responded to the sight of him, the heat of him. Her body wanting more of what it had been given in the library, knowing it was complicated, wanting it anyway. The desire spooling out of her like a cat batting around a ball of yarn. In the middle of it, wanting nothing more than to kneel for him.

Kierse shut it off again, this time with a gasp as she pressed her legs together.

Graves smirked. "You can kneel if you like."

She flushed from head to toe. Here in the back of a darkened limo, she could do it. She could fall to her knees for him. Let him take control. They had mere minutes before they reached the theater. How far could they get?

"You're considering it," he said with a sensual brush of his lips along her jaw.

"My absorption is up," she gasped.

Another kiss down her jawline. "I don't have to read minds to know that you want me."

She shivered. "Graves…"

"You do want me, don't you, Wren?"

"Yes."

He brushed his lips against the shell of her ear. "Lower your powers."

"More training?" she breathed.

"I want to try something."

She bit her lip, clinging to the memory of vault breaking, and then with a breath turned her absorption off.

Instantly, her memory vanished and another memory flitted into her mind. But this was *not* her memory. Her eyes widened as she realized this was *Graves's* memory. And it was of *her*.

She called his name, and he looked up, only to be blindsided by her beauty. She was standing on the staircase dressed as Titania in all her golden splendor. For a breath, she *felt* his desire for her. The need a bubbling, aching mess, trapped in a locked box, begging for her to break it open and steal it away.

And yes, he wanted her to kneel. As she had wanted to before him.

The memory melted, and her absorption snapped back on.

"Graves," she whispered, breathlessly. "How did you do that?"

"It's a new trick," he admitted. "From the solstice."

She reeled at the information. He had pushed a memory into her mind then, of the glen of wildflowers in Ireland that reminded him of her. But she hadn't known he could do it any time. As if *that* act had changed his powers in some way. Or did it just link them?

"Is that…how you see me?" she asked, looking into those dark eyes.

"Can you not see it for yourself?"

She had assumed all of those veiled words of interest were true but layered beneath Graves's carefully placed facade. This was stripped bare.

She swallowed as his hand trailed lower, tugging her off the seat toward him. The dress had no give to it. No slit. She could hardly move in it, and yet he repositioned her with ease. One hand putting her on her knees before him, the other wrapping loosely around her neck, a thumb to lift her chin up to meet his.

"There," he said. His hand grazed lower down between her collarbones, then between her breasts. "Just as you wanted."

She was breathless. Her body humming even before his lips met hers, his tongue arcing across her painted lips. She let him invade her mouth. A carnal moan left her at the first sweep of him against her own tongue, nerve endings sparking at the connection.

Fucking hell, she wanted this dress to be easier to get in and out of.

"If only we had more time," Graves growled, his finger skimming the underside of her breast.

Kierse spread her hands on his thighs and pushed them upward. She could feel the hard length of him in his pants. She may not be able to see into his mind, but she knew precisely what he wanted right now.

"You shouldn't start things you can't finish," she told him.

His eyes were liquid metal as he gazed down upon her. "You can finish whatever you like."

Her pulse jumped in her ears as she kneeled before her faerie king. They'd been tiptoeing around this since Paris. She could have been in his bed at any point, but there was a hesitation that had driven a stake through their affection. A winter god in the summer. His wren at the height of her singing season. She wanted to go to him. She wanted the distance.

And now there was no distance.

She couldn't escape him, and part of her wanted to see what he'd do if she reached for more. Her hand slipped up, wrapping around his cock through the fabric of his pants.

He grunted and stretched back, one hand twining in her hair and the other laid across the back of the limo. "Are you teasing me?"

"I'd never tease."

"A bold-faced lie," he said with mischief. "What am I going to do with you, Wren?"

"It's what I plan to do with you."

She was caught by his powerful grip. Not as in control as she claimed, but her chin was tilted up and she was challenging him. A challenge she knew he'd meet.

He didn't stop her as she reached for the button on his pants. They might look like leather, but they had regular fastenings, and they came apart at her touch. She slipped a hand beneath the material, and his erection sprang free between them. A mouthwatering display of girth and length that made her want to spread her legs and take him that moment. Maybe she would have, if her dress would allow it. But she was on her knees. She'd kneel for her king.

The first sweep of her tongue against the head of his cock had him bucking against her. As if he'd been dreaming about her sweet mouth. He tasted salty and purely Graves.

She wrapped her lips around him, slicking his head with her tongue.

Their mingled groans were audible. For so long she'd preferred eating out rather than blow jobs, but the satisfaction of being the one to drag that sound out of Graves? Divine.

"Take me all in, Wren," he purred, guiding her down onto him.

She swallowed as he flexed in her mouth. Deeper and deeper until there were tears glittering in her lashes, and she could feel him at the back of her throat. Then she pulled out and sank back down again. Her hand wrapped around his shaft, working him up and down as she sucked him off. His hips thrust up, meeting her demanding mouth. She could tell it was taking sheer control not to take over from her. Not to cradle her face in his hands and fuck her mouth like he did her pussy. She wanted that. She was wet at the thought. But she wanted this victory on her own.

"Wren," he grunted, deep and affected. "I'm going to come in your mouth."

She didn't let up, just took him deeper. Both his hands were in her hair and he thrust into her once, twice, three times before shuddering and releasing into her mouth. His cock pulsed into her as he groaned with pleasure. When he finally came down, his eyes met hers again, and she swallowed him down.

"Fuck," he ground out.

He withdrew his cock and replaced it with his thumb, holding her mouth open as if he wanted to see the site that had disarmed him.

"I've wanted to fuck this mouth for so long," he confessed like a dark secret. "I fucked myself thinking about it."

Her cheeks flushed. "Just my mouth?"

"I'll take your pussy, too."

"Now?" she pleaded.

"Can you ride me in that dress?"

She could not. He must have seen her despair, because he hauled her up next to him and slipped a hand under the sheer material. It bunched awkwardly around her knees, but he kept going upward against the resistance. "This will have to do until I can strip you out of the thing."

His thumb was on her clit. Deep, swirling strokes of her sensitive bud through her thong. A second later, he brushed her panties aside and thrust two fingers inside of her.

"Oh god," she gasped.

"So fucking wet," he praised.

He drew her out in sharp, delicious strokes. She was so turned on from the blow job that her body trembled at his touch, like she might explode any second. She writhed under him, wanting more, needing more. She wanted to rip this dress off of her body and slide onto his cock. But he held her pinned to the seat as his fingers worked her over. There was no escaping. There was no controlling this.

Then his mouth slanted over hers, rough and needy, like he hadn't just come moments earlier. And her orgasm hit her like a freight train. Her walls clenched around his fingers as she shuddered.

When she finally stopped trembling, he removed his hand and sucked his fingers clean. "Tonight," he promised as he hit the roof twice.

Kierse dropped her head forward. Her pulse was racing, and she needed to get herself under control. They had a mission. They had…work.

Graves lifted her head and stole another long, languorous kiss.

She fixed her dress as George pulled up to the front entrance to the New Amsterdam Theatre. The street had been cleared, and not a single tourist walked down this part of 42nd Street. Kierse could see the glow of Times Square in the distance, and still none of it seemed to hit the growing darkness of this block.

"Ominous," she whispered to Graves when he had finished adjusting himself and followed her out of the car.

"Ready?"

She pushed her shoulders back and took his offered arm, unable to deny that they looked a matched set. "Ready."

His hand touched her chin, lifting it slightly. "Tonight, *we* are the terror of the night."

Chapter Thirty-Four

The king and queen of faerie stepped into the midnight frolic.

All eyes turned their direction as they made their elaborate entrance. Fashionably late, with enough drama to feed those in attendance. Arms linked, heads held high, stride cool and confident. Imperious, deadly, superior. Whispers swirled the room like a vortex, collecting the myriad thoughts of the attendees on their elaborate attire and terrifying visage.

Graves's face was austere and arrogant. Kierse played the lady at his side with poise and allure. She had done this once before, but it had been a different game. At Imani's party, where she had proven her abilities by stealing furtive letters for Graves and had felt her magic blown to bits by the warlock's deadly wish powder, she had been a pet. A silly little wren at his side. She hadn't even known what a wren was to the holly king, then. But she had gone from plaything to queen within the year. A giant step up.

She would have happily played the pet tonight if it kept the most powerful beings in the city from sizing her up. Her entire life she had been a creature of stealth. Trying to fit into her new role was like stuffing her feet into shoes a size too small.

But she was on the outside of the game no longer. She was a player.

A waiter in a black tuxedo offered them champagne flutes from a tray. Graves took one and handed it to Kierse, who took a sip, tasting a floral hint to the dry refreshment.

The room was awash with in-bloom cherry blossom trees. The pink petals brightened the rooftop, heedless of the fact it was too late in the season for such flowers. She could almost scent the magic that had been used to create such a spectacle. The roof itself was made of retractable glass, halfway open to the midnight air for the guests, but covered over the theater performance. Tables and chairs were scattered amongst the costumed attendees, who were watching the folly and each other with unequal intensity.

"This place is stunning," she said, taking a sip of her drink.

"It's an exact replica of its Ziegfeld days," Graves said. "Impressive."

Kierse had only seen grainy photographs of what it had once looked like, but if Graves was awed, the similarity was beyond what she could discern.

The show itself was well into *A Midsummer Night's Dream*. Hermia lay on the forest floor in nothing but a silken night gown with her lover, Lysander, pressed against her breast. The girl was captivating to watch, dragging eyes back to the stage as she lay there disparaging the man for touching her, while her eyes longed for him.

"She's incredible," Kierse murmured.

"Lyra Anderson," Graves supplied. "I'm…acquainted with her parents."

"Of course you are."

"Her father, incidentally, does not want her on the stage," Graves added.

"What?" Kierse said with wide eyes. "Why not? *Look* at her."

"Are you speaking of her talent or her beauty?"

Kierse lifted her chin, a spark of mischief in her eyes. "Both."

"Her talent is unparalleled," he agreed. "Her beauty doesn't hold a candle to the sight before me."

"Are you turning into Shakespeare?" she asked with a flush to her cheeks.

"Certainly not. I know my strengths. I shall leave Will with his."

"First-name basis? Of course you knew him," she said with a soft laugh.

"I was there when the Globe burned down," he said with a shake of his head. "One of the times. And I confess," he said as his eyes lifted back to the stage, "she is a very compelling Hermia."

"Well, now I might be jealous," she teased.

His arm wrapped around her waist as he leaned in to whisper, "'Love looks not with the eyes, but with the mind, And therefore is wing'd Cupid painted blind.'"

Kierse had read that exact line earlier today while getting ready. It struck a chord within her when Helena said it to show that her love was not just rooted in attraction, but also connection and understanding. That Graves was quoting it now made her shiver.

"I thought this wasn't your strength," she said softly.

"I'll show you my strength later tonight," he promised into her ear.

The middle of a mission was not the time to fall at his feet. So she went for levity. "Is this how you tell me that you do not wish to bring Lyra to bed—yours or mine?"

His hands moved to her hips and tugged her back against his chest. "I have no interest in sharing you." His eyes lifted as he said, "With anyone."

Kierse's breath caught at the challenge in his voice. Then she turned to see where his gaze had moved, and she understood the meaning behind it.

Lorcan Flynn stepped into the room, looking every inch the Druid King in a sweeping forest-green cloak and brown leather clothing, a sword at his side. A gold torc adorned his neck, and a solid amulet hung low against his breast. His dark hair was pushed back, and a small golden crown sat on his brow. Those cerulean eyes immediately found Kierse in the dim light.

She swallowed at the look of possession on his face and watched it morph instantly at the sight of Graves at her side. One second, he could have stripped her bare and the next she wondered if he might draw that sword and run Graves through a second time.

"Don't," she said as Graves took a step away. Kierse put a hand to her chest and pushed back that same uncomfortable feeling beating at her breast. "We're not here for that."

"As you wish," he said under his breath, more threat than agreement.

Kierse tracked Lorcan as she and Graves circled the room, always keeping a sizable distance. The last thing she wanted was a repeat of the winter solstice. They were a few weeks too early for the summer solstice, and they might just kill each other instead.

As they mingled with other monsters, the play continued. Faerie mischief interfering with the lives of mere mortals. Robin Goodfellow, the oft' mentioned Puck, doing Oberon's bidding and only messing up the human relationships. Helena sobbed a bit too dramatically at Demetrius's confession of love, when only a few scenes earlier he had scorned her. A messy affair. Not unlike her own life.

Graves was acquainted with most of the humans and monsters in attendance. As many jockeyed for his favor as clearly despised him, but theirs was a mutual distaste that wouldn't breech the rules of propriety tonight. They were all here for a reason, and no one was leaving until after the auction.

"Well, this isn't a face I expected to see in polite company," Gregory Amberdash said as he approached them.

The wraith was swathed in all-black draping robes. His skin was sallow, and the thumbprints under his eyes were darker than ever. Kierse had almost trusted him for a time, until he'd betrayed her to Lorcan and sent her careening into this mess. Now she wondered how she hadn't seen that he would one day double cross her.

"Amberdash," Graves said, holding his hand out.

They shook once before his eyes returned to Kierse. "I was speaking of you, of course, Miss McKenna." Kierse took his offered hand and met his gaze with a steely look of her own. "Aren't you better off in darkened corners? Or are you here to rob us all blind?"

Kierse grinned. "If I was, I wouldn't tell you, now would I?"

Amberdash leaned forward, the waves of death rolling off of him. Wraiths fed off of human souls. They could drain the life out of a person piecemeal over years if they wanted to. Some humans even signed up for it, which Kierse had never understood. With his attention on her, she liked the thought even less than normal.

At that moment, she saw a glint of gold in the folds of his robes. She wouldn't have paid the small thing much mind if she hadn't been trained to put a value on everything.

"You're treading in dangerous waters," he said softly.

"Is that a warning or a threat?" she asked, moving in closer.

Graves stiffened at the comment. "I would choose your next words carefully."

Amberdash smiled, and it was all translucent white teeth and terror. "You know I am fond of you. I wouldn't want to see you get...swept away."

Kierse narrowed her eyes. That was *definitely* a threat. "I can take care of myself."

"Of course, my dear," he said, straightening. He turned to Graves then, all nonchalance. "Are you making an appearance at Monster Con this year? I heard the speakers are hush hush."

Graves settled back into himself as the mundane chatter of the night returned. Monster Con had been mentioned a few times in passing, but Kierse hadn't paid it much attention until it came out of Amberdash's mouth.

"I don't bother with those things," Graves said. "If you'll excuse us."

He put his hand on her back and urged her away from Amberdash. Kierse cast a furtive glance back at Amberdash, who was still staring at them as they disappeared. But his look was no longer diabolical—it was almost worried.

"What is Monster Con?" Kierse asked.

"An exclusive meetup for powerful monsters. The rich and entitled go there to gloat. It's supposed to be for both sides of the aisle to come together without fear of retribution."

"Both sides?" Kierse asked. "You mean monsters for and against the Treaty?"

"Among other things. No in-fighting allowed. It's supposed to be a sort of renaissance—or that's how it's pitched, at least."

"We have another problem," Kierse said.

"Many," Graves agreed.

Kierse raised the gold pin she'd lifted off of Amberdash. Graves saw what it was and laughed.

"Did you steal from him?"

"I wanted to see what he was hiding."

"Is that a...Men of Valor pin?"

"Yes," Kierse said softly, looking down grimly at the golden wings shot through with crossed arrows.

When she had killed King Louis in Third Floor, she had hoped it would be the end of the Men of Valor—a group of anti-human monsters who wanted to see the Treaty burn and monsters on top once more. But if Amberdash was wearing it, that only meant trouble.

"For another day," Graves said. "Stick to the plan."

She nodded grimly. "You're right."

The production of *Midsummer* was coming to a close with the final reveal of Theseus and Hippolyta's wedding. A union of power to contrast with the dream quality of the faerie realm. Only Hermia looked as if faerie still thrummed in her veins even as she fell into society's order and married Lysander. But perhaps that was just Lyra Anderson's star quality on stage.

The crowd cheered at the end, particularly loudly for Lyra's rendition of Hermia. A promise that the actors would mingle with the audience while the stage was set up for the auction.

Kierse met Graves's eyes. He nodded once. "Showtime."

Chapter Thirty-Five

Kierse caught the backstage door as a pair of actors exited in a hurry. The auction wasn't open for viewing until the item was presented by the auctioneer. So the only way she was going to get her eyes on the cauldron and its accompanying vault was to get into the auction room. While she wanted to move into stealth mode and hide amongst the shadows, that wasn't her role tonight. She wasn't here to steal anything, as much as she wanted to get a good look at the security system around the cauldron.

Her fingers itched for the chance to crack it. It felt like a challenge, and it only made her wrong smile appear on her face. The one that said if she did this she would be a legend. But she knew she shouldn't try. She didn't have the time or luxury to play tonight.

Still, she noted all the exits. There were very few ways directly off the roof—only a single elevator bank. However, the back side of the building was under construction and had scaffolding with stairs in the event of an emergency.

Now that Kierse was alone, she pressed a finger to the micro earpiece Graves had doled out to each of them before the party. The line switched on, and she heard Laz breathing softly on the other line.

"Laz," she whispered.

"Roger that," he said.

A second later, Graves said under his breath, "Here."

Kierse called up the blueprints in her mind and continued down a hallway that led to the area reserved for the auctioneers. She was almost there when a dressing room door banged open and out walked Lyra Anderson.

Kierse's breath caught at the sight of her. She truly was stunning, but Kierse noticed up close what she hadn't seen before...Lyra was a *vampire*. And not just any vampire—by the red rose necklace at her throat, she was part of the most elite Upper East Side clan. No *wonder* her dad didn't want her involved in the theater.

"*Love* your dress," Lyra said.

Kierse pushed all of that away and leaned into the character she had to play. "Thanks," she preened. "I adored your performance. I've never seen a Hermia quite like that."

"I appreciate that," she said, hand to her exposed chest. "Let's hope I get to continue to play the role."

"I heard that your father was interfering." Kierse hoped that was public information.

"Interfering is his middle name."

Graves cleared his throat on the line. A soft, "Get moving."

But Kierse couldn't just walk away from her without raising suspicions.

Lyra waved a hand. "But we're going to continue this run of *Midsummer* until the end of the month." She fluttered her long eyelashes at her. "Are you going to come to another show?"

Was Lyra flirting with her? God above, she was absolutely Kierse's type in any other circumstance. Not that she went for monsters, but one who looked like this…

"I sure hope so. My beau is a big Shakespeare buff," Kierse said.

Lyra stepped closer, her eyes wide, the scent of flowers on her pale skin. "Good. The show is all about messy relationships. Hopefully, I can serve the king and queen of faerie well." She winked as she strutted away.

Kierse liked her audacity.

Graves cleared his throat for all different reasons. Laz laughed softly on the line. Kierse got moving.

The security team consisted of six trained mercenaries—two goblins, a shifter, a half troll, and two mer, including Schwartz. The shifter and troll guarded the collection of items for auction while the two goblins brought each item forward. Kierse could already hear the opening invitation to bid on a rare painting by Monet. Schwartz and his comrade mer were circling the perimeter with automatic weapons. If their siren song didn't deter trespassers, the guns sure would do the trick.

The Monet sold for seven figures, and out came the next piece, a rare Filipino amulet with a robin's egg jade stone in the center, brought forward by one goblin while the second shadowed the exiting artwork. It was a smooth operation. Just as Schwartz had described.

Schwartz passed by on his next circuit of the room, and the slight tip of his head was the signal she needed.

She waited for him to pass, took a deep breath, and then walked straight into the back room. A gasp came from nearby, but she didn't look up. She didn't break stride. Her eyes clocked the box that held the cauldron instantly before she veered away and began to peruse the rest of the items. She went from one priceless artifact to the next like she was considering them at a flea market.

"Ma'am!" a harried assistant, who had hurried over from the auction room, said in a squeaky voice. "You can't be back here."

"What?" she asked, walking to the next piece. Farther from the cauldron, away from their real target. "I was just on my way to the bathroom."

"The bathroom?" the woman said, glancing around at the security guards.

A different mer guard took the first step toward her. His voice was hard. "You need to get out of here."

She steeled herself against the soft pressure of his siren song. He hadn't used it too obtrusively yet, probably thinking she was more a nuisance than a threat. "I'm just browsing. My husband has deep pockets, and we weren't informed of everything that would be up. I need to make a list."

"That's not what they're here for." He put a hand on her arm.

Kierse gasped dramatically and reeled backward. "Don't touch me! Don't you know who I am?"

"Rog," the assistant warned.

But already the other two guards were getting up from their positions to come see what all the fuss was about. Good. All Laz needed was a few minutes. She hoped that she could give him that long.

"Locking in," Laz whispered into her ear.

Kierse's heart rate kicked up as she started a mental countdown of how long she needed to keep them occupied. As they loomed over her, the threat was clear—she couldn't take down all these guards herself—but she didn't have to. The highbrow billionaire's wife she was playing wouldn't even consider it. She'd never think that someone would touch her. Kierse had seen enough of them, stolen from enough of them, to know the attitude.

"You need to leave," Rog said gruffly.

"I don't know who you think you are," she said with her head held high. "You couldn't buy a single *piece* at this auction, let alone all of them." She stepped forward like an entitled brat. "I could buy the entire lot of this."

Rog flexed his hand on his gun. The shifter came to his side. The half troll looked dumbstruck at her audacity.

Kierse waved a hand, dismissing them, and continued looking through the pieces, moving farther and farther from the closed computer bank where Laz was working. Away from his sneaking, probing fingers, reaching through their system to learn their secrets.

"Don't make me throw you out of here. I will," Rog said, still tailing her.

Kierse shot him a fierce glare. "If you lay one hand on me, it will be the last thing you do."

Rog jerked back in surprise. "I'm not afraid of some princess," he snarled.

"I could buy *you*," Kierse argued. "The whole dirty lot of you."

"We're not for sale," the shifter said with a gruff grunt.

"Another minute," Laz muttered. "If you can give it to me."

The shifter reached for her, grabbing for her waist.

Kierse took the opportunity to be as dramatic as possible. She slipped out of his grip and collapsed on the floor, careful of her dress. She immediately burst into hysterics.

"How dare you touch me! You *threw me on the floor*!" she gasped. She felt utterly ridiculous. Unhinged. This was so out of character for her, personally, that it was hard not to burst into laughter. "This dress cost ten thousand dollars. If you've ruined it, I am sending the bill to you."

"What is going on back here?" a harried auctioneer asked as he dashed into the back room.

Kierse was sprawled on the floor, trying to drum up tears as she looked at the man. "Your security threw me on the ground!"

"Ma'am, I am deeply sorry for how you have been treated," the man said obsequiously, offering her his arm. "Please forgive the security team. They're a little trigger-happy and don't know how to deal with high-end clientele."

"As I noticed!" she said as she accepted his help and rose laboriously to her feet.

"Almost there," Laz said.

But Kierse didn't have any more time. She was going to have to leave. She'd made enough of a scene to get in the way, and she couldn't ignore this man who was—finally, annoyingly—treating her like royalty. Fuck.

"I wanted one more minute," Kierse pouted, hoping Laz would understand.

"My apologies and deep regrets, but we are only showing the auction items as they come forward." He put a hand gently on her back and directed her toward the exit.

"Where was the restroom again?"

"I'll have an assistant show you," he said, snapping his fingers.

An assistant appeared to escort her away. She ground her teeth together as she followed the woman away from the scene.

"I'm out," Laz said into her ear.

"Did we get it?" Graves asked.

Laz was quiet a minute. "It was closed circuit. They hid most of the information off the system. I'll have to go through it."

Graves gnashed his teeth loud enough for the microphone to pick up. "Fine. Wren, make haste."

Kierse swallowed and continued down the hallway toward the bathroom. She wanted to ditch the assistant, but she was speaking animatedly about the entire collection and what Kierse could look forward to seeing. Since... she had been dumped on her rump before seeing it all.

"Thank you. That will do," Kierse told her, wanting nothing more than to leave this bullshit behind. She didn't like to be mean to innocents. It was the monsters and the billionaire humans who had her enmity.

But the assistant nodded and made a quick retreat. Kierse did the same.

Graves's voice came through the line. "Fuck. We have another problem."

Kierse burst through the stage door, only to find the problem ready and waiting for them.

"Imani is here," Graves said.

Chapter Thirty-Six

Imani Cato stood gloriously clothed in a white Roman sheath against her brown skin. Her head was shaved close and her expression fierce. She had absolutely not been on the guest list.

Graves's ex-apprentice was a master in her own right. After they had stolen from her, she had sought revenge against them by dosing Ethan with her wish powder and nearly killing him. Kierse had hoped that would be the end of her schemes.

"What the fuck do we do?" she asked Graves.

But he was already striding toward the other warlock. Graves was more powerful than Imani, but Kierse had a bad feeling about this. Something was niggling at the back of her mind.

Her champagne had been floral. The room had the same scent under the cherry blossoms. Lyra had smelled like flowers.

Imani's powers smelled like lilies. Kierse had been smelling it all night, but she had assumed it was the cherry blossoms. A convenient cover. She'd been so set on the plan that she hadn't realized what it was until it was too late.

"She dosed the party," Kierse said.

The moment the words left her mouth, Imani blew a cloud of red wish powder into Graves's face. He coughed and sputtered around it, throwing up his defenses to keep it from getting its hooks in him.

Kierse rushed forward. "Do you have the antidote?"

But before she could reach him, she slammed into another body. Strong hands gripped her bare arms. Kind blue eyes found hers. Her heart quickened, and she felt a squeeze in her chest like the air was being forced from her lungs. That smile, ever present on his face. Like he'd known the exact moment she would walk out of that door.

"Hello, little songbird," Lorcan said, "what trouble are you getting into tonight?"

"Let me go," she said.

His pupils were blasted out so large there was only a thin ring of blue around the edges. He smelled like lilies. Fucking hell, he'd been affected by

Imani's wish powder, too.

The potent red powder was her signature. She had figured out how to transpose her wish-granting abilities into a powder that could be inhaled or ingested for maximum effect. While she could grant any wish, in theory, her red powder homed in on…sexual desires.

"I'm persistent."

"This isn't *you* speaking," she told him.

Or maybe it was. Maybe this *was* what he wanted, but propriety kept him from indulging quite so dramatically. She remembered what it had felt like to be burned alive when she'd accidentally ingested a white powder so potent that it had overpowered her absorption powers and had turned her wish against herself. There was nothing Lorcan could *do*.

He laughed softly. "Who else do you believe you are speaking with?"

"You've ingested wish powder. You can't control what is happening."

She tried to move around him, but Lorcan's hulking form moved with her.

"Or perhaps I have just been waiting for the right moment."

"Don't do this," she warned him.

"I would if that was what you wanted," he said.

Kierse changed tactics and focused her powers, narrowing in on Lorcan. She could absorb the wish powder. She had done it for Ethan and saved his life. She could do it again if she had to. If there wasn't so much magic that it would incapacitate her.

But when she zeroed in on Lorcan, the golden glow and scent of lilies was all over him. She coughed at the noxious fumes that reminded her of her near misses with death.

No, he had way too much in his system. How had Imani done this without them knowing?

"You must know how I feel about you," Lorcan said like a confession.

A hand went to her jaw, tilting her face up to his. She felt frozen once more, as if she was suspended in place like a marionette and she had no idea who was holding the strings.

"Lorcan," she said, her heart beating furiously in her ears. "Do not do anything you will later regret."

"I could never regret this," he told her, dragging her closer.

He was going to kiss her. Oh God. She could see it there in his perfect summer eyes. That he had wanted to do it before, and today he would act on it because the powder lowered his inhibitions. And trapped in his gaze, she didn't feel like she could stop it.

A hand slammed down on Lorcan's shoulder, jerking him back from Kierse and breaking his hold on her.

"Touch her again and I'll fucking kill you."

Graves's voice was like dragging Lorcan's face across gravel. His body was tense, prepared—he'd come ready to make good on his threat, if necessary. Kierse came back out of the fog like coming up from underwater.

"You know that you cannot keep us apart," Lorcan said with a laugh.

"Funny," Graves said drily. "I can still taste her on my tongue."

"She is my chuisle mo chroí," Lorcan snarled, half ready to lunge at him.

Kierse tried to wedge between them. She was not ready for cosmic god magic to start shooting around at this goddamn party.

"What the *fuck* does that mean?" Kierse demanded.

Lorcan's eyes met hers, and again she felt that press against her chest, almost like she was going to be sick. "Do you not know?"

"Pulse of my heart." She whispered the words Graves had told her all those months ago. She hadn't taken them literally. She had assumed they were some Irish pet name.

"You are my soulmate."

Chapter Thirty-Seven

The word didn't compute. Soulmate.

It sounded like a joke. A punchline that wasn't particularly funny.

Except neither man looked like they were joking or like they were at all surprised. They looked like they believed this was a fact. A fact that both of them had already known. They'd probably known it since Lorcan had called her the Irish "pet name" last winter.

She understood why Graves would withhold that information. In fact, she remembered when she had come home from Brooklyn and he'd pushed her about Lorcan. Had he been fishing to see if Lorcan had divulged this piece of information?

He had not. And now he was dangling the word on a hook like it meant something to her. Like *he* meant something to her.

She took a step back. This was Imani's insidious magic warping their minds. They were fighting over her like she was a prize to be won. There was no *fight* here. Not one she wanted to be a part of. They were already enemies enough.

"I don't know what that means," she said finally. Lorcan opened his mouth as if he were eager to explain. "I don't want to know."

His mouth snapped shut. Graves looked smug.

"You two can fight this out without me. I want no part in this dick-measuring contest. We have more important things to deal with." Like where the hell Imani had gone.

Kierse tuned out the two men arguing over her protest and zeroed in on the goddess stalking toward the auction items.

Fuck. The cauldron.

Was that Imani's motive? Was she seeking revenge for what Kierse and Graves had done? Would she retaliate by stealing from Graves the thing that *he* wanted most?

"Graves, the cauldron," she said, trying to shake him out of it. But the magic had its hooks too deep in him. She pushed him again. "Find the fucking antidote and come back to me."

His eyes cleared for a second as the word "antidote" came out of his mouth.

Imani's power tightened its clutches and he was gone again. But at least he was fighting. She just couldn't wait for him to figure it out. Not when Imani was loose and the cauldron was within her grasp.

Kierse left them to duke it out, following in Imani's wake. "Laz, did you get out?"

"Just got into the car with George," he reported back. "I heard everything. Edgar has the antidote and he's on his way."

Kierse burst backstage, racing toward the back auction room. The auctioneers had already packed up and fled. The box that held the cauldron was missing. Kierse raced out the emergency exit leading to the rooftop. Schwartz had warned them that all the auction items had been brought up the back of the building on 41st Street with a pulley system, and Imani stared down over the rooftop where it had already been utilized.

"Fuck," she hissed.

Imani whirled on her. "Little wren, you're in over your head." Then she stepped off the edge of the roof and dropped.

Kierse's eyes widened in shock. She ran to the edge and found Imani clinging to the brick as she slid down. Whatever magic power that was, Kierse had never heard of it. Graceful falling?

But it was currently giving Imani the advantage on the cauldron.

Kierse could see a security team far below on the street loading equipment into the back of two cars. She knew that in the event anything went wrong, the team would extract the items and load them into separate armored cars, including both the cauldron and a decoy cauldron box.

They would be gone any minute. If Imani could reach the ground in time, she would have the cauldron within her grasp. And Graves wouldn't be able to shed Imani's magic before it was gone.

Going after the cauldron post-auction had always been an option if all else fell through. She had thought Graves would be coherent enough to make the call. Now it was *her* call.

The decision felt obvious.

"Imani is after the cauldron. If we don't go after it, we'll lose it," she told Laz. "Send George around to 41st."

"Confirmed. We're on our way."

Kierse hiked up her dress and tied up the train as she ran for the scaffolding on the back of the building. She ripped off her heels, mourning the beautiful gold shoes, then vaulted over the side of the building and took the stairs three at a time.

Too slow, too slow, too slow. Still she ran, feeling those wisp instincts kick in. Suddenly she was taking each set of stairs in stride, missing the entire set to land on the next platform. Her body felt primed and ready as if it had been made for this moment. Eleven stories and superhuman speed and she was still going to be too late.

Imani landed on the ground as they slammed the door on the remaining armored car and the first drove toward 7th Avenue. Imani never broke stride as she pulled powder out of a hidden pocket at her waist and flung it in their direction. Only one of the guards was brought to a stop. The shifter fell to his knees at her feet, writhing, and then the last door slammed shut and the vehicle took off in the opposite direction from the first.

A black car screeched to a halt before Imani, and she jumped in. Kierse landed on the ground as Imani's car pulled away.

"Fuck," she cried. "They're getting away."

"Almost there," Laz told her.

George rounded the corner, skidding to a stop before her. Laz threw open the back door, and she jumped inside as George followed Imani onto 8th Avenue at a dangerous speed.

"Does Graves hire racecar drivers?" she asked.

"Graves hires those he finds valuable," George said. "You're going to need to do something about that dress."

"You don't have pants in here, do you?"

A knife appeared in his hand, offered through the privacy partition.

"Right," she grumbled.

Then she hacked at the train of her dress until the thing went from full length to a mini dress in a few quick moves.

"Any word from Schwartz which vehicle we're following?"

"Even security wasn't informed which vehicle had the cauldron and which had the decoy," Laz told her.

Kierse groaned. "Great. Well, fifty-fifty shot, anyway. Best to stop Imani. She's on a long list of the last people I want to have an object that could make her more powerful."

"I'll get closer," George said, and he put his foot to the floor.

Kierse clung on for dear life as they sped south down the mostly empty streets. Luckily, Manhattan had developed enough in the intervening years that lights illuminated the darkened avenue. Neon signs glowed from buildings as they zipped past the entertainment district toward Chelsea.

Imani's black car was a block ahead of them, and the armed convoy was another block ahead of her. They'd have lost them both in the darkness if not for the city that never sleeps waking up again.

Madison Square Garden loomed ahead as they cleared the distance.

"Plan?" Laz asked.

Kierse shook her head. "Thinking."

"I suspect the boss would think this acceptable in this situation," George said and then pressed a button on the steering wheel.

A box slid out at Laz's feet. It hissed softly as it opened to reveal a handful of guns and ammunition.

"That's what I'm talking about," Laz said as he loaded one and passed it to Kierse.

She took it in her hand, knowing this was the turning point. Imani had changed the game. If the warlock got her hands on the cauldron, that was the end of the road. Even if Imani was simply doing this for revenge, she could *use* the magic of the cauldron to make herself more powerful. Like the spear, that power in the hands of the wrong person could prove deadly. Kierse couldn't let that happen.

"Back me up?" Laz said.

The sunroof slid open, and he climbed out like he'd done it dozens of times. They were really doing this.

Instinct took over, and Kierse slid through the partition into the front seat. She rolled the window down, hoisting herself out it and into a position to cover Laz. She'd always preferred knives to guns, but she'd had enough practice with them in her youth to find the handle comfortable in her grip as she leveled it at the back of Imani's car.

Laz opened fire on the vehicle, shattering the back windshield into a million little pieces. The car swerved and another figure appeared with a gun in hand, returning fire. George maneuvered smoothly away from the gunfire while staying on their tail.

Kierse ducked as a bullet whizzed past her. "Fuck."

She narrowed her eyes and felt her superior eyesight take over. She could see down the sights of the man leveling a gun at them. Not a face she recognized, but clearly one of Imani's minions. She could kill him. He clearly did not care whether or not he killed her. But that wasn't what she wanted. She wanted to stop Imani. She wanted to get the cauldron for herself.

There was another way.

Kierse dropped her gaze and opened fire on the soft rubber tires. The back one went flat, shredding into several pieces as it ripped out from under them. The car skidded sideways, making a horrible shrieking noise as it tried to drive on the dented, sparking rim.

She aimed again and released a volley of bullets until one landed in a front wheel. When the second tire blew, the driver lost control of the vehicle and sent it careening across multiple lanes. Bullets rained toward them, and George took the turn wide to avoid ending up in a collision.

A soft golden glow of magic suffused the car as Imani tried to salvage the damage. Then with a horrifying crunch, it slammed into a parked car in front of Penn Station. The car seemed to fold in on itself with a deafening smash.

The magical glow switched off like a light. Imani was out of the game.

As they passed the car, Kierse could see the driver had a bleeding head wound. Imani lay sprawled across him. The man who had been firing at them had been thrown from the car. Her husband, Montrell, was not among them.

Red-and-blue lights flashed a few blocks behind them. Kierse could hear the whine of an ambulance already in pursuit. Oh, how times had changed. A few years ago, no one would have come for help.

"Cops," Laz said, taking another clip from George.

"Continue to pursue the cauldron?" George asked for confirmation, unconcerned.

Kierse took a breath. The plan had gone to shit as it always did. She had learned to improvise on the job, and this was no different. They had known it might come to this. Not Imani, per se, but they'd known about the decoy and the chance to go after the cauldron. If they stopped now, what then? The cauldron was just gone?

"What about our intel?" Kierse asked.

"Half the files were corrupted," Laz said. "I didn't see anything about headquarters or the owner in all of it. I don't know about you, but I've been searching for this goddamn thing for Graves for nearly a decade. I'm not ready to let it go."

She wasn't ready to lose it forever, either.

"Do it," she told George.

Chapter Thirty-Eight

L az laughed. "Excellent."

George sped up again, keeping his eyes on the armored car in front of them. The vehicle cut right severely down 23rd Street toward the entrance to the High Line. Kierse had walked the repurposed raised railroad that had been transformed into a public park many times before the war had torn it up. It was a popular pickpocket spot until it had become a hunting ground for monsters.

Kierse reloaded as they caught up to the armored vehicle, which cut south again on 9th Avenue into the heart of Chelsea. This was Dreadlord territory. Kierse cut her eyes to the rooflines, wondering if wolves were watching.

"Here we go," Laz said.

They bumped the back of the vehicle with a screech. A goblin threw his head out of the side of the car and hefted a gun up. George veered to avoid him. Kierse glimpsed Schwartz in the driver's seat, his eyes straight ahead.

Right. Stop them. Don't kill the security detail.

"I've got this one," Kierse said.

She climbed all the way out of the window and clung to the side of the limo, waiting for George to draw into position. Then with all the force of her new abilities, she jumped from the car. Time slowed as if she'd switched into slow motion, though she hadn't. Her body hung in the air with her arms outstretched for her landing. On an exhale, she collided with the back of the armored vehicle. Her free hand grabbed the back handle, and her bare feet skidded across the ridged tailgate. She winced as the rest of her collided against the back door with a thud.

"Fuck," she spat.

Her feet slipped out from under her, and she dangled from one arm off the back of the car. She could feel the heat of the asphalt under her feet. For a second, she thought that she was going to lose her grip and fall.

She scrambled to regain purchase and hoisted herself back up. With a breath, she shook the locked door handle that had just saved her life. No give.

A thump on the roof told her that she wasn't alone and she needed to hurry. She could hear gunfire from ahead and the side, which meant Laz was now covering her. She shot a hole in the lock that secured the door closed, wrenched the handle upward on unoiled joints, and rolled it into place along the roof. The vehicle swerved, narrowly avoiding a collision, and Kierse was thrown sideways.

Her hip crashed into the doorframe as she flung herself inside the cargo hold, and she winced. That was going to bruise. Another thump closer to where she was sprawled out sent her scrambling to her feet. She pushed through the mess of boxes from the auction, looking for the large, slate-gray container that housed the cauldron. With enough time, she was certain that she could break it open. She didn't have to do it here. She just had to get it into their car.

"Kierse!" Laz cried as the second goblin dropped down into the back of the bay.

She whipped around, punching into her slow motion at the perfect time. His bullet had already been heading for her chest. She moved an inch to the right, trying to escape its path, but it skimmed her left arm. She cried out as it ripped through the muscle.

"Shit," she said as the pain careened her back into regular motion. At the same time, she lifted her gun and unloaded it into his chest. The goblin was wrenched off his feet, falling over the edge of the vehicle and crashing onto 9th Avenue.

Her breathing was harsh as she watched the goblin stay down, dead. It was far from the first person she'd killed. Jason had taken that pleasure from her. But it still didn't feel...great. The monsters she'd killed after Jason had all deserved it. This guy? A goblin mercenary working for the wrong person? He probably hadn't deserved it. But it was her life or his, and her survival instincts were top notch.

Now for the cauldron. She turned around, and there it was.

"I found it," she told Laz across the earpiece.

"I'll take out Schwartz."

"Make it look convincing."

Laz chuckled. "No worries there."

The cauldron was in a box with a number of fancy antitheft safeguards. She reached out with her mind, looking for a hint of magical deterrent. It was too good to be true that this would be just a simple robbery.

It came to her immediately. An almost familiar scent of pine and lemon threaded through with the gold wisps of magic. She squinted to see the warding marks etched into the side of the box, a pair of crossed swords, the mark of the maker. *Keep out*, it seemed to say, in that language that flew through her mind.

She reached through the magic, absorbing it as she went for the box. When her hand touched it, it was with a surprising silence.

The cauldron was a magical artifact of the Tuatha de Danann. The spear emanated an unrivaled amount of magical energy. With her new attunement to magic, she could feel the power radiating from her spear through the steel of its case. The cauldron should have been just as powerful—she should have been able to feel it. Instead, it was silence. Which meant only one thing…

"It's the decoy," Kierse said with a sigh, retreating.

"Fuck," Laz said, panting. "How do you know?"

A thud came over the comms, and then a body was kicked out of the car. Kierse jerked around to see Schwartz rolling down the street, alive but injured.

"Fuck, Laz."

"You said make it look convincing," he said as he took control of the vehicle and pulled to a stop.

Kierse took the box in her hands and jumped out of the back. "We should take this with us anyway. I want to practice on the locks."

Laz was already stepping out, opening the back door, and helping her get the fake cauldron inside the limo. "Fine. But the actual cauldron?"

"Gone," she said on a sigh.

"Not gone," another voice said on the line.

"Graves," Kierse said with relief. "What happened?"

"I'll fill you in later," he promised. "Schwartz got a tracker on both boxes. I'm sending the connection to George. I'll meet you there with Edgar."

"Got it, Boss," Laz said.

Of course Graves had a Plan D when A, B, and C went to shit.

George pulled away, heading south. Kierse kept glancing at the decoy box, wondering at the magical signature and whether she'd be able to break through the security. At first glance, it was deceptively easy, but she knew what sort of traps were locked into it. A dangerous smile came to her as she thought about learning its secrets.

George continued south until 9th Avenue turned into Hudson through the West Village, then veered left onto Bleecker Street. The darkness brightened as they entered the Village and its nightlife ignited through the charming streets and artists' center. Late-night restaurants were packed.

Music filtered out from the bars. A comedy club off of MacDougal had a line wrapped around the block.

Kierse gaped. "Wow."

"Looks like the tracker stopped," George said.

"Fuck," Graves growled on the line.

"What?" Kierse asked.

George pulled over, and Kierse glanced out the window. Her heart dropped. Graves was right. "Fuck" was absolutely the correct word.

Kierse stepped onto the cement behind the comedy club and looked up at the New York City entrance to Nying Market.

"I'm ten minutes out," Graves said.

"We don't have ten minutes," Kierse said with Laz at her back.

"Fuck," he snarled again.

George was suddenly at her side, offering her a coin and the phone tracking the cauldron. "Is there anything else you require?"

"Thank you, George. I think I have it from here."

Then she stepped into the goblin market, alone.

Interlude

George watched her disappear into Nying Market without a backward glance. Brave girl.

Boss was going to be furious.

He answered the phone on the first ring. "She's already inside."

"Do you have a second coin?" Graves asked gruffly.

"Just the one, sir."

Graves was silent a moment as if he was trying not to rip his hair out. George had known him a long time. He had never seen him quite like this until Kierse McKenna had entered his life.

It was a change for the better, in his opinion.

Not that anyone asked the opinion of the driver. They never had when he had been shuttling billionaires around for his father's business. He'd been just seventeen in San Francisco, and the only thing he'd wanted to do was escape. Take his surfboard and travel the world chasing the next big, daredevil maneuver. He'd tried skydiving, cliff jumping, and cave diving. His buddy had sold him a beat-up motorcycle that he'd fixed up with the scraps from his day job, and had been working on his pilot's license. Anything to piss off his parents, who wanted him to focus on school so he could graduate and take over for his father.

It had taken someone far more powerful than them to curb his enthusiasm.

After crashing his motorcycle in a street race, George had been forced to spend his spring break driving for his dad's business instead of on a surf trip with his buddies. He'd gotten Graves for the entire week.

The man was mercurial at best. George was intrigued despite himself by the strangely scary man who tipped generously and was always reading in the back of his limo.

Graves had gotten into the car on his last day in town. "How fast can you drive this thing?"

"Sir?" George had asked in confusion.

"I need to get to the airport as fast as you can get me there."

A slow smile spread on George's face at Graves's instruction. He'd driven for people who wanted him to do shady shit, but never anyone who wanted him to floor it to the airport. Could he get in trouble for that? Did he care?

"Yes, sir," he said smoothly.

He put the car into Drive and his foot to the floor. Someone was following them. Someone was shooting at them. He was pretty sure that something was blowing up in the distance. Was that the location they'd just left?

Not enough time for questions. Airport was all that had mattered. And he'd gotten there in record time. Not even a cop on their tail, miraculously. He'd followed Graves's directions to the private runway he'd rented for his jet and George had driven out onto the tarmac.

He'd calmly turned around with a wide smile, his heart beating to the tempo of the chase. "Was there anything else you require, sir?"

Graves had tilted his head at him. He'd assessed him, seen something there, something he'd appreciated. He'd offered George a job, a bargain, a life.

George had taken the deal and never looked back. Sure, while much of his job was still shuttling around a billionaire, there were times when he'd gotten to race in Monte Carlo or fly through Thailand or surf in Tahiti, and he'd known it was all worth it. Today proved it all over again. The adrenaline still hummed in his veins from the chase.

"What would you like me to do, sir?" George asked once Graves arrived at their location.

Graves ran a rough hand through his hair. He looked for all the world as if he truly had no idea.

"Can you trade for a coin?" George asked.

"They won't trade with me." He said it resolutely, as if he already knew that it was impossible. "I'll eat the goblin fruit."

Laz choked. "Boss, that's a death sentence."

"It's worse for humans," Graves said. "Magic users can fend it off better."

Edgar glanced at George and shook his head once. George cleared his throat. "Sir, she's already ten minutes ahead of you."

"I have the tracker's signal. I'll be able to find her."

He was serious. He was going to go in after her. Graves knew the consequences if he ate the fruit. He'd always had a coin nearby to get in—they had another back at the brownstone—but there was no time to return home.

"You don't know that she's in any danger," George said slowly.

Graves shot him a death look. "The *market* is the danger."

"Immediate danger," he amended. "And you trusted her to get this far. Trust her to come back out."

"He's right, sir," Edgar agreed.

Laz nodded. "I'd go in there to back her up in a heartbeat, but you know she doesn't need it. Not after what I just witnessed."

"Then you've never been in the market," he growled.

"But we know her," George argued.

Graves looked between them as if he couldn't quite believe that his staff was disagreeing with him. It had never *expressly* happened before. They had opinions, of course, but they generally let Graves do whatever was in his best interest.

This was not.

"You believe I should just stand here…and wait?" he asked gravely.

It was obvious that went against his sensibilities. He was clouded by his feelings for Kierse. It was a welcome change, but under the circumstances, George didn't want to have to find a new boss.

Not that anyone would be able to put Graves back together if something *did* happen to Kierse.

"Yes," George said. The daredevil asking for patience. How ironic.

"Edgar, go back for another coin. I'm calling Vale for backup," Graves said. His hands were fists at his side. "We'll wait here for my wren."

PART IV

THE CAULDRON

Chapter Thirty-Nine

The tracker directed her up. Past the main streets of the New York side of Nying Market, away from the elevator, to a set of laborious stairs. Up, up, up they went.

Her heart beat a fast staccato in her chest while the streets grew quieter, darker, more dangerous. She held her gun out in front of her as she navigated the streets with the help of George's cell phone. The red dot on the map was the only thing telling her she was going the right direction.

A pair of goblins rushed out at her on the next corner, and she leveled her gun at their heads. The first one reared back, stumbling into the second, who pushed him out of the way and snarled at her, "Pretty little thing's lost?"

"No," Kierse said. Her last market experience was traumatic enough to put steel in her voice.

She probably looked lost. Mostly naked save for the cutoff dress that hid next to nothing, walking barefoot in the grimy streets. It wasn't how she wanted to be spending the night, but she was going to leave the market tonight with or without the cauldron, and no goblins were going to stop her.

"Do you even know how to use that?" the goblin asked.

She fired at his feet. He yelped and jumped backward.

"Yes," she spat. "Now let me pass."

The goblins dashed away, a furious "crazy bitch" muttered under their breaths as they left.

Kierse didn't like that the sound of the gunshot would call attention to her, but she had bigger problems. The tracker had stopped.

She jogged forward, hoping to make up for their head start. Luckily, her speed had increased, and though she needed some concentration to see where she was going, she didn't let up. Just let the thrill of the chase rush through her as she promised herself that it'd only be one more minute. One more minute and then she'd have the cauldron.

She'd just need to get the thing out of here. A problem for later.

Kierse whipped around a corner, chancing a glance at the phone, and caught the moment the tracker blinked and then disappeared.

"No," she gasped.

This couldn't be happening. She was this close. Just around this corner.

Her breathing was ragged as she jogged ahead into a deserted alley. She turned in a circle, encountering only blank walls. Where could they have gone?

With a *crunch* she stepped on something with her bare foot and yelped.

She bent down to retrieve what she'd stepped on. She groaned. It was the tracking device. Busted.

"Fuck."

She didn't know what to do. The tracker was destroyed. The cauldron was gone. She'd come in here alone for nothing. Anyone who'd managed to get into the market after her would never find her now without the tracker's signal.

Kierse cursed softly under her breath. The alley was empty. Just a long stretch of concrete between two turns. It was strange, considering the rest of the market was packed full of monsters and storefronts and apartments, as if ants had been building on top of one another for centuries. How could everywhere else be alive and breathing and this backstreet be dead?

She turned in a slow circle. No, it was *more* suspicious that nothing was happening here on this strange, empty street. She focused her magic on the wall opposite her. Nothing. Just a wall.

But suddenly, pine and lemon wafted toward her—the same smell she'd gotten off of the decoy cauldron. She turned toward the scent and gasped softly.

There was a door.

A door, made out of the golden sheen of magic, with a glowing doorknob that seemed to beg her to turn it. Wards were etched into the otherwise blank wall, but they had been magicked to be unnoticeable. Kierse could sense them now that she was looking for them: little crossed swords swooped together by the language of warding.

The tracker had been dropped right in front of the doorstep. Maybe the security hadn't known about the tracker at all. Maybe the wards' magic had disabled it when they'd taken the cauldron through the door, doing their work to prevent intruders.

Which meant the cauldron was on the other side of the door.

A part of her knew that she should stop here. She had no clue what was beyond this door. And yet, the door called to her.

It didn't speak exactly, but there was something beyond it that lured her forward. Not like a spell, more like a magic she should recognize. Something that knew her, and wanted her to come. And she, too, wanted to answer that call.

Magic this strong should make her wary. Somehow, it did not.

She needed to tell Graves, but when she looked down at the phone in her hand, it was dead. She cursed and stepped a few feet away. Nothing. It was as if being near the door had shut off the technology. And she didn't have the time to wait.

She grasped the doorknob, knowing the warding wouldn't keep her out. She absorbed the magic around it, the scent of pine and lemon filling her nostrils. Then she turned it and pushed forward into the unknown.

The door swung open to a large antechamber. The floor was blanketed with moss and clover. The empty desk was made of oak. Hardwood doors led off to either side. The energy was still there, ever-present, like the beat of her heart, but she saw no answers in this lobby.

"Welcome," a voice said.

The woman before her was young. Perhaps younger than Kierse, only a teenager, with tight dark curls, light brown skin, and round glasses perched on the bridge of her nose. She sported a set of dark-green robes not unlike what the Druids wore, though hers were embellished with a tree on the left breast.

Her brows were knitted together. "Are you all right?" Her eyes widened as they narrowed in on Kierse's arm. "You're bleeding!"

"Oh," Kierse said, glancing down at the wound. She'd forgotten about that. She'd been so high on adrenaline that she'd shut off the pain in her arm. Now that she was looking at it, it did look extreme.

The woman hurried forward, taking Kierse's arm in her small hand. "This looks bad." She glanced up. "Is someone after you?"

Kierse hesitated before answering, "Yes."

"Come on. Come this way." The girl gestured for her to walk toward the far wall. "I am so sorry about whatever has been happening to you. I'll get you all cleaned up. You don't have to be afraid."

Kierse shook her head. "Wait...what?"

"I'm Maya, by the way. I know it's tough out there. The world hasn't been kind since the war." Maya glanced at the door again with a worried expression. "You're not the first person who has crossed our door and needed help."

"Where exactly am I?"

"A place that will help," Maya said. "Why don't we get you a bandage and a snack? You'll feel a little better with some food in you."

Kierse's stomach grumbled at that word. Oh, yeah, she'd been too hyped to eat before the mission and now it was hours later and she'd once again had nothing but half a glass of champagne. She *was* hungry.

But nervousness was beginning to curl in her stomach about wherever she had ended up. This was where the tracker had led her. The cauldron was gone, but she had a feeling that she had just inadvertently stepped into headquarters. And Maya had no idea. Maybe she could get some information out of her even if she couldn't get the cauldron itself. Stealth was, after all, her favorite pastime.

"A snack would be nice," Kierse admitted.

"What should I call you?"

Kierse knew she couldn't give them her real name, and she doubted Wren was on the table, either. She needed something else.

She swallowed and said, "Shannon." Her heart lurched at the sound of her mother's name on her tongue.

Maya smiled. "This way, Shannon."

Kierse hesitated for a second, looking back at the magic door. She didn't know if this was the right move and she had no one to ask. She was on her own, making her own decisions. She didn't need Graves's advice, but damn, she would have liked it right then.

She wouldn't get another opportunity like this. And if it gave them information on the cauldron or the Curator, it'd be worth it.

"Okay," she said, following Maya through one of the doors of the antechamber.

The back room was innocuous enough. Just a long beige hallway with connecting doors. None of the greenery from the lobby covered the floor. This felt more like an office building. A little less mystique. A little more practicality.

Kierse could still feel that magic pull that had led her through the outer door. She felt as if they were getting closer to its source. She wanted to keep moving forward until she found it, but Maya stopped at a plain door.

"Here we are," Maya said.

So far the girl had been nothing but kind. All smiles and cooing over her injury. Kierse realized that she probably wasn't supposed to be able to feel the magical pull, or at least wasn't supposed to know it was there, and she didn't want to tip Maya off that she was different.

Maya pushed the door open to reveal a small bedroom. "It's not much,"

Maya said as she walked inside. "But I figured you'd want solitude while I get supplies."

"Yes, thank you." Solitude meant Kierse could snoop around.

"There are clothes in the dresser if you want to get more comfortable," Maya offered. "But you can stay in what you're wearing if you prefer."

Kierse nodded as Maya left. She didn't even hear the click of a lock or see any magic on the door. Huh. So they really thought that she wanted to be here.

She turned to inspect the room. A simple twin bed with all white sheets and comforter. A set of chairs before a small table. A chest of drawers. A small sink for washing up. All of it was utilitarian and practical.

Kierse opened the drawers to find soft, comfortable clothes in multiple sizes. All of it cozy, soft, and warm. Gray sweats, white or black T-shirts, and the green robe Maya had been wearing with the little tree logo on it, which looked loose enough to fit over the tee. Kierse discarded her dirty and damaged dress for the more pragmatic clothing. She also found a pair of slippers, not unlike those at a spa.

While Maya was gone, she quickly searched the rest of the room for anything out of the ordinary. But to her practiced eyes, this was nothing but a small bedroom. There were toiletries and washcloths in a basin by the sink. Notebook paper and a pencil on the table. Nothing under the bed. No trap doors. No secret compartments. Not even any hidden cameras. It was just…a room.

Whatever this place was, it felt nice.

How many times had Kierse wanted something like this when she'd been abandoned? When the war had been raging? Brooklyn was the closest thing to a refuge like this. Lorcan and the Druids had done their best to keep the worst of the war out of their part of the city, but that didn't mean shit for the rest of them. Kierse hadn't even gone through the brunt of it, because she'd had Jason, as disgusting as the thought made her feel. She wasn't sure if she even would have lived without him and his thieving guild.

If this place had wanted her, she would have joined. In a heartbeat.

Maya knocked twice and only entered when Kierse said she was ready. She had a wooden tray in her hands with a jug of water, two metal cups, a half loaf of some kind of cake, and a host of disinfectants and bandages.

"Oh, Shannon! You found your size," she said cheerfully.

"Looked like there was every size," Kierse said.

"We do try to be size inclusive." Maya set the tray down and poured out two glasses of water. She passed one to Kierse and then took a long drink of her own before heading to the sink.

"This is a regular occurrence?" Kierse asked as she took a small sip. It tasted like a hint of lemon. Lemon all over this place.

"People find us when they need us," Maya said. "Sit here."

Kierse took the seat Maya indicated, staring at the cake with longing. She was a sucker for cake, but she wasn't sure that she was hungry enough to brave food in this place. It was still the goblin market, after all.

Maya pulled the other chair around the table and tended her arm like she'd done it a hundred times, wiping it clean with antiseptic and then applying a bandage to the wound. She tutted as she worked. "It might need a few stitches, but that's beyond me. I might have to bring Alex in, if that's all right. He's our resident doctor."

Kierse tensed. She wasn't sure about meeting someone else here yet. Every new person was a risk.

"Oh, he's a gentleman. There's nothing to fear from him. I know so many who have problems with those in medical professions, but he's the best," Maya said quickly. "And he's dealt with all sorts with abilities."

"Abilities," Kierse said cautiously.

Maya grinned widely. "Just the term we prefer to all of that monster business," she said with a laugh as she gathered her supplies and stood.

"You prefer 'abilities' to the word 'monster'?" Kierse asked in confusion.

"Well, there's no normal anymore, and we shouldn't treat each other like we're other." Maya shrugged. "Or at least, that's what I believe."

"So there are monsters...sorry, those with 'abilities' here, too?"

"Oh, yes. We have all sorts."

"Uh huh," Kierse said.

She was sure they were well-intentioned but changing the terms didn't exactly change reality or fix any of the problems.

"You're free to stay a while and meet them."

Kierse hedged, "I don't know."

"I get it. We're happy to help." Maya headed toward the door. "Eat some of the cake. It's cinnamon streusel and probably my favorite. You'll feel better with some food in you while I go find Alex."

It was tempting. A world where monsters and humans lived together harmoniously—not how it was happening in reality where monsters wanted to secretly kill everyone and only the treaty was holding together a tenuous truce. All because they *wanted* this life. It was a utopia.

And utopias were a fallacy.

Maya reappeared a moment later with Alex, a tall phoenix with flaming red hair. Kierse stood quickly. Phoenixes were unusually volatile and known to burst into flames at the slightest provocation. They weren't particularly common compared to other monster types.

"I get that a lot," Alex said with a grin. He had a boy-next-door look about him, aside from the red hair and wings, of course. His feathers were the same color as his hair, and the wings tucked tight against his back. Which must have made him very young, because most phoenixes could shed their wings and regrow them at will. Few kept them out like this all the time. It was beyond disconcerting.

"The wings don't get in the way, I assure you." He chuckled and set down his equipment. "I'm Alex."

"Shannon," she said softly, warily.

"I won't burst into flames, Shannon. This place unblocks all of that rage," he said with that same boyish smile. "Now, let me look at that arm." Kierse swallowed and then held it out. He removed the bandage and said, "Good thing you got me, Maya. A few stitches should shape this right up. As long as you're okay with that."

"Sure," Kierse said, surprised at his calm mannerisms. "If you think it needs it."

"It'll be quick," he told her. "Why don't you ask your questions while I do this?"

"Uh, what questions?"

Maya laughed. "Everyone has questions when they come to Sansara."

Kierse jumped at the word as the needle pierced her skin. "Sansara?" she gasped, hoping they would assume her shock was a reaction to the stitches.

"It's the name of our organization," Maya told her, shooting a look at Alex. He was too busy putting another stitch through her arm to return it. Kierse winced.

Sansara was the tree that Cillian Ryan had sucked dry of magic and left for ash before fleeing the druids. That tree was dead. Lorcan had claimed to have seen the ruin for himself. He'd tried to kill Cillian for years because of it. And yet here was a group of people calling themselves Sansara?

So many questions swirled in her mind, and she had a feeling Maya and Alex weren't going to answer them.

"Who runs this place?" she asked.

"We do," Maya said. "We take in travelers who are in trouble, not unlike yourself. Those who are weary of the world, cut to the bone, and jaded. Our mission is to help those most in need."

"But who is funding it? No one does this for no reason."

"Maybe not out there," Maya said. "But in here we all help each other."

Kierse could see how easily they twisted the questions around. They never directly answered what she really wanted to know, only gave her the comforting platitudes they thought she wanted to hear.

"I know it sounds unfathomable right now, Shannon," Alex said as he finished up the stitches. "But we really do want to help people."

"We're glad you're here," Maya added. "Even if just for long enough to fix you up and send you back out, if that's what you want."

"That's charitable," Kierse said. "What's the catch?"

Maya laughed. "No catch."

There was always a catch. Kierse hadn't survived on the streets without knowing the rules. This wasn't free, even if it would be amazing if something like Maya had described did exist.

Maya patted her forearm. "You look bone weary. I'd suggest you rest for the night, but I'll walk you back out myself if you want to go."

"If you want to stay," Alex added, "we'd welcome you."

"Thank you," Kierse said hesitantly. She looked between their two glittering, hopeful eyes and nodded. "I'll stay the night."

Maya stood up and clapped her hands together. "Excellent. We're so happy about that. We'll be back in a few hours to see how you're feeling."

"It was great meeting you, Shannon," Alex said.

"You, too," she said.

Maya gave her a thumbs-up, and then they were both gone, and she was alone in a room inside a…charity, named after a dead tree. Everything felt perfect. Except for everything that felt glaringly wrong.

The name. The location. The cauldron.

She chewed on her bottom lip as she planned her next move. She couldn't stay overnight. That much she knew. Even if she wanted to see how deep she could make it into this place, Graves was somewhere out in the market by now. She very much doubted that he would wait out the night before finding a way inside. He was powerful enough to break through the magic on the door. She didn't doubt him.

The clock was ticking.

Chapter Forty

The door was unlocked, not that a lock could have kept her in. She was glad for the change of clothes that would allow her to blend in with the rest of the charity's inhabitants. She knew where she was going—to find the source of that magical pull.

She strode down the long hallway as if she had every right to be there. She encountered a pair—a wraith and a human *laughing* together—and they waved at her as she passed. Seriously, what *was* this place?

It was a few empty, winding turns before she felt the strength of the power increase and she stopped. Large, wooden double doors stood between her and the dominating energy. They weren't guarded. There was no magical signature around them. Besides looking like the entrance to a vast room, there was nothing to suggest these doors were anything other than ordinary.

She hesitated with her hand on the doorknob. The physical pull of the magic was making her hand shake. She needed to get herself together.

Taking the moment steadied her. She focused on that memory of opening and closing the vault, using it as a meditation. Then she pushed the door open, just a hairsbreadth, enough to peek inside. What she saw took her breath away.

A sacred tree.

It grew endlessly toward the ceiling, surrounded by grass, moss, and clover. A small pool bubbled nearby. Men and women in green robes stood in a circle with their eyes closed, chanting softly in a foreign language. The scent of lemon and pine was strongest here. Her hand went to her chest as tears sprang to her eyes. It radiated unfathomable force that made it feel timeless. As if it had been growing since the dawn of life itself. Stretching its branches toward the heavens from which it came. It had a similar energy to the Oak Throne—holy, reverent, and awe-inspiring. She didn't want to say the name, not even in her head. Because it was not possible that this tree existed. And yet, she could not deny that the tree *felt* holy.

Sansara.

Could this be the tree? And if it was still alive, did that mean Cillian Ryan was as well? Did that mean he was here? Was his magic the pine-and-lemon scent she kept smelling?

As one, the chanters finished their mantra and then opened their eyes. Kierse nearly yelped in surprise, not wanting to be caught standing conspicuously in the doorway, she slipped fully inside, letting the door close behind her. Unfortunately, it didn't close silently the way it had opened. A ringing sound echoed through the chamber and the chanters turned in unison toward her intrusion.

"Welcome," a nymph said with a lilting laugh.

"I…think I got turned around," Kierse lied. "I didn't mean to interrupt."

"It's okay," a man said nearby. "You are free to join us in our meditation."

Meditating. Right. Not chanting to a powerful magic tree.

Well, if they were going to invite her in, then maybe she could get more answers. "Sorry." She glanced upward. "What's with the tree?"

The nymph chuckled. "Nature promotes healing. We all come from nature. We all return to nature. It's a calming exercise."

"Are you new?" another woman asked, stepping away from the circle to hold out a hand to Kierse.

"Just came in," she admitted. "I didn't really mean to sneak out, but…"

"We all did it," she said. "I'm Loretta. You can come sit by me if you like."

"I'm not big on meditating." Which was true. She'd always kind of sucked at it.

"Of course. Why don't I help you out of here, then?" Loretta said.

She glanced around the room at the group of avid meditators. All their eyes were slightly glazed, as if they were high on the power they'd drawn from the tree itself. Still alert enough, but not quite *here*. Something predatory filled the room. A vibe she couldn't quite explain.

Only that she wanted no part in this.

This had gone from a very nice charity to probably a…tree cult in a span of a few seconds. Would she have felt the same if she hadn't been able to feel the tree's magic? Could *they* feel its magic? Did they even know what it was doing?

Her eyes caught on the face of a man in the corner. She furrowed her brow. He looked familiar. Where had she seen him?

He must have noticed her at the same time. Their eyes met—his were a rich brown with that same glazed look to them. He was maybe thirty, with a goatee and shoulder-length brown hair. His tan skin spoke of a Mediterranean summer. So familiar, and yet she was uncertain.

"Kierse?" the guy said as if sparked to life.

Uh oh. He remembered her a little *too* well.

He took a step forward, and she retreated a step in panic. "Sorry. My name is Shannon."

Just then a second set of doors opened at the far end of the hall. Standing there was a pair of goblins. She recognized them—at least one of them had been at the auction—which meant...

"That's her! Get her!" he yelled.

Kierse's eyes widened in alarm as the group of happy meditators turned as one and rushed toward her. Loretta was closest to her and snatched at her arm, but she was just a human, and a slightly drugged human at that.

Kierse broke her grip with ease and fled from the room. Her cover was dashed to shreds. She needed to get the fuck out of this compound. She kicked off the stupid spa shoes, letting her stride lengthen. Within minutes, she was back through the corridors and into the lobby, the sound of pursuit behind her, as she whispered under her breath, "Please let the door be there. Please let the door be there."

The door *was* there, and it let her pass as if she'd been sucked through a vortex. Then she was on the other side. Her feet carried her forward, still at a run—and then she landed in someone's arms.

"Graves?" she gasped.

"I was about to break the door down," he snarled. "Are you all right?"

"We're about to have a cult come down on our heads," another voice said.

Kierse whipped around to see Vale with an enormous broadsword at the ready. "Vale? You called in Vale?"

"You went into the market alone," Graves accused.

"I'll cover your exit," Vale promised.

The doors burst open behind them.

"Run!" Kierse cried. For once, Graves didn't ask questions.

He took off after her, leaving Vale to distract the cultists. They raced down countless flights of stairs and across the New York–like streets inside the market. No one seemed to think it strange that they were running at top speed. Just another day in the market.

Kierse was panting and out of breath when they finally burst out of Nying Market and back into the real New York. Laz, George, and Edgar waited impatiently nearby. They all jumped up at Kierse and Graves's abrupt appearance, barreling toward the vehicles to get them started. Kierse finally looked over her shoulder and saw that the goblin who had blown her cover was still on their tail.

Graves jerked open the back of the limo, and Kierse fell inside. He jumped in behind her, and then the car was screeching away, back onto the Manhattan streets. They turned around and saw the goblin cursing at them.

"Thank fuck," she gasped. "I think we lost them."

"Yes," he agreed. His phone buzzed, and he checked the message. "Vale broke up the cultists. Only the goblin got past him."

"Good," she said. She collapsed back against the cushion of the limo, letting her breath return to normal before opening her eyes to look at Graves.

He looked paler than usual. "Are you all right? We lost you inside the market, and I was…" He didn't finish the statement. She could see the fear still on his perfect face.

"I'm all right."

His hand touched her cheek. He looked her over, verifying her claim. "I thought I lost you."

"You can't get rid of me that easily," she said, breathless for a whole new reason.

His storm-cloud eyes were serious, his mouth set in a firm line. "You went in the market…alone."

"There was no other way."

"You could have waited *ten* minutes for me."

"You could have trusted that I'd handle it," she fired back.

"I did," he said solemnly. "I waited outside for Edgar to get another coin. But it was my own team who kept me from eating goblin fruit to get to you."

She gasped in horror. "You wouldn't."

"I would have if they hadn't stopped me. I was that worried about you."

"I was going to text you," she conceded, "but George's phone died. The magic must have fucked with it."

"The market runs off of a different magical frequency. That happens."

But she was still stuck on goblin fruit. Graves wouldn't be stupid enough to eat the stuff. "Either way, you can't risk yourself like that."

His eyes widened. "And you can?"

"But goblin fruit." She bit her lip. "I wouldn't have wanted that, either."

He lifted an eyebrow. "And why is that?"

She choked on her words. "Because I don't want you to die!"

"It'd take a lot more than goblin fruit to fell me," he said, brushing a finger against her bottom lip. "I accept that you're independent, that you can handle yourself, that you're bloody reckless," he said, his British accent thickening as his emotions bubbled to the surface. "But you can't do this all alone anymore, Wren. At some point, you are going to have to let others help you. You're going to have to let *me* help you."

Kierse didn't have some witty comeback this time. He was right. She had been running on adrenaline, and going into the market alone was, frankly, stupid. It had seemed like the best choice at the time, but seeing it now through Graves's eyes made her reconsider. He'd feared for her life. He'd almost put himself in mortal danger for her.

She'd had her guard up for so long. Graves had hurt her and betrayed her trust. But he'd more than proved himself to her—he'd had her back in the market, he'd involved her in all the planning for the auction, he'd given pieces of himself that he never would have before. And tonight, when she'd recklessly walked into the market alone, he'd believed in her even through his fear.

She felt something break in her chest. Ice shattering from around her heart. She couldn't hold onto it all anymore—the anger, the fear, the hurt. She didn't *want* to have to hold it all anymore, alone.

So she would give it to him.

"Okay," she said. He must have seen the resolve in her eyes. "Okay."

Then his lips were on hers, slanting against her mouth and claiming her in one smooth motion. She leaned against him, into him, feeling his warmth radiate through her like a life force. The heat of the summer pressed all around them as the sun rose on the horizon in a shock of liminal dawn golds and saffron.

She sighed into him, running her hands up the front of his faerie king costume, which looked macabre in the early morning light. His hands fisted into her new green robe, those strong arms crushing her against him. She swung her leg across his lap, straddling his firm body, and continued to kiss him as if her life depended on it. Perhaps it did.

Tonight had gone to shit. It was hard to believe they'd begun the evening doing something very similar. Now she was trembling against him from hunger, exhaustion, and the hard comedown from adrenaline. Not to mention she'd been shot and now had stitches in her arm.

It had been a long night.

She wanted to shred his faerie costume and her cult uniform in the back of the limo in the heart of the Village. Oh, how she wanted it. Except she felt the small tremor in his hand. He was not feeling as well as he was pretending to be, and neither was she.

Slowly, she pulled back, pressing one last faint kiss on his lips.

Their breaths mingled as she stared down at him from her spot on his lap. The desire was plain on his face, but it was mingled with fear and fatigue.

"We should get you home. I think some reading will do you good," she told him, dragging her thumb across her bottom lip.

He caught her hand in his and pressed a kiss to her knuckles. "Are you babying me?"

"Perhaps you need to be babied," she said as he nipped at the pad of her thumb.

"I've lived a long time," he said with a slow, deadly smile. "I'll be fine."

"You ingested a lot of wish powder. The antidote only helps so much. You still feel like shit."

"I'll be fine," he repeated, going for another kiss. "I'm more worried about you."

"A little shaken up," she admitted.

"What happened in there? And what exactly are you wearing?" He tutted, fingering the little tree emblem. "I don't like you wearing oaks."

She laughed softly. "Well, you don't have a holly clothing line, do you?"

"I'll put it on the list."

"See that you do." She chuckled. The levity helped. "They're clothes from a tree cult."

Graves's eyebrows shot up. "Excuse me?"

"Yeah. Decided to join, in all my spare time."

"Wren." He twirled his finger around a lock of her hair.

"I think I know who the curator is," she said shakily.

He froze. "Did you meet him?"

"No, but the tree on this robe and the cult I just escaped—it was called Sansara."

Graves's eyes widened. "But Sansara was destroyed."

"So we were led to believe."

"And you think it's…"

"Cillian Ryan."

Chapter Forty-One

Half an hour later, George pulled into the underground garage. They exited the bullet-ridden limo without a backward glance and took the elevator into the brownstone. Graves grabbed two protein bars from the empty kitchen—Isolde had long since gone home and wouldn't be back for another hour or so—and passed her one.

"Gross," she said with a laugh as she tore into it on the way up the stairs.

"If you've lost half as much magic as I have, you're probably starving."

"Yeah. The cultists offered me cake, and damn did I want cake," she told him around a yawn. "You can win a girl over with some quality cake."

"Noted," he said with a smirk.

Kierse felt surprisingly better after having even the smallest amount of food. Her magic wasn't empty, but the events of the evening had been straining. She could feel it guttering with the need for recovery. Physically, mentally, and magically.

They reached the landing for the second floor only to find Gen passed out in a chair. Kierse shook her gently awake. "Hey, sleepyhead. We made it home."

Gen jolted awake. "Kierse, what time is it?"

"Morning."

"I didn't mean to fall asleep. What happened?"

"Plan went to hell. We didn't get the cauldron. I can explain more after we've all had some sleep, all right?"

Gen barely contained her yawn. "Yeah. Sleep. Good idea." She waved halfheartedly to Graves. "Sorry about the cauldron."

"Thank you, Genesis."

Gen crawled up the stairs and disappeared into her room. Leaving Kierse on the landing between the library and Graves's quarters. Her bedroom was a floor above them. She disliked the thought of being a floor away from him, wondering if he was sleeping soundly while he recovered. But there was still distance there. A bridge they'd teased around but hadn't crossed.

Graves grasped her hand. "Come with me."

She laughed as he tugged her forward. "Aren't you tired?"

"Exhausted."

Then they were through the door of his inner sanctum. A large bedroom with a four-poster bed, wooden dressers, and a million little details that were completely Graves. A collection of Edgar Allan Poe's poetry with "The Raven" featured prominently sat on his nightstand. His carved wooden bird collection had grown since she'd last been in here. She recognized that the coins she'd previously thought were European had one or two Nying Market coins in them. As if they were trinkets and not priceless. She loved the portrait of Anne Boleyn—the queen, not the cat—on one wall, and on another, a landscape of a field of wildflowers in an Irish countryside with two figures lying on the hill reading a little green book. It was all familiar and all new.

"Do I belong in here?" she asked, a touch teasing, a touch of true hesitance.

"You belong everywhere I am," he said.

She flushed, running a hand over the cornflower-blue comforter. "Everywhere?"

He bent to press a kiss to her neck. "Everywhere."

She turned in his arms as he threaded his fingers up into her hair. He met resistance and then slowly, with controlled care, began to remove each little pin. One tendril loose and then another. A wave of hair falling down her back like a cascading waterfall as he released all the tension on her scalp.

He dipped his head down to taste her lips, and she sighed into him, pressing their bodies together. His lips were hot and pliant, his magic a gentle warmth and not his regular inferno. Not a good sign, but she knew they were safe and he would be back to normal after scouring his library.

"This way," he said.

He guided her away from the bed and into the bathroom. It had a large sunken tub with a turquoise mosaic on the bottom and a white stone walk-in shower the length of the room, stone seats on opposite sides.

Graves turned the handles in the shower to reveal multiple hidden spray jets and a waterfall feature. The water heated almost instantly until the shower was fogged and steam billowed out into the room.

His hands were gentle as he stripped her out of the cult clothing. First the robe, which she thought he might burn in protest. Then the shirt.

His fingers fluttered gently over her bandage. Worry crinkled his brow. "You're injured?"

"Just a graze. They gave me stitches."

"A graze," he said darkly. "From a bullet."

"You were busy. I was holding down the fort."

"Busy," he said. "Not quite the word I'd go for. Absolutely fucking furious and fighting Imani's magic tooth and nail."

"What are you going to do about her?"

"That's a later problem," he said as he dropped to a knee and removed her sweats and underwear. "Shower first."

She stepped inside, letting the spray run down her body. She dragged a hand across the glass to get a good look at Graves. He removed the faerie king top first. It had hidden seams and seemed to simply unravel before dropping to the floor in one long piece.

Her mouth went dry at the sight of him. The tattoo that started at his wrist. A circle of holly vines with their piercing thorns digging into his skin like a living mural of his tortured pain. They snaked up his forearm, across the curve of his bicep, around the bulge of his shoulder, and swept out across his chest. He was broad and muscled and utterly delectable. She wanted to run her tongue along the dips and valleys of his pecs and across every ridge of his abs to the Adonis lines that led down into those inscrutable pants.

She watched her devil release his trousers and drop them to the ground. Her eyes widened. All muscled quads and narrow waist and thick, long cock, hanging heavy between his legs.

"You're joining me?" she asked, a little breathless.

Her eyes darted down and back up again. Heat was already pooling in her core. She hadn't thought she had an ounce of adrenaline left in her body, but here she was, ready to drop to her knees again for this man. Monster. God.

Water cascaded down his muscled form as he entered the shower. All sleek skin and utterly inviting torment. She wanted to run her hands down him and feel his smoothness. Take his cock in her hand and slide it home into her where it belonged.

"Soap first," he said, his voice husky as if he could see the desire in her eyes.

He reached for a bar, lathering a washcloth and then running it carefully across her skin. Every sense was heightened at the feel of his hands on her, cleaning away the night's excursions. He was cautious of her bullet wound, treating it with tender care, before continuing on. When he was finished, he began to scrub at his own body as she washed off the soap under the spray.

She held out her hand. "Can I?"

He offered the washcloth to her without comment, and then she was running soap down Graves's chest. Her heart beat a furious tempo as she moved along his legs and up across his arms. He turned for her, letting her marvel at the planes of his back and the tight clench of his ass. God, it was fucking magnificent.

His cock lengthened further at the sweep of her fingers and brush of her palm and the soft notes of pleasure she made at the simple act of getting to touch him. Finally, she had soaped every inch of him, and he stepped into the showerhead, washing away the evidence of her fingers. She eyed the water with barely suppressed jealousy.

"If you keep looking at me like that," he said, low like a warning.

"Then what?"

"We have to wash your hair." As if he was physically restraining himself so that he could take care of her.

She didn't argue. Just turned her back to him and let him lather the dark strands. His hands massaging her scalp were sweet heaven and pure torture.

She moaned. She couldn't even help it. It felt fucking incredible to have those hands working her over. Fingers that knew the world's secrets, releasing all of her tensions.

His cock pressed into her ass at the sound. As if he, too, couldn't help himself. She shivered at the need they both clearly felt crawling up and out of their chests. Like a bird trapped in a cage, beating its wings to be set free.

"Wren," he ground out.

She hummed at the sound of her name on his tongue as he washed the shampoo out of her hair and went back for conditioner. It smelled like honeysuckle, sweet and pungent, and she couldn't imagine him using it, but she loved it. Like he'd had it waiting here for her all along.

When the conditioner was finally washed out, she kept her eyes closed, letting the water rain down on her and whisk away the events of the evening.

Graves sucked her nipple into his mouth. She gasped but kept her eyes closed. Let him lead, if he wanted. She'd let him do anything right now. Anything at all.

His fingers replaced his mouth and then his tongue swirled around the other nipple until it peaked. They'd built up and up and up, the need a physical pain hovering between them, as if at any moment they might both explode and lose their minds without the other. She'd held out because of her anger, but it had cooled. And in its place she'd found...a partner.

One who had trusted her in the market and with the plan and with his heart.

She wanted this. She wanted him.

His hands ran down across her stomach and over her hips. Gone was the methodical cleaning, and here was worship. It was slow and intent and made her ache in all the right places.

His fingers slipped between her legs, finding the apex of her thighs and sliding over the wet folds of her body. He dragged his palm hard against her clit, grinding it there until she was shaking at the pleasure. Then, and only then, did he push two fingers inside of her, spreading her wide.

"Oh," she gasped softly.

She opened her eyes to find him on one knee before her. His glittering dark eyes met hers as he stroked deep into her core. "I should towel you off and put you to bed."

"Uh huh," she whispered.

He speared up into her again. "But I can smell your desire." His tongue laved at her nipple again. "And this cunt is so wet for me." He dipped lower, brushing his tongue over her clit. "And your reactions are so needy. Are you needy?" he asked, swirling his tongue on her clit again. "Is this a needy little cunt?"

"Yes," she told him with no embarrassment. No flush. He was right. She wanted him. She wanted him more than anything in the world. And she'd never sleep anyway without using her hand to get off thinking about him. "I need you inside of me right now."

"Fuck," he said as he slipped his fingers out of her.

He stood and grasped one of her legs, lifting it up over his hip as he all but hauled her off of the ground in the slippery shower. The head of his cock was poised at her entrance. "Say it again."

"I need you," she gasped as she reached down and slowly lowered onto the head of his cock. "Fuck me, Graves."

He thrust upward in one swift motion, spearing her open and leaving her gasping. He was massive. A fact that she hadn't exactly forgotten, but her body had clearly not reminded her until he was inside of her. She felt weak and on fire and like a mewling mess all at once.

"God fucking damn," he said into her shoulder. "You feel so fucking good."

"Yes," she gasped.

He pulled out and then thrust back into her, hard and unrelenting. "Such a good girl," he praised. "Taking all of my cock."

"Fuck," she panted.

"So." *Thrust.* "Fucking." *Thrust.* "Good." *Thrust.*

It was brutal and unrelenting and the best fucking feeling of her entire life. She was going to explode any second, and all he had to do was keep up this pace. She'd give him everything that he was taking from her. Meet him as an equal.

"Close, close, close," she chanted.

The bastard pulled out.

"No!" she gasped. "Graves!"

He laughed softly as he dropped her leg, whipped her around, and bent her at the waist. Her forearms landed on the granite bench with her ass high in the air. His hands spread her cheeks wide, and he slapped one side, then the other.

"This is how I want you. Bent over so I can rail you."

"Have me however you like. Just let me fucking come."

His next thrust sent her to the moon and then to Saturn. She was in outer space amongst the stars, reveling in the planetary alignment. Her mind so far gone that her body's only response was to unleash.

She screamed into the shower as her orgasm ripped through her, torquing like a vice grip. A torrent of wild lust that started in her core and wrenched out of her like a burst of magic. And Graves couldn't hold on any longer than her in the wake of her explosion. He roared and came hard and fast, pistoning into her a few times before collapsing forward.

They both breathed the same breathless air. No words could begin to explain the hunger that had overflowed into something more. Something bright and inviting and raw settling between them.

She wanted to languish here forever. Live with him hard and urgent inside of her and forget the rest of the world.

He must have felt the same, because it was several minutes before he finally slid free. Her legs turned to jelly, and she went limp, only managing not to fall when Graves caught her around the middle.

"Easy," he whispered gently.

"Feel…hungover?" She hung her head forward and felt what she could only assume was a sex coma.

Graves chuckled softly. A pleasant, melodic sound that almost sounded happy. Joyous.

"I fucked you senseless," he preened like it was such an accomplishment.

"Do it again," she teased.

"Don't tempt me. You're about to pass out. I need to take care of you first."

He lifted her up and set her on the plush rug outside the shower. With a big, fluffy white towel he dried her off, taking care with the curls in her hair before wrapping her up like a burrito. After quickly toweling himself off and slinging it low across his hips, he hoisted her into his arms and carried her back into the bedroom.

"Your bed?" she slurred.

"I almost lost you tonight, Wren. You can't imagine I'm letting you sleep elsewhere."

He pulled the covers back and set her down on the bed. Graves slipped her out of the towel and then pulled the sheets up. She was nearly asleep as soon as her head hit the pillow. Like he really had rendered her senseless. She snuggled down, inhaling the scent of leather and books and a hint of the clean laundry detergent.

She could vaguely sense that he was hanging the towels up, setting his phone to charge, and turning off the light before he crawled into bed behind her. He rolled into her, one arm falling across her chest and tugging her gently against him.

His warmth and scent and the feel of him all combined. She was sleepy, disoriented, and exhausted, but his cock was pressed against her ass, and maybe she had just enough sense left in her to take him one more time.

"Wren," he groaned as she wiggled her ass against him. "You need sleep."

"Mmm hmm," she murmured.

She dragged her hand down his arm, repositioning his fingers over her breast. His head dipped into the valley between her shoulder blades. He inhaled sharply as he felt her peaked nipple.

"You can barely form sentences."

Kierse didn't care about any of that. So she did the unexpected—she switched her absorption off.

Graves went *very* still. His body a rigid form behind her, his cock lengthening at the memory she sent down the line: looking down at him as he fucked her against the shower wall. The moment he flipped her over and split her apart. The roar of her orgasm as he undid her very being.

"That...is...cheating," he growled, his cock hard and aching against her backside.

Her mind pushed forward. Not a memory this time—a thought. Her very vivid imagination. Of him lifting her leg and sliding his cock home into her.

"You're dangerous," he growled.

But he was already moving, shifting his body so he could ease his cock into her pussy.

He pushed home and growled into her shoulder, "This is what you wanted?"

"Oh," she gasped. "So full."

The distance between them was nonexistent. He kept an arm banded across her chest, using it as leverage to rock back and forth into her. She met each stroke, pushing backward onto him. There was nowhere to go or move or breathe. Just the heat of him all around her and the feel of his cock filling her.

She was fully in the moment and hadn't even realized that she'd kept her absorption off. Letting him see her as she saw him, her mind wide-open for him to revel in. A trust she never would have given him before the events of tonight.

Then he sent an image into her mind so she could see what *he* was seeing as he fucked her. As if she were the most precious and incredible thing he'd ever laid eyes on. How her body felt like returning from a centuries-long hell to touch heaven. And how he'd burn down the entire fucking world to keep her.

At that thought, he laid her flat on her back so he could get better leverage, hoisting her legs over his shoulders and slamming into her. Mere seconds of the increased friction and she was crying out into the darkened room again, him only a second behind her as they finished together.

Flames danced in his irises as she watched the entire world burn, knowing she'd let him do it.

Chapter Forty-Two

"So let me get this straight," Gen said a few days later as they waited for everyone to gather in the library. "You're Lorcan's soulmate?"

Graves stilled at the word as he poured himself a drink.

Kierse cursed softly under her breath and lifted her head from her work on the decoy box. Edgar and George had brought it up for her to tinker with, to see if she could break through the Curator's security.

"That's what you got out of all of that?" Kierse asked as she reached for the tray of biscuits—cookies—that Isolde had brought up earlier. She snagged two of Isolde's favorites—a jammie dodger and custard cream. Recovering from the weekend had been tougher than she'd thought. "Not the wish powder or car chase or goblin market or the *tree cult*?"

"Yeah, yeah," Gen said with a wave of her hand. "Business."

Gen was right. That had been business, and while it had been full of action, it had not been what Gen's romance-loving heart cared about. And while Gen had healed her bullet wound earlier in the week, she'd been mostly interested that Kierse was now sleeping in Graves's bedroom.

"Okay but *soulmate*?" Gen said with a shake of her head. "Why didn't you tell me about this earlier? What the fuck does that even mean?"

"I've been trying not to think about it," she admitted.

She returned to her work. She'd already dismantled the safety features, but it had taken the better part of an hour, and she was thankful she hadn't tried to do this while at the venue. It was going to be many, *many* more hours before she got through the biometrics and combination lock. But she enjoyed it.

"How can you not think about it? It would be all I was thinking of. Soulmates are like...soulmates. Do you feel different when you're around him?" Gen wrapped her arms around Anne Boleyn and hugged the damn cat to her chest. "Tell me everything."

Graves leaned back against the table and brought his drink to his lips. When Kierse met his gaze, he arched an eyebrow. As if challenging her to answer those questions while the thought of his cock inside her every night still resonated through her.

"Uh, can I get a raincheck on a feelings conversation?" She reached for a chocolate biscuit and finished it off with some steaming hot tea.

Gen glared at Graves. It didn't exactly have the heat she intended in pink leggings, holding a cat. "Could you be a little less...*you* right now?"

"No?"

"If you weren't here, she'd give me all the details," Gen told him.

"She is free to give you all the details right now," Graves said. He lifted his shoulders, unconcerned. "What is she going to say that I don't already know?"

"Well, I don't know," Gen said. She glanced at Kierse. "What doesn't he know?"

Kierse laughed. "Don't I wish I knew the answer to that."

"A chuisle mo chroí is a magic bond. I've seen it a few times." Graves's eyes were hot on her face as he continued, "It usually creates a strong connection, an awareness of the other person that might feel physical in the chest. Touch is almost like being intoxicated. Sometimes you feel a loss of your own will."

Her hand went to her chest at the words. She remembered the ache there when she'd been in Brooklyn. The way she'd felt like she couldn't physically pull away from him when he'd reached for her at the Frolic. And even all those months ago, when she should have feared him for all he'd done, and somehow she'd believed all the lies that had come out of his mouth. As if even before the spell had broken, the link had been there, but muffled.

"That's why you broke his contact with me at the party," Kierse said.

"I would have taken any excuse to hit him," Graves said casually. She raised her eyebrows, and he conceded, "But yes, I knew what he was doing."

"And you still let me go to Brooklyn."

He chuckled grimly. "As if I could keep you from doing anything."

"Aww," Gen said with wide eyes. "He trusted you to come home."

Kierse swatted at Gen. "You're getting us off topic."

"Am I? Are you going to see him again?" Gen chanced a quick glance at Graves. "You have to, right? We need to see Ethan after the last disaster."

"We do need to see Ethan."

"Aren't you curious what he's going to say?"

Kierse shrugged. She *was* curious. And it wasn't like Lorcan hadn't already made contact—he'd reached out the day after the auction, asking to see her. She'd left him on Read. And while she knew she needed to see him, she didn't even know where to begin with this soulmate situation.

"Well, I'm curious," Gen said.

"If we're going to see Ethan, then yes, I'm going to have to see Lorcan, too."

"When will you do that?" Graves asked.

"Before the engagement party?" Gen suggested.

Kierse nodded, thankful to have Gen directing this conversation. Her eyes met Graves's across the distance and added, "Once I'm back to full strength."

He nodded. "Understood."

Gen looked between them warily and opened her mouth to ask more, but the door burst open, and in strode Laz and Schwartz. Laz was clearly bullying the taciturn mer, who looked one jab away from pummeling his friend. He probably deserved what was coming to him after he'd thrown Schwartz out of the car. George and Edgar trailed behind the men in a much more dignified fashion.

"Oh look, the testosterone has entered the room," Gen said with an eye roll.

Laz grinned wide and strode across the room to sink into the seat next to Gen. "Admit it. You missed us," he said with a nudge to her shoulder.

Kierse pushed the decoy box away from her for the start of the meeting and slid down the couch to make room. Schwartz sank into a nearby chair. George and Edgar remained standing, waiting for Graves to call things to order.

"Maybe Schwartz," Gen said. Her eyes slid to the mer, taking in his state. "Do you want me to try another healing?"

He shook his head. "Just have to heal it up the rest on my own. Appreciate you taking away much of the pain, though."

Gen grinned. "Good. I was glad to help."

"You've gotten really good," Kierse said.

"I've been...seeing Niamh," Gen said casually.

"As if I hadn't noticed you sneaking out," Kierse said with a laugh. "How is *that* going?"

"We're just training!" Gen said quickly. "I hope you don't mind. I know how you feel about the Druids."

"Yeah, but I love Niamh, and you should train," Kierse insisted. "The rest of us are."

Gen gave her a small smile and fell silent as Laz started ragging on Schwartz again, triumphantly reenacting throwing him out of a moving vehicle.

"If you're all done," Graves said drily. Under his breath, he added, "Why did I ever decide to get a team together? It was so much quieter working alone."

Kierse grinned. He was saying that, but she could tell something had thawed since their frozen winter. She liked the change.

"Where should we start?" Graves asked. "Laz?"

"Gotcha, Boss," Laz said, leaning his elbows onto his knees. "The good news or the bad news?"

"Good news," Gen said cheerfully.

"Well, I did some decrypting on the files we got at the auction. It's not much, but you were right that they never intended to sell it. They wanted to see what the interest would be. The Curator is showcasing his entire collection at the Monster Con."

Graves sighed. "Including the cauldron?"

"It was on a list of items to be shown the first night of the con."

"Monster Con," Graves said. "It's at the Plaza this year?"

"Yep," Laz said. "In the heart of our dear city, on the night of the twenty-first."

Kierse could see Graves's mind working. The cauldron at the Plaza the day of the summer solstice. It was a setup. She could already feel the trap closing around their heads. And yet...how could they walk away?

"We're going to steal the cauldron at the Monster Con?" Gen asked.

Everyone turned to look at her, speaking the quiet part out loud. And then back to Graves, waiting on bated breath for his confirmation.

"Yes," he finally said.

Gen nodded. "Well, fuck."

The rest of the room laughed at her, but Graves was already strategizing.

"The bad news?" he asked.

"We need another tech guy," Laz admitted with a frown. "I'm not the best in the world by a long shot, but I get by. I'm not sure getting by is enough for this Curator guy. He knows what he's doing. We need someone better."

Graves nodded once. He'd probably already had that thought.

Kierse had another one. "We know a tech guy. One of the best in the business."

Graves met her eyes. "No."

"But..."

"I know what you're thinking."

"Then you know that we need him."

"Who?" Gen asked, glancing between them.

"Walter Rodriguez," Kierse said.

"Who?" everyone repeated.

"It's not an option," Graves added.

Kierse huffed. "Walter was Graves's apprentice before me."

"Were you fucking him, too?" Laz muttered under his breath.

Graves shot him a sharp look, but the rest laughed. The fact that they could even joke with Graves was shocking. Revelatory.

"He has the ability to push his force-field magic into wards and combine it with computer systems. He kept Graves out of Third Floor. If he's that powerful, we want him on *our* side," Kierse told him. "If we leave him to himself, he might start working for them again."

"If he helps us, we let him in on the take, and he could become that much more powerful."

"Are you worried he would rival you?" Kierse challenged.

"No," Graves said slowly. "I do not worry about that. But I am not in favor of giving more power to people with questionable loyalties."

"They were all *your* apprentices, Graves," she said with pointed look. "Maybe the common denominator is you."

"Maybe it is, but it doesn't change that Walter is a liability. He's powerful enough."

"You don't even know if he'll ask for more power. Just because it's what you're after."

Everyone held their breath, waiting to see how Graves would react. They could needle him, but Kierse was the only one who pushed. She was right about this. Laz had admitted he wasn't the best. They needed the best.

"I'll find out what he wants," Graves finally said.

A breath released from the room. Kierse felt it a victory he'd given in, ever so slightly.

"Schwartz?" Graves asked.

"If I'm healed up in time, then I'm on the detail for the next assignment," he said. Then tipped his head at Gen. "Thanks to your little healer, I should be a go for the con."

"Good. You'll be on duty, though. We'll need backup. Possibly someone else invited to the event," he said softly. His gaze slipped to hers. He sighed like he hated the question he was about to ask.

"What?" Kierse asked warily.

"Nathaniel O'Connor?"

Her eyes lit up. "You want to *work* with Nate?"

Last winter he'd gone ballistic at her for working with Nate, and now he wanted to bring him *into the fold*?

"'Want' might be the wrong word," Graves admitted, "but he's the Dreadlord alpha. He'll have an invite, and he's on our side, right?"

"My side, at least," she agreed.

"Good enough for me," Graves said. "Would he do it?"

"I can ask him," she said.

"We're going to his engagement party next weekend," Gen said brightly. "You should come."

"To the party?" Graves asked. His eyes were curious as they swept to Kierse.

"If you want," Kierse added quickly, knowing he never would. That was *not* Graves's world. "But I can ask him there regardless."

"Good. Schwartz, you have your assignment. Kierse and I will bring on our next two members. Laz, I have an idea for you, but I might need to call in a favor. Keep combing through the files to see if there's anything else in them in the meantime. Send them to me to review."

Laz nodded.

"Is your warlock friend going to continue to be a problem, sir?" George asked from where he'd been standing silently.

"No," Graves said gruffly. "I've dealt with that."

Dealt with was a word for it. Montrell had shown up one night, an apology on his lips. Imani was badly injured, and her magic was on the fritz from the car crash. Graves had told him that if Imani ever set foot in his city again, she was going home in a body bag. And because of their previous affiliation, that had been as much leeway as Montrell would ever get from him.

"Edgar, any luck with the stakeout?"

"No one came or went from Sansara in days, sir."

"So they're self-sustaining?" Schwartz suggested.

Graves pursed his lips. "It's possible."

"Or they moved the door," Kierse said.

Graves nodded. "That's also a possibility."

Since currently only Graves and Kierse could see magic, one of them would have to be the one to look into it.

Before Kierse could even volunteer herself, Graves said, "I'll look into it. Thank you, Edgar." Edgar nodded his head once. "Kierse has gotten us one step toward the Curator," Graves continued. "We're going to do some work to verify the information she provided." By work, he meant digging around through her memories again. "Anything else?"

No one said a word. The plan was coming together. Kierse could see his mind working, and already she had ideas to help. She'd broken into the Plaza with Jason. She knew the layout like an old friend.

"Get to work," Graves said, clapping his hands to end the meeting.

George and Edgar promptly left. Laz hassled Gen out of her seat, insisting she come downstairs for some biscuits with him and Schwartz before they headed out. Kierse stood and stretched her arms overhead. She could still feel the strain from her wound, but Gen had fixed the bulk of the damage.

When everyone was finally gone, Graves's eyes met hers again. "Are you ready?"

"Are you?" she teased.

He shut the book he'd been looking at. "Always ready for you. Lay down and let's get started."

Chapter Forty-Three

K ierse was flat on the chaise. Her heart raced, and she couldn't seem to calm it down. There was no reason for fear. It certainly wasn't about Graves, but more what she might find in her broken memories. Cillian Ryan had put this spell on her. He'd been the one to hide her from the world. And she was almost certain that he was the one running Sansara. There were too many coincidences for it to be anything else.

The only way to find out was to go through.

"Breathe. You look like you're about to panic. I'm not going to torture you."

She narrowed her eyes at him. "I'm not panicking."

"I've seen it with others," Graves said casually. "You're going to show me something you don't want me to see if you're not relaxed."

"Should I meditate like the tree cult?" she asked, feeling snippy.

He sank down onto a chair opposite her. He looked at her for a long moment before leaning back. "Are you nervous about what you'll find? Or about seeing Ethan again?" He paused again. "Or Lorcan?"

Kierse let the tension drop from her shoulders. "I don't know. All of the above."

His expression was serious. "That's understandable. Ethan is your friend. Things will work themselves out. Having Gen there will help." His eyes darted to the closed door. "Are you sure you haven't trained her in espionage? She's incredibly adept at getting information out of people."

"That's just Gen." Kierse shrugged. "She's too good for this world."

"Hmm," Graves said uncertainly. "And as far as Lorcan…"

"I can handle Lorcan," she told him.

"The soulmate bond is powerful. He's going to try to use it against you."

"You talk about it like it's a weapon to be wielded."

"I wouldn't underestimate him," Graves said solemnly.

Kierse lifted her chin. "I have no intention of falling prey to him."

"Prey don't have as many teeth as you."

"Then don't worry about me. If he can use it against me, I can do the same."

He was silent a moment, as if refusing to say he *did* worry about her. Especially when it came to Lorcan. The connection was strong, and she didn't know what that meant for her uncertain future.

Finally, Graves nodded. "I believe that you believe that."

Which was not the same as saying he believed she wasn't in danger.

Still, she let it drop. She didn't want to discuss Lorcan any more than he did. Lorcan was a thorn in her side that had released a drop of blood but hadn't yet ripped her open.

"As for my work," Graves said, transitioning smoothly. "You didn't want me in your head at all. Now we're not just skimming for memories of your parents." He grinned devilishly. "Or during sex."

"No, that part I do not mind at all," she said with a choked laugh.

"This is deeper work. I'd be remiss to not warn you that it may be trickier."

"Why?"

"You don't have any memory of Cillian. As far as we know, you only met him once. While we have his magic signature and the knowledge that he put the spell on you, you don't remember anything else about him. It's very little to go on. It might take a few tries to get to the night that it happened."

"Okay," she said, breathing out harshly. "But we will get there."

"Yes, we will." Graves ran a hand through his hair. "Also, I heard from Mafi."

Kierse's head jerked up. "About the psychiatrist?"

"She's back in the city."

She relaxed back down, her mind spinning. This whole thing with therapy and doctors still freaked her out. She couldn't explain it, except that it had been so hard and expensive to pay for doctors for so much of her life. She wasn't sure how to trust or open up to a paid professional. It was hard enough doing it with people she cared about. To think of Graves in her mind digging for answers.

"If you want to see her," Graves added. "Mafi said we could come in whenever we wanted."

"I'll think about it."

He acknowledged her and then went straight to business. "What are you going to focus on?"

Kierse bit her lip. "My parents. The night they left your house."

"That's as good a place as any. We can try to skip forward until they reach him."

"Should I think about the smell at Sansara, too?"

"Let's try this first. We don't know exactly where we're going, and too many points of entry could drag us to the wrong person or time." He slid his gloves off. "Whenever you're ready."

She slowed her breathing. She could do this. She flipped that switch on her absorption, feeling it give as smoothly now as her slow motion. She turned it to off and let Graves's magic settle into her skin.

She was leaving the library, a yawn escaping her little mouth as she walked between her parents to the elevator. She stumbled from exhaustion, and her dad picked her up. She laid her little head on his shoulder and fell asleep as if the night had been peaceful and she was safe and loved.

A tear leaked from the corner of Kierse's eye as the memory faded to dreams.

"Should we stop?" Graves asked, pulling back.

"No." She replaced his hand on her arm. "We need to keep going."

"I'll guide from here," he said, his voice taking on a smooth, melodic tone.

How many times had he done this before? How often had he stolen information from someone's mind by *guiding* them? Enough. Enough, and it didn't matter, because they needed the information. *She* needed the information.

"You just woke up after leaving the library. What do you see?"

Kierse distantly felt his magic entangle with her consciousness, encouraging her to show him what he wanted to know. She also felt an immediate instinct to fight his touch and cast him out, but she pushed that down and concentrated on what he wanted.

Her dad was putting her to bed on the couch, tucking a blanket around her shoulders. Her eyes fluttered open, and she yawned. "Did I fall asleep?"

"It's okay," he said, pressing a kiss to her forehead. "It's late."

He ran a hand through her hair, and she closed her eyes again. But she was restless, once more opening them to look up at him.

"Is Mum going to be okay?"

"Don't worry about your mum. She's a strong one."

"But if they're after us…a spell isn't going to hide her, too."

"No," he told her truthfully. "We'll figure something out."

It was the first time she realized that her father was lying to her.

She fell back asleep, but Graves's voice was in her ears, already guiding her to a different memory. "You went to see the Druid, Cillian Ryan. Your parents took you to see him."

Her mind whirled, sorting, processing, coming up blank. It was like a computer search engine looking for a name and finding nothing. But there shouldn't have been nothing.

Her absorption switched back on, and Graves leaned back. He passed her a chocolate cookie. "Eat something. Switching your powers on and off will drain your magic."

She took the offered food and finished it before sighing. "There's nothing there."

"We don't know that. It was our first try. The rest has worked."

She huffed in frustration. "Okay. You said it'd be harder, but…"

"This is not the toughest interrogation that I've done. It can take some time to get where we're going. Trust me."

And she did. He was darkness and winter and the villain of his own story. And yet she put her trust in him.

She listened in on her magic and saw that Graves was right. Using her absorption like this was draining her. They couldn't do this all day.

Her powers winked off once more, and Graves was back in her head. That slight push as he directed her into her little New York apartment. Time seemed to move in fast forward.

Kierse recalled through his magic the rest of the next day with brilliant clarity. Waking up to her mum making an Irish breakfast, her dad complaining about missing the food from home. Dough proofing in a bowl nearby—her mum only baked when she was nervous, and today, she was making Kierse's favorite: cinnamon babka. She'd have it ready after school.

Kierse went to school. She was a silent type who knew all the answers but refused to raise her hand. Hour by hour, her fear grew, and by the end of the day she sprinted out of the building and ran home.

Her parents were there. The babka had just come out of the oven. She had an afternoon snack. They were speaking in careful, cool tones. Low enough she couldn't hear even with her advanced wisp powers. Well, they weren't *that* advanced yet. Her mum had told her they'd get stronger.

"…tonight…" Mum said.

"Let's see what happens tonight," Graves said, burrowing deeper.

The memory flitted forward. It was dark outside. Kierse was wrapped in a coat as they got off the subway in an unfamiliar part of Manhattan. It was drizzling and cold, fall pressing in on them as winter approached.

She wanted to go home. She didn't like it here. When she looked up at her parents, their brows were creased, their mouths set in firm lines.

They stopped at a large, red-brick building that looked like it might have once been a warehouse but at some point in the last hundred years had been converted into condos or lofts with the fall of manufacturing in the city. Kierse shuffled forward into the dingy vestibule, and her mum pressed a button on the door. A buzzer went off, and her dad heaved the door open to let them into the drab lobby.

There was no elevator. She panted up the many, *many* stairs. Daddy offered to carry her, but she didn't stop. Just trudged along until they reached a long corridor with flickering overhead lights that smelled of piss and vomit.

She pinched her nose. "Gross."

Mum put a shaky arm around her shoulders, and they continued down the hall. A woman stumbled out of an apartment up ahead, cursing in a foreign language, before careening past them.

"7016. 7018," Mum said. "Next one."

Suddenly, the memory yanked her away. She was standing on the street. The rain was coming down in sheets. She had no umbrella, and everything was strangely muted. She couldn't hear. She couldn't smell. She couldn't sense the air around her. The tops of her ears felt weird when she touched them, and not just from Mum's glamour. For *real*.

Kierse cut it off.

"What happened?" she asked.

Graves shook himself out of her mind. "You moved forward. After the spell."

"I didn't do anything. It just jumped."

"That sometimes happens."

She took a bottle of water from him and drained half of it. "Let's try again."

He placed his hands back on her. Kierse went under. She was at the end of the hallway. Her breaths came out in hard pants. The woman fell out of the room. This time Kierse deduced that she was speaking in an accented Spanish. She walked past on heavy feet.

Adair put his hand on his belt as if to pull out a weapon at her approach. Shannon was trying to stay calm, collected, but Kierse could see the hover of her magic around her, at the ready.

"7016."

Mum put her hand on Kierse's head.

"7018."

She chanced a glance at her husband in fear.

"Next one."

Kierse was jerked away. She stood in her living room. Mum leaned heavily against the countertop, tears in her eyes. Daddy was speaking to her.

"We had to."

"I know," Mum said. "But what do I do? We knew he couldn't put the spell on a fully developed magical user."

"Shannon, we will figure this out."

"I'm a danger to her," she said with a sniffle. "My magic will lead him here. I have to go."

"Shannon…"

"It's safer for her."

"I'm right here!" Kierse burst out. "I'm standing right here. Don't talk about me like I'm somewhere else." She ran into her mum's arms. "You can't go."

"I love you," Mum said as she stroked her hair.

Kierse let her absorption drop again. Her head hurt like someone had driven a knife through her temple. Her magic was considerably more drained than she'd expected.

"What the fuck, Graves?"

Graves stood, striding across the room and returning with a box of tissues. "Here." She stared at it in confusion. He gestured to his nose. "You have a nosebleed."

Kierse ripped a tissue out and touched it to her nostril. It was a slow drip, but she wasn't susceptible to them.

"Why is this happening?"

"It could be because of me. It's happened before," he admitted. "Though I'm not sure if it's me or you."

"Me? How could it be me?"

"Mafi did say that trauma could block the memories from resurfacing."

Kierse bit her lip. "But they were working before. It's just this one room."

"Then it could be whatever is behind that door is too traumatic for you to witness."

She shook her head. "No. It doesn't feel like trauma. It feels like…" She wiped at her bloody nose. "I don't know. Like the spell is still there."

"The spell was broken."

"It feels like there's still something there. Some kind of block."

He shrugged one shoulder. "It does feel like we hit something when we almost get to that room in Tribeca."

"Tribeca? Is that where we were?"

"Yes, I recall the building," he said.

"Could we go there?"

"It was twenty years ago. And it was destroyed in the war," Graves said with a sigh. "No luck there, I'm afraid."

She swallowed her disappointment. "It was a long shot, anyway." She rolled her shoulders back. "Let's go again."

"Try to think of the magical signature you sensed in Sansara. We'll see if that breaks through the block."

Kierse took a deep breath. "I can do it."

Her absorption dropped away. Graves's hand was on her, his voice in her ears. "Take us back to the hallway."

Kierse focused and let the hallway reappear before her. She'd time looped through it twice now. She knew the moment when the door opened and the woman spat something in Spanish. The fear across her mother's face. The steel in her father's. They were ready to fight if this went down.

"7016." Her hand came down onto Kierse's head.

"Pine and lemon," Graves breathed so softly that for a second she could smell it again.

"7018." Mum looked backward with alarm.

Kierse focused here. Let her wisp senses stretch. What had she detected in that hallway? What had she known even without knowing it? She wasn't blunted yet. She didn't have the spell on her. There was something under the fear.

"Next one."

There.

The next door.

She could see it ahead. The 7020 on a little plaque on the front door. A little glow of magic around the frame. Warding, just like Mum could do. Just like in the library from the night before. And a smell...

Pine and lemon.

Just like in Sansara.

She was ripped away from the scent of that magic, as if she wasn't supposed to have remembered that part. She landed on the streets of New York. She'd just pickpocketed an unsuspecting tourist for money for lunch. She was six and starving. Her mum had died in childbirth. Her daddy had abandoned her without a word. She had to survive. She couldn't die. She touched the wren necklace against her chest, the only thing she had left of them. It had been her mum's. That was all she knew.

Survival was what mattered.

"Hey, kid," a voice called. "Neat trick."

Kierse whipped around as fear pierced through her. A man was smiling down at her. He had dark features—dark hair and eyes—with an angular face and a kind look about him. His hair was groomed, beard shaved clean, and he was dressed in nice clothes. Nothing fancy, but cared for. Nicer than anyone living on the streets would wear, but not like the clothes of the people she stole from. Nondescript.

"What do you want?" she asked, mimicking a cool, adult voice.

"I can show you how to get better at that," he said with a dark grin.

Jason.

Kierse dropped the connection. More blood trickled out of her nose. Enough that Graves passed her a second tissue with a concerned look on his face.

"It was him," Kierse said. "Cillian Ryan. I smelled it."

"We should stop there for today."

"I can keep going," she whispered.

"I don't think so." He handed her another drink. "We pushed too hard."

Her head was pounding a quiet rhythm against her skull. She needed a break, and yet she couldn't stop.

"Not hard enough," she gasped as she downed the water. "We still didn't see him."

"We may not see him, Wren."

She closed her eyes, unable to believe that. She had to see him. He was there in her memories. And yes, she had the confirmation she'd needed that the person who put the spell on her was also the person running the tree cult. Which meant he was the Curator and he would be at Monster Con.

But she wanted more.

"There was a guy in Sansara who recognized me," Kierse said. "I thought he looked familiar, and then he said my name."

Graves narrowed his eyes. "You didn't mention that."

"I forgot. We were in a rush, and it just came back to me." She ran a hand back through her hair. "We should look for him. Maybe he's a key from my past to unlock this."

"He could be *anyone*," Graves argued. "You have no idea where you know him from. Maybe he wasn't even connected to the Curator when you knew him."

"I know, but he's the last connection I have. Can we at least try?"

He stared down at her like he wanted to dismiss the scenario. Perhaps if it was anyone else, he would have. But he yielded for Kierse.

"We'll try."

Kierse sighed with relief and closed her eyes again. "I'm ready."

Graves had her pull up the image of the guy she had seen in Sansara. He still seemed vaguely familiar, but no more recognizable than before. No idea how he knew her name.

She was sluggish as she searched through that memory for something familiar. She latched onto his face as Graves guided her forward, slipping through her murky thoughts like through sewage.

"Where have you seen him before?" Graves asked.

But she hadn't seen him before. She didn't remember, and Graves's magic couldn't seem to coax it out of her. Frustration bit at her as she pressed and pressed and pressed…

She was in the hallway again, staring up at the next doorway: 7020. The magic signature coming off of it—the warding in place—all the answers right there before her. She pushed and pushed and pushed, felt the memory almost *crack* along a fissure. She was going to get in. She would be able to open that door. To find her answers.

Then the memory physically drove her backward. She gasped at the rebound, and Graves hastily severed the connection.

"Fuck," she hissed, bending forward and cradling her head in her hands.

Her vision went blurry. Jagged edges sliced through her brain. She winced and shielded her eyes from the dim lighting. This was turning sharply into migraine territory.

And she was bleeding all over Graves's chaise. Not just from her nose but from her eyes. She'd never fucking bled from her eyes.

"You are *done*," Graves said firmly as he bent to one knee and pressed a tissue to her nose. "For at least a few days. This shouldn't be harming you this severely."

He handed her another one that she used to wipe at her eyes. Tears streamed from them now, mixing with the blood. They ran in pink stains down her cheeks.

"We were close," she whispered. "I felt it start to crack."

"I am going to prioritize your health the way I wouldn't if you were anyone else."

There were shadows in his eyes at the proclamation. Fear. He'd hurt people with his powers before. Maybe many people. He knew the signs.

And if he wanted to keep her safe, he would. Even from himself.

She nodded. They'd pushed too hard. Even if she wanted to try to get through the crack in that memory, she couldn't do it today. She could barely think. Her magic was shot like touching a frayed electrical wire.

"Why did it react like that?"

"We were pushing against something." He took a fortifying drink of liquor. "Take a moment. Why would you not be able to get past that? Especially with *my* help."

"He...he fucked with my head," she guessed.

"Either the spell erased that memory or...he did."

Kierse frowned. She had been so focused on *how* to get past the block that she hadn't stopped to consider the why. The why that had been plaguing her since the beginning of all of this. Why would someone erase her memories? And why *this* memory?

"You think he didn't want me to remember him."

"That's a theory." Graves took another drink. "And with the power of Sansara, on a full moon, at the fall equinox," he said, rattling off parts of the memory that she hadn't even put together, "he'd be capable of it."

"So what's behind the door that he doesn't want me to see?"

"That's the question, isn't it?"

She wiped her nose and met his eyes. He nodded as if he wanted her to say it first. "So where do we go from here? Maybe if we just tried again."

"No," he said sharply. "I won't let you continue to bang your head against a brick wall. We need another solution."

She stared up at the ceiling. "We could go back to Covenant."

He arched an eyebrow. "You're ready for that?"

"Maybe Mafi is right. Maybe this is partially my brain holding back traumatic memories. She said we could come in whenever. Maybe we should go now?"

"Then let's go."

Chapter Forty-Four

M afi met them at the back entrance to Covenant. Her hijab was a riot of sunset colors, and her eyes were dark and disbelieving as she eyed Kierse up and down. "Didn't think you'd be back."

"Didn't really want to," Kierse admitted.

In fact, she'd been chewing on it the entire drive to the hospital. She couldn't ignore the stigma she felt was attached to needing *help*. Her. Kierse. As if *help* was something she'd ever been allowed to ask for before. She'd once had the flu and been bedridden when she'd been working with Jason. It was the most helpless she'd ever felt, and she'd reviled every second of it.

It was one thing to ask for help with her memories when she had thought they were a magical problem. It was another thing entirely to think she'd done this to *herself*. Hidden her memories from her own mind so she didn't have to look at them. Objectively, she knew that wasn't her fault, but it didn't make it any easier to confront.

"But I'm here," she said with a shrug.

"Guess you discovered that his powers aren't endless," she said, shooting Graves a look.

Graves arched an eyebrow. "Who said they weren't?"

Mafi scoffed. "You never change."

"I'm here," Graves said. "With her."

Mafi pursed her lips. "Well, come this way."

Graves put his hand on the small of her back, and together, they followed Mafi into the hospital. Kierse didn't know what exactly to expect, and she was jittery with nerves as they headed down a long, narrow hallway. It felt the same as when she was about to jump into a heist, except instead of excitement she only felt a foreboding sense of dread.

Mafi took them into a room that was less hospital and more therapist office. It was painted in soft blues with dim lighting illuminating the client couch, rows of low bookshelves, potted plants, and a tea kettle. It didn't have the antiseptic smell of the rest of the place, but rather a warm sandalwood scent. It was meant to be inviting.

"You'll wait here. Make yourself comfortable," Mafi said.

Kierse took a seat on the couch, crossing and uncrossing her legs. Graves went immediately to the bookshelves. He scoured the shelves with a neutral expression.

"Anything interesting?" she asked.

"Lots of self help."

"That makes sense, considering…"

He tilted his head as he explored the next shelf over. "This one has books on how to improve your sex life." His eyes lifted to hers, and a smirk played at the edges of his pretty mouth. "I don't have any of these in my library."

She flushed. "Pretty sure we don't need any help in that area."

A knock at the door interrupted whatever was going to come out of his mouth next. The door opened, and Dr. Carrión entered the room. She wore a knee-length skirt with a blue blouse tucked into it and her white coat over top. Her black hair was curly and shoulder length, framing her light brown face. She wheeled forward in her wheelchair and held her hand out. "You must be Kierse."

Kierse stood and shook her hand. "Hi. Yes, that's me."

"I'm Dr. Camila Carrión. It's a pleasure to meet you. I'm glad you decided to come back to the Covenant and apologize that I was back home in Peru when you were last here."

"That's all right," Kierse said.

"And you must be Graves." They shook as well. "Nice to meet you, too. Mafi speaks quite highly of you."

Surprise flickered across his face for the span of a second. Kierse had literally never heard Mafi say so much as a kind word to Graves, let alone about him.

He held out his gloved hand. "Correct. How was your trip to Peru?"

"Productive," Carrión said with a smile. "I'm glad to be back in the city, though. As Dr. Mafi might have mentioned, I'm specifically studying monster mental health in a post-Monster War New York. Though my practice is much broader than that, and I'm happy to have you here today. I've reviewed your file, Kierse, and Dr. Mafi filled me in on your history with memory issues." She turned to Graves. "It was nice to meet you, but I'll continue the rest of the meeting with my patient."

Graves straightened his cuffs. "I'll clear the room," he said smoothly. "I'm just here for her."

The doctor smiled up at him. "Excellent. There's a waiting room down the hall with refreshments and a television if you head to the right out the door."

He held up a book he'd pilfered off of her desk. "I have my entertainment." His gaze shifted to Kierse. "I won't be far."

The implication hung in the air as he exited the room. Dr. Carrión wheeled into a spot across the room from Kierse. "He's quite charming."

Kierse laughed. "Most people find him intimidating."

The doctor grinned. "I could see that. Though he doesn't appear to intimidate you."

"Not anymore."

"That's good. Would you like some tea?" she asked as she poured tea into a mug.

"No, thank you," Kierse said.

"Why don't we start at the beginning? Tell me how this all started in your own words."

Kierse took a deep breath and then released it. "A magical spell was put on me by a Druid when I was a child. I didn't realize that I had magic at all until I met Graves last winter. It turned out the spell dampened my powers, and they returned to me fully once it was gone. Around the same time, I started having nightmares, which ended up being memories of my past with parents that I didn't have any conscious memory of. All I knew—or thought I knew—at the time was that my mom died in childbirth and my dad left me."

"But that wasn't the case?"

"No. They fled with me to New York when their families rejected their marriage. With the help of a potion I got from the goblin market and Graves's powers, I've been piecing back together what happened. But I keep going back to the night the spell was put on me, and there's a block. I get to the room where it happened, but I can't go inside."

"What do you think you'll find in this room?"

Kierse shrugged. "The person who did this to me."

"What will it accomplish if you find them?"

"I'll finally have answers," she tried to explain. "Maybe the person is still alive and I can ask them why they did this to me. I mean, I know that my parents asked him to put the spell on me. To hide me from someone who was trying to harm my family. But I don't know why they made me forget my past in the process."

"What could be a reason that person would want you to forget your past?"

"I don't know," Kierse said. "The why is evading me. I need more information. Maybe the spell was just protecting me. Maybe the general memory loss is part of the spell. Like to hide my magic, I needed to forget all magic."

"So it could be nothing more insidious than a side effect of the protection."

Kierse bit her lip. "It could be, but something tells me that there's more. My memories are starting to come back, but *this* memory is still stubbornly stuck. And I don't know why. So it could be that the Druid didn't want me to see that memory, or this is some side effect from when the spell broke, or like Mafi suggested, my mind won't let me see it."

"And you believe your mind is shielding you from what?"

"Seeing the spell being put on me," she guessed.

"Hmm. Do you think that was particularly traumatic for you?"

"I don't know," she said slowly. "I don't remember."

Carrión glanced down at her tea. "But your parents died shortly after that, correct?"

"I...think so," she whispered.

"Or at least, they abandoned you to the streets and you presumed them dead."

"Right."

"How does that make you feel?"

"Feel?" she asked uncertainly.

"About your parents and their abandonment."

"I don't know," she said slowly. "It's not...great, but I survived."

"Of course you did. You're a survivor. But what if you had children, would you want them to have the same upbringing as you?"

"No," she said automatically, half coming out of the chair in horror. "Children should never have to go through what I went through."

"No one should have to endure a loss like that." The doctor's face was open, and Kierse could see no judgment. "In my experience, the trauma of the loss of a parent, the loss of security, the loss of love is one of the deepest we could ever go through."

Kierse choked as she tried to swallow. "Yes."

"And with that in mind, we need to consider that the trauma you endured may have some impact on why you cannot get past that mental block." The doctor set her tea down before asking, "Is it possible that they died in that room?"

Kierse's chest tightened. "No, I can get *past* that night. I can see me leaving with them after the spell is put on me."

"That's good. That you can move past it." She tapped a finger on the arm of her chair. "Do you have a memory of their death?"

Kierse froze. She had been so hung up on the block that she and Graves hadn't gone further. The thought made her sick to her stomach.

"I don't know," she finally whispered. "I don't think I want to see it."

"And why is that?"

"Would *you* want to see your parents' deaths?" she gasped.

"Both of my parents are dead. I watched my father pass during the war and my mom at a young age. I was there, and it was terrible. The grieving process was excruciating. But that isn't what happened to you. You were never able to grieve their losses for what truly happened. A new history was constructed around you. That is not the same thing. Just because you have learned how to live with what happened doesn't mean that you've healed from it."

Kierse reared back as if struck. That was what she'd done. She'd learned to live with it. And reopening that wound was like someone stabbing her repeatedly. She didn't want to know the future. She didn't want to see it. Whether that was the block or not, she didn't have it in her.

She stood abruptly. "I don't… I think…we're done."

Dr. Carrión frowned. "I understand that what we're discussing is deeply troubling. But you need to face what happened so that you can move forward."

Kierse swallowed. That was what she'd said she wanted, why she'd come. But she hadn't thought it had anything to do with her parents' deaths. She just wanted to get into that stupid room.

"Before you dart out of here, I'm interested in trying something. Are you opposed to doing a spell?" Dr. Carrión reached into her bag and removed a small cauldron, a lighter, and a bag of herbs.

She hesitated. "What does it do?"

"This will clear the mind. It works by releasing trapped energy through its natural pathways. It might help you to see through the block."

"That's possible?"

"Sometimes," she said with a laugh. "This facility is science and magic combined. My medical degree can take me far, but when it comes to magic and monsters, a blend is usually a more elegant solution."

Dr. Carrión set up the spell, turned off the lights, and then spoke a few words over the burning herbs. A cloud of purple smoke puffed out of the pot and suffused the room.

"Breathe the smoke in and then go to that spot in your memory where you are stuck."

Kierse inhaled and let the rich scent fill her lungs. She closed her eyes and tried to think about the apartment that she had never been able to enter. She could see her parents, the woman yelling in Spanish, the dirty hallway. She could sense their anxiety and pain and fear. But the door lurched toward her, and then...she just moved past.

To the street with her blunted senses. Then to her parents' apartment. People in the room, a strange voice issuing a command, blood on the floor. She quickly looked away from it. Then suddenly the street where Jason had found her.

Kierse gasped as she wrenched herself away from it. That time had been different. She still hadn't gotten into the room, but she'd seen something else...something she hadn't seen before. Yet another thing that didn't make any sense.

The doctor turned the lights back on and spent a few minutes in silence as she sifted through the smoke. After a few moments, it began to dissipate, and she sat back heavily in her chair as if the weight of the magic settled into her bones.

"That was...disorienting," Kierse said, feeling her back coming up. She didn't want to ever do that again. "It happened so fast."

"But slowly enough for me to see that there are two blocks," the doctor said.

"What? Two?"

"One is a magical block. I could see it when you hit it like a physical force. But there's a second one around what happened to your parents."

Kierse shook her head. "I don't know what happened to them."

Carrión frowned with a sad expression in her eyes. "You're going to have to face what happened to your parents," she said. "You've looked away from the truth for so long that facing it will be difficult."

Kierse stood again as tears pricked her eyes. "I don't *want* to look at what happened to my parents. Do you even know what you're asking of me? I just want to remember that they loved me. That they left me. Isn't that enough?"

"You have much darkness in your past. I can understand that facing it alone would be difficult. Therapy is a great resource to support you through it, and I'd be happy to continue these sessions with you."

"I don't know," Kierse said. She already felt ready to flee.

"Talking to a professional will help. A way for you to untangle all those events that you would never want your children to experience. But, either way, know that this was all done *to* you. You were just a child who deserved better from a hard world."

Kierse could hardly breathe at those words. This had been done *to* her. What a simple thing to say and something that was so hard to look at. She'd been so independent, on her own two feet for so long, it was hard to even consider that she was this way for a particular reason. That she might have turned out differently in a softer life.

She thanked the psychiatrist and went in search of Graves, uncertain if she would ever return to this place. He must have seen it on her face as he rose to his considerable height.

"Did she help?"

"She said that I had a second mental block that I need to untangle before I'd have a hope of unblocking the magical component."

"A block around what?"

"What happened to my parents."

"Ah," he said slowly. He drew her to him and wrapped his arms around her. She rested her head against his chest, feeling the heat of him against her. She took a fortifying breath. "Take all the time you need. I'll be here when you're ready."

Kierse nodded, uncertain if she'd ever be ready to face that, knowing it was the only way to get what she needed from her memories. A paradox that kept her up late into the night.

Chapter Forty-Five

"A re you sure this is a good idea?" Gen asked as they hopped off the subway in Brooklyn, dressed to the nines for Nate and Maura's engagement party.

Kierse had spent the time since her meeting with Dr. Carrión working on her memory fortifications. She wasn't ready to face what happened with her parents. But she couldn't sit around and do nothing, either. So she'd gone out and pickpocketed a few unsuspecting people to boost her reserves. But it didn't help her mental capacity. She'd hit the wall, and the wall had hit back.

Thankfully, by tonight, Kierse was feeling herself again. Well enough for a quick stop before the festivities.

"Define good idea," Kierse said.

"Won't Lorcan know that you're here?"

"Yes, but we've got that covered," Kierse said. "Just stick to the plan."

"I don't like the plan," Gen admitted.

Kierse huffed, tugging down the hem of her black mini dress. "It was *your* plan."

"I know. This is why we let you plan things. You're good at that part."

"It's fine. The whole thing is going to be fine." Kierse winked at her. "Let Operation Jail Break commence."

Gen laughed and followed her down the Brooklyn streets. Kierse clocked a few patrols on rooftops—not that the Druids needed them to give the boss a heads-up she was in their territory. The second she'd crossed the bridge into Brooklyn, she could feel Lorcan.

Now that she knew what this was between them, that pressure in her chest made perfect sense. It was like a fishhook caught against her breastbone, and she just needed to follow the string back to its owner to find Lorcan.

She pressed her hand against her chest. Not yet.

"You okay?" Gen asked.

"Yeah," she lied.

Gen pursed her lips. "You can feel him?"

"Over there," Kierse said, pointing vaguely in the direction of his headquarters. The direction they were circling toward.

"It's that specific?"

"If I think about it," she admitted.

"So he'll be on us soon," Gen realized.

"Guess we'll have to be quicker."

Gen sighed. Always finding Kierse's propensity for danger unnerving. "Hurry."

They rounded another corner before hitting their drop point. Niamh's head appeared at the back entrance of a building, her burgundy hair up in a complicated braided twist. Her red-painted smile widened as she saw them.

"Hello, girls," she said with a wink.

"Niamh," Kierse said as she ducked inside.

Gen shot her a shy smile. "Hi."

"My little acolyte," Niamh said. "Never took you to be a rule breaker."

"I make an exception for Ethan," Gen said with her head lifted high.

"Then let's get going."

Kierse and Gen followed her through the labyrinth of Druid corridors—a bunch of empty office spaces and then closed apartment doors—before getting into more familiar territory.

"You might have to do some offensive work," Niamh warned Gen. "As we get closer."

Gen bit her lip. "You can't?"

"Oh, I *can*. But I'd like to see how my pupil is progressing."

"Offensive work?" Kierse asked. She glanced between Niamh and Gen in alarm. "What exactly are you teaching her?"

"You'll see," Niamh said with a smirk.

Gen muttered a few words to herself and took a deep breath as they continued forward. They were nearly to the barracks when a pair of Druid guards appeared in their way.

"Gen," Niamh said.

But Gen had already moved in front before either of them could react to intruders. Her eyes were closed and she moved on instinct, sliding through dance-like steps as she got in close to the two guards.

"What the…?" the first man asked.

Gen touched her finger to his throat and whispered, "Sleep," under her breath.

The woman next to him watched with wide eyes as she realized who she was dealing with. Kierse could see surrender in her eyes, but Gen wasn't looking at her. She wasn't looking at anything, in fact.

Then she clipped the girl in the kidneys and said, "Down."

She only opened her eyes after they both collapsed to the ground. Kierse's jaw was on the floor.

"What the fuck was that?" Kierse demanded.

"Healing," Niamh said simply.

"That...doesn't look like healing."

"There are two sides to healing," Gen said. Her eyes drifted to the pair of Druids with a frown, but she recited the words rote. "Sustaining the body and relieving the body. All life is a circle, an ouroboros, birth and life and death. You cannot learn only parts of the practice or else it stunts all growth."

"Precisely," Niamh said with pride in her voice.

Gen preened under Niamh's praise.

Niamh nudged Kierse with a laugh. "Stop looking so shocked. They're just sleeping. We also don't have unlimited resources. We don't want to have to do that with everyone."

"Well, at least I know you can handle yourself," Kierse said once they'd moved the guards out of the way and continued on at a faster clip. "If you're learning *death* magic."

"We don't wield that," Niamh said automatically. "Only to ease suffering."

Kierse had doubts. If someone could use the magic, then they would. Of that she was certain.

It was only a few more minutes before Niamh stopped in front of Ethan's room. Kierse focused her mind on the hook in her chest. Lorcan had moved, but he wasn't heading their direction just yet. They had a few minutes before her part began.

Gen knocked twice on the door. Her hand still hovered in the air when it was wrenched open.

Time froze as the three friends looked between each other. Ethan, who had always been gangly, standing there all beefed out, wearing a green T-shirt a size too small to make him look even bigger and fitted running shorts. Gen with a hand toward him, almost as if she couldn't believe he was real. And Kierse, trying to fight back the hurt of their last interaction, hoping Gen could heal it like she always did.

"Gen!" Ethan gasped, throwing his arms around her. "What are you doing here?"

Gen buried her face into his chest and squeezed. "We came to see you."

"We should get inside," Niamh warned.

"There's not a lot of time," Kierse added. She put her hand on her heart again. It was like she could feel that *soulmate* bond tugging closer.

"It's not much," Ethan said, self-conscious of his space as they barreled inside.

In fact, it made the attic look like luxury. There was a narrow twin bed against one wall. A utilitarian desk next to that with a wooden chair. Papers were neatly piled on the desk, and an ink pen rested on top. A chest sat at the end of the bed with drawers for his provided clothing. There were no familiar touches. No pictures. No books. And worst of all for Ethan, no plants.

"Where are your plants?" Kierse asked on instinct.

"There's a greenhouse," he said quickly. "It's part of classes."

Kierse eyed him skeptically. "You're okay only seeing them during classes."

Ethan tensed at the words. "Are you second-guessing the curriculum or are you just here to argue with me again?"

"Stop," Gen said.

Kierse's back went up immediately at his words. She could see Ethan was ready to bite again if he felt his place as a Druid was threatened. And that *wasn't* why they were here.

"I'm not here to fight. I never want to fight with you," she said softly.

"We're here because tonight is Nate and Maura's engagement party," Gen told him.

Ethan's jaw dropped. "They're *engaged*?"

"Yes. The wedding is in a few weeks," Gen said. "After your boot camp thing is finished. We thought you'd want to come to the party tonight."

"I do," he said automatically. Then he wavered. "But…"

"What's the worst they can do to you?" Kierse pushed.

Ethan's eyes lifted to Niamh's. "Well? Would they kick me out?"

"Maybe," she conceded. "But you're a strong talent. And you're kind of essential in several ways."

"The triskel magic," Ethan conceded, looking between them. "Which we should be training."

Kierse wrinkled her nose. "Yeah."

"But also because you're important," Niamh said, pointing at Kierse, "to her."

"What does she have to do with it?" Ethan asked, still sullen.

Kierse sighed. "I'm Lorcan's 'soulmate.'" She mimed the quotes around the word.

Ethan's stunned expression was almost satisfying. His religious-like fervor for Lorcan, however, far from pleased Kierse. Lorcan was charismatic and beguiling in many ways. She wasn't sure how to keep Ethan from falling any farther under his spell.

"You can get out for a night," Niamh promised.

"Come with us," Gen said, grabbing his hand. "Just for tonight. We'll have you back in the morning."

"Like Cinderella," he mused.

Kierse could already see him bending. He'd always been persuadable. It was both an advantage and a flaw. Much like Kierse's own cynicism.

"Please," Gen said softly.

"Fuck," Kierse said, eyeing the door. "He's on the move. I need to go."

"Go?" Ethan asked.

"Please come with us," Kierse said as she headed toward the door. "I'm sorry about what happened last time, but I miss you. We both miss you. We want you there."

"Plus, Corey is going to be in attendance," Gen dropped casually.

Ethan's eyes widened further. "Really?"

"Yes," Kierse confirmed. "I'll see you on the other side. I hope, at least. Because I'm about to brave Lorcan to let you sneak out."

Then she was through the door, crossing her fingers and toes that Ethan would bend and join them for a night. Maybe then the fissure that had appeared between them wouldn't turn into a chasm.

Kierse rounded the corner, jogging to get out of the building. It had been Gen's idea to use Lorcan's connection to her against him. After she'd heard Graves mention it, she'd thought maybe Kierse could be bait, luring him on a wild goose chase away from Ethan so that they could sneak him away.

She wasn't sure it had worked until she'd dropped out onto Broadway a fair distance from Ethan's building to find Lorcan loitering against the brick wall next to the door. Her traitorous heart skipped a beat at the sight of him.

He smiled, broad and predatory, as if he felt it. "Hello, little songbird."

"Lorcan," she said softly.

He dazzled in a summer gray suit. The jacket open to reveal a crisp white button-up with the top two buttons undone, his dark hair was windswept off his forehead. Those glittering blue eyes traveled over her like sunlight kissing across her exposed skin.

When Gen had suggested this, Kierse had thought this would be easy. That *knowing* she could manipulate him the way he had been manipulating her would make it so. Standing in the presence of the Oak King, she was less certain.

"You dressed up for me," he said with a smirk as he eyed the short black dress and knee-high boots.

She cleared her throat. "Engagement party, actually."

"Ah, your little wolf friend."

"Indeed."

"You thought you'd swing by before you go so I can see your outfit." He twirled his finger in place as if he thought she might actually turn for him.

"Not exactly."

"No?" He chuckled. "Well, you've been on quite an adventure."

"Have I?"

He pushed off the brick and approached her. She had to tilt her chin up to meet his inimitable gaze. "Did you get what you were looking for?"

"Are you so sure that isn't you?"

He laughed softly. "You never responded to my messages and have been dodging my surveillance."

"We already had this conversation," Kierse said. "If you want your men to follow me, then you're going to have to send out better recruits."

"You also recommended that I stop stalking you." His hand swept up as if to brush her hair off her face. Fear racketed through her. What if he touched her and she couldn't say no, couldn't escape, didn't have anyone there to stop him? His hand froze, his head tilting almost as if he could see the thoughts painted clearly on her face. "You think I would hurt you?"

"No," she said. "Not on purpose."

"Those are two different things."

"I've known you to be the type of person who believes the ends justify the means."

"Never with you," he promised.

He dropped his hand and took a step back. The pressure in her chest dissipated so she could breathe. Had it gotten stronger?

"I wanted to apologize," he said, meeting her gaze. "I never wanted you to find out about our soulmate bond that way."

"Yet you didn't tell me yourself when you had the chance."

"I wanted to tell you when I first realized, but then you were gone to Dublin. When you returned...I didn't want to unduly influence you."

"That's rich, coming from you."

Lorcan straightened to his full height. "Why are you hell-bent on making me the villain here?"

"I'm not."

He shot her a look. "I've been heavy handed, I admit, but I haven't lied to you. As you are lying to yourself right now. As *he* has lied to you."

Kierse bristled at the words. "Don't bring him into this."

"How can I not? You're acting like he's innocent. Like he didn't hide your heritage from you and lie to you about your abilities and hold you back from progressing." He spread his arms wide. "I'm standing here offering you all of that and more—a place among your family, safety, security, and all the knowledge I have of your people. If that's not enough, we are magically bonded."

"What's the catch?"

"You have been so hurt all these years you cannot see that the people who care for you want nothing from you. Just you."

"And that's what you want?"

"I cannot deny it." His hand landed on her chest right where the thrum was loudest. "And neither can you."

The contact went straight through her. Her head felt fuzzy. Her body yearned. It would be so easy to give in to this feeling, to the need that shot through her body and burned her nerve endings and made her question everything she had done to get her to this moment.

"What would it have been like if you had found me first?" she whispered.

"Bliss."

She believed him. It would have been everything.

And then he released her.

His fingers brushed her chin upward, and he pressed the softest of kisses into her forehead. His hand shook slightly.

"You can take Ethan tonight for your party," Lorcan promised. He'd known all along. "Have him back before morning meditation."

Kierse broke free from him, feeling shaky and uncertain. "Okay."

"And Kierse," he said softly, "come back to me."

Chapter Forty-Six

Kierse met Ethan and Gen at the subway station. Ethan had changed into khakis and a green polo with the Druid acorn on the breast. She would have rolled her eyes at him if they weren't in a fight.

"We're all good."

Ethan looked skeptical. "Lorcan just let you leave?"

"He told us to have a good time." She ruffled his hair. "Just have to get Cinderella back before morning meditation."

"He *knows*?" Ethan looked horrified.

"Yeah, I don't know how, but he was fine with it."

"Anything for you," Gen teased as they trotted onto the M line train.

"Niamh decided to stay?" Kierse asked.

Gen purposely looked out the window. "She said it probably was for the best. Pupils and students shouldn't fraternize or something."

"Never stopped me," Kierse muttered.

Gen shrugged with a half smile. "If only we all had your audacity."

"Personally, I don't want to hear about your fraternizations," Ethan said.

"Why not?" Kierse asked, bristling at the implication.

"Don't pick a fight with her." Gen poked a finger into his stomach. "This is a happy night."

Ethan leaned back in the empty subway car. "Can we talk about how the fuck you and Lorcan are soulmates, then?"

"No," Kierse said automatically.

"It's new," Gen warned him. "She only recently found out."

"How's that possible?"

"It's always been there," Kierse said, her gaze wandering back out the window as they passed over the East River. "At least, I think it's always been there. It was muffled by the spell, but even when I was around him last winter, I was drawn to him. I kept feeling like…he wasn't a bad guy. Despite all the harm he was causing me and you, I still felt something there that didn't make any sense to me, because I was so angry with him all the time."

Gen leaned her head onto Kierse's shoulder. "You still are."

"Maybe more so. He knew. He's known since the spell came off what was there and didn't tell me."

"As if that would have made anything better," Ethan said. "You told him you'd kill him the next time you saw him. Telling you then was a death sentence." Then he added almost as an afterthought, "And…he isn't the bad guy."

"I don't know. I don't want to think about it."

"That won't make it go away," Gen said softly.

"Yeah. What else should I do? We're in the middle of…" She glanced at Ethan warily. She wasn't accustomed to thinking of him as the enemy. "Work," she finished.

Ethan blew out a breath. "What are you stealing now?"

Kierse's lip quirked up at that. "Something fun."

"You always think it's fun," he argued.

"Because it always is."

"Maybe after, then," Gen said.

"Which is when, exactly?" Ethan asked. "Because we should start training our magic together *now*. I have weekly private lessons with Lorcan on my growing powers and the abilities of a triskel. You know he was part of a triskel?"

"Yes," Kierse said. "He told me."

"Well, he's the only person still alive who was part of one. He's the only one who can train us."

"That isn't true," Gen said automatically.

Ethan looked like he was going to argue, but somehow Kierse knew where she was going with this. "Niamh was part of it?"

Gen nodded. "A Druid, a High Priestess, and a wisp."

"And Lorcan's wife was a wisp," Kierse said, letting the pieces fall into place. "They were a triskel until she was killed."

"That's why Niamh has been in Dublin. She finds it…difficult to be here, around Lorcan, after Saoirse's death."

Kierse imagined one of her two best friends dead for a hundred years and how she would still feel the pain of that for all the years to come. She couldn't imagine that weight. Didn't want to have to imagine it.

"So Niamh could train us," Gen added quickly. "If Lorcan is the problem…"

"Why is Lorcan the problem?" Ethan asked in a huff. "He's your soulmate. Shouldn't you be like jumping for joy and moving into Brooklyn and shit?"

Kierse shot him a look, and Gen burst into laughter.

"When has *anything* been that easy with Kierse?" Gen asked. "As soon as it looks too good to be true, she's side-eyeing everything."

Ethan breathed out with a small smile. "That's fair."

"We do need to train, though," Gen said softly. She glanced up and met Kierse's gaze. "It saved your life. Imagine what else we could do."

"So much more," Ethan agreed.

Kierse sighed. The last thing she wanted was a reason to spend more time in Druid territory. Her relationship with Lorcan was complicated enough without adding time spent in Brooklyn where she could *feel* him under her skin at every moment. But Gen and Ethan were pleading with her, their eyes round and open. She wanted this with them more than she hated dealing with the discomfort of Lorcan.

"Fine," Kierse said. Because they wanted it. And she had a hard time telling them no.

Gen leaned her head on Ethan's shoulder, and he threaded his fingers through her hair like he always had back in the day. For all intents and purposes, everything was back to normal. Kierse knew this was a hesitant truce with Ethan, but her capitulation had brought them closer together again. Maybe that was part of the reason she'd done it. She missed him. She missed them all being together. Life had gotten much more chaotic since they'd left the attic.

When the M dropped them off, they left the platform and walked out onto the streets of Midtown. East 53rd Street was the sort of glam that Kierse avoided unless she needed some easy pickpocketing and was willing to put up with the mess of tourists. The subway exit let out in front of a chain store that sold luxury watches and somehow had survived the war, and across from a tech company that had overtaken a historical 5th Avenue building.

People crawled all over the sidewalks, and the trio huddled together as they traversed the crowds, turning left onto 5th and then crossing the street to 52nd. Nestled in amidst the high rises was a five-story building with a wrought iron gate and handrail up the stone steps—the entrance to Club 21. The front edifice was all floor-to-ceiling windows looking out on an elegant front porch. Known more commonly as 21, the club had been a speakeasy in the 1920s and a place for celebrities and politicians to dine and drink over the years. While it had closed its doors during the war, it, too, had made a revival in this newfound peace.

Gen and Ethan climbed the stairs first. Kierse put her hand on the railing absentmindedly as she followed, then quickly pulled it back, hissing.

"Are you okay?" Gen asked.

Kierse glanced down at her hand. It was red and irritated, but not bubbling or blistered like it felt like it should be. But damn, this iron was *not* her friend.

"Just...iron."

Ethan tilted his head. "What's wrong with iron?"

"Having a bit of an allergy since the spell came down," she admitted. She showed them her hand. "Drains my magic, too."

"I can fix the first part," Gen said, murmuring a few words.

Her palm miraculously healed over, erasing all the pain.

Ethan's eyes grew wide. "Whoa! Look at you!"

Gen flushed. "Yeah. I've been training, too. Maybe you'll show us what you can do other than strut around with all those muscles."

Ethan rolled his eyes. "We're doing more than just working out."

"Doesn't look like it," Kierse teased.

The front door opened as they approached. Standing in the doorway was Nate's second-in-command, Ronan. A cigarette was already dangling from his pouty lips as he strode outside.

Ronan's dark eyes tracked the three of them before landing squarely on Gen. "Hey, there," he said with a hunter's smile.

"Hi," she squeaked, suddenly shy.

"I was hoping you'd show up," Ronan said.

Kierse and Ethan shared a look that filled her with glee. Of their trio, Gen had always been the least interested in relationships. It was delicious to watch her deal with Ronan's attention.

"We'll meet you inside," Kierse told Gen and then pushed Ethan across the threshold.

The interior was every bit as beautiful as the exterior. A large, circular bar took up the center of the establishment, and model airplanes and boats, football helmets, and other toy paraphernalia hung overhead. There were a dozen circular tables covered with gingham tablecloths. The chairs were filled with Dreadlords and their friends and family, the restaurant full to bursting with those eager to celebrate the happy couple.

Corey jumped to his feet when Kierse and Ethan stepped into the bar. His jaw dropped as he took in Ethan from head to toe through the dimly lit bar. Ethan jerked forward like he was going to run to him. Kierse wanted to encourage him, but she knew her own history with Ethan was murky. She didn't know how Corey felt about it all, only that he loved Ethan very much. The rest Ethan would have to figure out.

"Hey," Ethan said as they approached. His Adam's apple bobbed with discomfort. "It's good to see you."

Corey, to his credit, flashed him a too-pretty smile. "Miss me?"

Their builds were more similar now than they had been months earlier—

they were both stronger since the split but emotionally injured from the break. Yet where Ethan's prized curls had been shaved down, Corey had let his glossy dark hair grow nearly to his shoulders. Different, and yet the same in all the ways that mattered—at least, Kierse thought so.

Ethan dipped his chin at Corey's tease. "Every day. You don't hate me?"

"I might have cursed you and your ancestors for a few months."

"My poor ancestors. What did they ever do to you?"

Corey arched an eyebrow. "Allowed you to get away with this stupidity."

"Well…"

"I thought you had a few more weeks."

"I do, but…"

"We broke him out," Kierse interrupted. "Enjoy!"

Corey pulled her into a hug. "Thank you. The Roulettes owe you one. *I* owe you one."

Kierse would have gladly accepted a favor from the Roulettes, the gang on the Lower East Side that Colette partnered with for protection for the brothel, but she didn't feel that this was an owed moment. "I just want you both to be happy."

Kierse left them alone, grabbing a snack from the bar as she wandered deeper into the bar. She'd been so hungry lately. Using her magic all the time was exhausting.

She surveyed the room, finding the leader of the Roulettes, Carmine Garcia, perched on a chair some distance away. He had smooth, light-brown skin and wore his thick, black hair slicked back. He was leaning toward Colette as if she were his entire world. They had been having an affair for years. Colette never admitted it was exclusive, even though Kierse suspected it was, aside from client work.

And there was Madame Colette—the earth and moon paused in their orbits to revel in her loveliness. Gen was so much her mirror, and so much a mashup of whoever her father was. Colette wore a flattering maroon dress with little tassels that swayed with her figure. Her milky skin was unlined and her lids a deep blue of the ocean right before a storm. When she set those eyes on Kierse, it was like coming home.

"About time you showed your face," Colette said as she rose to her feet.

"Did you need someone to properly pour your brandy?" Kierse asked with a smile.

"At least you remember your place."

Her smile stretched wider.

"Did you bring my daughter with you?"

"Genesis and Ethan both," Kierse told her. "Though they each got a bit…distracted."

Colette's gaze followed her to where Ethan was in deep conversation with Corey. She sighed as if aggrieved. "Youth."

Kierse extracted herself from Colette and went to congratulate Nate and Maura. They were seated at the front of the room surrounded by Dreadlords and a handful of Maura's nursing friends, who kept eyeing the wolves with interest.

"You made it!" Maura cried as she jumped up to hug Kierse. She was dressed in a stunning salwar kameez—a two-piece garment comprised of long, flowy pants and a knee-length sheath of off-white and gold, embroidered with shimmering beads. The sleeves were sheer with intricate embellishments. A cream shawl draped across her narrow shoulders. Matching dangly earrings and bangles completed the ensemble.

"Good to see you," Nate said with a grin. "I see you got Ethan out, too."

"We did."

"Any trouble?" he asked.

"Always."

Maura laughed. "You should know better than that, Nathaniel. This is Kierse McKenna we're talking about."

"If you weren't my favorite kind of trouble," Nate said, pressing a kiss to Maura's wrist, "it would certainly be Kierse's bullshit."

Maura rolled her eyes and yanked her arm away. "Where is your plus-one? Tall, dark, dangerous." She waggled her eyebrows. "I thought you'd bring him along, too."

"Uh, yeah. He's not like…social."

Nate coughed into his beer. "That's a word for it."

Maura pouted. "I was *so* looking forward to meeting him."

"Next time," Kierse said uncertainly.

Even though she very much doubted that Graves would brave a wedding, either.

She was about to change the subject when the front door opened again, letting the last lingering bits of daylight into the darkened room. Kierse only turned because the rest of the room had gone quiet.

A nightmare had walked into their midst.

Graves.

Chapter Forty-Seven

Kierse was sure that she was seeing a mirage. But no, it was Graves in the entrance to Club 21 for Nate and Maura's engagement party. He was dressed in a classic black suit with a black button-up and tie paired with fitted black gloves. He looked every bit as threatening and terrifying as she'd ever seen him. Those thunderstorm eyes assessed the room for a challenge and found none. He didn't need a weapon on hand. He *was* the weapon.

The tension released from his shoulders like a snake uncoiling.

Her breath caught as heat pooled in her core. She could practically feel him pressing against her mind, offering her a glimpse into what he wanted from her. How he wanted to take her. Or was that just her mind running away from her? How quickly could she get him out of this room to ease the ache in her?

Graves stalked across the room. The crowd parted for him as if they could feel the weight of his oppressive gaze on them. She shivered at his approach, wondering exactly how this was going to go down. Graves had a charisma that she could not deny, but she had never seen him in this sort of situation. Only in ones in which he was in command.

Here he was in *her* world. Not his.

His hand slid around her waist, and he pressed a possessive kiss to her lips, claiming her before the entire room. "Wren," he said against her mouth. "Sorry I'm late."

"Late," she breathed, suddenly forgetting how words worked.

"I went to check out the door. It's gone. Curator must have moved it."

"Oh." She brought herself back to the present. "You went into the market alone?"

"I met Vale," he reassured her. "I had to pay him for his help last time anyway. I was planning to be here when Gen mentioned you would arrive, but I got held up."

"Gen mentioned?"

"She gave me the information," he said casually. A smirk on his lips said he'd wanted to surprise her. "I was invited, correct?"

"I have a plus-one."

"You weren't planning to bring anyone else?"

"I had another offer."

His smile faltered. "I bet you did."

"Didn't take him up on it, though," she said, threading her fingers through his tie. It wasn't a flat black like she'd expected but instead was embroidered with holly vines. Apropos.

"I'm sure he loved that."

"He didn't, but I bet you do."

Graves smiled. A real genuine smile that made her heart stutter. "I do, Wren. I very much do." He gestured to her waiting friends. "Now are you going to introduce me, or should I take my gloves off?"

Kierse laughed, an emotion that made Graves almost glow. "I can do the intros."

"About fucking time," Maura said, nearly jumping up and down. "I'm so excited to meet you!"

Graves held out a gloved hand, and Maura put hers in it without hesitation. She could see that was a novelty for Graves. People didn't touch him if they knew who and what he was. But Maura didn't seem to care.

"The pleasure is all mine," Graves said gallantly.

Nate rose to his feet. "You know," he said, when he shook hands with him, "she normally dates girls. This is a huge downgrade."

Kierse sighed heavily. "Nate!"

Graves smirked. "To be fair, I typically date men."

Nate's eyebrows shot up at that. "Well, she is special."

"She is," Graves confirmed.

With the tension defused, Nate and Maura pulled them into their circle of friends. They sank into chairs and faced the couple as conversation resumed around them. People still glanced over at Graves as if uncertain when the bomb was about to go off in the room, but otherwise, it was as if they were any other couple at the party.

The whole thing was a novelty. Having Graves at her side. His arm across the back of her chair. Their legs brushing under the table. Him listening intently to everyone's conversations, though only speaking up when a question was directed at him.

With his general aura of command, she had never considered him an introvert. But of course, he lived alone and had for years. He didn't like large crowds of people and wanted his silence and privacy. Was this draining him to be around people he didn't know? A million questions she had never considered. A million experiences she had never thought she'd have with him. The possibility of each one as captivating as the next.

It was some time before Ethan and Corey reappeared in the speakeasy. Gen had ditched Ronan at some point to speak with her mother. And now all three of her friends rounded the table and took a seat in front of Graves and Kierse. Ethan sat stiffly across the table from Graves, his chin held high, eyes watchful and alert. Corey shot him an exasperated look before slouching back next to him. As if they'd already had this conversation and Ethan was being ridiculous.

Kierse didn't doubt they'd all talked about Graves's appearance and decided in advance what to do about it. But Gen had spent enough time with him now that she was almost...not afraid of him. Corey looked as if he believed Ethan's fear was overstated. And Ethan...well, he looked like he'd rather be doing anything else.

"So," Graves said, placing one gloved hand on the table. Ethan's eyes shot to it as if it were an affront. "Are they still making you run miles at midnight during the full moon?"

Ethan's eyes widened. "What?"

Gen furrowed her brow. "Who is?"

"The Druids," Graves said.

Kierse glanced at him, wondering what his game was.

"How do you know about that?" Ethan demanded.

"So yes?" Graves said with a long-suffering sigh. "That was the worst part. As if we weren't already training our mind and body and magic from dawn until dusk—then to wake us up to run by moonlight." He looked at Ethan with a forlorn expression. "'Course we at least got to run through Wicklow with the Irish wind whipping across our faces."

Ethan's jaw dropped. "*You* trained with the Druids?"

"What? They didn't tell you that part?" he asked, knowing full well they had absolutely left that out.

"Don't tease," Kierse said. "Graves trained with Lorcan when they were both teenagers. They came up in the Druidic Order together."

Ethan looked like his mind was going to explode. "But you're not a Druid!"

"Not anymore," Graves agreed.

"How could you have been a Druid?" Ethan demanded.

Kierse and Gen exchanged a grin. Well, that had gotten Ethan talking.

"The same way that you are," Graves said. "My mother was a High Priestess."

"How do you know who my mother was?"

Graves raised an eyebrow. Knowledge himself. He'd gone digging.

"I'm naturally curious," he said.

"Cat," Kierse muttered.

"No wonder Anne Boleyn picked you," Gen said. "I had been wondering."

"Anne goes where she will."

Ethan chewed on his lip like he wanted to say more. Finally, Corey sat forward and put his arms on the table. "Can you just tell him about your training? Otherwise he's going to torture himself all night wondering what it was like but refusing to ask."

"Corey," Ethan groaned. He ducked his head into Corey's shoulder. "I'm fine."

"There were fewer of us back then," Graves said. "Magic was still a big fear in the countryside, and we had to hide our existence. The Druids had a stronghold outside of Wicklow and another within Dublin. We switched between the two for training. There were five of us who were close at the time. Two Druids, two High Priestesses, and a wisp."

Kierse stilled, enraptured as he spoke about a time that she'd rarely heard him discuss. Let alone to a *table of people*.

"Myself, Lorcan, Niamh, Emilie, and Saoirse," Graves said like he had gone very far off. "Saoirse and Niamh were best friends then. They'd grown up together. Lorcan was in love with Saoirse right away, though that took much longer to develop. Both Niamh and Lorcan were in love with the wisp at the center of their triskel."

Gen and Ethan glanced at Kierse, and she held her hands up. "I already have enough to deal with."

They laughed. A sound that was so familiar it warmed her heart. She wanted to bottle it up so she could listen to it anytime she needed.

Graves looked like he was going to say something more about Emilie, but instead he kept going, describing the grueling routine they'd followed. Ethan interjected now and then to explain the differences. A picture built of the respite Graves had had in the countryside, with friends and a family she knew he'd never had before or since. It was a glimpse into a different time and a different world.

"I can't believe they had you get *high* on the full moon to unlock your magic," Ethan said with wide eyes. "Like psychedelic mushrooms!"

Graves shrugged. "It was a different time. It calmed us down enough to let us reach further."

"Don't get any ideas," Corey said with a laugh. "I cannot imagine you on psychedelics."

Ethan started to argue with Corey about the idea. Kierse leaned into Graves and smirked. He arched an eyebrow in response. If he'd had his gloves off, she could have lifted her absorption and known exactly what was running through that mind, but as it was, she was pretty sure she already did. He'd built a bridge. A small but necessary one.

The night continued on with laughter and joy. Ethan and Corey got up later to dance. Gen twirled the room with Maura and her nursing friends. Graves slid his hand into Kierse's and surveyed the crowd, an almost contented look on his dark face.

Nate was slightly inebriated when he approached them late in the evening. "So, this is really happening?"

"It's happening," Kierse agreed. Graves nodded. "Actually, we have business to discuss with you, if you're sober enough for it."

Nate laughed. "I'm probably not."

"You'll want to hear this," Kierse said.

Graves nodded. "We should go somewhere private."

Nate gestured to the party. "Where exactly would that be?"

"I know a place."

Graves came to his feet, offering his hand to Kierse to help her up. Then they headed across the room, dodging the drunk partygoers and bypassing the restrooms. Kierse glanced sideways down the darkened hallway. Gen had disappeared some time ago and had never returned.

Her eyes widened as she saw Ronan had her pushed up against the wooden paneling of a back hallway, their mouths connected and limbs entwined. As if they were trying to get as much out of this kiss as they could without shredding each other's clothing.

Nate guffawed behind them at the display. Kierse grabbed his arm before he could say anything. "Leave them. They've earned it," she hissed.

"Fine," he grumbled.

Kierse didn't know what was going on with Gen—if Niamh's rejection had pushed her into Ronan's arms, or if Ronan was what she really wanted. But Kierse had too many relationship problems herself to interfere where she wasn't needed. Gen was an adult and could figure it out herself.

Graves turned to a hardwood door labeled CELLAR. He pushed against it, but the door was locked. Kierse grinned, stepping around him to pop the lock with one of the pins in her hair.

His eyes shot to hers. "You're a little too good at that."

"You like it," she teased.

"Sure is handy," Nate agreed as they started down the set of stairs.

Graves flipped a switch to reveal the massive cellar stocked floor to ceiling with fancy, vintage wines. "Used to house old presidents' and movie stars' wine collections," Graves told them. He continued past the exclusive tasting table set for a dozen to an upper right corner of the shelving. "Ah, here we go." He removed a bottle the color of blood. He plucked a wine opener from a nearby tray and began to uncork it. "I left a few bottles here in the eighties," he said as he poured a small amount into two glasses and passed them off to Nate and Kierse.

Nate gulped it back and frowned. "I'm too drunk to know if that was good."

Kierse chuckled before taking a sip. "Whoa. It's so smooth."

Graves poured himself a glass and tasted the wine. "Ah yes, just as I remembered it. I'm not sure how many bottles are left of this."

"Are you trying to butter me up?" Nate asked. "You could have started with this when you arrived."

"I came to the party for Kierse," Graves said.

"I came for business," Kierse said, elbowing Nate and then took a refilled glass from Graves. She leaned into the table. "We need your help."

Graves sighed. "'Need' and 'help' are probably the wrong words."

"Wait," Nate said after downing half a glass of the expensive wine, "are you bringing me into the inner circle?"

Graves shot him a look.

"We want you to help us with a heist to steal the cauldron," Kierse said. "It's going to be at Monster Con. We're putting a team together. We know you have an invitation, and we need back up inside the Plaza."

Nate looked between them for a moment, suddenly focused, his brilliant mind strategizing the way she'd seen him do so many times. "I have an invite. I assume you do, too?" Graves nodded. "How are you getting her in to steal it? No guests are allowed. Security is tight."

"We're still working on that," Graves assured him.

"I'll get in if I have to come through the vents," Kierse assured him. "I'm not worried about the Plaza."

"Hmm...how dangerous is this going to be?"

Kierse winced. "If we do it right, not at all."

"And if we do it wrong?"

Graves shrugged. "We'd be going up against a room full of the most powerful monsters in the city."

"Great. Sounds like a good time. Where do I sign up?" he asked sarcastically.

"If we succeed, I'm offering everyone the same thing," Graves said slowly, swirling the wine in the glass. "A chance to use the cauldron once when we have it."

Nate blinked from Graves to Kierse. "What does it do, exactly?"

"It has power beyond comprehension—healing, food, magic. It provides."

Kierse leaned forward, resting her hand on Nate's. "I asked Graves about the incubus curse, and he said there was no known cure."

Nate slumped, deflated. "I knew, but...I still hoped."

"But the cauldron might help."

Nate didn't pull back, but he looked at her in deep confusion for a moment before it dawned on him. "You're sure? You're not just giving me false hope?"

Kierse turned to Graves then. She *wasn't* sure. Neither of them had ever laid eyes on the thing. But the legends hinted at the possibility.

"It's not a guarantee," Graves said. "But these are magical artifacts of the gods. The sword alone was able to break the spell put on Kierse. If I had it in my possession still, I'd see if it would also work to break an incubus curse. However, it is no longer in my possession. So, if you help me get the cauldron, we can see if it heals magical curses."

"All right. Yes," Nate said automatically. He held his hand out to Graves. "Count me in."

Chapter Forty-Eight

Graves finalized plans with Nate while they polished off the bottle of wine. She hadn't been drinking much before this, but the vintage wine hit her harder than she had expected and now she was pleasantly buzzed. Once Nate made his way out of the cellar, all thoughts of leaving with him vanished.

"You handled that well," Kierse said, setting down her empty wineglass and walking toward Graves.

"He would have done it for you without an incentive."

"Perhaps," she said. "How did things go with Walter?"

Graves sighed. "Walter's different. I'm still not sure if he's on our side."

"Can you blame him? His magic burned out and you kicked him out when he was at his lowest." She arched an eyebrow as she ran a finger down his tie. "Who does that sound like?"

"Do not compare us," he said.

"I just mean that he's hurt by what you did. He doesn't trust you."

"I don't trust him, either."

"We need him."

Graves bit down a curse. "I know."

When Gen had invited Graves, Kierse hadn't thought he'd show up, let alone charm her friends and *belong* in this world. Never in a million years had she thought he would go this far out of his element. Only a few months earlier he'd refused to even have anyone in the house.

She liked this side of him. She liked it a lot.

"Thank you for what you did with Ethan."

"Which is?"

She raised her eyebrows as she drew him in by his tie. "Told him about your past. Talked to him about being a Druid. By telling him the truth, he didn't see you as the monster they paint you as."

"That's a problem," Graves said, his lips an inch from hers, "because I am a monster."

"My monster."

"Whatever you want me to be."

Graves swept his hand across the table and sent the glasses and dinner plates flying, shattering as they fell to the ground. He grasped her ass and lifted her into the air. She hastily wrapped her legs around his waist before he set her down on the edge of the table. He dragged their mouths together, stealing her breath. She wanted to taste every inch of him and not stop until she was through. It was all tongue and teeth and longing as he clenched his hands in her dress. Her fingers grasped the lapels of his suit coat, wanting nothing more than to strip him out of it.

"I've been wanting to get under this dress all night," Graves told her.

He slid between her legs, rucking her dress up to her hip until it barely covered the tops of her thighs. His kiss was tender but unrelenting like he wanted her to know how much she meant to him and at the same time he wanted to devour her whole. Fuck the rest of the world. He just wanted *her*.

Graves's seeking fingers slipped under the hem of her dress, and she lifted first one hip, then the other, helping him shuck off her black thong. He tossed it to the side and immediately slid his fingers between her wet folds before slipping inside of her. Her head tipped back on a muffled moan.

"The room is soundproof," he promised.

She felt the kiss of his magic brush against her skin. She could be as loud as she wanted and no one would hear or dare disturb them.

He only gave her a few harsh strokes with his fingers before he released his cock and fit it to the entrance of her pussy. They both groaned with pleasure as he slid into her inch by glorious inch.

"Yes," she gasped as he worked up to filling her fully.

"Fuck, you're tight," he said.

He dug his fingers into her hips as his cock slipped through her folds again and again. They both gasped as he finally drove fully into her and stilled. His head tipped forward, that midnight-blue hair obscuring his eyes, pure pleasure playing across his features.

"You feel amazing," he ground out.

He hadn't moved. As if he wasn't able to with how delicious her pussy felt wrapped around his hard cock, like he wanted to revel in the sensation as long as possible. She squirmed, wanting him to take her, fuck her. Needing the release and wanting him to draw it out of her.

"Fuck, Wren," he said. "You're so greedy."

Then he put a hand behind her knee and lifted one of her legs up, using the new angle for leverage, and began to move within her.

"Oh fuck," she gasped.

All thoughts vanished. She'd deal with everything else another day. Right now it was only Graves moving inside of her. She might have started as his wren, belonged to him in that way, but she was not a pawn for the Holly King. She wanted this, and she couldn't imagine another world where she didn't want it.

"God, you're close," he said as he slammed back into her.

"You have your gloves on," she teased.

"I can feel your cunt gripping me."

"Fuck yes," she groaned. "Harder."

He obliged, leaning forward and carefully placing a hand around her neck. He looked down at her as he continued to fuck her with a question in his eyes. But she would take everything he would give her. Everything and more.

He increased the pressure slowly, choking her as he pumped into her at an increased pace. Her body was all sweet pleasure, a hazy, delightful mess of emotions. The added feel of his grip around her throat—him claiming her, her wanting nothing more than to be claimed as his.

She came undone all at once with a vicious cry, and he milked her orgasm for all it was worth, using her body to draw out his own. With a grunt, he unloaded into her until he, too, was spent.

He collapsed forward over her body. Their panting breaths mingling in the empty cellar. His lips pressed against her neck and across her collarbone to her shoulder, laying claim to all of her.

Chapter Forty-Nine

The next morning, she woke with Graves's head between her legs. She murmured softly as the feel of his tongue swirling around her sensitive clit pulled her from her dreams. Then the murmurs turned to mewls and the mewls to moans.

"Morning," he said into her thigh, pressing firm kisses down to her knee. His gray eyes looked at her with a predatory glint. "Wanted to break my fast with my favorite meal."

"You didn't finish."

His fingers slipped down her inner thigh, teasingly avoiding the one area she wanted. "Show me what you do when I'm not here."

"I'm too busy with your cock to touch myself."

"When you were gone, then," he said devilishly. "Did you touch yourself thinking of me?"

Yes.

The word caught in her throat. She had. So many times. No matter how furious she was with him, he'd still been the best fuck of her life. And that wasn't something a girl just forgot.

He grinned like a Cheshire cat. "Show me."

Her hand slid down her stomach before parting the flesh and slicking her fingers through her own wetness. She was soaked from Graves's ministrations. She hadn't been that far from coming when he'd stopped. She brought her finger back up to the apex of her thighs and swirled it around her clit.

A soft sigh left her mouth as her pleasure ricocheted through her. She was so sensitive and so turned on and so ready to orgasm already. Graves watched her, fascinated by the sweep of her fingers and her pants and the rise and fall of her chest.

His cock lengthened, thick and heavy as he watched her. As if he could hold out no longer, he took it into his hand and pumped it up and down to the time of her circles. He could have fucked her at any point, but instead he watched. His fascination with the sight of her pleasuring herself was a pulse between them.

And she, too, was mesmerized. Watching his cock disappear in and out of his hand. Hands that had blackmailed and tortured and killed people. That had made her scream her pleasure and find her memories and held her safe. A duality that she couldn't begin to disentangle. Maybe she never would.

"Oh God," she cried out as her orgasm hung by a string. "I'm close. So close."

Graves was pumping even faster. One hand parted her legs, slipping fingers inside her wet pussy. The added friction tipped her over the edge. She came with a fury, clenching around his fingers. He continued jacking off, watching her orgasm with a renewed fervor. Then he unloaded, hot come spurting out of him to land on her chest and stomach. Sticky white seed smeared all over her.

When he finally finished, he looked down at her through bedroom eyes and said, "A masterpiece."

She laughed. "I'm covered."

"I fucking love it." He ran a finger through his own come from breast to belly button and down further. "If I had it my way, I'd have you filled and covered in come every weekday and all weekend."

"Oh my God," she said with an eye roll. "What are you, marking your territory?"

He grinned. "Maybe I am."

She laughed because there was nothing else to do. She couldn't believe the girl who had always been more into girls and half hated the idea of a guy coming in her was now coated in the stuff and contemplating when she could have it happen again. Asshole.

Graves pressed a kiss to her lips. "We need to clean up. We have company."

"What?" Kierse asked.

But no matter how she tried to wheedle an answer out of him, he carried her into the shower and cleaned her off. He had her bent over the bench again, pumping into her until they both came hard and fast. A desperate second orgasm that he milked out of her with precision.

She toweled off and changed into a black tank and shorts. Graves claimed that he had one more thing to do in his office and then he'd meet her in the library. He offered for *her* to be the one more thing he had to do, and oh how the idea had been tempting. She pushed him toward his office and left him to his work. She was starving and…a little hungover. How potent had that old bottle of wine been? She'd definitely been buzzing, but now her head hurt. So, while she wanted to find out about their company, she needed food first.

Kierse stopped in the kitchen to find Isolde with a spread already laid out. "I see you're enjoying cooking for more people."

Isolde brightened. "We're like a bed and breakfast."

Kierse laughed at that assessment. "Don't tell Graves."

"Never," Isolde said conspiratorially. "We don't want to disrupt him."

Isolde hummed happily as she kneaded dough for a cinnamon babka. She was trying to match the recipe to the one Kierse loved from her favorite bakery.

"You were famished," Isolde said when she downed a whole plate of eggs, bacon, and pancakes and went in for a second.

"Hangover," she told her with a yawn.

"Ah, take some of the biscuits to go with you. Gen really likes them."

"Everyone likes your cookies," Kierse said.

Isolde straightened at the word. "We'll have you using the proper words eventually."

Kierse laughed as she grabbed the tray and took it upstairs and into the library.

When she pushed inside, she'd honestly been expecting Graves's mentor, Kingston. Graves didn't have many other friends in his line of work. Just a long list of enemies, broken hearts, and staff. Kingston was the closest thing he had to a friend, but they hadn't heard from him again since the ominous roses when they'd first returned to the city. And he wasn't here today, either.

"Walter Rodriguez," Kierse said.

Graves's old apprentice was seated cross-legged on the couch, a laptop open on his knees. Gen sat next to him, stroking Anne's head. Anne hissed at Kierse as she approached and trotted off into the stacks. One day that cat was going to like her. She swore she was.

"'Sup," Walter said, pressing his black-rimmed glasses up his nose as he buried his head back in the computer. He wore a gray T-shirt with a comic book character Kierse didn't recognize on it, black jeans, and black high-top sneakers.

"Surprised to see you here."

Walter shrugged. "No one more than me."

She set the tray down on the table and put a hand on her forehead as she dropped into a chair. She grimaced at the decoy box in front of her, which she was still having trouble with.

"You woke up late," Gen said.

"Late night," Kierse said. *Lots of sex.* "And a hangover. Do you think you could...?" Kierse gestured to her head.

Gen snorted. "You earned that hangover. You can live with a rough morning."

"I had a rough night." She winked at Gen, who blushed.

"I bet," Gen said with an eye roll.

"What about *you*? Did you and Ronan do the dirty?"

Gen flushed. "No!" Then glanced sideways at Walter and back. "But we did hook up."

"Ahhh!" Kierse said. "Tell me everything."

"I can hear you," Walter promised. "And I do not want to know, respectfully."

"Sure. Sure," Gen said. "We just met, but I've heard a lot about you."

Walter looked up at her with a tilted head. "All bad, I presume."

"Heard you're really strong."

"Huh," Walter said and then went back to his computer.

Kierse fiddled with the combination lock. She'd spent the last couple weeks dismantling the thing piece by piece, but the lock still eluded her. It was infuriating. She felt like she was missing part of the puzzle. It had been *years* since a lock had messed with her this much. Not since she'd been a child, working with Jason as he trained her through the intricacies. And she felt again like that small child again as this lock refused to open for her.

"So, Walter," Gen said amicably, "you decided to join Team Holly."

Kierse nearly choked on her own spit. "Team Holly?"

"What? It works! I even designed a logo." She turned over the notebook she had in her lap to reveal a little holly leaf with the berries in the center, TEAM HOLLY written in block text over top. "I thought we should get T-shirts."

Walter stared at Gen as if she were some bizarre sort of creature with horns sprouting out of her head. He shrugged. "I'd wear a T-shirt."

Kierse sputtered. "You just joined!"

"I try not to do things half assed. If we're getting team shirts, I want one."

"I like him," Gen said with a wide smile.

"How did he convince you to work with us?"

"He didn't," Walter said into his computer.

Gen and Kierse exchanged a look. "What convinced you?" Gen asked.

"You did," Walter said.

Kierse frowned. "Me?"

He looked up at her very practically. "You could have killed me at any point. You can get through my force fields. You can bypass my wards. You are a weapon. Graves should have used his weapon to kill me, which would have deactivated my wards. Then he could have walked in and taken the spear himself."

"But he didn't," Kierse realized.

"You didn't kill me. Graves didn't want me dead," Walter said simply.

"Huh."

Sometimes she forgot that Graves could have been even more of a villain. For whatever reason, he didn't want Walter dead, and Walter knew that. If Graves was asking for his help, Walter also must have calculated it was better to work for the biggest bad on the block than get stuck in someone else's machinations.

"While we're on the topic of not killing people," Gen said matter-of-factly.

"Yeah?"

"Triskel training."

Kierse groaned. She'd hoped to never think about triskel training again. "Do I have to?"

"You agreed."

"Yeah, but…"

"Niamh said it's best to start on the full moon, because we'll be at full strength. That's Tuesday."

"Okay," Kierse said with a sigh. "I'll need the week to prepare to see Lorcan again, anyway."

"And Niamh," Gen said softly.

Kierse nodded at her friend. They were both a little fucked.

Graves stepped through the door of his library. His hands were bare, and he ran one through his dark hair. The sight of him in that suit with the ferocious look on his face just made her want to drag him back upstairs.

"Everything all right?" Kierse asked.

"Laz is in place," Graves said without preamble. "Schwartz was taken off of security from the Curator."

"What?" Kierse and Gen gasped at the same time.

"Since the auction, the Curator decided to go with in-house security," Graves said. "We're going to have to find some other way to get him inside."

"Fuck," Kierse grumbled.

"And *you* inside," Graves added. "Since we thought Schwartz would be able to bypass security for you."

"Double fuck."

"Plus, I just got the final information from the con. Increased security, due to the nature of the business—monsters—and the new collection being showcased."

"Curator," Gen said with a sigh.

Graves nodded. "No plus-ones are allowed inside the conference space at any point. Everyone will have a badge given to them at check-in with a bar scanner that matches a picture verification."

"So Walter just adds me to the list," Kierse said.

"Then they'd know you were there," Walter said. "The uninvited thief."

"Correct." Graves glanced at Walter. "Rodriguez, you got anything for me?"

"In fact, I do." He pressed a button, and a small printer Kierse hadn't noticed at his side whirred to life. "This is the Monster Con schedule."

"You had no difficulties getting into the con network?"

Walter looked up at him with skepticism. "Should I have? It took about three minutes."

"Good," Graves said. His eyes shot up to hers, and she mouthed, *I told you so.* He tipped his head at her in concession.

"I've reestablished your security net and reinforced it with my warding. I'm working on the problem of the Curator now. That might take me a little longer." Walter ripped the papers off the printer and passed them to Graves. "I'd print the list of registrants, but it's hundreds of monsters long. If you're looking for anyone in particular, I can do a search for you. Otherwise I'll send it to your email for review."

"Excellent."

Graves scanned the schedule that Walter had given him. Kierse abandoned the decoy to take a look at the second half of the papers and see what all the fuss was about.

SATURDAY, JUNE 22ND 11:00 A.M.

THE RISE AND FALL OF VAMPIRES: A COMPREHENSIVE LOOK AT THE CHANGES IN BLOOD COMPOSITION BY LEADING EXPERTS IN THE FIELD, INCLUDING EX-VISAGE SCIENTIST HARRY HAYWARD.

SATURDAY JUNE 22ND 11:00 A.M.

THE MONSTER TREATY: PROS AND CONS FOR WRAITHS INCLUDING PANELISTS GREGORY AMBERDASH, MICHELLE LOMBARDY, JAMES VAN

DYKEN, AND ANDERS LARSSON.

SATURDAY JUNE 22ND 11:00 A.M.

MONSTERS IN ACADEMIA: A WHO'S WHO OF TENURED MONSTER FACULTY INCLUDING WAYLAN YARROW, BASTIAN WILLIAMS, IFETAYO MUSA, SAMANTHA SMITH, AND JORIE NGUYEN.

SATURDAY JUNE 22ND 12:00-2:00 P.M.

LUNCH SERVED IN THE OAK ROOM. DIETARY RESTRICTIONS PASS REQUIRED.

SATURDAY JUNE 22ND 2:00 P.M.

BLESSED BE THE PEACEMAKERS: THE ROLE OF HUMAN RELIGION IN UPHOLDING THE MONSTER TREATY WITH HARVARD ANTHROPOLOGIST EUGENIE ETHRIDGE

SATURDAY JUNE 22ND 2:00 P.M.

DON'T SAY THE M WORD: HOW TO TALK TO HUMANS ABOUT MAGIC WITH THE LEADING FAE FOLKLORIST, ANDREA CHAPMAN, PAIRED WITH HUMAN/MONSTER PSYCHOLOGIST HENRIETTA SANCHEZ.

The list was endless. Every time slot had six to ten different panels of varying topics for monsters.

"This is…exhausting," Kierse admitted as she continued to flip through the pages.

"Yes. Everyone who is going is required to speak. It's the bipartisan contribution, blah, blah," Graves grumbled.

"*You're* speaking?"

He glanced up at her. "On Sunday."

"We'll have the cauldron before that."

He smirked. "Exactly."

She flipped through the pages until she found the list for Sunday. She almost missed it twice because there was no name associated with it.

SUNDAY, JUNE 23RD 8:00 A.M.

MONSTERS NOT MAGIC: A COMPREHENSIVE LOOK AT THE MYTH AND LIE OF THE MOTTO FEATURING A SURPRISE GUEST, A RENOWNED MONSTER TREATY SPECIALIST.

"You got your name removed?" Kierse asked.

"*I* did," Walter said with a grin.

"Worth his weight at least," Graves said.

"Eight in the morning," she said with a snort. "They should have known you'd never agree to that."

Gen snorted. "Facts."

Kierse went back to where she'd left off. She already had more questions than she could keep in her head all at once. Amberdash would be there, which made sense. He wouldn't be able to avoid being included in something like this. A Fae folklorist sounded like someone Kierse should corner in a bathroom for information. The dietary restrictions card had her worried. She knew what monsters ate—who they ate—and what that card must look like. She doubted it was just gluten free.

"Oh," Graves said softly.

"What's oh?" Kierse asked.

"I might have found your way in."

Kierse peered over his shoulder and saw that his finger was pointing toward the Friday night entertainment. "A welcome reception benefit for the arts?"

"That's where the Curator is going to be showcasing his collection."

"How is that going to get me inside?"

He pointed at the next line: "Including the cast of New Amsterdam Theatre's Aerial Garden reproduction of *A Midsummer Night's Dream*."

Kierse's mouth formed an *O*.

"Lyra."

Chapter Fifty

Lyra Anderson on stage at the New Amsterdam Aerial Gardens theater, playing her rendition of Hermia, was a revelation. Kierse had thought she was a triumph on their opening night during the auction. With a few weeks of regular shows, she had transformed into an otherworldly creature. The crowd grew still and silent every time she appeared on the stage.

This was the fourth show that Kierse had seen in so many nights. Graves had gone to the first with her, and he was here again tonight. His hand rested on her inner thigh under her dress as they watched from a secluded table to the right of the stage, closest to the backstage door.

"You think this will work?"

"After what she said to you at the auction?" he asked with a smirk.

"I *am* irresistible," she teased.

His hand inched higher. "You are."

She spread her legs wider under the table and let him find that she'd opted out of panties for the night. The dress was a form-fitting navy silk that showed every line and curve. She hadn't had a single pair of underwear that worked with it.

Graves stilled the second he found out. "Wren…"

"Hmm?" she asked coyly.

"Can you be quiet?"

She shook her head but didn't stop him as he slid his fingers higher. She inhaled sharply, feeling the flex of his magic surround them. She could still hear the stage performance, but no one would be able to hear them. That wouldn't keep her face from revealing what he was doing to her, however.

His eyes were trained on her as she tried to hide her emotions. His fingers thick and slippery deep inside of her. His thumb pressing insistently against her clit. Anyone could see their secret intrusion. She hoped that the evening darkness hid them. She wasn't sure that it did.

And still Graves didn't let up. Nor did she want him to.

She bit into her lip, stifling a cry that only they would be able to hear.

Graves pressed his lip to the shell of her ear. "Are you going to come for me, Wren?"

"I..." she gasped.

"Let your powers down."

She let him into her mind. Showed him how close she was, how she could barely contain herself, and the look on his face as he stole her breath. She wanted to say fuck it all and have him spread her open on this table.

His eyes turned dark at the thought. "I could oblige."

She wasn't sure if he was teasing or serious. But just the thought sent her over the edge. A breathless gasp ripped out of her as she came against his fingers.

"Pity," he said as he slipped free of her and reached for a napkin.

She crossed her legs and waited for her breathing to return to normal. She felt shaky from her orgasm.

"We're supposed to be working," she accused him.

"How can I resist when you're on display for me?" he asked as he slipped his arm across her shoulders.

"You're filthy."

"Is that a complaint?"

He knew it wasn't.

"You can finish again after we complete our work," he said with that dangerous smirk she so adored. He *tsk*ed her. "You're so distracted."

She snorted. "I think you were the distracted one."

"Well, when you fail to wear underwear...who can blame me?"

Kierse turned her attention back to the stage as the fifth act began—the triple wedding as the Fae depart from their mischief. All was right with the world. Kierse always got a little bored with the ending. She understood it, but she preferred the mischief. Perhaps that was in her nature.

"What do you know of the triskel training?"

"Little," Graves admitted.

"But Lorcan, Niamh, and Saoirse were already bonded when you knew them before?"

He frowned as if he didn't want to discuss this. She knew him well enough to know when he was hedging.

"I want to be prepared for what I'm walking into with Lorcan," Kierse said. "I have to go back to that place on Tuesday for my training. And I don't know what to expect."

"They weren't a triskel yet when I knew them. It didn't begin until after Lorcan and Saoirse's wedding," Graves told her. "I was already cast out by then."

Kierse frowned. "Because of Emilie?"

Graves said nothing as Theseus monologued. He didn't speak again for several minutes. "In part because of what happened with Emilie."

She wanted him to say more. To explain what had happened. Lorcan had accused him of killing her. What led them on this path?

"They never wanted me to be a part of the Druids, though," Graves said. "They would have found any reason."

Kierse knew that feeling. It was one that had connected them from day one. It didn't answer her questions, but she knew he would tell her when the time was right.

"If you had to guess, what do you think the training will be like?"

He released a soft breath. "I wouldn't worry about the training. It's going to be about connecting your powers and learning to use them together. You've already done it, and I suspect it will be like riding a bike. Especially with the full moon."

"Yeah. I guess I'm not looking forward to whatever stunt Lorcan is going to pull when I see him next."

"I'm sure he'll try to convince you of the binding ceremony."

Kierse furrowed her brow. "What binding ceremony?"

Graves jerked his head toward her. When he realized she knew nothing, he smiled, slow and smug. "Oh, look at him, keeping secrets." He laughed softly. "Classic."

"Uh…I'm not going to like this, am I?"

"The soulmate bond has to be bound in a ceremony to reach full potential," Graves explained.

"A ceremony…like what? Like marriage? Or like a werewolf mating?"

"Both and neither," Graves told her. "It's a magic bond. All magical creatures have a magic signature. The Fae gave Druids access to magic, and so Wisp and Druidic magic can be connected."

"But you said both and neither. They're connected to be more… powerful? For more powerful children?"

Graves eyes darkened. "I'm sure they believe that's a benefit. Though wisps don't have many children. A sacrifice of being long-lived."

"So Lorcan has been planning to bind our magic together all this time and never mentioned it?"

"Probably," he admitted.

"And you didn't tell me why?"

"I thought you already knew. He's the *hero*, right?" Graves said sardonically.

"I'm not going to do it."

"You don't have to," he said with a sigh. "It was required when a bond mate was discovered in my day. But you're not part of the Fae Council, nor did you grow up in their ranks."

"No, they tried to *kill me* as a child. I can't think they'd sanction this if they were still alive."

"But they're not," Graves said.

"No," she said, deflating at that reality.

She was the last wisp. She had a soulmate bond to the most powerful Druid. Something in that made perfect sense, if it was a continuation of a line. Natural selection. It didn't make her hate it any less.

"Just ask him about it," Graves said through clenched teeth. "I bet he bends over backward to reassure you about it."

Kierse didn't doubt that for a second.

The show came to a close with that anger and indignation still rattling her bones. She and Graves stood with the rest of the audience for a standing ovation. Lyra's eyes swept to the seats that Kierse had purchased for the entire week. She had noticed them before, but the intrigue was more intense this time. A question in her perfect dark eyes.

"Ready?" Graves asked.

"I'll meet you in the limo."

Kierse waited for Lyra at the backstage door. Nearly the entire cast had left before Lyra appeared, dressed in a tight black dress with a large designer bag slung over her shoulder. She didn't look surprised to see Kierse.

Despite that fact, she still flushed slightly at the sight of her. "Hey."

"You kept me waiting," Kierse teased.

"You waited," Lyra noted.

"I did."

Kierse fell into stride with her as they headed for the elevators.

"Where's the guy who is always with you?"

"I sent him to the car," Kierse told her.

"Hmm."

They stepped into the elevator, and they were halfway to street level when Lyra pressed the hold button.

"I don't need a patron or money or anything," Lyra said quickly. "I know the last time that we met, I was really forward, but I don't actually...do theater like that. I'm a professional."

Kierse almost laughed. "I can see that."

Historically, so much of the backbone of the theater had been held up by, essentially, prostitution to the wealthy. Patrons had come into fashion once more, to allow actors and artists to continue to work. Most of them were not entirely altruistic.

"I'm just being honest."

"I believe you. Nor am I hoping to pay to sleep with you." Kierse actually did laugh then. "Does it look like I've paid to sleep with anyone?"

"No," Lyra whispered.

"Nothing against sex workers. The oldest job and everything. I used to live in the attic of a brothel, and the workers were all incredible people. But I'm not propositioning you like that. I'm just interested."

Lyra took a step back as if that were the last thing she had expected. "Oh."

Kierse pressed the button that let the elevator drop down to street level. She gestured to the awaiting limo. "This is my ride."

"You're just going to go?" Lyra asked in confusion.

"I'll be back tomorrow," Kierse promised with a wink. "Unless you need a ride home?"

Lyra looked at the limo for the invitation it was. Kierse could see the moment she wavered. But she also knew Lyra's backbone was strong and that she'd decline the help. Thinking that giving in to them too easily would lose her ground.

"No, thank you. I can get to the Barbizon on my own."

Barbizon. Kierse filed that name away. She'd heard of the place. It used to be an all-women's hotel where artists could feel safe in the city during the Roaring Twenties. It had been reopened recently for human and monster women to have a safe place of their own again. It made sense that someone like Lyra would be living there. And that she was definitely interested, if she gave Kierse that name so willingly.

"Suit yourself," Kierse said and reached for the door of the limo. She was about to pull it open when she acted like she'd just remembered something. "You're going to be performing at the Monster Con, right?"

"Oh, yes, we were just given the date for that. Will you be there?"

"Well, my beau is speaking," she said, gesturing to the interior of the limo. "But I don't have an invite. So, not sure yet. Hopefully we'll see you there."

Kierse could already see the wheels turning in her head. A night off from the show run, a performance where they'd have a room in a five-star hotel, and Kierse needed a way in.

She'd let her come to the conclusion on her own.

Kierse stepped forward, kissing both of the girl's cool cheeks. "See you tomorrow night."

Then she ducked into the limo and forced herself not to look back.

"Well?" Graves asked.

"It worked."

"She confirmed that she'll get you in?"

"Not yet, but she will." Kierse was certain of that.

A yawn escaped her as George pulled away. She'd been going to so many midnight showings and not sleeping long enough during the day.

"You look like you're about to pass out."

Kierse stifled another yawn. "I'm fine."

"You've been burning the midnight oil."

"I'm a creature of the night." He shot her a look, and she grinned. "Just as much as you are."

He held his arm out. "Come here, creature of the night. Your work is done. You can relax."

Kierse shifted across the leather in the back of the limo and into his arms. He tucked her in close as she rested her head against his shoulder. Her eyes immediately felt heavy. As if the weight of the world dropped off her shoulders, and there was just Graves's security.

When she opened her eyes again, she was in the hallway.

Kierse glanced around, taking in the dirty drug den at the heart of Tribeca. She noticed the numbers on the doors. Her father's anxiety flowed from him. A woman yelled out in Spanish.

But she clutched onto her mother's hand and headed toward the middle of the hallway. She could see the door that they were trying to get to. She knew that something was waiting for them there. All she had to do was grasp the handle and push.

The world felt fuzzy at the edges as she reached for the door. She needed it. She needed to know what happened. 7020 was *right there*. All of her answers were within her grasp.

At the first touch of cool brass, she was elsewhere. On the ground, staring up at the building. Her parents were gone. This didn't feel right.

She took a step and was in the apartment. Her parents' apartment. Tears in her eyes. A flashing light meant something…something important.

No, no, she wasn't ready. It couldn't be now.

A hand shook her, and she burst back into consciousness. She was heaving as she leaned forward and put her head between her knees. Her vision was black at the edges, and the world seemed to waver.

"Wren?" Graves asked.

"A dream." She brushed her hair off her face. "A nightmare."

"The room?"

She nodded. "And then…an apartment. There was an alarm of some sort."

He was silent a moment before asking, "Do you want to talk about it?"

"What's there to talk about?"

"Your parents," he said. "And what happened to them."

She shook her head. "No."

He rubbed gentle circles into her back. The silence dragged on, but it wasn't uncomfortable. He was a comforting presence. Not pushing her to discuss what had happened. Not forcing out her own unspoken fears.

"What if I don't face it?" she whispered into the silence, her eyes squeezed shut.

"You will."

"How do you know?"

"You're too brave and too stubborn to do anything else."

She laughed. "I don't think most people consider a thief brave."

"I'm not most people, and you're not most thieves."

"Once I know," she said, meeting his gaze, "I'll know forever."

"Yes."

"I can't undo it."

"I know, Wren," he told her, brushing her hair from her cheeks. "You'll know when you're ready."

"You're not going to push me to do memory work?"

"No." He drew her face up to his and planted a kiss against her lips. "I trust you."

And she saw in his thunderstorm eyes that he meant every word.

Chapter Fifty-One

Kierse wasn't ready. That much she knew. And since Graves didn't push, she opted out of more memory work for the time being. They had enough to deal with planning the heist that the memories could wait. Or at least that was what she told herself when she went for another performance of *Midsummer*. And another after that.

By then, Lyra had come around. She was the one who suggested Kierse enter the con with the theater troupe. Kierse acted surprised at her suggestion, as if she hadn't been banking on it, and then readily agreed. Her entrance was secure.

With that out of the way, she set herself to conquering the decoy. She even consulted Walter on some of the specifics. While he couldn't break locks, he designed computer systems, and had ideas that she'd never considered. She was sure it would unravel any day now.

And while she might have been avoiding memory work, she couldn't avoid the triskel training that she'd agreed to. Tuesday was the full moon, and she and Gen were set to return to Brooklyn. She was still upset with Lorcan for keeping the binding ceremony from her. After he'd made it out, time and time again, like he was a good guy. A fucking savior complex if she'd ever seen one.

Gen kept glancing at her and bouncing her leg as they took the subway into Brooklyn. "Maybe he has a good reason for keeping it from you."

"Maybe," Kierse said, meaning *no, he doesn't.* "Let's just get this training over with."

They hopped off the train and headed down Broadway. Niamh had suggested they meet her and Ethan outside Williamsburgh Savings Bank at dusk. The full moon was tracing an arc across the night sky as they stepped up to the large building.

Declan stood at the entrance. His beefy arms crossed, his eyes trained on her and Gen as they approached. A gun was holstered at his waist.

Kierse sighed heavily. Lorcan's second had kidnapped her and held her at gunpoint. He'd disrespected Niamh in her presence. To say she wasn't particularly fond of the man was an understatement.

"Declan," Kierse said.

He sneered down at her. "You're late."

"Lorcan has you on guard duty?" she said with a smirk. "Good dog."

His glare was ferocious as he took a threatening step toward her.

"Stop instigating him, Kierse," Gen said, pushing her backward. "It's good to see you again."

Declan raised his eyebrows. "Is it?"

"No," Kierse muttered.

"It is. I know you were just following orders," Gen said, ever the peacemaker.

The door to the bank opened, and Niamh appeared. She wasn't in the school-girl attire she'd worn in Dublin, or the cool business-casual look she'd adopted with the Druids. Tonight, she was in all-black athletic clothing—flared leggings, a tank top, and sneakers. She grinned down at the girls. "Having fun with the rabble?"

Declan shot her a glare. "Your *guests* have arrived."

Niamh patted him twice on his arm. "Thanks, Dec." She turned to Gen and Kierse. "Are you excited to get started?"

"I am," Gen said. She pointed her thumb at Kierse. "She has beef with Lorcan."

"Don't we all," Niamh said with a laugh. "What did he do this time?"

"Yes," Lorcan asked as he stepped into the doorframe. "What have I done?"

Kierse faltered at the sight of him. She had to physically hold onto her anger like lightning in her chest. Because he, too, was out of his characteristic suit and instead wearing black joggers and a fitted gray T-shirt that stretched across his muscular chest. His dark hair was loose against his forehead, and those piercing blue eyes shot straight through her. The pulse of their connection was a brand against her sternum.

"You were supposed to wait inside," Niamh chided him.

Lorcan didn't even spare her a glance. "And you expected me to listen?"

"He never listens," Niamh muttered under her breath. "Why don't you two have it out, and I'll get Gen and Ethan set up inside?"

Gen nodded vigorously. "Sounds like a plan."

They darted inside, letting the door fall shut behind them.

Lorcan didn't even look at Declan while dismissing him. "You're no longer needed."

Declan gave him a little salute before wandering off, his eyes continuing to look back at them.

"So, are you going to tell me what I've done?"

Kierse ground her teeth together. "The binding ceremony."

"What about it?"

"You didn't *tell* me about it."

He shrugged. "So?"

"So?" she asked in disbelief. "That's all you have to say?"

"We don't have to go through with it anytime soon," Lorcan said, taking a step down toward her. "It doesn't change what's in here."

He reached out to touch her chest, and she took a step back.

"Anytime soon...isn't never."

"No, it's not."

"*So*, when were you going to tell me?"

"When I thought you might agree to it," he said simply.

"What if I never agree to it?"

He smiled then. That blinding, happy smile that said he'd never suffered, even though she now knew that he had. "She said the same thing, once."

Kierse faltered. "Who?"

"Saoirse."

"Your wife."

"Saoirse hated me when we first met. It's almost funny to think about, considering we were married for nearly four hundred years." His eyes went distant. "But the first time magic flared between us, she told me she'd rather die than be bound to anyone."

"Wait..." Kierse said as confusion bloomed in her stomach.

"Oh, yes, we were soulmates." This time when he reached for the place they were connected, she let him touch her. "And you have her magic."

"I have...Saoirse's magic?" Her voice cracked as she asked desperately, "How?"

"I don't know. I knew it the second that I saw you without the spell. This magic between us had already been connected once before, and it was calling back to me."

"That's impossible."

"I thought so as well. I've spent the last six months scrounging through everything we had on reincarnation."

Her eyes widened in alarm. "I am not...reincarnated."

"You may not *be* her, but you have her magic. That's why the bond is so strong. Saoirse needed time to process and come around to the idea." He spread his arms wide. "All I have is time, Kierse. I'm happy to give you as much as you need to do the same."

She tried to wade through this new information. Graves had said Lorcan would twist his explanation to make himself the good guy. But fuck, no one could have prepared her for this. She had the magical signature of his *dead wife.*

And not just that, they had been bound in the past *and* a triskel. No wonder things were so intense between them. No wonder she could barely escape him every time.

"You don't have to make any decisions today," Lorcan promised her. "The Oak Throne will wait."

He held his hand out for her, his face contemplative and open. Damn him.

"You're not playing fair."

"I never said I would," he said with a smirk.

She put her hand in his. "I'm just here for training."

"As you say."

"Not for you."

His smile widened as he brought her fingers to his lips and pressed a kiss there. "If that's what you have to think to convince yourself."

She bit her lip at his audacity and let him draw her inside. Gen, Ethan, and Niamh were standing in a tense circle, waiting for their return. Niamh rolled her eyes at their approach.

"About time," she said. "We only have one full moon."

"All good?" Gen asked.

Kierse nodded once, extracting her hand from Lorcan's. "Yeah. What's the plan?"

"Lorcan is going to stand over there," Niamh said, pointing away from them. "I'm in charge."

Lorcan crossed his arms and refused to move. "I was as much a part of this triskel as you were."

"Yeah, but I'm in charge."

"Maybe in Dublin. Not here."

Kierse would have thought that this little showdown didn't mean anything. But this *was* a powerplay, jockeying for position, and the whole thing maybe wasn't as light as they were playing it.

"It's fine. He can stay," Kierse said to defuse the situation.

Niamh sighed tightly. "Fine. Lorcan stays."

A circle had been drawn in chalk on the bank floor. Niamh directed the trio to stand in spaces around it to form an equilateral triangle. Their positions had been marked for precision.

"The ritual helps to keep everything in balance," Niamh explained when she directed Kierse onto her spot. "We want to make this as easy as possible. The full moon, the positions on the circle, the connection to the cosmos. It all makes the magic simpler and less draining."

This part of Druidic work Kierse had never experienced herself. Magic was just something that she had. There were rules to follow for when she was drained, but using it didn't require all this pomp.

"Ideally, as you get stronger, you won't need any of this to use your triskel powers. They're a muscle, and like any other muscle, it takes work to reach that point."

"We did all right the first time," Kierse said.

"With my borrowed magic on the winter solstice and under a full moon," Lorcan reminded her.

Niamh shot him a look but continued, "Yes. You had the Oak King magic inside of you, which made it easier for Ethan and Gen to connect to you. The solstices are the most liminal times of the year. A point when the veil between worlds is at its thinnest. Any of these thresholds make the magic more potent. They enhance what is already there."

Ethan nodded encouragingly. "When to do a spell is almost more important than what spell you choose."

"Normally," Niamh said. "With you three I'm hoping it won't matter as much, but we're taking precautions." Niamh moved to the position opposite Gen. "The point of a triskel is combined powers are stronger together. You will be able to do things together that none of you could do alone. Separately, the source of each of your abilities focuses on healing, nature affinity, and absorption, but when you're together all these will be amplified." She looked at Kierse. "Your absorption is key to this link."

"How so?"

"When you absorb more magic, you can use it to amplify the other's powers."

Kierse bit her lip. She wasn't sure if she completely understood, but maybe she would have to do it for it to make sense. After all, during their last linking, she'd been unconscious.

"Since Gen was the one who managed the link last time, we should start with her."

Gen twiddled with her fingers before nodding. "All right. The same thing I did last time?"

"Yes. Start by projecting your energy toward Ethan and Kierse. Find the center of magic in them and try to touch it," Niamh instructed. "It's best to start with one person at a time probing forward so none of you gets overwhelmed. And know it's okay if you don't get it the first time. This is advanced magic."

Kierse didn't feel anything for several long minutes. She could see that Gen was concentrating on Niamh's suggestions, but if she was managing it, Kierse couldn't tell.

Finally, she huffed out a long breath. "I can't do it," Gen gasped.

"It's okay," Niamh said reassuringly. "It's much harder under these circumstances."

"Because last time, if we didn't make it work, Kierse was going to die."

"That's right," Niamh said. "You're in no immediate danger."

"I can try," Ethan said. He looked sheepish as he added, "We've been working on projecting our magic, and I've managed it with a handful of my plants."

But no matter how Ethan tried, the connection wasn't there.

"Kierse?" Niamh said. "Your turn."

"All right," she said with an unconcerned shrug.

When she reached for her powers, they slid against her skin with ease. She'd been working with Graves on her absorption for weeks. This was not so different than turning it on or off with him, only this time she wanted to link with the people who could touch her magic. A thing she and Graves couldn't do.

Kierse found the sources of Ethan's and Gen's magic like a brush of a feather compared to Graves's torrent—such small and fragile things, it seemed as if they could be snuffed out with a whisper against the flame.

She gingerly reached for them, trying not to blow them out. As one, Ethan and Gen yelped. Gen put her hand to her chest, and Ethan stumbled out of the circle.

Kierse retreated. "Sorry. Sorry. Too much?"

Gen rubbed her chest. "It was like a sucker punch."

Lorcan took a step toward her. "What were you thinking about?"

His eyes probed hers as if he could read her thoughts. Immediately, the memory where she opened and closed the vault sprang forward, a reflex. But no one was trying to get inside her mind. This was an exercise in lowering her defenses to let people in, and she had been doing that successfully for weeks.

"I was worried I would snuff out their magic. It was so light."

"You went straight to the source like you'd done it before," Lorcan said.

She had. She'd reached for Graves's magic.

"I've been training, too," was all she said.

He pursed his lips in disapproval, but Niamh took back control of the session.

"Good. Let's try that again, but instead of thinking about avoiding snuffing out their magic, think about offering a hand to it. You don't want to sucker punch them," Niamh said with a quirk to her lips. "You want them to come to you."

"I'll try again."

This time she reached out for their magic but ignored that hers felt like an inferno in comparison. These were her friends. Her best friends. They had saved her when all was lost in this world. She would choose them every time. She always had. No matter what came between them. And they would choose her, too.

When she offered her hands to them, their magic embraced her like an old friend. The link settled into place like they were physically holding hands and not standing several feet away from one another.

"Yes!" Niamh cheered. "That's it. Now hold it steady."

Kierse kept her hand up, holding the line for all of them. She wasn't sure either of them had enough magic to link them together normally. Not without some real strengthening. Kierse was naturally gifted, and she hadn't quite realized it until this moment. Not when she was surrounded by Graves's raging magic all the time.

"Excellent," Lorcan said. "Should we try to power share?"

Niamh frowned. "No. Let's unlink first and do this again a few times before they move on."

"What's a power share?" Kierse asked as she let the link drop.

Ethan and Gen gasped as they nearly doubled over from the effort. Kierse had been the one holding the whole bond up. While she did feel marginally drained, she wasn't going to collapse. Not compared to doing draining mind work with Graves. Had he been leveling her up?

"You move up and down the bond," Lorcan explained. "Kierse would give power to Ethan, who would pass it to Gen and back. Then vice versa. You want to get used to feeling the sense of the bond and sharing the energy."

"We should try it," Kierse said excitedly.

Niamh looked at the other two charges. "Just linking for a while."

They linked over and over and over again, until Kierse was pretty sure she would be able to link with Ethan and Gen in her sleep. Still neither of them were able to initiate. Niamh insisted that they would get there in time, but for now Kierse made it happen.

By the time Niamh agreed to try power sharing, Kierse could feel her own power drain begin. Hours had passed, and her friends looked rough. As midnight approached, Kierse felt a burst of energy hit her. That liminal space giving her enough power to keep going.

She linked with her friends, letting their magic settle. She did as Lorcan had suggested—she sent a small grain of rice down the thread. Just enough magic that Ethan would feel it, but not enough to overwhelm him. She'd realized over this training that any little bit could do damage. It took a good deal of tweaking to make it safe.

"Holy shit," Ethan murmured as the magic hit him. Tears sprang to his eyes. "Is this…is this what your magic feels like?"

"I don't know—what does it feel like to you?" Kierse told him.

"It's beautiful," he whispered. Their eyes met, and he swallowed. "Really beautiful."

"Can I feel?" Gen asked.

Kierse sent a grain to her as well—just a touch of magic. Gen's eyes lit up in wonder. It was like the two of them were refreshed after hours of hard work.

"Wow," Gen breathed.

Lorcan and Niamh exchanged a look. One of deep, unabashed wonder and terrible inalienable grief. Kierse hadn't considered how hard this might be on them.

"We should end there for tonight," Niamh said on a small sniffle.

"I can take over if you need a break," Lorcan said.

"No. I think they've done enough. They look beat."

"We'll have to wait another month for this opportunity. They're not strong enough to do it any other time. We should keep going."

"Lorcan," Niamh warned.

"We can do it," Kierse said.

Gen and Ethan, flush with her magic, nodded.

"Fine. Let me just take a restroom break." Niamh disappeared to get herself back together.

Lorcan took over. He had them run the magic between them like they were throwing a ball across the circle. Back and forth and around and around. Sometimes it was more magic, and sometimes less. They worked until even Kierse was feeling the fatigue of it all.

Then he moved into transferring powers from the other person.

When Niamh returned and saw them fumbling through it, her eyes widened. "They're not ready for that."

"Under dire conditions, they need to be able to take power to use for themselves," Lorcan said. "They need to know how to do it."

"Next time," Niamh insisted.

But Ethan was already reaching with his tiny tendril of energy toward Kierse, like a good little soldier. Kierse was so open that she hadn't even planned for what that would feel like. An invasion of her powers. The snap came so quickly, with their link wide open, that she couldn't stop him from taking and taking and taking.

"Ethan!" Gen cried.

"Ethan, stop," Lorcan commanded.

But it was Niamh who physically tackled him to the floor, throwing him out of the circle and breaking the link.

Kierse wavered unsteadily on her feet. Her magic empty. Her absorption off. Her vision blurry.

They needed to link. Ethan needed to put it back. He hadn't...meant to go that far.

"Kierse," Lorcan said, his hands gripping her shoulders, ducking so that he was looking into her face. Only his arms were holding her up. "Are you okay?"

"Sure," she whispered.

He released her tentatively, and the force of having to hold herself up sent her toppling forward. Lorcan caught her again, lifting her up in a wedding carry. She could smell his magic—spring rain and summer sunshine—envelope her as she disappeared into oblivion.

Interlude

"Well?" Lorcan demanded.

Niamh felt Kierse's wavering pulse and sighed. "She'll be fine. She's just at magic burn. She didn't burn out, but she's drained."

"There's nothing you can do?"

"No," Niamh said. "I've done what I can. She needs rest to recuperate. She'll need to focus on building her magic stores back up."

Lorcan looked half ready to pull out his hair. Like he might go back downstairs and throttle one of his own Druids for doing this to Kierse. Even though Ethan hadn't done it on purpose *and* he'd done it on Lorcan's orders. That had to be the worst of it.

There was always a risk when linking powers. This was what she had been trying to avoid. When they were all low and exhausted, those risks became reality.

Now here Kierse was, in Lorcan's bed like sleeping beauty. Niamh didn't know how long she would be out, which was an even bigger concern.

"We're going to have to tell Graves," Niamh said.

Lorcan snarled. "He can fucking deal."

"You know he won't."

"She is perfectly safe with me."

"This is *Graves* we're talking about," Niamh said. "You two and all your bullshit. He's going to blow your stupid truce and barge into Brooklyn and *take* her from you. Is that what you want?"

"Let him try," he snapped.

Niamh didn't want that. Not for Kierse or Lorcan or the Druids. She would like to avoid an international incident if at all possible.

"I'm going to have Gen call him," Niamh said. "Okay?"

"Do what you think is best. But if he tries to take her when she's like this, I'll kill him," Lorcan said, his eyes still on Kierse.

Niamh touched his arm. "She's not Saoirse. You know that, right?"

Lorcan looked like he'd been slapped. "Of course I know that."

"Okay," Niamh said, dubious.

She headed to the door and left him sitting at Kierse's bedside.

Sometimes she hated Lorcan for acting as if he were the only one impacted by Saoirse's death. As if Niamh hadn't loved her first.

They had been neighbors in their small village on the western coast of Ireland. Back when Niamh had still been figuring out that the world might see her as a boy, but she had always known that she was a little girl. She had played house with Saoirse instead of fighting with her older brothers. Eventually, her mom had stopped giving her britches and started to make little dresses for her. She'd gone through a handful of names over the years since her birth name never fit quite right. It wasn't until she met Oisín that she realized that the name she had been looking for all along had been Niamh.

And Niamh she had always been.

In those early days in Dublin, Niamh and Saoirse had been inseparable, and what Niamh had thought was simply unrequited pining had finally blown over into something…more. When Lorcan had shown interest in Saoirse and declared their soulmate bond, she had cried herself to sleep in Niamh's arms. She'd asked her to run away. Niamh still sometimes regretted not doing it.

In that time, a soulmate bond was sacred and special. Niamh couldn't be the one to take that away from her love.

It had all gotten complicated the day that Lorcan had brought Graves into their midst. A secretive and melancholy youth with none of the ease and humor the rest of them had. Only Emilie seemed to be able to draw him out of his shell in those early days.

In the end, it was Emilie's death that had brought Lorcan and Saoirse together. After their wedding, the triskel appeared, drawing her into their merry union. Something she thought would be awkward but was as easy as breathing. She finally had her love back. Saoirse the center of both of their entire worlds.

Until Saoirse's death. And then being around Lorcan was like a knife through her chest. Every look from him said, *It should have been you.*

"Is everything okay?" Gen asked.

Niamh pulled herself from her old thoughts. Nothing could be done about the past. Only about the unsteady future.

"She's in magic drain," Niamh said.

Gen was another problem. Like the way she made Niamh's heart beat wildly in her chest as if she'd resurrected the decaying thing. The only way Niamh knew how to survive that was to push Gen away. She'd lived a long, full life with the love of her life. She couldn't watch a second one die.

"Is there anything I can do?" Gen asked with those wide, earnest, clouded eyes that saw so much.

"Actually, I need you to call Graves and tell him that she's going to have to stay here until she wakes up."

Gen bit her lip. "He's not going to like that."

"No," Niamh agreed, glancing back at the closed door where Kierse lay in Lorcan's bed. "He's really not."

PART V

MONSTER CON

Chapter Fifty-Two

"I don't care what he wants!" a voice yelled. "I am not moving her!"

Her body ached all over. Like someone had sat on her chest and crushed her ribs in. Her fingers and toes tingled as if they were coming back online. Her head pounded.

And yet she was comfortable. The bed she was in was warm and soft and pliant. It smelled like rain and soap. She could have buried her nose in it and inhaled. For some reason, it was like coming home.

Her eyes peeled open slowly to take stock of where she was. Unfamiliar. Everything was unfamiliar.

She stiffened when she didn't recognize the bed or the room or anything inside of it. The space was all exposed red brick and floor-to-ceiling windows with long, gauzy drapes. The bed was a mahogany four-poster with an olive comforter and crisp white sheets. A desk sat against one wall, covered with old dusty tomes and a large ledger. The door next to it was cracked to reveal a bathroom.

She focused on the present. She was in a stranger's bedroom. It smelled like summer and looked like…an old Brooklyn warehouse.

The pieces began to slot into place. She gasped and tried to jerk upright. Her body screeched in pain at the overuse, and she flopped backward.

She was in Lorcan's bed.

She was *in* Lorcan's bed.

Oh, fuck, *she was in Lorcan's bed*!

How long had she been here? What was she doing here? What the fuck had happened?

She didn't remember exactly. Only that she was in a long, white button-up that must belong to him. Had he changed her? Oh dear God, she'd need to process that some other time. At least the other side of the bed looked unslept in. She must have had the bed to herself. She fucking hoped she'd had it to herself.

Gingerly this time, she righted her body, waiting for the pounding in her head to slow to a small pulse. Then she kicked her feet to the side and tried to stand, holding onto one of the posts for support.

At first her head swam, but slowly her vision cleared. Pieces of the night came back to her. The triskel training. Magic sharing. Ethan.

Oh.

Ethan had drained her magic. Accidentally. She didn't think he'd known how to do it on purpose. Yet he'd still done it.

"Yeah, you can tell him to go fuck himself!"

Kierse narrowed her eyes. Lorcan. That was Lorcan.

And if he was arguing with someone…that meant…

"Graves," she whispered.

She was halfway across the room when the door creaked open again and Lorcan padded forward on silent feet. He froze at the sight of her standing in the middle of the room in nothing but an oversize button-up.

"You're awake," he said, his eyes traveling down her legs.

"Is he here?"

He huffed. "No. Even he isn't that stupid." Kierse took a step toward the door and then stumbled. Lorcan was there an instant later, catching her. "You should be in bed."

"I'm fine."

"You just fell walking."

Her head felt fuzzy all over again at the feel of his hands. She wanted him to stop, but at the same time it did steady her.

"How did I end up in here?"

"After you collapsed, I carried you up here."

"How long was I out?"

"A few hours. It's just past dawn," Lorcan said, guiding her back to the bed.

She took a seat if for no other reason than to get away from his distracting hands. But now he was standing over her while she was in his shirt, the hem dragging up her thighs. His eyes gleamed with devotion and desire.

"How are you really feeling?" he asked, concern sweeping away everything else.

She cleared her throat. "Like I hit magic burn by way of a trainwreck."

"Been there." Then as if he couldn't help himself, he pushed her hair back behind her ear and said, "You know if we were bound, I could replenish you."

"I can replenish myself," she told him, brushing his hand aside.

He heaved a long breath and stepped back. "All right. I can have some soup and bread brought in." He walked to a side table and poured her a glass of water. She took it from him. "How do you recharge?"

"Stealing."

He chuckled. "That sounds right. Well, once you can walk on your own, have at it."

"Can't I reabsorb what Ethan took?"

He frowned at the question. "Well, for one, you can't relink without the full moon. Two, you don't have any magic to link with at this point."

"Oh. Right."

"I didn't know you could absorb consciously. I thought it was still a passive power for you."

"I've been practicing. Turn it on, turn it off like a switch," she told him in between sips of water.

He tilted his head. "Why would you need to turn it off?"

"Because sometimes I'm going to hit magic burn and people are going to be able to use their magic against me," she reminded him, gesturing to herself. "Like right now. So it's best to be prepared."

"All the more reason not to let you leave anytime soon."

She knew what he meant—more reason not to let Graves in her head. If he only knew.

"How are Gen and Ethan?" she asked, changing the subject.

"Sleeping and exhausted. Ethan burned off a lot of the magic right away. So he's fine, but Gen stayed up and watched over you until Niamh made her sleep." He refilled her glass of water. "And you should curl back into my bed and do the same."

"What are you going to do?"

"I'd be happy to join you."

She rose to her feet unsteadily. "I'm going to head out. You get that sleep. You don't look like you slept at all."

"I didn't. I watched over you the entire time."

She flushed at the comment. She needed to leave. Nothing good could come from staying another minute in Lorcan's bedroom.

"Do you have my clothes?"

"If I tell you I destroyed them, will you keep wearing my clothes?"

He ran a hand along the collar. Her legs felt like jelly. She needed to find out how to get out of this building and to a subway. Fuck, she couldn't ride a subway in this state. She couldn't brave a troll.

"Stay," he pleaded. "You're not well."

A part of her wanted to listen to him. To fall back into that spring rain and let the summer sunshine lull her into submission, but she couldn't. So she shook her head, not trusting the words that might come out of her mouth right now.

He sighed and retrieved her clothes, offering them to her. "You're not a prisoner."

"You sound so convincing," she joked as she padded into his bathroom.

She slid out of his shirt, leaving the soft cotton on the counter and pulling her leggings and tank back on. They felt dirty and constricting in comparison. She forced herself not to look back at the shirt she should never have been wearing.

Her phone had been stashed inside the pile of clothes, and she cringed as she turned the thing back on and saw it light up with texts and calls from Graves.

She jotted out a quick message, letting him know she was fine and on her way back now.

The phone immediately rang in her hand. With a sigh, she answered, "Hey."

"I'm on my way," Graves said. "Where should I pick you up?"

"Do you really think you should drive through Druid territory?"

"Do you think I give a fuck?"

"No," she muttered.

"Where are you right now?"

She bit her lip. "I'm not sure, actually. I'm in Lorcan's bathroom."

Graves was silent a moment. "I know where his building is. I'll meet you downstairs as soon as George gets us across the bridge."

He'd been waiting. Her heart warmed at that thought. She figured if it had been anyone other than Lorcan, he would have already barged in and rescued her.

"See you soon." She hung up the phone and exited the bathroom.

"He's on his way?" Lorcan asked with distaste.

"Could you two put your hate on hold for a minute?"

Lorcan shot her a look that said that was never happening. "Don't ever forget what he's capable of."

"I don't," she told him as she pocketed her phone. "Nor what you are."

"I'd never hurt you."

Kierse almost believed him. Almost.

Chapter Fifty-Three

Graves's limo was waiting at the exit to Lorcan's building. Graves leaned back against the door, utterly unconcerned. Druid patrols stared down at him with open enmity, guns trained in his direction. And on his part, not a single fuck was given.

"Wren," he said, breathing a sigh of relief at her presence. "Let's get you home."

He yanked the door open, letting her slip inside. He smirked up at the patrols before sliding in after her. He tapped the roof twice, and George pulled away.

Graves was utter stillness next to her. She could feel the waves of death emanating from him. The nightmare that she'd first known. As if he couldn't control the power that whirled like a tornado, threatening to take down the entire Druid compound.

"Are you okay?" she asked softly.

"Am *I* okay? You were the one who was injured."

"Do I look injured?"

"Yes," he said flatly.

"Did Lorcan tell you what happened?"

"Gen did," Graves said. "As best she could. She did not see the danger that I did."

"What danger was that?"

His gaze finally shifted to hers. "Your magic was drained. Your absorption was off. Anything could be done to you."

"Do I seem different?" she asked, not discarding his fear. He had a reason for this, clearly. His feelings were valid.

"You *smell* like him," Graves growled.

Kierse bit her lip. "That...would make sense."

"Explain."

"I woke up in his shirt," she told him. "In his room. In his bed."

Graves clenched his jaw. "We need to turn around. I'm going to kill him."

Kierse laughed. "We'll shower when we get home. I can start smelling like that honeysuckle and jasmine stuff you got me again. Will that make it better?"

"He's goading me," Graves said.

"Yes. But he was also trying to take care of me and was worried about moving me. I am still not that steady on my feet."

"He has ulterior motives."

She scooted across the seat and leaned her head against his shoulder. "So do you."

Graves slipped his arm across her back and pulled her in tighter. "Yes, but you are my wren."

"Mmm," she agreed without argument, letting her eyes flutter closed.

It wasn't that much later when Graves was carrying her out of the limo and up in the elevator. She snuggled tighter into him as he hefted her up the stairs to his bedroom. She thought he might force her to shower to get the smell of Lorcan off of her, but he just yanked the sheets back and tucked her into the comforter.

She yawned dramatically. "Bed?"

He kicked his shoes off in response and began to undress her slow and methodically. Once she was down to her underwear, he tucked her back into the bed, removed his clothes, and crawled in after her. Her back was to his chest, and everything felt exactly as it should.

She hated how out of control she felt in Lorcan's presence. And how much easier it was when there was a major body of water between them.

Graves pressed a kiss into her shoulder. "I hate that, too."

She shut her mind down, finding that space where she could open and close her vault with ease. Not that she really thought she could keep Graves out, but...she hadn't meant for him to hear that.

"I already know how you feel about him," Graves told her. "I've seen it before."

"Stop reading me," she said, shifting away from him.

His eyes clouded. "Of course."

"No, wait..." She reached for him. "I didn't mean..."

"I understand," he said, keeping the distance. "It's less fun when you can't choose it."

That was true, but that wasn't the problem. It was the hurt on his face.

"I don't feel for Lorcan what I feel for you."

"I know," Graves said evenly. "It's more complicated than that."

"Yes. It's..."

"Intense," Graves finished for her. His gaze dark as he stared down at his bare hand.

"Sometimes," she admitted, willing him to meet her eyes again.

"Compulsive," he added. "Complicated. Painful. Wanton. Frustrating."

She hadn't even been thinking about how the bond made her feel. Was she that transparent?

"Did you read all that off of me just now?"

"No," Graves said slowly, looking up at her finally. "I read it off of Emilie."

Kierse swallowed hard as realization dawned. "Emilie had a soulmate?"

"A Druid named Tadhg, who was rising in the ranks. He was a decade older than us at the time. It doesn't feel like much now, but it did then."

"You're a few centuries older than me," Kierse said with a laugh.

"Precisely." He lifted a shoulder. "At the time, a decade felt like an eternity. Especially when you're in love with someone else."

Kierse had a dawning realization. "You were in love, but she had a soulmate that was someone else."

"Yes."

"Much like…"

"You and Lorcan," he confirmed.

"Fuck," she said. "You really reach for the worst hand in the deck every time, don't you?"

His lips quirked at the flippancy. "They're always drawn for me."

"I know that feeling."

"Emilie was my first love. I thought she was the entire world. I wanted to believe that the soulmate was wrong, but it was an *honor* back then. We decided together to petition for a marriage."

Kierse could hear the heartbreak in his voice. The girl he'd loved and no one would take them seriously.

"We thought it would change their minds. It did not."

"I'm sorry," she told him truthfully.

His expression was flat as he added, "No one would have done it anyway. I wasn't really one of them."

Kierse frowned. She didn't feel the writhing pit of jealousy she thought she would at hearing Graves discuss his first love. She'd rescued Torra months earlier and had once wanted that to be her entire world. This was centuries before she had even been born. She couldn't be upset about a life that he'd lived before her.

All she felt instead was understanding and sympathy. That so many people had hurt Graves, rejected him, and created the monster they thought they were protecting themselves from.

"It was a long time ago. What should have been clear to me but wasn't until it was too late was that Emilie could never be mine." His eyes were hard and flat at the words. "Now I'm wondering if I have once again convinced myself of the impossible."

Kierse's heart was stuttering at those words. "Which is what?"

"That you could be mine."

Their eyes met across the small distance. She watched him bare his soul to her. With open fear in every interaction, and still he was trying.

Kierse reached out then and took his hand in hers. His eyes widened at her as she opened herself to him. Not at the confused feelings for Lorcan that were distorted by whatever connection was between them, but deeper, to the core of what she felt for *him*. For *Graves*.

"There is no organization forcing anyone to be together. A few hundred years have passed since that time. There is no Fae Council. The Druids don't control me. Nothing and no one controls you. The only people who get to choose anything are the two people in this room. All right?"

"I much prefer that," he said, sliding his hand up her arm and around to her back, pulling her into him.

"Good."

His lips brushed hers as he said, "Just know, you are my choice. Every time."

Chapter Fifty-Four

A few days later, Kierse was fully recharged and hunched over the decoy box. The heist was only a matter of days away, and she was running out of time and down to the last digit of this combination. She could feel the thread like it would come apart for her at any second. The anticipation was killing her.

Then with a little hiss, it popped open.

"I did it!" Kierse gasped.

Gen startled awake. "I wasn't sleeping."

Kierse laughed. "You so were but look!"

Walter lifted his head a fraction above his computer. "Did what?"

Gen straightened. Anne Boleyn hissed at her side. Gen stroked her back and leaned forward.

"Oh!" she gasped. "You got it open."

"Nice," Walter said, returning to his work.

"What's inside?" Gen asked.

"Let's find out."

Kierse gingerly opened it all the way up to reveal…an empty box.

She deflated. She'd known it was a decoy—she hadn't been able to feel the cauldron inside the box—but a part of her had still hoped for *something*. The only thing she could sense was a lingering scent of lemon and pine. The Curator's magical signature.

"Well, that was anticlimactic," Gen said with a laugh.

"All that work for an empty box."

"Yeah, but you proved to yourself that you could do it."

"A for effort," Kierse grumbled. "Now, I just have to reset it. At least that won't be the same as dismantling it."

Walter glanced up. He'd taken up essentially permanent residence in the seat opposite them. The computer systems ever-expanding across the table. "We have a problem."

"What kind of problem?"

"A big one."

Kierse sighed. "Should I get Graves?"

"I've already alerted him. He should be here soon."

"Is this better or worse than Schwartz being kicked off the security team?" Gen asked.

"Worse."

Graves threw the door to the library open. "A manual switch on the cauldron system and you *just* found out?"

"It looks like it was added recently," Walter said with a shrug. "We're going to need someone inside security to dismantle it if we want to get Kierse inside."

"And we fucking lost Schwartz," Graves grumbled.

Gen raised her hand slowly.

Graves shook his head. "You don't have to raise your hand."

"No. I was volunteering."

"For what?" Kierse asked.

"To turn off the security system," Gen said.

"Do you know anything about security systems?" Graves asked.

"Well, no, but everyone else has a job to play tomorrow."

"No," Kierse said automatically.

Gen sighed. "You don't get to make the decision."

"You're not part of this."

Gen whipped around to face Kierse. "I sat through every meeting. I live here. I am every bit a part of this as you are. I have magic, and I can handle myself. I want to do this."

"Why?" Graves asked before Kierse could object further.

"What do you mean, why? That's an artifact of my people's history, too, right?"

"So, you want to use the cauldron?"

"No," Gen said slowly. She lifted her chin and met Graves's imperious look. "I don't need to be healed. I am a healer."

Graves's brow cleared in understanding. "Ah, you want to learn from it."

"If I can…"

"I can't promise it will teach you anything," he said.

"You're actually considering this," Kierse said.

It was unfathomable. Not because Gen wasn't competent. She was and always had been. She had an inner strength that many people underestimated. She was the backbone of their trio. Kierse had seen how well she could use her new magical abilities, but she still couldn't help but want to protect her. It wasn't that she was an innocent, not with her upbringing, but she was pure in so many ways. Untouched by the horrors of the world. Even Anne Boleyn loved her. She was the best of them.

"I will consider all options," Graves said. "But we do need an extra pair of hands now that Schwartz is out. You and I are stealing the cauldron. Laz is already in the hotel putting together the warding system from Walter. Nate is controlling our exit. George is the getaway car. Edgar has to be there for loading and unloading and Schwartz will be covering him. Isolde is baking. Walter is running security. Do you have someone else in mind?"

"No," Kierse said. She knew the plan. They'd gone over it a hundred times, tweaking until they were sure they'd considered every possible angle. This new wrench certainly didn't help anything.

"I can do it," Gen told her.

"I know you can," Kierse told her. "I hate risking you."

"You don't have to worry about me."

Kierse grasped her hand. "We worry about each other. It's how we survive."

"Gen should be fine to manually switch off the system. I can walk her through it," Walter said.

"In two days?" Kierse asked with a sigh.

"I. Can. Do. It," Gen repeated.

"There's another issue," Walter said.

"What now?" Graves grumbled.

"Kierse was going to be the distraction for the Curator while you switched out the boxes," Walter said. "But the window just closed."

"What does that mean?" Kierse asked.

"I ran some numbers and estimate it at four minutes and thirty-four seconds on average." Walter looked at their blank faces. "That's how long you'll have to get the cauldron out."

Kierse and Gen exchanged confused looks, but Graves got to the conclusion first.

"Kierse has to steal it," Graves said slowly.

"Yes," Walter said. "The Curator will need to be elsewhere. And we'll need the more talented thief to make the switch."

"And a bigger diversion," Graves said.

"Schwartz might be needed after all."

"Are you saying that I won't be able to talk to the Curator?"

"It's that or the cauldron," Graves said.

Kierse stilled under those words. She hadn't had any more success with her memories than she'd had before the psychiatrist. She'd thought that speaking to the Curator might be a way around her mental blocks. She could learn straight from the source about the night he'd put the spell on her. That chance, or the cauldron that Graves had been after forever—she didn't want to make that choice. And yet she felt as if it had already been made for her. She wouldn't meet the Curator. She'd have to find the memories the old-fashioned way.

"Fuck," she said, pacing toward the closed window at the back of the brownstone.

"Gen, you're in. Walter will fill you in on the system," Graves said. "I'll call the rest of the team in for a meeting." She heard the door open and close behind them and the soft tread of Graves's shoes as he approached her. "This doesn't have to be the only way you meet him."

"Yes, because after we steal one of his most prized possessions, I can just schedule a meeting." She shot him a look.

"When you're long lived, you have more than one opportunity to go after the things you want."

She hung her head. Getting the cauldron was the priority, but she didn't know if she *would* have another shot at getting to meet the Curator.

"We have to try again," she said on a sigh of frustration.

"To get past the block? Are you sure you're ready for that?"

"What other choice do I have?"

"You just recovered your stores," he said. "And you need them all for the heist."

"Then I can go out and steal to replenish them."

He studied her. "All right. I do think that it's better for you to face this fear and try to break through the barrier than to walk into the heist wanting to meet the guy."

"I wouldn't jeopardize the mission."

He raised an eyebrow. "Oh, really?"

She laughed. "I never *plan* to go off script."

"The script just happens to be in rewrites whenever you're on screen?"

"Exactly," she said with a grin. She dropped her head and sighed. "All right. We'll try again."

"Good," Graves said, guiding her back toward the chaise. "Where do you want to start?"

Kierse didn't know. The doctor said that she needed to face what happened to her parents. But she didn't know how to do that or even where to start.

Graves gave her a moment and then seemed to know she couldn't answer. "Why don't we just go back to the hallway and see if we can make it to the room? Don't push against the block. I don't want you bleeding all over my rug."

She rolled her eyes at him and laughed. "Charming."

His lips quirked. Kierse lay back on the chaise and closed her eyes. The hallway. She wanted to go back to the hallway. She didn't know how to face it, but what other choice was there?

She started to tremble. There was a reason that she'd been avoiding this. The fear seemed to creep up her throat until she felt like she was going to scream.

Was this what the trauma felt like? This relentless fear that she was going to see something truly awful and never be the same again? She'd survived abandonment and an abusive thieving guild and the Monster War. How much worse could it be?

And why did her brain say that this would break her? That this would be the thing that finally put her in the ground?

"Wren," Graves said softly.

His bare hand touched her arm, but she hadn't pulled her absorption down. She reached for it and nothing happened. Silence filtered through the buzzing in her ear. She couldn't touch her magic. No, she could touch it, but it wouldn't release.

"I can...I can do it," she whispered.

With what felt like a rip, she tugged her absorption free and Graves's magic settled into her.

She dropped into Graves's library. The same place she was currently sitting, but it was her younger self looking up at him through suspicious eyes as her parents negotiated for him to take care of her.

She hadn't meant to take them there, but the smell of the library had taken over her senses. They were back at the beginning again.

"Did you bring something to barter with?" Graves asked.

"Yes," Shannon said.

Her father removed a hunting knife from a sheath at his belt. He dropped the heavy tool onto the table. It was long, sharp, and used, the leather of the handle worn. An emblem—a stag's antlers inside a Trinity Knot—was burned into the metal.

"Is this sufficient?" Adair asked. "It was blessed by the Fae."

A sob escaped Kierse's throat at the sight of her parents there together. Her father offering his own hunting knife for her safety.

The connection broke, and her absorption snapped back into place. She covered her face as all the joy of their faces bled from her.

"Hey," Graves said, reaching for her. "This is too much. You do not have to do this right now."

She looked up at him with glassy eyes. "You said yourself, I'll have it at the back of my mind the whole time I'm at the Plaza if I don't face it."

"You might. But if you're this upset at this one memory, will we be able to be able to work through the block? Will you be better or worse if we accomplish what we're after?"

She bit her lip, unable to answer. She felt like she was going to crack in two at the very thought.

"Worse." The word escaped her lips before she could stop it. She didn't feel ready. She felt like she had to do this thing to get past it. Not that she was prepared.

"That's all I need to know." He retreated with a nod. "Let's get through the heist. We can deal with the Curator and your memories after."

Chapter Fifty-Five

Stealing from tourists wasn't doing it for her today. She needed to be back at nightfall for the final meeting before Monster Con tomorrow, but she still wasn't fully recharged. It should have been easy enough to walk around Midtown, considering the size of the crowds, but she'd gotten bored. And most of the Upper East Side was away at the Hamptons or wherever the ultra-rich jettisoned to escape the summer heat.

Kierse sighed as she sank into a seat on the Mall in Central Park. Bustling tourists paraded through the avenue lined with park benches. A saxophonist played across from her. A female mer swirled a soapy, five-foot loop of string on two poles, creating child-size bubbles. A nymph breakdancer was showing off farther down. Monsters and humans. As the Treaty had always promised them it would be. And yet it all felt tenuous.

Maybe it was just frustration. Another failed attempt with Graves. Another block in her memory. Another day with no answers.

She tilted her head back and looked up at the summer sky. Here she was in Central Park, and still she felt heartache for a past that was stolen from her and she couldn't even remember.

Her phone pinged. She pulled it out to see a text from Gen. She still wasn't exactly used to getting to message her friend whenever she wanted. Technology had been so expensive and difficult to get your hands on after the war, and having money was still new.

Gen: *Are you still going to see Ethan?*

Kierse groaned. Or maybe she'd been spending all day avoiding this. She had to go back to Brooklyn.

Kierse: *Yeah. Do you want me to pick you up?*

Gen: *I have to work with Walter until I figure this out. Will you tell him I'm sorry? I really wanted to go to see him after graduation…or whatever the Druids are calling it.*

Kierse shot back a text agreeing to tell him and then skipped through the park to the nearest subway station at 72nd Street. She descended into the depths, wondering if she should try stealing from the resident troll, when she nearly skidded to a halt.

There was no troll.

In fact, there was nothing standing in the atrium between the stairs and the turnstiles. She re-pocketed the cash she'd already reached for on instinct. She cast her eyes around the whole area as if the troll was going to jump out at her. But there was none.

It was so disorienting she almost missed the symbol spray painted in gold on the floor where the troll typically sat. It was an arrow shot through wings. Kierse's stomach curdled.

Men of Valor.

She'd already known they weren't gone, but she didn't know what it meant that they had put their logo over the place where a troll had sat. She snapped a picture of it and sent a text separately to Graves and to Nate with the caption, *Trouble.*

Nate: *Fuck*

She hopped on the B train toward downtown, switching to the M at Washington Square Park before she heard back from Graves.

Graves: *I'm on it.*

She didn't know what that meant.

But she'd known the city felt too quiet. The truce too perfect. After what happened this winter, she had been expecting bedlam. Not this cookie-cutter shit. As the heat of the city intensified, she felt the meddling underbelly boiling and ready to burst.

Kierse was well acquainted with the Broadway stop in Brooklyn now. And how her chest started to tighten the closer she got to Druid territory. Except today...Lorcan wasn't here.

She had never walked into Brooklyn and not immediately known where Lorcan was. It was disconcerting. And considering the Druid acolytes had graduated today, she would have thought he'd be around...congratulating them. Or something.

So she actually felt light—and weirdly empty—as she walked down the street. None of the Druid patrols even blinked at her. She even bypassed Declan giving orders. He glared at her but said nothing. She walked right into headquarters and found Ethan in his room.

"You came," he said with a laugh.

"Of course."

He looked behind her. "Where's Gen?"

"She told me to tell you that she's sorry, but she got caught up."

"Oh," he said, disappointment etched into his features.

She laughed. "Well, at least basic training didn't remove your heart from your sleeve."

He wrinkled his nose at her and grabbed a hat, slinging it on backward. "Doesn't look like you've added one to yours."

"Doesn't sound useful," she teased.

"Jerk."

"Hey, you're the one who stole all my magic and knocked me out."

"Well, I didn't mean to do that."

"I know you didn't," she said, falling into step with him.

He pulled the door closed and tipped his head to the side. "Come with me."

There was still distance between the two of them. She wasn't sure if there always would be from now on. They weren't holed up in the attic anymore, completely reliant on one another. But at least they were trying. It was better than when she'd first come home and they'd argued. She'd do anything to erase that.

"Where are we going?"

"You'll see," he said with a smirk and barreled down the hallway.

Kierse recognized the same route she had first taken with Lorcan when she'd returned. Down a set of stairs and into the long hallway that bypassed his underground vault. Kierse paused at the sight of the thing.

"Think I can get inside?" Kierse asked, her fingers itching.

Ethan grabbed her hand. "Let's not find out."

"Why not?"

"I don't particularly want all of the Druidic Order coming down on us."

Kierse mock-gasped. "You think so little of me?"

"No. I think so highly of them."

She laughed. "The brainwashing is intense."

"Pot meet kettle," he said, pulling her away from the vault.

She was still arguing with him about going back when they made it into the bank.

She froze.

Where before the mosaic tiles had once been perfectly aligned, a *tree* rose out of the ground. As if its roots had sprung up through feet of cement and cracked the floor to burst fifteen feet into the air.

"There is a tree in the middle of the room."

"That's what I wanted to tell you and Gen."

"That somehow a *tree* is here?"

"Our tree," Ethan explained. "It's our magic."

She glanced at him in confusion. "What do you mean?"

"When we were connected as a triskel, I took way too much and blasted the magic into the floor. You'd already passed out by the time it happened. We all left, and when we came back, a tree had appeared where I released the power. It's been growing steadily ever since." Ethan touched the trunk and closed his eyes as if connecting with it. "It's part of us now."

"How?"

"Niamh thinks our triskel magic created a new sacred tree."

Kierse's eyebrows shot up. "Is that possible?"

"It hasn't been done before, but they said that a triskel can do great magic."

Kierse stepped hesitantly forward and put her hand on the tree. It reacted to her magic with a sigh. No, it wasn't reacting to her magic; it *was* her magic. Primarily hers, at least. There was a tiny thread of Ethan and Gen in there, too. Just like when they were linked and she was the torrent of power that suffused them.

She could hardly believe that this great thing had come out of their joining. She knew that a triskel had saved her life. But this somehow felt so different to that. So precious.

Her mind recalled another sacred tree she'd seen—Sansara. Had Cillian Ryan channeled his own magic to recreate the tree he'd destroyed? Was that how Sansara still stood? Was that even *possible* without a triskel?

And then another question—could Cillian Ryan be part of a triskel?

"Thinking deep thoughts," Ethan said.

"It's been one of those days."

"Are you going to tell me about it?"

She sighed. She *should* confide in Ethan. She always had before. "I have a block in my memory."

Ethan's brows furrowed. "Gen said that you were starting to remember things from before. I can't believe the spell took your memories."

"Yeah," Kierse said on a sigh. "How much did she tell you?"

"That you went into the market to get a memory potion and you remembered that they'd had the spell put on you. I didn't know you'd done more than that."

Kierse shrugged. "Well, with Graves's help."

Ethan sighed. "Do I even want to know?"

"Maybe not," she said with a laugh. "But it's been fine. He's just helped me recall the rest of my memories. And there's a block when I try to remember the moment when the spell was cast, like a skip in my mind. I can't get through it to see it happening. No matter how Graves or I push, it's not there."

Ethan looked uncomfortable. He'd come around a little on Graves, but Kierse didn't know if he would ever be fully convinced.

"You know what, forget about it," Kierse said with a shake of her head. "This is why I didn't tell you to begin with."

"No, I'm sorry," Ethan said quickly. "I want to know more. What does that mean? That the memory isn't there?"

"That he erased it, or the spell did. I'm not sure."

"But you're going to find out."

"That's the plan," she conceded. "When we get to that point in my memory, it always jumps forward. And that's when I hit a second block. Graves took me to the hospital to see a psychiatrist."

Ethan's jaw dropped. "Really?"

"Yes. Contrary to Druid training, Graves cares about me. The psychiatrist said that my brain was shielding me from a traumatic incident. And I think it's how my parents died."

Ethan's face dropped. "Oh, Kierse."

"I know," she said, sinking to the floor and putting her back to the tree. Ethan dropped down next to her. "Going through memories is never great, but I just...don't know if I want to even see that."

"Maybe you forgot them for a reason. Maybe it's for the better."

"Maybe, but the psychiatrist said that I needed to face what happened to me." She shrugged. "All of it's fucked up."

"I'm sorry I haven't been there for any of this," Ethan told her.

"I'm glad you're here now."

Ethan wrapped her up in a hug, and something seemed to fit back together inside her.

They were silent a few minutes before Kierse nudged him and asked, "So, are you going to see Corey tonight?"

Ethan ducked his head. "We might have made plans."

"And you're coming to the wedding?"

"I'll be there." He removed his hat and ran a hand over his hair. "Going to need to get a new fade first."

Kierse laughed. "Ah, there's my vain boy."

Ethan pushed her shoulder. "Remind me why you're my friend."

"Because you love me."

"I do," he confirmed.

Kierse sighed with relief. Maybe finally the thing between them was getting back on track.

"Oh," she gasped. Her hand went to her chest.

"Are you okay?"

She rubbed the spot reflexively. "Lorcan's back."

Ethan's eyes widened. "I didn't know he was gone."

She shot him a look. "You think we would have done all of this without interruption otherwise?"

"I guess I didn't think about it." He frowned. "You really hate that you're connected, don't you?"

Kierse rose to her feet and dusted her hands off on her shorts. "It's complicated."

"Is it because it's Lorcan? Would you be fine if it was Graves?" he asked through gritted teeth.

"I don't hate Lorcan," she said automatically and was surprised to find it was true. "Maybe he isn't as bad as I've made him out to be. He took care of my best friend, after all."

Ethan grinned. "That he did."

"But I don't want anyone or anything to tell me what to do."

"What else is new?" he said with a laugh.

Kierse shoved him. "Shut up."

"You're just so predictable. You get the best thing in the entire world with one of the best people in it and you're like, 'Oh man, I'd rather make the worst decision I can instead.'"

She snorted. "Wow. Thanks for the show of support."

"What would it hurt to give Lorcan a chance?"

"If I ever need a wingman, I'll tag you in," she promised. "Until then, stay out of my love life. Deal with yours first."

Ethan laughed and held his hands up. "Fair. Fair. But...you are going to see him, aren't you?"

"Yeah," she admitted, heading across the bank floor. "I guess I am."

She left Ethan at their tree and followed the invisible string that drew taut between her and Lorcan. Back through the tunnel to the large wooden double doors that he had brought her to the first time she'd shown up in Brooklyn. Behind these doors was the Oak Throne.

Which could be hers.

She put her hand against the door. She could feel him on the other side, though she was uncertain what he was doing in there. Ethan's words about giving him a chance rang in her ears.

"Fuck," she muttered.

Then she pushed the door open.

Chapter Fifty-Six

Lorcan looked much like a spoiled prince, lounging across the Oak Throne. One foot braced over the wooden armrest. His head in his hand propped up by his elbow. A navy three-piece suit draped across his powerful figure. All he was missing was the crown slipping over his brow to complete the modern Renaissance painting.

"Heavy is the head that wears the crown," Kierse said as she stepped into the room.

Lorcan sighed heavily before glancing up at her. "Are you mocking me?"

"Would such a visage deserve mocking?"

"And what visage is that?"

"A king sitting upon his throne," she said, gesturing to him as she stepped up to the dais. "All you need is the crown."

Lorcan swirled his fingers in front of him. The golden glow of his magic materialized as he spoke a few indistinguishable words. The scent of summer rain and sunshine hit her afresh as the glow solidified into a crown made of magic. Something solid and yet insubstantial. Ephemeral and molten. It was a shiny gold piece interwoven in intricate Irish knots. He lifted the piece to his brow where it fit her pretty picture perfectly.

She smirked. "There it is. I'll remember you like this forever."

He gestured flippantly. "As a king?"

"Irreverent."

He made a second circle, breathing life into a second crown. This one much smaller and almost dainty, yet powerful. It was a mirror to the first, with the same knots throughout. He held the second piece in his hand. "Then I would need an irreverent queen."

She laughed. "Could you imagine me in a crown?"

He stood smoothly and took the step down the dais. She froze under those crystal-clear eyes as he settled the second crown easily into her dark hair.

"It suits you."

She removed it, running her thumbs over the intricate metal work. "How'd you do it?"

"Magic is easier right now," he said with a shrug. "Give it a day and I'll be scrounging for summer magic."

She'd been ignoring the approaching solstice, uncertain what exactly was going to happen this year. She didn't want to ask. She didn't want to know. And yet she couldn't.

"How does it normally work? The Oak and Holly King battle. Are you always together?"

"No. Almost never. The magic releases and one of us is weakened regardless of whether the fight is physical."

"I've read all the books about it," Kierse said. "The scant few I could get my hands on, at least. They didn't really explain how this started."

Lorcan turned back toward the throne. "That is a story for another day, I'm afraid. I don't have the patience for it today."

"Is the Oak Throne also part of being the Oak King?" she asked, staring up at the massive thing.

"No. I was the Oak King first," Lorcan told her. "The throne is for the ruler of the Druids. Only I can sit on it." His eyes flicked back to her. "And my queen."

"So why aren't you in Dublin, then?" She glanced up at the throne. "Why isn't the tree in Dublin?"

Lorcan flicked his eyes to her. "You know why."

Graves. He was here to watch the Holly King.

He sank back into the throne, leaning his elbows on his knees and staring down at her with those imperious eyes. "And why are *you* here? Don't you have a big party tomorrow?"

Why was she even surprised that he knew?

"Yes, I'm aware you're going after the cauldron," he said with a shrug. "I won't interfere. Though you shouldn't give it to him. As if that really needs to be said."

She arched an eyebrow. "Last I checked, I don't take orders."

"I wasn't giving any. I know what he wants from the cauldron, what he wanted from the spear, what the sword refused him."

Kierse refused to be baited. "Do you keep the sword in that vault? Is that why you showed it to me?"

"Would I be that stupid?"

"Yes," she teased.

He leaned backward, smirking. He draped his hands over the armrests, and now he looked every inch the Oak King. As if he might crumble mountains with a look and bring her to her knees with a second. "Go open it and find out."

"Another day, perhaps."

"Looking forward to it."

He returned to his slumped position, lying across the throne as if it weren't full of magic and sacred to his people.

She should have walked away then. Let him mope, or whatever was going on with him. But her feet carried her up the dais, where she set the golden crown down on the armrest.

"What's going on with you?" she asked.

"Are you suggesting that you care?"

"I'm the only one here."

He laughed sardonically. "Ringing endorsement."

Kierse couldn't help it; she smiled. A real smile. It was like seeing behind the curtain. For the first time, he wasn't showing her the smooth and suave leader of the Druidic Order. He wasn't trying to seduce her or win her over. He was irritated and a little petulant. She kind of liked it.

He glanced up at her as if he could sense her change in mood. "You actually want to know?"

"I guess I do," she told him.

"There was a troll revolt today. The trolls all abandoned their posts in the subway at once. The entire group of them worked as one and left. Men of Valor logos were spray-painted over a ton of the entrances. The whole time it's been quiet in the streets, they've been consolidating power in the background."

"I saw the spray paint and a missing troll at the 72nd entrance," Kierse said as she tried to comprehend it. Trolls were singular in nature. They rarely, if *ever*, worked as a unit. It was why each of the various gangs had been able to have a different troll guarding their entrances. "So the trolls are where, then?"

"No one knows, but I would wager they're working with the Men of Valor now."

"What are they hoping to gain? The end of the Treaty?"

Lorcan nodded. "That was always their aim. There's a convocation coming up to discuss the Treaty, and delegates from each side are going. Apparently two are chosen at the Monster Con this weekend. I would bet good money that they're putting their representative up then."

Kierse's head swam. *"Fuck."*

"Yeah. So that was what I was dealing with while you were gone."

"Are you coming to the conference, then?"

"Yes," he said flatly.

She needed to get home. Graves likely already knew this, but it was going to change things for the heist.

"I need to make sure that my people will survive the fall out," Lorcan said, his finger slipping into the center of her crown and swirling it in a circle. "The last thing I want is another war."

"Same."

"So, if you need to go, then you should go. I have shit to do."

But she physically couldn't move. The connection in this room was almost overwhelming. She had been trying to ignore it while they talked, but there was no denying that she felt rooted to the ground.

When she didn't leave, Lorcan's gaze shifted up to her again. "What is that look?"

"I've never seen you like this."

"Like what?"

She shrugged. "You're not trying so hard."

Lorcan lifted an eyebrow. "Are you saying you…like me more like this?"

"I didn't say that."

He shifted to sitting again. "You do."

She bit her lip. "I mean, you were *intolerable* when you were trying to win me over."

"I just needed to be an asshole this whole time?"

"As if you could be an asshole," she said with a laugh.

"Hmm," he said and then stood from the throne.

He took a step toward her, bridging the distance smoothly, his frame towering over her. The crown was still in his hand, and he set it on her head. The weight was almost a comfort. It had been made for her, after all. His hand moved to her chin, tilting her head up. She shivered under that gaze, the touch igniting under her skin.

"Do you feel that?"

"The…the magic?" she breathed.

"*Our* magic," he told her. "My chuisle mo chroí."

Between one breath and the next, his mouth landed on hers. Her head went fuzzy at the contact. She couldn't think or move or breathe for anything except him. His other hand wrapped around her back, crushing her against his chest. His lips were warm and pliant, and as he slid his tongue in her mouth, she tasted summer heat.

She was frozen there in the midst of that kiss. Her mind still under the weight of their soulmate bond and her body reacting to the connection with *more*. She didn't know which way was up and which was down. She couldn't begin to process how she even felt about it.

Intense. Compulsive. Complicated. Painful. Wanton. Frustrating.

The words came to her unbidden from a memory that she could barely grasp onto. But they explained it perfectly. The physical intimacy was almost too much. It nearly tore her apart. It made her want to rip her clothes off and have sex right there on that throne. But it *was* complicated and frustrating, and she shouldn't do this. She shouldn't want to do this.

Her fingers tangled in his suit coat as he tilted her body, aching for deeper access. He groaned into her mouth as everything intensified. Until their magic swirled all around them. A cloud of golden light that circled and circled like a mini tornado in the center of this sacred space.

There was no right or wrong. No good or evil. Only this connection burrowing down between them and attaching tethering hooks to their souls. The perfect one made for the other. Two matching crowns of gold.

Binding.

The word came out of the abyss.

There was a binding ceremony. And she had to agree to it for it to happen. Only...only was this her agreeing?

Because she didn't agree. She *couldn't* agree. There was a reason for that.

She wracked her mind, trying to find the reason in her brain, but there was nothing there. Just this room and Lorcan and this kiss.

Then she felt a familiar memory, one she had gone over again and again and again. She opened a vault and closed it. Opened it and closed it. Open and close. Until that was all she saw and knew. The rest slipped away.

And she was inside her head, separate from her body. She remembered everything.

Kierse pulled herself away.

"No," she said as the connection abruptly severed and the crown slipped from her head.

Lorcan's pupils were blasted out, and he looked ravenous. "Did you just...feel that?"

"You were in my head."

"You were in mine," he countered. "We were connecting even without the ceremony."

"That wasn't the ceremony?"

He shook his head, visibly stunned. "It was just that intense."

"I can't do this."

His gaze shuttered. "This?"

"Whatever this is." She took another step backward. "I can't do it."

"Everything says otherwise."

Her arms wrapped around her middle. She couldn't stomach what had just happened. It wasn't that it had felt wrong, but that it had felt right. Like the most-right thing in the entire world. Which made her wary. Things that looked too good to be true usually were.

Not to mention Graves.

"I'm sorry," she said softly and meant it.

"Is this because of him?"

"Yes," she told him truthfully. "I should go."

She turned to leave, but he followed her down the dais and across the moss-carpeted ground.

"He's doing it again," Lorcan said with a snarl. "He's ruining it like he did with Emilie."

"He's not doing anything. I'm making a choice that Emilie wasn't allowed to make." She reached for the door handle. Lorcan slammed his hand onto the door before she could leave.

"Emilie didn't make any choices, because he killed her."

Kierse shot him a pained look. "I'm sorry about your sister. That doesn't change what happened between us."

"I suppose it doesn't." He loomed over her, and she lifted her chin, meeting his look with a dark one of her own. "But I'm certainly not going to sit around and wait for him to kill you, too."

"He's not the same person he was when you first knew him."

"No, he's worse," Lorcan argued. "When I first met him, he was as close to me as a brother. Now, he's a fucking monster."

"We're all monsters," she told him. "Now, let me leave."

Lorcan's arm dropped from the door. She wrenched it open, and he reached for her instead. "Hey."

"Lorcan…" she said, retreating to that place in her mind. Fear that she'd lose control again coursing through her.

"Just…be careful. Okay?"

She nodded once and then slipped through the door.

Chapter Fifty-Seven

Kierse was still rattled and angry when she made it back to Graves's brownstone. The team meeting was supposed to start any minute, and she was surprised that it was so quiet. Maybe she wasn't the last person to arrive.

"Oh Kierse, you made it," Isolde said with a smile as she came out of the kitchen carrying a tray of drinks.

"Let me take that," Kierse said.

"Thank you. Oh! Do you want to see the cake?"

Kierse grinned and followed her into the kitchen, where a stunning, multilayered cake sat on the counter. It was several layers of white buttercream with a wave of roses falling down one side like a river of blood.

"It's stunning."

"Ready for my delivery tomorrow," Isolde said with a wink. "Now, let me grab the snacks." She hefted a second tray into her arms. "Here we are. Let's go to that meeting."

"Has everyone already arrived?"

"I believe they were still waiting on Mr. Schwartz," Isolde said.

Kierse smirked. Mr. Schwartz sounded like Schwartz's father. The thought of calling him that almost jogged her out of her bad mood. But it didn't explain why the library was so quiet. With that many people, she should have been able to hear with her enhanced abilities.

They had begun their climb to the library when the elevator dinged and Schwartz appeared.

"Sorry I'm late," he said, catching up to them. "Allow me."

He took the tray from Isolde, and she kissed his cheek as she headed upstairs with them.

"Of course," he said with a short bow.

"Busy?" Kierse asked.

Schwartz huffed. "Purchasing explosives last minute raises flags. I had to call in some favors."

"Oh, explosives," Kierse said. "Fancy."

"Hopefully, it's enough," he said with a shrug.

Her unease intensified as they reached the second-floor landing to continued silence.

Schwartz raised an eyebrow. "Are we the first ones here?"

"Isolde said we were the last," Kierse said as she pushed the door open.

Everyone was seated at the center of the massive library. In fact, an extra couch and chair set had been brought in to accommodate the additional members. Anne Boleyn lounged languidly between Laz and Gen. Walter sat across from them in front of his computer setup. Nate sat on the other couch with his ankle crossed over his knee, typing away on his phone. George and Edgar stood sentinel in a corner. Isolde headed over to them. Graves had his arms crossed over his chest as she stared at the girl sitting opposite him—Lyra Anderson.

"What the hell did we miss?" Kierse asked.

Schwartz deposited the tray of food and then did the same with Kierse's full of drinks. He took the open chair, leaving Kierse standing beside Lyra's seat in confusion.

"We have an interloper," Graves explained.

"Opportunist," Lyra interjected.

Kierse glanced between them. "What happened?"

"She was snooping around."

"Trying to get your attention," Lyra corrected.

"Why would you do that?" Kierse asked.

"Because I'm not an idiot," Lyra said, breaking Graves's gaze to look at Kierse. "Look, I was interested in the offer and everything, but I was raised to ask questions. And the more questions I asked, the deeper I got into whatever *this* is, and I want in."

"Why?" Graves barked.

"Why *not*?" Lyra asked, arching an eyebrow at him.

"This isn't fun and games," Kierse argued.

"Who said it was? My parents did this sort of shit all the time, and I grew up on stories of the scary motherfucker who helped them." Lyra gestured to Graves.

"Your parents were not doing anything like this," Graves assured her.

"Mind if we know who her parents are?" Laz asked.

Nate scoffed. "You don't recognize the vampire princess in our midst?"

Kierse glanced between Nate and Lyra. She knew that his family had connections with the Andersons.

Laz shrugged. "Fill me in."

"Beckham and Reyna Anderson," Lyra muttered.

Schwartz whistled low. Laz looked impressed. They were sort of legends for their part in the first vampire war.

"*Anyway*," Lyra said. "If they can do it, then so can I. Plus, if you're going to use me anyway, then I at least want a cut."

"That's fair," Kierse admitted. It would be simpler for Lyra to be involved than to use her and ditch her the way they'd planned to. A lot fewer questions.

"Fine," Graves said with a shake of his head.

"Oh and…maybe don't mention this to my parents," Lyra added with a wince.

Kierse bit back a laugh. She was all hard-hitting confidence until it came to her parents finding out what she was doing. Joining the theater against their wishes was one thing. This was something else entirely.

Graves's eyes met Kierse's. The look curdled the laughter inside of her. She had to tell him about Lorcan. They had to talk about what had happened. And he had gotten much better at reading her without ever laying a hand on her.

She broke eye contact and sauntered across the room to take a seat next to Nate. Right now was neither the time nor place.

"You seem tense," Nate said, throwing an arm across her shoulders.

"We're stealing the cauldron *tomorrow*."

Nate arched an eyebrow. "Normally you're hyped up for this shit. Jonesing for some thievery."

Damn her friends for knowing her too well.

She shoved Nate's arm off her with a good-natured laugh. "I'll be there tomorrow."

"Suit yourself," Nate said.

Graves cleared his throat. "Let's address the new factors. The troll revolt and the Men of Valor logos spray painted in the subways. It's unclear if they're going to make a move at the conference while we're busy, but it is a possibility. Nate and I will be on high alert throughout and we'll have Walter with eyes in the sky. Otherwise, proceed as normal."

"Lorcan will be there, too," Kierse added.

Graves's eyes skipped to her, and she looked away. She didn't want him to see whatever was on her face. "Wonderful," he said drily. "He better stay out of our fucking way."

"He's there to counter the Men of Valor. So I'd guess he's on our side."

When Kierse glanced at Gen, her best friend was staring bullets into her.

There were questions in her eyes that Kierse had no answers for.

"Similar objectives doesn't put him *on our side*," Graves said.

"Okay," Kierse agreed.

Graves was silent for a few seconds. She hoped he wasn't piecing together something she didn't want him to look too closely at. But eventually he moved on. "The convocation seats add a new layer to the plan," he said, glancing to Nate. "There are two seats up for grabs. We know the Men of Valor are going to try to get both of them."

Gen bit her lip. "How do we stop that from happening?"

"Nate is going to put himself forward for one of the seats."

Nate jerked around. "What?"

"You were part of the treaty signing. You are well liked. You have an army of wolves behind you," Graves said. "You're an obvious choice."

"But I'll be busy with this," he said, gesturing to the heist party.

"Voting will be after," Graves said. "You'll do your job with this, put your hat in the race, and all goes well, we'll be voting you in to the convocation this weekend."

"Fuck," Nate said. "Maura is going to kill me."

"She'll be fine with it," Kierse told him.

"You're perfect for the job, Nate," Gen told him.

He groaned. "Fine. I'll do it."

"Good," Graves said. "Everyone else set? Laz?"

"All wards are in place. I'm set for transport tomorrow."

"Schwartz?"

Schwartz nodded. "Explosives purchased. I'm laying them tonight."

"Gen?"

She gave him a thumbs-up. "Laz got me a uniform and a pass to access the security room. Walter showed me what I need to do."

"Nate?"

"Besides the new problem of dealing with the Treaty issues, I'm good to go. But if they need me to vote..."

"We'll deal." Graves turned his attention to Kierse. "You'll have Lyra with you. Fill her in on specifics. She'll be your backup and diversion now."

"Will do."

Kierse watched Graves survey the room full of people. A few short months earlier, he wouldn't have trusted one person, let alone an entire room of them. Any of them could betray him in the middle of this. But it was their chance to get the cauldron, and everyone had a necessary part to play in the scheme. Graves simply couldn't have done it all alone. It was good to see him accept that their little family had grown to eleven.

He opened his mouth as if he were about to give a closing speech, but he stalled and looked upward. "Edgar, someone is at the door."

A few seconds later, the doorbell rang.

"How does he know?" Lyra whispered.

Kierse didn't have it in her to explain warding to the girl. She might be a vampire princess, but Kierse had a strong bet that she didn't understand magic in the slightest.

"Who is it?" Kierse asked, standing.

Gen came to her side and placed a hand on her arm as if she was going to pull her away to ask questions. But Kierse absolutely could not stomach questions.

Walter choked. "Uh…Graves…the security footage."

Oh right, he'd installed cameras.

Graves walked around to look at the screen and closed his eyes briefly. He looked half ready to shred anyone who spoke to him sideways. "Fuck."

"Who is it?" Kierse asked, pulling away from Gen. She took one look at the man in the top hat and repeated Graves's epithet.

"The meeting is adjourned," Graves said. He found George where he was waiting in the corner. "Get rid of everything that makes it appear like we're working in here." George nodded and began to collect the paperwork. "Walter, you need to move your computer equipment elsewhere. I'll delay him as long as I can, but make it quick. Laz and Schwartz will help you." He glanced up at the rest of the confused faces. "The rest of you need to leave out the back way."

"There's a back exit?" Gen asked in confusion.

"I'll show them," Isolde said, gesturing to the men. "Come with me."

"I have to deal with our…guest," Graves grumbled.

"I'm coming with you," Kierse insisted.

Graves glanced back at her before nodding. "He'll expect you."

"Kierse, wait, we should talk," Gen said.

"After," Kierse promised.

She hurried after Graves and out of the library as the rest of them hustled to clean the place up.

Edgar had just thrown the front door open, and in strode the English gentleman who upended Graves's life.

"Kingston," Graves all but growled.

Chapter Fifty-Eight

"Graves, my boy!" Kingston crowed.

"Kingston." A smile appeared on Graves's face, almost unbidden. He was clearly displeased with his mentor's unannounced arrival, and yet somehow, Kingston could still manage to get a smile out of him. "What are you doing here?"

"You didn't think I'd miss this Monster Conference that you're hosting."

"I'm not hosting," Graves said.

"It's in your city!" Kingston said, pulling his top hat from his head and tucking it under his arm. He was a penguin of a man, the picture-perfect caricature of a British gentleman. Complete with suit tails, crisp white cravat, and shiny black cane.

"That doesn't mean..." Graves began.

But Kingston cut him off, turning to face Kierse. "Hello, my dear."

"You remember my former mentor, Kingston Darby," Graves said. He gestured to Kierse. "Kingston, my apprentice, Miss McKenna."

The formality took her by surprise. She had been so used to him using her first name or even her nickname that her last name felt like a barb.

"Kierse," she said quickly as she held her hand out. "Feel free to call me Kierse."

Kingston took it and shook vigorously.

"I certainly do remember her," Kingston said. His smile was wide and sharp as knives. "When my apprentice takes on his own apprentice, it is always of note. Though I believed you a wren." Kingston glanced at Graves and back. "You managed to keep one alive."

"Barely," Kierse joked.

Graves shrugged. "We'll see for how long."

"Charming," Kingston said with a laugh as he clapped Graves on the back. "Well, the pleasure is mine as always, Kierse. Are you attending the conference as well?"

"I'm not," Kierse said.

"Well, that's a bloody shame. We could use some more warlocks present."

"That's questionable," Graves said, glancing at Kierse, silently willing her not to contradict the statement.

She wasn't stupid enough to do so. Graves only trusted Kingston about as far as he could throw him. He might like the man and open up around him, but trust was a different matter. Yet another thing they had in common.

"You never did like the thought of our kind being out amongst the other monsters," Kingston said.

"Indeed," Graves agreed. "Bottom feeders."

"Well, I won't disagree with that sentiment. Most monsters are self-centered and single-minded."

"Not so different than yourself," Graves muttered.

Kingston guffawed. "I have my moments."

"As does Graves," Kierse said easily. "How long are you staying?"

"Well, I certainly can't leave before the festivities," Kingston argued.

"Go home," Graves cajoled.

"The convention is only a few days, and you'll need more voices of reason with this Treaty discussion happening."

"Which is precisely why you should leave."

"I am reasonable," Kingston argued with a laugh.

"You have different rules in England. You should keep them there," Graves told him.

Kingston waved his cane around. "You could learn a thing or two from us."

"We learned to get rid of you," Kierse said cheekily. "Tea in the harbor. Red coats going down with them. All that."

"Got a backbone on this one," Kingston noted with a laugh. "Well, it's only a few days. And I didn't bring a red coat." His smile widened.

"I very nearly sent Imani home in a body bag," Graves growled. The warlock territorial nature rearing its ugly head. "I didn't *ask* for visitors in my city."

Kingston straightened, finally perceiving the threat. "Are you suggesting that I'm not welcome?"

"I'm suggesting that you should give notice," Graves said.

"Since when have *I* had to give notice?"

"I'm working."

"You could use a vacation," Kingston quipped.

"You were my mentor," Graves said. "You were there in my formative youth. That is the only reason that I am not demanding you leave my city on the next plane for England. I don't have the patience for this."

"You're always so touchy when the solstice is approaching."

Graves sighed like he found him insufferable. "Just go."

Kierse thought Kingston might actually go at Graves's insistence. It was his city, after all. While he was not at the height of his power by any stretch of the imagination, he was still formidable, especially in his own home.

Then Kingston laughed, slapping Graves on the back again. "I do love your antics. I'll take my usual room until I can get into the Plaza tomorrow. Make a reservation for me at the Met in the morning. I want to recharge before I go." He dropped his hat back on his head. "Will Isolde be cooking tonight or should we go out?"

Graves looked like he wanted to bury a sword through his mentor's back as Kingston headed toward the stairs.

"I'll have Isolde prepare dinner," Graves told him.

"Jolly good!" he said, waving his cane.

Kierse watched him go in shock. Kingston was the only person Kierse had ever met who threw Graves completely off guard. He could get away with things no one else could.

"You're letting him stay," Kierse said in surprise.

"Did it much look like I had a choice?" Graves growled.

"Without wasting a lot of power…no."

"It'll be easier to deal with him quickly and send him on his way. Just another fucking complication." He pinched the bridge of his nose and released a breath. "Follow me."

Her stomach dipped in anticipation as she went upstairs with him and entered his personal office. He shut the door behind them, and the buzz of his magic enveloped the room as he made the room soundproof.

"What happened?" he demanded.

"Happened?"

"With you. Something happened. You're being avoidant."

"Yes," she agreed. "I…didn't want to say anything in front of anyone else."

He went around to his desk and leaned against it, waiting for her response. "No one else is here now."

"Right."

Still she said nothing. Her silence was deafening, and he finally dropped his head with a sigh.

"What is Lorcan's plan?" Graves asked. "He's coming to the conference. So you spoke to him. What did he say?"

"Well," she said gently, "it isn't to mess up the heist."

His eyes crawled over her as if he wanted to read her thoughts without touch. "Are you okay?"

It was then that she realized she was shaking. That she was terrified. Of what had happened and Graves's reaction. Telling him right now was probably not the right time to do it, and yet there was no other time.

She was not okay. She had kissed Lorcan under the influence of some stupid soulmate magic. She had gotten herself out of it, and she had walked away. But she had still kissed him. A part of her had *wanted* to kiss him. A part of her hadn't wanted to leave at all.

"Lorcan kissed me."

A soft laugh of disbelief escaped him. "Of course he did."

"Graves, it was…" She shook her head. "I can't explain it. Maybe you should just read me."

"Forgive me. I don't ever want to see that."

He reached into his desk and pulled out a disassembled handgun, working over the parts with expert precision.

"What are you doing?" she asked slowly.

"What does it look like I'm doing?"

"Putting together a gun." She took a step toward him, hand raised. "I'm not sure tonight is the night to go after him. He's at the height of power right now."

"He's expecting me," he said as he inserted the magazine with a soft click.

"I wouldn't be so sure," she said.

"And why is that?"

"Because I walked away," Kierse said. "There was a—I don't know— magic connection when it happened. Like the binding was trying to happen without the ceremony. I used your technique to regain control and broke it apart."

"You *resisted* a binding?" he asked in apparent shock.

"I guess so. He didn't think that was even possible without the ceremony."

"It shouldn't be."

"I guess it's because I have Saoirse's magic."

Graves's eyes widened. "You *what?*"

"Uh, yeah. That's what Lorcan said. That's how he knew immediately after the spell. Our magic was already connected once, and it was like… reincarnated into me."

"Oh," he said as if that made perfect sense. "That explains a lot."

"Anyway, I told him I was making the choice that Emilie couldn't."

Graves paled at those words. "What did he say to that?"

"That she couldn't make a choice because…"

"Because she's dead."

"And you killed her," Kierse whispered.

"Ah," he said, setting the gun down between them. "That I did."

"Do you want to tell me what happened?"

"I tried to use my magic to break the bond," Graves said, staring down at the weapon. "She asked me to do it when we ran out of options. I thought I had that kind of power. I was so arrogant."

Kierse's stomach twisted at the thought. "Did you do it?"

"No. Well, I thought I had started to make it work, but it went all wrong so fast." He shook his head. "I removed memories of the bond and her soulmate and everything related to it."

"I didn't even know you could do that."

"It is delicate work, and I rarely use it anymore. One change can have a ripple effect through the entire mind. It can crush a mind. The one memory taken from you has left a ripple," Graves explained. "Just touching it causes you physical pain."

"And that's what happened with Emilie? You did too much and she died from it? That sounds like an accident."

He looked directly into Kierse's eyes when he said, "I want you to understand that I am not the hero."

"None of us are heroes."

"I am what he says I am in this. I was overly confident, arrogant, and convinced of my rightness. I kept pushing and pushing and pushing. Trying to do anything to shred the bond with my own crushing power." His eyes never left her face as if he wanted to impart the truth to her as clearly as possible.

"But that still sounds like an accident," she tried to argue.

"It was not an accident," he said, his voice stern. "I decided while it was happening that I'd rather she was dead than with him."

Kierse's heart ached for him. "You were so young. That doesn't sound like the reason it happened and more like your own self-loathing."

"I should loathe myself after what I did. What Lorcan says is correct. I robbed her of her choice. I killed her, Wren. I did it."

Her stomach twisted.

"And I swore I wouldn't make that mistake again," Graves said, reaching for the gun. "I'll kill *him* this time."

She laughed as she put her body between him and the door. "That's ingenious. Killing him *would* solve this problem."

"I'm glad you agree."

"I don't," she said, putting her hand to the front of his suit. "Lorcan isn't the problem." Graves scoffed. "He's not. Even if he was, now is not the time to kill him. Not this close to the solstice. Not with the heist tomorrow." She swallowed as she took his hand in hers and let her absorption drop. "Not when I love you."

Graves's brow furrowed. His perfect lips opened in incomprehension. "You...love me?"

"I do."

And then she stood on her tiptoes and pressed her lips to his.

Chapter Fifty-Nine

With her magic down, he could read her thoughts, and he'd taught her many tricks since they started training. If she wanted to control what he saw, then she just had to focus on it...so she did.

She showed him the first time she'd seen him and how terrifyingly beautiful he was. The moment he'd held her crying in the subway tunnels for the first time. The trust she'd given him before their first mission. The sight of him calling her *wife* in the halls of Versailles. The knowledge that he had her back no matter what. And then every single minute look and detail she could conjure up since they'd returned to the city. How she felt about every facet of him.

The villain he claimed.

The monster she desired.

The man he'd become.

He'd changed. While he may still be dangerous, he was not dangerous to her. Everything had shifted in their time together.

Graves lifted her by her hips and settled her on the lip of his desk where her ass dug into the edge of the gun. His mouth was open and pliant. His tongue roving. His hands mapping every inch of her body.

He didn't interject in the middle of her parade of memories. He didn't force any thoughts into her head. He let her feed him the knowledge that he so desired.

After he'd had his fill, she pulled back to look at him. "No counter arguments?"

"None," he said as he lifted her shirt up and over her head, leaving her in nothing but a black, lacy bralette.

She grinned. "You're usually so eloquent."

"You said all that needed to be said." Then he laid her out across the hard leather.

She wiggled against the gun. "This is in the way."

"And here I thought weapons got you off," he teased, slipping the gun out from underneath her. "Hold this."

He settled the gun on her stomach. The cold steel drew a hiss from her as it touched her bare skin. Its weight against her did somehow turn her on. Fuck him for knowing it.

He smirked at her reaction and then lifted her hips to shuck her shorts onto the floor. "Something to say?"

"You're dangerous."

"Me? Not the gun?" He lifted her ankle onto his shoulder and began to lay kisses down her calf, sliding to his knees before her.

"We both know what the most powerful thing in the room is."

"Oh?" His eyes were contemplative. "You believe it's me?"

"Obviously."

"A weapon is only as powerful as its weakness, and you are mine."

She shivered at those words. "What does that make me, then?"

"The most powerful thing in the entire world."

Her heart swelled. His weakness. His power. She was all of it. And he was everything to her.

He nipped at her inner thigh, and she yelped. "You're going to leave a mark."

"Many," he agreed.

He slid her thong to the side and ran a finger down the center of her. She gasped and tipped her head back, body on fire.

"So wet for me," he breathed.

"Yes," she panted.

He slipped two fingers inside, curling them upward. She squirmed underneath him, wanting his cock and not just his fingers, but also desperately wanting everything he'd give her.

"What got you so riled up?" he asked as he circled around her swollen clit. "Was it the gun?" He reached up and took the handle in his palm, dragging the hard metal down her stomach, across her pelvis, and down over her wet pussy.

She shuddered. "Graves!"

"Or was it me?" He slid his tongue up over her exposed clit. "You choose."

"Yes," she gasped.

"Yes, I should fuck you with this gun?" he asked a mischievous look on his face as cold metal touched her exposed skin again.

She had to clench her entire body to keep from jumping at the touch. But she couldn't stop her reaction. There was something heady about him touching her with it. The dangerous thing as if they couldn't both kill her. As if she didn't want him to keep going.

The metal pressed against her sensitive clit, and she gasped as the friction hit her in all the right places. The nerves sparking to life at the fact that he was even doing it. He curled his fingers in at the same moment he moved the gun against her most exposed spot.

"Fuck," she cried as the orgasm hit her unexpectedly.

"Fuck," Graves echoed as he discarded the gun and stood.

"More," she pleaded.

He unfastened his pants and let them fall to the ground. His cock strained against the fabric of his underwear, and she sat up on one elbow to reach for him. He grasped her wrist tightly in his hand as he let his cock spring free. Then he wrapped her hand around his shaft.

"Oh, you're so big," she whispered at the hard feel of him. She shot him a dirty smirk. "Was it the gun?"

"The thought of killing for you," he promised.

"Kill me instead," she pleaded, angling his cock to line it up with her body. "Kill me like this."

At the first touch of him against her, they both groaned. She didn't know how they'd held out this long as it was. She had been ready to ride him the minute he'd seen into her mind. She just needed completion to consummate the match.

As he slid home, it all came together. Their bodies perfectly aligned, along with their hearts.

She looked up into his face and saw none of the danger always lurking at the edges, only desire. His hands gripped her hips as he started a rhythm. In and out. Her hand still lingered between them, feeling the slippery wetness as he pushed inside her body. The tightness as he stretched her fully. Feeling *him*. And she wanted more.

Her finger touched her clit, circling it as he thrust into her, the movements barely restrained. Their eyes locked. She was already on the edge and wanted him to come over with her. She was going to have to stop touching herself or it'd all happen too fast.

"Don't stop," he said, still reading her thoughts. "Come for me."

At his words and the hard slam of his body and their ritual joining, she unleashed. Roaring into the stillness of his office. With her still clenching around his cock, he hoisted her up and into his arms, kicked open the door that led into his bedroom, and then dropped her into the middle of the comforter. After shucking off the rest of his clothes, he crawled in after her.

"Say it again."

"What would you like me to say?" she asked as he caged her in against the pillows.

"You know."

"I love you," she breathed.

"Again."

"I love you."

His head dipped into her neck, kissing down her clavicle and to her breasts. He released them from her bra as he said, "Again."

She said it into his mind this time: *I love you. I love you. I love you.*

His smile was the first cool dip of winter chill. A promise of the change of seasons. A hope for hibernation and relaxation before coming out of the dark. It was sunshine on fresh snow. The whip of a cool breeze in her hair. He was her winter god, and she'd worship at the altar until the end of days.

He lifted her up and flipped her on top of him. "Ride me."

She wiggled her hips against his lengthening cock and then slipped onto him, inch by delicious inch. When she was fully seated, her head fell back with a moan.

"Dear God," she groaned. "You feel incredible."

"I could live like this forever," he said by way of agreement.

She leaned her hands against his chest and slowly rocked her hips forward and back. His fingers inched higher up her thighs until they landed on her hips, taking her weight and increasing the tempo. Panting like she'd run a race, she bounced atop him. His cock burying deeper and deeper with each thrust. Until she once again felt so close that she might fall apart.

Sensing that, Graves flipped her over again and drove in at a quicker tempo.

Their eyes locked as his hand touched her cheek. "Let me show you."

There was no linked connection. No magic that twined like a braided string. But there was something more, something deeper, crashing together as their bodies joined. As if summer and winter had met at the heart of the calendar year and colossal storms raged in the midst of their collision. It was life and death and trust and lust and hope and sacrifice.

In all of it, it was love.

She saw what she looked like through his eyes. The first night they had met. The night she had played the part of his pet and he'd known he was a goner. The feeling of holding her in the subway tunnels as she cried. Thinking he'd lost her forever not once, but twice. And the long months of planning to make it all right. The weeks together where he'd proven himself to her.

They finished together, riding a tidal wave down to the shore. As their breathing slowed with their hearts joined as one, the rest of the world disappeared entirely.

Graves swept her hair out of her face, placed a soft kiss on her tender lips, and said, "I love you."

Her eyes lit up, overcome by the admission. "I love you, too."

Chapter Sixty

I t was several minutes before either of them had the ability to move. Kingston was waiting somewhere above them. They didn't have endless time. And yet neither seemed like they wanted to relinquish this sanctuary.

Finally, they cleaned up, and Kierse changed into one of Graves's shirts. He returned from the closet in boxer-briefs, his holly tattoo visible as it threaded up his arms to his chest. He held a package out to her.

"What's this?" she asked, sitting on the bed.

"Before…this," he said, gesturing all around them. "I had a present for you."

"A present? What is it?"

"Open it and find out."

She took the box gingerly in her hand, removed the gold ribbon, and then tore into the shiny black paper. Inside was a flat black velvet box. Jewelry? Something to wear tomorrow?

She glanced up at him, but he signaled for her to continue. She lifted the lid, and her heart leaped into her throat. Nestled inside was a knife.

Not just any knife—her father's knife.

She removed it, holding the worn handle reverently. It was the wrong fit. Her father had been a giant of a man. But still…her father had *held* this knife.

Her finger moved to the blade, and she hissed as it pricked her. It was still sharp to the touch. She sucked the blood away as she looked over the symbol carved into the metal—antlers around an Irish knot.

"It was his war band," Graves said. "The symbol of his people."

Kierse looked up hopefully. "Are they still around?"

"A few of them."

"I could meet them?"

He nodded. "Though they were monster hunters and likely disagreed with your parents' marriage as well."

"Of course," she said in understanding. But there was still hope. There might be family out there somewhere. "You kept this all this time?"

"I'd forgotten about it until the last time we did memory work and you recalled it," he said. "It should belong to you."

"Thank you." She pressed the knife to her chest as tears came to her eyes. "It's the best gift you could have given me."

She had so little of her parents. She hardly even had memories of them. So much had been taken from her. All she had was this knife and her wren necklace.

She wanted more.

Suddenly, holding the knife, she felt as if she was ready. Ready to face her past. To face what happened to her parents.

"Graves," she said, gripping the knife hard between her hands. "I think I'm ready to see that last memory."

That didn't seem to be the reaction he'd expected. "Now?"

"If we have time. I know the heist is tomorrow and Kingston is here… and everything could go wrong."

He stopped her with a kiss. "We have time."

"Should we go to the library?"

"I think we can do it right here," he said, gesturing to the bed.

"Okay," she said as she settled into the pillows. Graves sat next to her, his hand reaching for hers and squeezing.

"Whenever you're ready."

She swallowed. It was time. Time to find out what happened to her parents after the spell was put on her. Her hands shook slightly at the thought, but there was no use holding back any longer. She needed the truth.

"Ready," she said and lifted her absorption.

"Let's start in the hallway," Graves's silky voice said.

She swallowed and pushed forward to the point right before they reached the doorway.

"7016," her mother said.

Kierse leaned into the memory. Cillian Ryan had taken her memories from her for the spell.

"7018."

She just needed to *push through*. If she knew what had happened, then maybe she'd have the answers she needed to be able to move on. She wanted to find out what happened to her parents. She wanted to know so much more than this…

"Next one."

Kierse pressed against the crack in the memory, smelled the lemon and pine, saw the crossed swords warding. All she had to do was walk into that room.

It wouldn't bring her parents back. Nothing could bring them back.

But she wanted answers. It wasn't too much to ask.

The memory gave, and she seemed to slip right through it like jelly and then past it. They were back in the tiny apartment. It was so like the night that the wisps had shown up to their place in Scotland. The wardings were failing.

"I thought we had more time!" Shannon cried. "Take Kierse and run."

"What about you?" Adair asked.

"He's here for me."

"Mum!" Kierse cried, rushing for her mother.

Shannon bent down and pulled her into her arms. "Listen, love, you have to go with Daddy, okay?" She wrapped Kierse's little fingers around the wren necklace at her throat. "This was given to me by my mum. It's a wren, you know that?"

"Yes," Kierse said through tears.

"My mum always said that wrens sang open the doors to faerie. That one day a wren would take us home," Shannon said, wiping the tears from Kierse's eyes. "So hold onto this and it will take you home, too."

"Okay, Mum," she whispered.

"Adair."

Her father took her out of her mother's arms, and Shannon grabbed a backpack, heading for the door.

"Mum!" she cried.

"I love you," Shannon said.

Adair hurried Kierse into a closet. "Just like we practiced, remember?"

Kierse nodded and huddled in the corner, folding herself up as small as she could while her father piled their clothes and coats on top of her. The door to the closet shut just as their front door burst inward.

She could hear her mother's shrieks as a soft *pop* sounded twice. A loud thump that Kierse now realized must have been her mother's body.

"Shannon!" Adair cried.

Another pop. Another thump.

"Was there a third?" a distorted voice asked.

"I heard there may be a child," a woman said.

"Can you feel them here?"

There was a long pause. Kierse's younger body shivered under the weight of the coats, trying to keep from breathing too loudly, terrified they could hear her heartbeat.

"No. There's no other magic in the apartment," the woman said.

"Good."

Then the door opened and slammed again.

Kierse yanked free from the memory. Blood ran out of her nose, over her lip, and down her chin. Tears coated her lashes. Graves handed her a tissue.

"I remember. I remember it all," Kierse whispered as she wiped at her nose. The rest of the memory rang through her like a gong. "I think I've known for a while. The Fae Killer showed up. That's who that was."

"Yes," Graves guessed. "Your mother didn't leave soon enough, and he found you."

"How?"

"I think the woman with him senses magical signatures. Possibly she can hunt them. Though I haven't heard of any warlock with that ability."

"I see," she said softly. "I remember the rest. The block—I think the block is gone. I came out of the closet, and they had bullets in their chests. I ran out to the street to tell someone what happened, but as soon as I was away from my mom, I forgot what wisps were. I forgot I had parents," Kierse told him, staring down at her hands. "Like the spell wrapped itself around me like a cloak once I was free."

"He made you forget magic. So your past would disappear as well."

Kierse nodded. She glanced up at him. "He stole everything from me." She set her mouth. "I would like to find out why."

She'd witnessed her parents' deaths. Now and in the past. And no matter how much her mind had shielded her from it, how much the spell had removed, it still lived in her. No wonder she'd had trouble opening up. No wonder she struggled to accept love. From Gen and Ethan and now Graves...

Her hand went to the wren necklace at her throat. Her mom had said that a wren would sing open the door to faerie. That she should follow it, and it would take her home. Was that literal? Or metaphorical? Prophecy? It sounded like an old wives' tale.

"Not everything," she corrected. She touched the necklace. "I kept my wren, and it brought me to you."

"It did," he agreed.

"Had you ever heard that tale, about wrens opening the doors to faerie?"

"Never," he said. "Not in all my years."

It didn't even make sense, but she would have to investigate it once they'd gotten the cauldron. That was still the most important thing.

Graves drew her into his chest. She'd thought she would feel worse after finding out about her parents. And while she was melancholy, it was a relief to have the truth. That was all she wanted. The Curator had the rest of the answers.

"We need to get the Curator alone. I want to ask him questions."

"I have some questions for him as well," Graves said, flexing his hands. Kierse had an idea he had a very specific kind of *questioning* in mind. "Let's secure the cauldron. Then I'll use my resources to track him down and get your answers."

"Deal."

"Good," he said and kissed her again.

Tomorrow their world would change, but this…this would stay the same.

Chapter Sixty-One

K ierse adjusted the elaborate mask on her face. "Is it right?"

Lyra turned to her, and Kierse got a full look at Lyra's mask—a half face of gold with a turquoise gemstone between her brows and brushed turquoise metallic paint along her cheekbones. It had golden wings from either side, made of a wired tulle that shimmered with the same turquoise glitter. The whole thing matched the fitted turquoise dress she'd had designed for the theater benefit tonight.

"It's not tight enough," Lyra declared and twirled her finger.

Lyra retied Kierse's mask, which was black metal that almost molded to her features. It was filigreed with rose gold along the edges and had rose-gold beaded fringe dangling from the bottom of the mask, obscuring the bottom of her face. One side had black feathers splayed out up and over her dark hair. It was beautiful but deceptively heavy.

Lyra tightened the string to the point of pain across Kierse's temples, but she held back any complaints. This was the only way inside the building during Monster Con. The security for the conference was too tight.

"Better," Lyra said, adjusting a string on Kierse's sumptuous, rose-gold gown. "You fit right in."

It was the first night of the con, and all three theater companies were here for the charity benefit to raise money for the arts. And, unbeknownst to them, make it easier for Kierse to sneak in unnoticed. Which was key. She was hiding in plain sight.

The previous night, she and Graves had dined with Kingston on Isolde's delicious cooking. Kingston had left for the museum in the morning to restore his magic—persuasion was his main power, but he had portaling as a secondary magic, and it took almost all his reserves to travel the Atlantic. Graves hated the ability. Kierse coveted it. But it was convenient in this case to have Kingston out of the way while they got everything in place for the heist.

She needed to keep her head in the game. This wasn't like last year when she and Graves had singlehandedly broken through King Louis's defenses. This was an entire operation by a talented team. Every person had their own part. She was in position, and now she just had to wait.

A voice crackled to life on their shared channel. Isolde said, "Cake delivered."

Kierse resisted the urge to tap the earpiece in her ear as Walter fired back, "Acknowledged. Laz, you're up."

She could practically see the multi-tiered cake that Isolde had created for the event. Nate had convinced a friend who worked for the con to hire the faux bakery, Cake & Cake, off of the advice that they were making the cake for his wedding. Isolde *was* baking Nate & Maura's cake, but there was no Cake & Cake business. Isolde only worked for one person. And now that cake was in an enormous box with the faux Cake & Cake logo Gen had designed printed on it in baby blue. There was also a second, smaller cake in a second, smaller box that was being held until closing. A little decoy box, if you will.

"Cake in my possession," Laz said over their earpiece.

"That's our cue," Kierse said.

Lyra adjusted her basket of roses and then looped her arm through Kierse's as they headed together toward the ballroom.

"Let's try not to get held up by some handsy monster."

Lyra's eyes were dark and piercing. "I was trying to get held up by *you*."

"I know."

"We still could," Lyra offered under her breath. "I don't bite."

Kierse laughed softly. "I think you do."

Lyra grinned, showing off her elongated canines. "Only if you ask me to."

Damn Lyra for being 1,000 percent her type.

A throat cleared abruptly on the line. Graves was clearly listening in on their conversation. Lyra bit her lip and then pulled Kierse toward the exit.

"Hurry up, girls," a manager said as he yanked open the door that led into the ballroom. "You're missing a basket." The man stuffed a basket full of masks into Kierse's hand. "Hand those out and don't come back until they're gone."

Lyra waved her hand. "Of course, Jeremy."

Then they were through the door and into the mass of people. Kierse's jaw dropped. She had known from the start that the Curator was showcasing his collection of famous artworks, priceless jewelry, monster artifacts, and magical objects—including the cauldron, which would be unveiled after the dinner—and while she'd memorized the layout of the showcasing room, it was nothing to the actual display.

The Curator had earned his name honorably. The pieces on display were beyond stunning. Kierse had walked the halls of the Met with Graves and Kingston not six months earlier, enamored and a bit overwhelmed. The Curator's was nearly as splendid. They passed a towering renaissance sculpture, crown jewels in a glittering necklace and earrings set, and a long, golden staff from an Egyptian monster hunter. Each item more dazzling than the next.

"How did they even get him to show all this stuff off?" Lyra asked.

"He volunteered," Kierse said. "Guess he was tired of living in the shadows with his prized possessions."

"How do you think he even got all of it?"

Kierse shrugged. "He's a Druid. Long lived."

Lyra wrinkled her nose. "Thank fuck my parents aren't like this."

"Can we focus?" Graves said over the line.

Nate appeared then, taking a black mask out of her basket and covering his face. "All set here," he said with a wink.

"Noted," Graves said.

"See you soon," he told Kierse before blending back into the crowd.

Kierse glanced across the room full of bespoke suits and custom gowns. Her eyes found Graves at the edge of the party with Kingston gesturing wildly next to him. She would have rather had him watching her back, but they needed Lyra for an alibi. With the arrival of Kingston, it was more imperative than ever that Graves be seen in public at all times. The last thing they wanted was for anyone to get suspicious.

Graves seemed to feel her gaze and looked up with a dangerous smile on his face. The one that said his enemies would not bend but break under his gaze. She loved it. She loved *him*.

"That's the last attendee," Walter said in her ear. "Doors will lock soon. Kierse, Lyra, get moving. I'll give you a countdown."

Kierse would have known someone had just entered even if Walter hadn't told her. If she was honest, she had known for a while that Lorcan was getting closer, and now that he was in the room, her hand itched to press against her chest. It felt like a lightning strike as his attention shifted fully to her. That kiss had altered something. Clicked something together that made her want to run across the room right this very minute.

Lyra tugged on her arm. "Come on. We need to duck out."

Kierse resurfaced as if coming up from a deep swim. They meandered the enormous ballroom, bypassing enchanted swords and sneak cloaks and a black-and-white photograph of the city from on high. Lyra paused with her mouth agape.

"How did he get this?"

"What is it?"

Lyra blinked. "It's a photograph my father took before the first vampire war. I thought he had all of them."

"Maybe he sold one."

"I don't think he did," Lyra said contemplatively. "I'll have to ask him."

The line in their ear came alive with a burst of static before Laz said, "Box secure."

Kierse and Lyra veered to the exit when a throat cleared over a microphone. "Thank you so much for coming to the first official Monster Con since the war."

Applause rose up from the spectators, most of them hidden behind the masks the theater performers were handing out. Half of Kierse's basket was empty, and she could see black-and-gold masks everywhere.

"I'm happy to present to you our first keynote speaker. You may know him as a Midtown businessman, the man who can make anything happen. But what you may not know is that he is also the new head of the elusive society, the Men of Valor."

Another roar of approval. Kierse jolted to a halt.

"Please give a warm welcome to…Gregory Amberdash!"

Kierse's jaw dropped as her former employer strode onto the stage, taking the microphone seamlessly from the presenter. She knew that this place was for all monsters, regardless of affiliation. That was sort of the point, to allow discourse without repercussion. But how in the hell had Amberdash taken control of the Men of Valor and then been given a platform? What else had he accomplished silently in the background all these months?

"Welcome!" Amberdash said. The wraith held an arm wide as if he could truly welcome the group before him and not like the soul-sucking wraith he really was. "What an honor to be speaking today before all of you and to have the distinction of announcing my new role within the Men of Valor."

"Wren, move," Graves said in her ear.

Kierse wanted to march up there and demand answers from him. He was the one person she trusted after she'd gutted Jason and left him for dead. Amberdash had continued to work with her. He'd sold her out to the Druids, sure, but he'd given her a warning first about how deep in shit she was. She might have died without it. He wasn't a good monster—there were no good monsters—but she was surprised how much she hadn't thought him capable of this.

Power ruined everyone.

"Kierse," Lyra said, tugging on her arm.

She couldn't. She couldn't go up there. Least of all because she couldn't blow her cover.

"I'm moving," she said finally. She let Lyra lead her away from the crowd of monsters.

"While I'm pleased to bring in all monsters of character who were guaranteed a spot at this convention, I'd also like to welcome those who are not members of the Men of Valor into our ranks. Join us!"

Kierse ground her teeth together. Cut off the head of a snake and another one sprang up. Killing King Louis hadn't meant the demise of the Men of Valor, despite how good it had felt to slice his head off with the spear. The spear that she was desperately missing right now. With it in her hands, she wouldn't have been able to resist the call to finish Amberdash's bullshit reign.

"You know our values. They're yours as well. Monsters should rule themselves. Humans should rule themselves. The problem lies in treating us the same," he said, his gaze shifting across his captivated audience. "When we all know that we are far superior."

A cheer ran up at those words. She didn't know which way the wind would blow for them, but none of it was good.

Amberdash continued his speech over the cheers. The last thing she heard before slipping from the room was, "Which is why I put forth my name—Gregory Amberdash—for consideration to be your voice at the Monster Treaty Convocation."

Chapter Sixty-Two

"What the fuck?" Kierse hissed.

"That's not good," Lyra agreed.

They ditched their baskets of masks and roses as they slid out a back entrance. Kierse touched the small coin-size mark on the door twice—the signal Walter had given them when the doors were clear.

"Wards going up in three, two…" Walter said. "And they're up."

They looped their arms and stuck close together. Just two girls from the theater in masks, sneaking out together. Nothing to see here. Security turned a blind eye to them except for one guy who leered at the way they clung to each other. Then they rounded the corner, and the security thinned. They were too busy watching the room of guests to bother with entertainers. Just as planned.

"How long do we have until they figure out they're locked in?" Lyra asked.

"Long enough."

Walter had rigged his force field warding into a series of coins that Laz had systematically attached to the various ballroom doors over the course of the last couple weeks. Once activated, no one could go in or out until he took them down. Which meant Graves and Nate were stuck in there unless things went really wrong. If things went that sideways, then it wouldn't matter if they let loose the entire ballroom of monsters.

Soon enough, Amberdash would finish his horrific speech, the lot would move into the next ballroom for dinner. That combined dreadful affair would determine the length of time they had to get things done. Once people finished their "meals," they would want to return to peruse the showcase or, worse, leave. Kierse would need to be done long before then.

"Schwartz reported in," Walter told them. "He's in position at the Curator's compound. Waiting for Gen to call in. No security footage on that level, either."

Worry crept into Kierse's stomach even though she knew Gen could take care of herself. She wished she could be there, but she couldn't be in two places at once. This was the moment she really wished Ethan was in on their mission. She would have trusted him to have Gen's back.

"Here we are," Lyra said.

Kierse glanced at the pair of security guards at the end of the hall. They immediately jumped to attention as Kierse and Lyra headed their way in their fancy ball gowns.

Before they could get up in arms, Lyra gestured to the gender-neutral bathroom with a giggle.

"Come on," she said, going full Hermia in a split second. Her gaze shuttered, and her mouth turned soft and pouty. Her lips pressed to Kierse's shoulder, a kiss against the skin.

"They're watching," Kierse said, loud enough for the guards to hear, and promptly looked away, feigning embarrassment.

"Let them look," the actress said as she pushed the bathroom door open and tugged Kierse inside.

As soon as Kierse pushed the door closed, she flipped the lock. "Time to get changed."

Lyra winked at her. "There are easier ways to get me out of my dress."

Kierse snorted as she gratefully removed her intricate mask. She wiggled the metal trash can attached to the bathroom wall until it popped out of the frame supporting it. At the bottom of the attachment was a bag, which Kierse opened to find their change of clothes. This time she wouldn't have to do elaborate theft in a ball gown and high heels. She vastly preferred it this way.

She stripped out of her dress and slipped into black leggings, a black tank top, and sneakers. Lyra changed into a white coat and dark pants that mirrored the kitchen staff. Originally, Kierse had been planning to do both parts, but Lyra *was* the better actress, and now she didn't have the time.

"How do I look?" Kierse asked.

"Like you are about to be very sneaky. And me?"

"A kitchen princess."

"Perfect," Lyra said with a laugh.

Kierse bounced from toe to toe as she waited for a cue from Walter. They were running low on time. If Gen didn't make it to the security system and disarm it, Kierse was going to have to do something drastic.

"Come on, Gen," she muttered.

"I'm here," Gen whispered in her earpiece. "Sorry."

"Can you confirm location?" Walter asked.

"I," Gen began, huffing as if she'd just been in a fight, "uh, I'm close. Give me another minute."

"What the hell happened?" Kierse asked.

"Guards," Gen said.

"Are you all right?"

"I may be…bleeding," Gen said. "And I can't heal myself…or not something of this magnitude."

"This magnitude," Kierse repeated in horror. "Where are you bleeding?"

"Knife wound. Side," she said matter-of-factly.

"Fuck. Do I need to send someone to get you? Gen, you can't…"

"I'm working on it now," Gen interrupted, her breathing labored.

"Excellent," Walter said. "They closed the doors for dinner. The clock is ticking."

The silence was deafening as they waited for Gen to bring down the security system. After that, they had minutes to steal the cauldron. It all relied on her.

Kierse could hear her friend's labored breathing on the line. It felt like everyone was waiting on bated breath.

"Gen?" she whispered.

"It's almost down." She sounded horrible. Kierse hated every minute of it.

"I'm sending Nate as soon as he finishes in that ballroom," Kierse told her.

"Don't…you…dare."

"Nate," Kierse said.

"We're almost done in here," Nate told her. "I'll head to the basement."

"I don't…need…you."

"I'm backup, and I say you do," Nate said.

"Gen," Walter said. "We're running low on time. Vampires eat fast."

"True," Lyra said with a frown.

"Why aren't your parents here anyway?" Kierse whispered at her.

"Oh, they don't get *involved*," she said. "One war was enough for them."

"That's not factual," Graves came over the line. "Can we focus?"

Silence again. Fuck. This wasn't good.

"Done. It's down," Gen said, her voice thin and strained. "Send…send Nate."

And then there was a crash, followed by deafening silence.

Chapter Sixty-Three

That sound echoed through her bones.

"Gen!" she gasped, trying to stay quiet in her panic.

"I'm on it!" Nate said through the line.

There was nothing she could do about Gen, and she couldn't jeopardize the entire mission. Still…she wanted to.

"What do you want to do?" Lyra said, fear in her face for the first time. This had all just become very real.

Kierse bit her lip. "There's nothing we can do. We have to move forward. Four-and-a-half minutes are on the clock."

Walter said, "Schwartz, fire at will."

There was no answer from Schwartz on the line as he was too far from the Plaza to be online with the rest of the team. He was only directly connected to Walter, their eyes in the sky.

Kierse and Lyra glanced at each other as if any moment they would be able to feel Schwartz blowing up the Curator's compound. Walter was the one who had found the location in the midst of all the coded details Laz had stolen at the auction. None of them had known what they were looking at until Schwartz had done recon to discover a residential front for some sort of warehouse drug operation. Schwartz had made sure the building was clear of people, and then he'd detonated enough explosives to cause the diversion they needed.

It was far enough away that the explosion would only be known to those associated with him. Which meant if they were still following the protocol Schwartz had been given when he worked their security…

She tensed, waiting to hear footsteps pounding on the ground outside of the bathroom. But there was nothing.

"What's happening?" Lyra asked.

She didn't know. They couldn't see what was happening on the other side. There were no windows in the tiny bathroom.

"Walter?" Kierse asked.

He was silent a moment before saying, "They're not moving. I'm checking in with Schwartz and trying to hack their system to see if I can get them out of there."

"Fuck," Lyra muttered. "How long will that take?"

Walter didn't answer. Lyra shot her a confused look. Time was ticking away. They couldn't wait.

"Fuck it," Kierse grumbled.

She shucked her clothes back off and changed hastily into her pretty party dress and heels.

"What are you doing?" Lyra asked.

"Someone has to make them leave," Kierse argued.

"So it should be *me*," Lyra said.

"You're the better actress, but you have another job."

"This isn't to script!"

"We're not in a play," Kierse countered.

Graves's sigh was audible. "She never follows the plan."

Kierse shot Lyra a cheeky grin and turned around so the mask could be retied. "See. He knows me."

"Don't die," Lyra said as she cinched the ribbon.

"Walter?" Kierse asked.

"Security footage loop running in your section," Walter informed them. "Go."

Kierse pushed the bathroom door open and sauntered down the hallway. Both men tensed at the sight of her. They were both human. One of the problems the Curator hadn't considered when he'd fired his band of monster mercenaries was that human men were incredibly vulnerable in this world. They might have weapons, but none of them were prepared for monsters.

"Ma'am, the party is the other direction," the first man said.

She executed a drunken stumble. "I thought it was this way."

"No," the second guy said. He pointed the other direction. "Back the way you came."

"Oh, sorry." She might not be as good of an actress as Lyra, but she'd nearly reached them, and that was all that mattered.

"Ma'am," the second guy tried again.

Kierse let her Fae reflexes take over as she launched herself at the first guy. She jabbed her hand into his throat, and as he was gasping for air, she brought her knee up between his legs. He doubled over in pain. While he put his hand on his jewels, she retrieved his gun and slammed it down onto the top of his head. The poor guy dropped like a sack of potatoes, unconscious.

She whirled to face the second man, who was still fumbling to react and draw his weapon, and trained the gun on his head. He raised both of his hands in horror. She ripped the earpiece out of his ear.

"What are you?" the guy asked with wide eyes.

"A goddess," she said with a grin.

Then she stepped into the man's guard and brought the gun down against his temple. He collapsed next to his colleague.

"We're good, Lyra."

The girl dashed out, and together they hauled the unconscious men into the bathroom. Kierse quickly frisked them, using their own handcuffs to tie them to the grab bar affixed to the wall in the accessible stall and removing their communication devices and weapons.

"Excellent work," Lyra said with appreciation.

Kierse curtsied.

"Get moving. You have two-and-a-half minutes," Walter said.

Kierse and Lyra hurried out of the bathroom. Nearby was a loading entrance into the kitchen's walk-in cold storage. Laz had placed wards on those locks as well so only the team could go in and out of them. Lyra disappeared inside and came back with the second cake box, Cake & Cake in a pretty blue font on the lid.

"Shall we deliver our cake?" Lyra asked.

"We shall."

Lyra opened it to reveal the cauldron decoy box. Kierse felt the gentle hum of magic as she took it out of the cake box. It had been her idea to load an amulet with an absurd amount of magic and insert it into the center. Since she'd known immediately that it wasn't the real cauldron just by touching it, *their* decoy would be much more deceptive if it gave off at least somewhat of a magical aura, instead of being completely empty.

Lyra took the empty cake box and hustled back to the bathroom where she'd also change back into her ballgown and be lookout, or a diversion if necessary.

Kierse could see the Curator's magic all over the door—the wards with the crossed blades at the center and a *strong* scent of pine and lemon. He really didn't want anyone in this room. It must be draining to hold up wards like this. Kierse reached out and put her hand on it. Her absorption moved through it with ease, just like normal. Good.

She twisted the handle and found it locked. Well, at least that was predictable. She picked the cheap, hotel-grade lock with ease. She glanced back once before pushing the door open and stepping inside, tensing for an alarm. They'd tripped an alarm last heist, and Kierse had been certain to check the plans this time. But nothing went off. The only indication something was wrong were the red emergency lights illuminating the small space.

At the center of the otherwise empty room sat a box the exact size and shape as the one she was holding. And inside was the cauldron.

Kierse could sense the magic within before she even put her hand on the box. She mirrored the energy between the two boxes and decided it was close enough. There was no way for her to reopen it to feed it more magic, anyway.

She set the decoy on the floor and reverently reached out for the real thing. She breathed a sigh of relief when the magic didn't change when she touched it. Considering what the sword and spear did upon contact, she wasn't certain that it wouldn't try to talk to her through the metal. The spear didn't, but she didn't know if "didn't" and "couldn't" were the same thing.

With the real cauldron in her possession, she put her decoy back on the pedestal. A light flickered to life.

"There's a light. I think it's a weight sensor. Walter?"

He was silent at the word. "I don't have an alarm on my end."

Which was good. That meant that the Curator couldn't see it on his end, either. She hoped.

"How much time do we have?" she asked, staying calm in the face of this new problem. If someone walked in here and saw the light, they'd know. Or as soon as the manual system rebooted, it would let them know. She had to fix it now.

"Down to a minute," Walter added.

If the decoy didn't work, they might get caught walking out of the hotel. The whole place could go on lockdown. Everyone would be compromised. How quickly could the rest get out of here before that happened?

No one spoke. Protocol dictated what to do in case anything went wrong. Remove earpieces. Destroy them, discard them, get out. All she had to do was make the call.

Fuck, fuck, fuck.

Kierse tested the two boxes in her hand. They were identical in every way, except the cauldron was in one. She didn't think it was even a noticeable difference in weight. She dropped the decoy box back on the pedestal and ripped a pin out of her hair. She set it on the sensor and held her breath.

The light flicked off.

She breathed out. "Fucking hell."

The last thing she wanted was to leave her hairpin behind. But it was that or immediately be discovered when the system came back online. Leave *one* clue, or lose everything.

The decision was made.

Walter began to countdown in her ear. "Fifteen seconds."

She turned and fled.

"Ten seconds."

She reached the door.

"Five seconds."

Kierse pushed it open.

"Four. Three."

She twisted the lock from inside.

"Two."

The door closed behind her, and the hum of the security system came back online inside the room.

"One."

"It's done."

Kierse rushed down the hallway and burst into the bathroom, expecting to find Lyra. Except there was no Lyra, only the two guards groaning faintly as they started to come to. She should have come back in here when the countdown began to prep for her next part.

"Lyra?"

"She's holding up more guards who came to investigate when the others stopped communicating," Walter said over comms.

"Fuck."

"Laz is almost in position."

Kierse fled the bathroom with the box in hand, pushing through an employee door that led to an empty hallway. She could see a back entrance to the kitchens and a bellhop walking toward her, holding a designer hat box.

"Laz," she said with a sigh.

He opened the designer box, and Kierse set the cauldron inside. They covered it with fancy fabric, dropped the lid back on top, and Laz nodded.

"Luggage secured."

Kierse nodded. "See you on the other side."

"I'm on my way now," Graves said.

They'd gotten away with it. She'd stolen the cauldron right out from underneath the Curator's nose. Laz would take the box to a full luggage cart and carry it out to Graves's awaiting limo, where George would play getaway car. She and Lyra would exit through the back door with the rest of the performers. Already the rest of the crew were reporting in that they'd gotten out of the building.

Kierse took a deep breath and stepped out into the hallway.

"Kierse," a voice said behind her.

She turned in surprise. For a second, she didn't recognize the man. Then it hit her—this was the person who had known her name at Sansara. The one she couldn't find in her memories.

"Sorry, I'm not…"

A cloth was put over her nose and mouth from behind. She struggled for a minute before her head went fuzzy, her limbs limp. She stared up into the eyes of one of her attackers, wondering how she knew him and once again coming up blank.

"Don't worry," he said. "The Curator has been waiting for you."

Interlude

Laz was more spy than thief.

Infiltrating the Plaza was probably beneath him, but it had brought back joy in the assignment. While he didn't mind friendly car chases through the city streets, he preferred taking on a new identity and not getting caught. He and Kierse had that in common.

He dropped the designer hat box on top of more designer luggage. He'd already prepped the luggage cart in advance with a pile of expensive luggage, waiting for him to complete the last part of the job.

"All set," he said to one of his colleagues.

The guy clapped him on the back. "Rich fucks, huh, Andrew?"

Andrew was the name that he'd gotten the job under. It had been relatively easy to become him.

"Tell me about it. Smoke break later?"

"I'm off the fucking clock."

Laz nodded at him. He'd known that. Which was why he'd asked.

"Next time, then," Laz told him.

He took the luggage cart and headed toward the Plaza entrance. Ten years of searching. Ten years of undercover work. Ten years, and today it would be all over.

He'd met Graves on a mission in Bucharest. In Romania, the story of Vlad the Impaler and, more specifically, how he inspired the character Dracula some couple hundred years later, was inescapable. While he might have birthed the most famous story about vampires, Laz hadn't believed a single word of the propaganda that the Ottomans and his other enemies had written about him. Vampires were real, but Vlad certainly hadn't been one.

Or at least that was what the CIA had drilled into their heads. And Laz had believed them, up until he shipped out on that assignment.

They'd sent him to spy on a potential uprising in the northern reaches of Romania. The details were sketchy, but an underground group was taking up in Vlad's name and causing distress across the Romanian borders. The last thing they'd needed was problems with Ukraine. It was an election year, after all.

Bucharest had been a bust, except for a rumor Laz had sniffed out claiming the group had some mysterious artifact. They'd called it magic. Laz would believe it when he saw it.

Monsters might exist; magic certainly didn't.

So he'd followed the trail of whispers. It had taken him into the region of Transylvania, back to Vlad's original hometown of Sighisoara, a medieval walled citadel. He'd scaled the small wall. He'd entered the compound. He'd found the sacred ceremony. And he hadn't been the only one.

Even disguised in one of the cult's ritual costumes, Graves had looked out of place. The group had been too stupid to see the fox in the hen house. Laz hadn't been stupid.

But before he could act, the magical artifact that he'd been certain was a fake had lit up like the Fourth of July. All of the worshippers fell to their knees as their life force was *siphoned* out of them and pulled into the magic artifact. The entire sect fell over dead.

Graves walked over to the table and picked up the artifact. He sighed, resigned. "You want to take this back to your boss?"

Laz stepped out of the shadows, gun raised. "What are you?"

Graves wouldn't have an answer for him for many years. "It's a cheap knockoff. It isn't supposed to kill everyone." He tossed it to Laz, who caught it on instinct.

Curious, despite himself, he asked, "What's it supposed to do?"

"They claimed it was an amplifier, a tracker. Supposedly, it was how Vlad destroyed so many of his enemies," Graves said. "Couldn't be that he was just a vicious son of a bitch clinging to power in uncertain times."

"How were you involved with the cult?" Laz asked, gun still trained on him.

"Same as you. Infiltration." Graves shrugged off the robes, revealing the suit beneath. He wiped his hands on the expensive material. "Though I'm not a fan of the dirty work. Looking for a job?"

"I have a job."

"The CIA. I know." Graves grinned at him, dangerous, powerful. "Want to work for me instead?"

Laz should have said no. There was no reason for him to risk his career for this egoist who had infiltrated a Vlad the Impaler cult for an artifact that he didn't even believe would work. But he'd seen magic when he'd always been assured there was none. And by the end of the night, he'd said yes.

Graves looked exactly the same as that day in Romania all those years ago. He lounged back against his limo in his tailored suit, typing away on his phone as if he didn't have a care in the world.

"Your luggage, sir," Laz said.

"The trunk. Thank you," Graves said. "I'll keep the hat box up here."

"Of course, sir." Laz brought him the cauldron and carefully placed it on the backseat. "Kingston?"

"Occupied for now. Kierse?"

"Exiting through the back as arranged."

"Excellent." Graves took out a folded hundred-dollar bill and handed it to Laz. "Good work."

"Thank you, sir," Laz said as Graves smoothly sank into the back of his limo.

Laz shut the door tight and watched for a moment as the cauldron left the premises. They'd done it. It had gone off without a hitch.

Laz deposited the cart at the entrance and headed for the break room.

It was only then that Walter's voice came over the line. "I've been booted out of the system."

He had just gotten inside and asked, "You've lost the footage?"

"It's gone. Everyone out now."

Edgar grabbed the last remaining things from his locker, ready to exit the premises, when Walter said, "Kierse has gone offline."

And Graves was already gone.

PART VI

THE SUMMER SOLSTICE

Chapter Sixty-Four

K ierse's head was pounding. Her mouth felt like she'd swallowed cotton balls. Her eyes stung like she was cutting fresh onions. She could still smell the laced chloroform. It turned out she could still be knocked out by the shit, even as a wisp. Good times.

"Graves," she said out loud.

No response. She couldn't feel the earpiece in place anymore. Fuck.

She peeled her eyes open, but she might as well not have. The room was pitch black. She could only make out that she was in some kind of conference room from the strip of light coming in under the door. The only sound was the air-conditioning system blowing cold air on her face. She was tied to a wooden chair with some kind of thick rope. She wiggled against the bindings and immediately hissed as they dug in.

Not just ropes. Iron.

She froze like a deer in headlights. Who else knew what she was? That iron would be a better restraint than rope?

They had been careful. She'd been wearing her glamours all the time around New York, just as she had in Dublin. The only people she'd told she was Fae, besides those who had been there the night she had discovered her identity—Graves, Lorcan, Ethan, and Gen—were Nate, Colette, Oisín, and Niamh. None of them would betray her.

But that wasn't true, was it? Rio knew. Though she doubted this was their handiwork. No, there *was* one other person in Manhattan who knew her identity. The person who had put the spell on her to begin with—Cillian Ryan.

The cultist's voice came back to her then: *The Curator has been waiting for you.*

Fuck.

Fuck, fuck, fuck.

They'd been so careful. And still, somehow, she'd been caught in the trap. She might have been strong enough to burst through rope, but the iron had enough of a dampening effect to make her nauseous. Or was that the drugs? Maybe both.

The question was: what was he going to do with her?

Kierse started to tremble. How long before anyone noticed she was missing? She was supposed to get herself out of the Plaza. Graves would be back at the brownstone already. Lyra had been dealing with a diversion. Everyone else had their own getaway plans. She was alone.

Fear filled her lungs and wracked her nerves. The darkness was normally her friend. She needed to get it together. She would not be the girl afraid of the dark. She was a survivor. She had gone through worse than this. Jason had beat her senseless and left her for dead. She'd nearly *died* from god magic last year. What was a little darkness when she was already filled to the brim with it? She had embraced the darkness long ago.

She would get herself out of this situation. She just had to wait. It was a common tactic. Sensory deprivation. Leave a mark alone with their thoughts long enough and they'd sing whatever tune you wanted.

Kierse wasn't one of them. She went deep within herself. To the vault that she opened and closed and opened and closed. The memory that grounded her, that had *always* grounded her. The thing she had thought about when Jason had hit her was the same place that brought her out of the magical connection with Lorcan was the same thing that kept her mind clear of panic.

Kierse jolted at that thought. She and Lorcan were connected. She could sense him, but only barely—maybe he'd already left the Plaza but wasn't yet back to Brooklyn. They weren't bound through the ceremony yet, and she had never tried to reach out to him. But if there was ever a time...

She closed her eyes and let her breathing even out. She ignored the feel of the iron biting into her skin and went deep into her magic. She felt that connection at the center of it all. The thrum that beat against her breastbone like a second heartbeat. *Lorcan.*

It purred to life at the acknowledgment.

It didn't get any stronger, though. Still just a soft hum. She focused her entire attention on it. She let it build inside of her. Coaxed it to life in a way she never had before. The only time it had felt like this was when he was touching her.

She hesitated. She needed the connection to be stronger. As strong as when they kissed. But to do that...she'd have to let her mind go there. She'd have to think about him...*want* him.

Her stomach twisted. She didn't want to want him. But if she wanted his help, then she would have to try. She'd have to let herself delve into that place she had ignored all this time. She had no one else she could reach right now. There was only Lorcan.

She let her defenses down, peeling back the layers of her mind until she exposed that small part of herself that *did* want Lorcan. And maybe… it wasn't that small. Maybe it wasn't just a sliver she ignored. Maybe it was all of her in that moment.

She swallowed hard as she let that connection, that feeling, that man flood through her. All the things she had ignored and pushed aside and cut off from herself. The first time he'd smiled at her when she'd met him at his restaurant. The way he'd caught her stealing. How he could barely keep himself from touching her. The ease of his presence when they talked. The look on his face when he'd realized who and what she was in Graves's library.

Even then, she'd known. Deep down, she'd known. Her anger had been a living, fire-breathing dragon inside of her, and she'd refused to see it. Now she couldn't ignore it. The feel of his hands on her skin. The summer sunshine on her face. Those cerulean eyes boring through her. His insistence that she should live in Brooklyn with him, with her family, with his family. That they were connected and she couldn't deny it. Now she wasn't denying it. It was there.

Still, she pushed further. To that moment by the Oak Throne, wearing his faerie crown, his hands cupping her face. The devotion in his eyes. The irreverent king wanting nothing more than his irreverent queen. Then the kiss. His lips against hers. The way her entire being had been turned inside out. She shuddered at the memory, at the way his touch, the way their magic rose up, could conjure a storm within her. It ached to look at the memory. She'd made her choice, and still, *this* was here. This thing she couldn't seem to carve out of herself.

The magic rose like the tide. The connection strengthening in a way that she feared she wouldn't be capable of dissipating. But that was a fear for another day. Not when she was bound by iron and helpless.

Right now, she needed him.

Lorcan, she pleaded silently, reaching through their connection. *Please. Help.*

She waited and waited and waited. Nothing happened. She didn't know what it would feel like for him to hear her, or if he could even reach back through. Could he talk to her? Were her words reaching him? Still she pushed, pleading and begging and coaxing, using the force of their connection to reach for him. Anything to get him to come back.

Don't go to Brooklyn. Don't leave me, she said in her mind. *Come back. Help me.*

The lights flicked on.

Her eyes were closed, and still she winced at the sudden brightness. It severed the connection to Lorcan she'd been trying so hard to hold on to. The magic faded back to its normal dullness as he continued to get farther away. She hadn't reached him at all.

She slowly peeled her eyes open and got her first real look at the hotel meeting room. She was facing the door with her back to most of the room. There was a kitchenette against one wall stocked with drinks, and a small round table and chairs. She tried to wrack her brain for the floor plan and guessed she was on the second or third floor, in one of the smaller rooms off the ballrooms. The hallway outside connected to elevators near the bathrooms. If she could just…get out, then she could escape.

But there was no time for that. The door was creaking open. A black boot appeared through the gap. Kierse rattled against her bindings, ignoring the pain that shot up her arms and legs as the iron worked hard against her skin. But it was no use. There was no escape from whatever was about to come.

The man who'd knocked her out stepped through first. She still didn't know why he seemed familiar. Maya followed behind him. She pushed her glasses up her nose and smiled warmly at Kierse.

"Good to see you again, Shannon," Maya said as she took up a position to Kierse's left. The other man stood sentinel to her right. Two other guards she didn't recognize took up stances by the door.

"Her name isn't Shannon," the guy barked. "It's Kierse."

The *tap, tap, tap,* of a cane against the floor announced the arrival of their leader. "Shannon was her mother."

All of his goons dropped to a knee and said as one, "Curator."

Kierse froze at the sight of the man who entered. The Curator. Cillian Ryan. A rogue Druid and the powerful magical user who had cast a spell on her and stolen her memories. She recognized the face that hadn't aged in the nearly ten years since she'd stabbed him in the back and left him for dead.

"Jason?"

Chapter Sixty-Five

"Hello, Kierse."

Jason was larger than life, his upper body broad and muscular, clothed in a sharp black suit. He'd always hated ties, and he didn't wear one now, just had his button-up undone at the neck. He'd scrapped the clean-shaven look she'd seen recently in her memories for a full, dark beard. His eyes were as dark and deadly, but a new scar ran through his eyebrow and lid toward his jaw. A scar she had given him. His mouth was set in a way that had always made her walk on eggshells. The tilt of his head revealed the clever snake hidden in his mystique.

No wonder she hadn't been able to place the familiar Sansara goon. He was one of *Jason's* from the thieving guild. She hadn't even known his name.

"What…what are you doing here?" she asked. She willed her body to stillness, but it wasn't listening.

She had *killed Jason*.

It had been her only mission after he'd beat her to within an inch of her life and left her for dead. Gen had found her and saved her. She hadn't understood why Kierse had wanted revenge, but she'd needed it to be able to move on.

She'd tracked him down. With her own two hands, she had sliced into his face. He'd tried to fight back. He was bigger than her, stronger than her, and now she realized, he'd had magic to repel her. She'd probably absorbed any attack he leveled against her. He'd gotten his hands on her throat to finish what he'd started. Her knife had been out of reach. She'd managed to push him off her. He'd gone for a gun on the bedside table. She'd put a knife through his back before he could get to it.

Her body trembled at the memory. Of watching the blood leak out of his body and the life leave his eyes. The only father figure she'd ever known. And all of it had been an elaborate lie.

"Surprised to see me?" He looked down his nose at her. "I thought you might be. Worthless piece of shit."

She flinched. She was a little kid all over again, getting scolded by the one person she looked up to. The person who threw her off a building and broke her arm and left bruises in his wake. The fear was innate. Ten years away from him didn't change a thing.

"I killed you."

"Not quite," he said on a laugh. "Just paralyzed me from the waist down... for a time."

She shook her head. "I watched you die."

"Then we're even, right? You were supposed to be dead, too."

She was, but Gen had found her. She'd taken her revenge. Was this his?

He leaned the cane forward, resting both his hands on it. "It took hours of physical therapy and rehabilitation and more magic than you've ever seen in your life to get me back to where I am today." He lifted one arm wide. "Am I everything you remembered?"

"I remember killing you."

He smirked. "Try again."

"What do you want?"

Jason laughed. "You know the answer to that."

Kierse refused to be baited. He always played these games. Made them guess, and the guess was never quite up to his satisfaction. She was trapped in her own personal hell with her very real nightmare.

"Not going to answer?" He clenched his jaw. "Then I suppose I should just finish what I started."

He nodded at the goon to his right. The man drew a gun and put it to her temple.

"Wait!" she gasped.

He tutted at her, holding a hand up. "Don't make me go to such extremes. Why do you always make me do this?"

Her stomach flopped at the words. The bullshit manipulation she had endured so savagely for so long. It had taken her years to accept affection. Only with Graves's help had she learned to want something more in her life. She hated how small she felt in his presence.

"I don't know what you want. Revenge?"

Jason laughed. His gaze cut her down. "Did you think this was some elaborate trap just for you? That I give a fuck?"

Kierse *had* thought that. All the rare and priceless pieces he'd had on display. They all made sense if they belonged to Jason. He was the most talented thief she had ever known. Well, after her...

"I don't know," she said softly, letting herself look small to him while her mind raced ahead. "Your people said you'd been waiting for me."

"Not *you* specifically," he said with a snort. "You, the little thief who thought they could best me. And then look at the shit that appeared before me." He gestured to her. "My thieves don't get *caught*. Did I not drill that into your head enough?"

She cleared her throat. "I guess not." Inside, she was furious. He *had* taught her that. He'd taught her all of his tricks. But that didn't mean that he knew all of hers. She was going to find a way out of this.

"So where is it?"

"Where is what?"

"Don't play dumb with me," he said, taking a step toward her. "I know you can't help it, but I trained you. You're better than this."

"The cauldron," she guessed.

"Ding, ding, ding." He leaned forward. "Where is it?"

She shrugged. "Gone. Guess I wasn't too bad of a thief, after all."

"I see. She doesn't know shit."

He turned his back on her as if he really were ready to discard her. She couldn't let that happen.

"Why did you do it?" she asked him before he reached the door.

He stopped. "Do what?"

"Erase my memories after you put the spell on me."

He whirled around. Surprise lit his face. "So the spell *is* broken?"

"Yes."

All the puzzle pieces fit together, suddenly. Graves had never met Cillian. He wouldn't have known Jason and Cillian were the same man, the one who had stolen her life away twice. Lorcan had said Cillian was dead—someone had killed him during the Monster War. *She* was that someone. After she'd paralyzed him, he must have gone underground. Scrubbed his identity and started a new life. One where he was still a thief, but no longer the one who got his hands dirty. It was just like him. Everything fit—and still, the question lingered…

"Why did you do it?" she asked again. "I know that you're Cillian Ryan. A Druid, cast out after you drained Sansara. You were doing dirty underground work using magic while you started your thieving ring. Before you became this…"

"Is that what you think? I was *saving* children like you." He gestured to her. "You were never going to amount to anything. You weren't going to do anything except die like the rest of your kind. Just like the rest of my little ring of thieves."

She bristled with indignation. "I'm a survivor."

"You were a half breed," he snarled. "Half of anything is a whole of nothing."

"But you could have *told me*," she yelled at him.

He shrugged, unconcerned. "Then what use would you have been to me?"

And it was that simple. He'd stolen and used children as a way to bring in followers who were devoted to him. As she had been. As had they all. Now he had a cult around him and his stupid tree. More power, more followers, more devotion, just like he wanted.

This wasn't how it ended. This couldn't possibly be right.

"So, that's it. You did it to get followers. You couldn't earn anyone's respect, so you stole our memories and made us your little devotees."

"Not everyone," he said with a one-shoulder shrug. "Just those with magic."

"But you *have* magic. You're a Druid. You have Sansara!"

"Power begets power," he said. "The more power I had, the more likely I was going to be able to replant Sansara's power, making my own power infinite."

"But why would hiding our magic, taking our memories, give you anything?"

"It gave me *everything*," he said with the calm assurance of someone who had been doing this so long that he was fully convinced of his righteousness. "Just like draining Sansara did."

She stilled at the smug look on his face. The spell. The block. The reason she couldn't see into that room.

A horrible thought hit her. She had been weaker with the spell over her, but she could still access her powers. As if the spell had only been a dampener. But with Jason standing before her in all his pomp and egoism, she had another thought.

He'd siphoned away the magic of Sansara, letting the tree crumble to ash, and then *retained* those powers for years, making him one of the most powerful people in the city. Then he'd rounded up a ton of children and made them his thieving guild. He could have had anyone at his side, but he'd chosen the most vulnerable.

A power source.

The spell hadn't hid her magic at all. It was…a siphon.

"The spell wasn't what you told my parents at all, was it?" she asked in horror. "The room in Tribeca…"

Shock flashed across Jason's face for the span of a second. "You shouldn't be able to remember Tribeca."

"You took the memories, because you didn't want anyone to be able to piece together what you'd actually done." She looked up into his eyes. "You were siphoning my magic."

He leaned against the cane and clapped twice, sardonically. "Took you long enough to figure out."

"My magic flowed into you, continually replenishing you. When the spell broke, you knew, because you felt the loss."

It was only after the spell was lifted that she'd had the full force of her magic. She'd thought that was because the spell was hiding her. But it was just that she was no longer continuously giving most of it away.

"I was powerful enough by then with Sansara regrown that it was but a blip," he told her.

"And I wasn't the only one." She glanced at the two guards at his side. Likely other magic wielders who he was stealing from. "Just the strongest. Especially considering my absorption was a standby effect and could draw in powers for you at any time."

"That was rather useful," he agreed. "Though you were hardly the strongest."

She didn't believe him. She could read him too well.

She didn't believe in good guys. People like Jason, they always won. That was how her world worked. But for once, just once, she wanted it to be the case that what was dead stayed dead. She came out ahead. This bastard didn't win.

"All of this, just for your own power?" she asked him. "That can't be your end game. You've built too much to keep it hidden and unappreciated. Do you want to take on the Druids?"

He scoffed. "As if I care about them. They lost long ago with their 'goodness above all' attitude."

"That's not exactly how they've appeared to me."

"You've had interactions with Druids, have you?" he asked, leaning toward her with a smirk on his lips.

"Unfortunately."

"That's my girl," he said with a laugh. "Always did have a problem with authority."

She didn't know how she had gotten to this point. Jason's head games always gave her a headache. One moment degrading her, the next praising her. She was done playing with him.

She rattled against her chains, trying to use her magic.

Jason laughed. "Oh, I have missed you, Kierse. You always were entertaining. And I'll let you in on a little secret." She bared her teeth at him. "You owe me."

She narrowed her eyes at him. "Why?"

"Because I saved your life. The Fae Killer destroyed your kind, and if it wasn't for me, you'd have died alongside them."

"You didn't save me. You destroyed my life," she accused. "You're spinning more bullshit tales to make yourself feel better about stealing the powers of *children*. You're pathetic."

Jason stalked toward her like a predator, but she saw him for what he really was. "You're the one currently tied to a chair."

"You're just a man desperate for attention and caught up in your own grandiose fantasy. A narcissist who preyed on children," she snarled at him. "You think this means you win? Because people worship you?"

"Better to be worshipped like a king than be another sheep in the herd," he told her, leaning down until they were at eye level. "You wouldn't know anything about that, would you? Who would follow you?"

Kierse boiled with rage at the sight of his smug smile. She wasn't the same girl she'd been when she'd gotten out. She'd been sixteen and still both enamored and terrified of him. She'd had enough gall to try her hand at killing him, but she knew now that she should have put a bullet between his eyes just to be safe. And she fucking intended to this time.

She reared forward and slammed her head against his nose. The *crunch* as his nose broke and blood spurted was extremely satisfying.

"You fucking bitch!" he cried, reeling back and reaching for his face.

All that remained after her fury was her magic. Not the place she'd gone while trying to reach Lorcan, but the center of her wisp powers. They were weakened from the iron, but still vibrant enough from the heist to latch onto. The guards rushed to Jason, who yelled and sent Maya off for medical help. The other goon fretted over him, and Jason pushed him away. He never could stand looking weak.

She smiled. Let that energy rush to her fingertips. The burst of power came to her like an emotional avalanche. He thought he was just going to get away with it. He was going to leave like he hadn't destroyed her life.

No. The answer was all she needed.

She pushed like she had never pushed, sending herself into slow motion with such force that time stood still. The drop of blood stalled at the bottom of Jason's chin. His goon's outstretched hand froze. The clock refused to tick.

Between one second and the next, Kierse shifted forward, her body a blur as she went from tied to the chair with iron to standing on her own two feet. Magic suffused her bones and whipped her hair around her face and sang a sweet tune. The scent of Irish wildflowers blooming in the spring burst across the room. Golden magic mingled with blue down her limbs.

She dropped her slow motion. Time ticked forward.

Kierse had phased from one place to the next.

Chapter Sixty-Six

Jason's jaw dropped in horror as he jerked backward. "You…can't do that."

"It seems that I can."

The power was a torrent through her. She didn't know how long she could hold onto it. Not long.

"The iron…"

"I'm only half Fae," she snarled. "Half of anything is a whole of nothing."

"That's not what I meant," he said carefully. The mean and ugly persona he'd been spitting at her when he'd had her cornered disappeared in the wake of her power. She watched him try to bring back the charming guy he'd always used to win people over. "You don't want to use those powers too much or the Fae Killer is going to find you. That's what I saved you from, right?"

Kierse's eyes narrowed. "The Fae Killer is still out there? Aren't all the other Fae dead?"

"He's still out there," he assured her.

"Do you know who he is?"

Jason's lip quirked up. "I do. And I think you do, too." He straightened up to make himself look more important. "If you kill me, you'll never find out."

"Fuck you, Jason," she said, taking a step forward. The force of holding her powers in her hand was like trying to lift a car over her head. "Your death belongs to me."

Jason's eyes darted to his followers. "Don't just stand there! Stop her."

Then like the coward he was, he fled the room. She rushed after him, but his followers came out of their stupor all at once. There were only three of them, but they had guns. As they fumbled for them, Kierse had only one chance.

She'd never used her magic in this way before. She didn't even know if wisps could *do* what she had just done. Phasing wasn't exactly part of the repertoire, but if she could do that, then she could do more. She had enough energy to push herself to the brink. Anything to stop Jason.

Her absorption had always been passive. But over the weeks she'd learned how to turn it on and off, how to use it as an amplifier in her triskel, how to feed the power she absorbed to others. This time she only had herself.

She needed to be her own amplifier and her own power source.

Grasping her power tightly in her fist, she turned her palm out toward the Sansara cultists and unleashed her energy. Like a fire hose, it rushed out of her skin and hit the first guy hard in the chest. He wrenched backward into the other two guards.

One had already gotten her gun up and aimed for Kierse's chest. She punched another bout of magic toward the woman. It hit her the same moment that the bullet punched through Kierse's shoulder.

They both screamed. Kierse dropped her magic and clutched her shoulder. Blood poured from the wound. At least the bullet had gone straight through. If it had lodged in, she would have been extra fucked. But her strength wouldn't hold up long without a healer.

There was no time to waste.

She grabbed a gun from the first guard, shoved it into the back of her pants with her good arm, and grabbed a second to carry. She stepped over the pile of guards, blood seeping down her fingers as she tried to hold herself together and head toward the elevator bank. She was weak. Too weak. She couldn't do much more from here, not without assistance. But she had to kill Jason. That was her only mission.

The elevator doors dinged as she reached them. She fired the weapon a few times through the small crack and watched the shots ping wide. The smell of lemon and pine rose up strong. Jason had used his magic to redirect the bullets. His smug face disappeared as the doors closed.

"No!" she screamed, hitting her fist against them.

There was no light that told her what floor he was going to. This wasn't the movies where she could figure it out and magically appear. She had to make a choice. Up or down. Up meant ballroom levels that led out to the main hotel. Down meant the loading docks and bigger exits. With a bloody nose and in a hurry, he'd go down.

Kierse whipped around and rushed into the nearest staircase, taking them two at a time toward the basement levels. Her legs felt like jelly, and she had to focus on her Fae instincts to get her body to keep moving. She wasn't going fast enough. There was no way around it. The blood loss and magic loss was taking a toll. She had two more floors to make it.

"Keep going," she whispered to herself. "Just keep going."

When she hit the final landing, her knees nearly collapsed out from underneath her. She held onto the railing for a second too long before pushing out to the loading docks. Because of the late hour, there weren't as many people working, but it wasn't empty, either.

"Your shoulder!" a man said with wide eyes. "You need a doctor."

With her gun held at her side, she marched forward. Her head was spinning, but she couldn't stop. At least she'd chosen right—gold magic floated around Jason's legs as he used it to help himself into the van.

She lifted her weapon and fired at him. Shouts rang from the workers as they all ducked behind equipment and hid. Her shoulder screamed as she tried to hold the gun steady and continue toward the van. Jason ducked down out of sight. The door to the van slammed shut. The tires screeched as it backed out of the loading dock. Kierse kept firing. She tried to focus on the tires like she had when she'd chased Imani, but her vision was blurring. Was that blood loss? Magic drain?

"Fuck!" she screamed as her bullets embedded into the side of the van, but it continued out of the dock and onto the streets.

She ran to the exit only to watch it disappear from view.

He was gone. Jason was gone. All of that and he'd gotten away. She dropped to her knees as the adrenaline slipped away from her. She was in a bad way. She needed…

What did she need?

Graves.

A way to escape this.

The workers were still cowering, glancing over the tops of boxes to see if the worst was over. They'd all been so conditioned by the Monster War that no one had even intervened. Which benefited her, at least.

She wouldn't make the blocks north to get to Graves's brownstone. Not on foot, at least. She needed a cell phone. She needed—

With all the adrenaline gone, another pulse of magic hummed louder. She'd been so caught up in the ordeal with Jason that she hadn't been able to focus on anything else. Now, as it was all going dark, she realized that Lorcan had gotten closer. Very close. Had he heard her plea?

A black van stopped in front of the docks, and the passenger door ripped open. Her magic went wild, pulsing in her chest to the tempo of her blood flowing through her veins. She brought her gaze up to meet the blue eyes of her rescuer.

"I've got you," Lorcan said.

He lifted her up into his arms. The connection between them picked up from trot to a gallop.

"How did you know I'd be here?"

"I heard you call for me," he said. "I'll always come."

She stared up into his face for a moment before giving in and leaning her head against his chest. He carried her to the van. The door to the back slid open. Niamh was perched inside, her face a mask of worry.

"Hurry. She's lost a lot of blood," Niamh said.

Lorcan lifted Kierse inside. Then he hoisted himself inside as well. "Declan, move," he barked.

His second grumbled something under his breath but got the van moving out onto the street.

Lorcan cradled her head into his lap. He brushed her hair out of her eyes as Niamh went to work ripping away part of her dress to get a look at the damage. So many beautiful dresses she'd ruined in the past few weeks.

"You're okay now," Lorcan told her.

She hissed as Niamh began to work on her wound. She didn't understand the healing magic, only that it was *not* painless like she'd thought.

"Sorry," Niamh said quickly. "Think good thoughts. The rest might hurt."

"Thank you," she whispered to both of them.

"Close your eyes. You're safe."

Safe. She was safe.

She didn't feel safe. Jason had gotten away. He was still out there, and she didn't know what he was going to do next. The Fae Killer was out there, too. Jason knew her true identity. Would he…tell him about her? She needed to talk about this with Graves. He'd have answers. He always had answers.

"Graves," she said through gritted teeth as Niamh worked on her arm. "I need you to take me to Graves."

Lorcan sighed heavily. "I'm afraid that I can't do that."

"I need to…I need to get back to him. He doesn't know what happened."

"Lorcan, hold her steady," Niamh said.

Lorcan's hands grasped her sides as he kept her from shaking. The contact made her jump. It was like a pipeline had opened that she no longer had a way of closing.

"Just rest," he said softly, his fingers splaying across her skin. "After tonight, you won't ever want to go back to him."

"What does that mean?" Kierse asked, jerking against him.

He nodded at Niamh, who frowned at the gesture but put her hand on Kierse's temple. "Sorry," she whispered. Then she said the word, "Sleep."

Her anger at Lorcan's betrayal dissolved into the fading light.

Chapter Sixty-Seven

For the second time that night, she awoke in an unfamiliar place. She was lying on the ground with her cheek pressed against the earth. The scent of freshly tilled soil and green grass and something that she could only ever begin to describe as Ireland. Which made no sense. She was certainly not in Ireland.

It was the pulse of energy all around her that finally made her open her eyes. She was lying on a blanket of moss. Her gaze lifted to see the Oak Throne in all its glory. Seated on the throne was the irreverent Oak King. She blinked, and that vision of him was gone, replaced by the ruler of the Druids sitting imperiously in his place.

The duality of Lorcan was not lost on her.

She had been reeled in by that glimpse of him, only to fall victim, once again, to who he truly was—the self-righteous ruler.

His eyes cast down upon her, and she shivered. The force of that look was staggering, as if he could see straight through her, to the heart of who she was. Their connection that had been growing was now an open tap. All she had to do was turn the dial and the whole thing ratcheted up to dizzying levels.

"Hello, little songbird," he said with a radiant smile. The one that should have won her over, but only made her stomach dip in warning.

She'd known he was an enemy. She'd known he would do anything to get what he wanted. She shouldn't have forgotten.

"Let me go," she rasped.

"You're not a hostage."

She pushed herself up onto her elbows. The pain in her arm was gone. She looked down to see that first, she was dressed in new clothes—a loose, white silk dress—and second, the bullet wound in her shoulder was completely healed.

"Niamh is extremely talented," Lorcan said. "The process is draining, though, and you were already on reserves."

Kierse reached for her magic and saw that what Lorcan said was true. She was beyond low. She was nearly completely drained. All that energy she'd gotten from stealing the cauldron had been used to phase out of her chair and blast aside the guards. The little she'd had left, the healing had clearly tapped.

For a second, she considered the sacred tree that was not far from here. The one that had been created out of the triskel. But while it should have been easy to feel at this distance, it was like a block had been set around the room. She could no more reach for that tree than anything else outside of this room. Great.

Standing before Lorcan on the summer solstice, at the *height* of his fucking powers, with her tank on empty. This was going to be…fun.

Slowly, she eased to her feet. The white dress fell to her knees, the material soft and comfortable. Her feet were bare. All her jewelry had been removed, including her wren necklace. She brought a hand to her hair and felt that the top layer had been braided into a crown around the top of her head, while the rest fell loose to the middle of her back. She looked and felt…younger in the outfit. Not like the hardened girl she was, but rather someone she could have been in a different time and place. Either way, it didn't feel like her.

"What's with the costume change?"

"Today's important," he said as he stood from the throne. Despite her carefree summer vibes, he was still in a navy suit with a white button-up and leather loafers. The crown was gone from his brow, but somehow he looked even more formidable, as if the magic swirling under his skin was threatening to unleash.

"Maybe for you," she said. "But if I'm not a hostage, then I'm going to go."

Lorcan slipped his hands into his pockets. "Back to him."

It wasn't a question. They both knew the first place she'd go.

"Yes."

He tilted his head thoughtfully. "Have you wondered why that is?"

"What do you mean?"

"Why him? After what he kept from you at the last solstice, the way he used you, the pain he caused you," Lorcan said, taking a step down from the dais.

"As if you haven't done the same."

"I came when *you* called," he reminded her. "I kept you safe. Explain how that's remotely similar to what he has done."

"I'm not arguing with you about Graves."

"Good," Lorcan said with a deadly smile. "Because you were the one who bridged our connection without a binding ceremony. You reached deep enough into our bond to access me. You begged me to come."

She flushed at the memory of doing just that. "I was being held hostage with iron. I would have done anything to escape that fate."

"Still, I came at your command. I brought a healer with me. I saved your life."

"I saved my own life," she snapped back at him. "I managed to escape the Curator's clutches. Who, mind you, is actually Cillian Ryan, who masqueraded for years as my thieving master, Jason. So forgive me if I don't care about your self-righteous bullshit right now, Lorcan."

"Cillian Ryan is alive?" he asked coldly.

"Yeah. Remember how you said someone killed him during the Monster War? That was me." Lorcan's eyes widened. "I put a knife in his back, but it paralyzed him instead of killing him. He got away just before you showed up."

"How did you get out of the iron?"

Kierse hesitated. She didn't know if she wanted Lorcan to know how she had done it, but there was no way around it. "I slowed time enough that I could push my body out of time and out of the chair."

His eyes widened. "You phased. That is incredibly advanced. Only Saoirse had that power, and it took her a hundred years to develop."

Kierse stilled at those words. A century. Meanwhile Kierse had discovered it out of necessity. Was it because she had Saoirse's magic, or was it because she'd had no other choice?

"This makes sense to me," Lorcan said quietly, almost to himself. "But you haven't answered my question. Why do you think it is that you keep going back to him?"

"I don't want to do this with you. I don't know why I'm here or why you changed my clothes or what you think you can possibly gain from this. But I made my choice. In the end, it's still mine."

"Is it?"

"What does that mean?"

He prowled forward. "I've had some...musings over the last couple weeks. Something felt off. I couldn't quite put my finger on it. Niamh said you were adamant that you didn't want to work with Graves again. That you didn't trust him. That there was nothing to worry about, and yet you were staying at his brownstone. You were with him. And every time I saw you, your feelings toward him changed."

Kierse flushed. "There's plenty of reasons for that—*he* changed."

Lorcan laughed. Then his face fell. "Oh, you're being serious." He ran a hand back through his hair. "Fucking hell, how much damage has he done?"

"Damage?"

"Let me draw you a picture," he said as he began a circuit around her. "You leave for months and refuse to talk to him. He shows up unannounced and convinces you to come back to New York with him. Niamh mentions that you've lost some memories. You mention to me that you've learned how to turn your absorption off. Gen mentions to Niamh that she's worried about you and Graves after what happened last time."

Kierse bristled at that. "Did she?"

"Yes. She said she's worried he's not telling you everything. Then Ethan comes to me and tells me that Graves is helping you remember your parents." His hands clenched into fists. "He's worried by what that means. That Graves could be in your head."

"That is *none* of your business."

Lorcan stopped at her back. His words were hollow as he asked, "Did he ever tell you how he killed my sister?"

"Yes," she whispered. "But he'd never do that to me."

"Would you even know if he had?"

Kierse clenched her jaw and turned to look at him. "Graves has not done anything to our bond, if that's what you're insinuating."

"How would you know?"

"He told me that he'd kill you first," Kierse argued.

Lorcan chuckled. "Of course he said that. Yet I'm alive, and the only thing that has changed is you. How you claim to feel about him. What your *choice* is."

"You just can't accept that you lose, can you?"

"I can't accept that in the entire universe, I was given exactly one person, and she was torn from me. Except then I find out I have a second chance, after decades of mourning. Someone who is made for me," he said. He reached out and rested his hand on her breastbone, intensifying their connection. "Who I am made for. And you don't even want to consider it. That's not possible without his interference."

It took her entire force of will to pull away from his hand. "I'm not Saoirse, and I can make my own choices."

She turned away from his downturned face and headed toward the double doors. He'd said she wasn't a hostage. Well, then she was going to leave.

"His entire job is to manipulate minds," Lorcan said, stalking after her. "He has spent his life perfecting it to get what he wants. And what he wants most in this world is you. You think he wouldn't use his power on you?" Lorcan grasped her arm and whirled her back around. "Do you think he'd even be able to help himself?"

She stood firm at those words. Glared up into his perfect blue eyes. Her anger a blur inside of her. "You weren't there when he was using his powers. He refused to push me too far. He took care of me. He was teaching me how to keep my guard up against anyone who was in my mind."

"Did it ever work on him?" Lorcan shot back.

Kierse narrowed her eyes. No. He'd always said that there was no way to keep him out. She'd always assumed he meant because he was so powerful. He was too good at it. "He was training me against someone else. Someone like you."

Lorcan raised an eyebrow. "I don't have that power. *He* does. So if he wasn't training you to keep himself out of your head, then he wasn't training you at all."

"*I* kept us from binding in this very room."

"The binding that initiated without even a ceremony. That both of us clearly wanted. The universe wanted. But sure, Graves didn't get in your head to stop it."

"That isn't what happened."

"You won't even look at the truth right before your eyes."

"This is *your* truth," Kierse argued.

She'd learned to trust Graves in those sessions in her mind. Learned to let her guard down around him. Watched him change into the person he was—who fed her information for free, brought her into his inner circle, learned to work with others, and learned to love. He'd fought for her. He'd done everything in his power to be the man she deserved. She couldn't be fooled into believing that.

Lorcan's hand cupped her face, his eyes imploring. "You let a monster in your mind. You shouldn't be surprised when he shreds it to pieces."

Kierse shivered. "He wouldn't…"

"Are you sure you'd know?"

She hesitated.

"That's what I thought."

She didn't want to consider it, and now she had to. Would she know if Graves had fucked with her mind? Her gut said he hadn't. That he wouldn't do that to her. She had changed her mind about him all on her own. She'd trusted him to have her back. After seeing the memory where he helped her parents, she'd let him in. The rest had been a natural domino effect after her strong feelings last winter. It wasn't… It couldn't be… There was no way it was anything else. Right?

"The binding can stop it," Lorcan said softly, reaching for her hand. His fingers entwined with hers. His eyes pleading. "We can keep you safe."

She shivered at those words. "No."

"Kierse…"

"Let me just talk to him."

"I was afraid you'd say that," he said, his head bowed. "I've lost too much. He'll kill you before letting you go. I can't risk it."

His expression was determined when he looked back up at her. He took her other hand in his. "Tonight we'll be bound."

Chapter Sixty-Eight

K ierse tried to yank her hands back, but it was like trying to move a mountain. His power wrapped around her wrists. She couldn't break through his magic. Not today. Not when he was at his most powerful. Just as Graves had been the night they stole the spear. Lorcan had his robin as a power booster like Graves had his wren. The summer solstice was upon them. Even if she had been at her strongest, she wasn't sure she'd have been able to get free.

So she needed to try to reach the sensible man he impersonated.

"What happened to letting me make my own decision?"

"You've proven susceptible to corruption," Lorcan said.

"What about having all the time in the world to let me come around?"

His expression didn't change as he met her gaze. "I would have waited until the end of time, but I will not sit by and let him destroy you the way he did Emilie."

The doors opened at some unseen command. In walked Niamh in traditional Druid robes. Her burgundy hair long and flowing. Her expression troubled. Behind her came a cadre of Druids in green robes belted at the waist. Declan led the Order into the room, taking up spots inside as if they'd all prepared for this moment. Declan stopped at Lorcan's side. He sneered at her as if he thought this was what she deserved.

"In position, sir," Declan said, nodding to Lorcan.

"Is she ready?" Niamh asked.

"Yes," Lorcan said at the same time Kierse said, "No!"

Lorcan dragged Kierse toward the center of the room. "It's as we thought. He got to her."

Niamh bit her lip as she and Declan followed them. The swagger was gone from her step, and she looked between Kierse and Lorcan as if she didn't have a clue in the world what to do.

"Why are you helping him?" Kierse demanded of Niamh. "You told me in Dublin that he wasn't really in charge. You said he didn't have power over you. You don't have to do this."

Niamh wavered. "He's in charge here," she said with a sigh. "And he's right anyway. I've been worried about you."

"Worrying about me and kidnapping me are sort of different extremes."

"I know. If we could have done this any other way, we would have," Niamh promised her.

Niamh removed gold, braided string from her pocket and nodded at Lorcan. He lifted their hands, and Kierse pulled against his magic. She didn't have any energy. The little she had was like throwing pebbles into the ocean. Little good it did.

"Please don't," Kierse whispered.

"I'm sorry," Niamh said. "I was convinced we wouldn't have to do this, but Ethan came to us so scared for you."

Ethan had betrayed her trust, and now they were here. The wound stung. She couldn't believe he'd done that to her.

"Ethan doesn't know what he's talking about," Kierse said. "I'm not corrupted or whatever Lorcan is saying."

"I know how insidious he is," Niamh said softly. Her eyes cut to Lorcan, who lifted a brow. "Lorcan isn't all good, but he's never done anything like Graves. He'd never hurt you."

"Believe it or not, *this* hurts me," she told them, gesturing to their joined hands.

Niamh hesitated. "Lorcan…"

"The ceremony is an honor," he said. "It's sacred."

"It's sacred," Niamh repeated. She began to twine the golden thread around their wrists.

"You might not be in my head," Kierse said flatly, "but you sure as hell are manipulating the rest of them."

"This is a handfasting," Niamh continued as if she hadn't heard Kierse at all. "It's a traditional Celtic wedding ceremony but is used symbolically in this ceremony to express the union of two souls."

"Please," she pleaded with Lorcan. "Don't do this."

"It'll be better when it's over."

The Druids began to chant in an ancient language. She remembered the small lesson Lorcan had given her on Druidic spells—self, spirit, and sacrifice. The self was inherent magic of which Lorcan was at the peak of his. Spirit was time, place, and the cosmos of which today was the summer solstice. And sacrifice was what was given to power the spell. Here, it was the chanting and the ribbon tying them together and the promise of a queen to the Oak Throne.

Wind whipped inside the building like they were outside on the day of a hurricane. Her hair flew around her face, cutting into her eyes and obscuring her vision. Lorcan stood firm against the squall. The mountain in the storm. Magic crawled up their bodies, a swirl of gold and blue glittering in the dim lighting. It started at their joined hands and stretched outward toward her chest. The most beautiful sight she'd ever seen. And the most terrifying.

The chanting increased in volume. Niamh's words as she read off the spell were lost to the volume of the wind. Still it continued, eating up inch after inch of her wrist and then her arm and up to her shoulder. She panicked as it reached for her. She tugged against the bindings, but all it did was tighten the string, pull them closer together. Still, the magic embraced her body like an old lover. Warm and inviting. It wanted to lull her into submission. And it felt good.

It would be so easy to give up. To let him win. Because there was that piece inside her that said this was what she was made for.

The last wisp.

The most powerful Druid.

They were destined. And once they were bound together, the world would be set right again.

Except when she looked up into blue eyes, she wished for gray. When she saw his dark brown hair, she was missing the midnight blue. When she saw his navy suit, she wanted the black. She wanted the darkness. She wanted Graves.

"Stop," she begged.

A tear tracked down her cheek as she yanked on her wrist, pushing against his shoulder with her other hand to try to get away from him. Still it didn't move. The magic only crept closer, crawling across her chest and down her torso. As if she were being dipped in glowing light.

"Please, Lorcan, put a stop to this." She tugged some more. "I don't want this. I don't want to be bound to anyone. You can't just take my autonomy."

"It's too late," Lorcan said. "The ceremony has already begun."

"We can undo it. We can undo it together."

"What would you do if we did? Run straight back to the problem? No. I'm not going to let you get yourself killed."

"He's not going to kill me," Kierse argued. "But this is *worse*. Can't you see that?"

"How could this be worse than what he did?"

"You're taking away my choice!" she screamed at him.

"He was stealing your mind," Lorcan roared back. "He was going to push too far and he was going to kill you. Do you want to be dead? Is that better than being with me?"

"This has nothing to do with you and everything to do with your fucked-up power. Your vengeance against him. You don't want *me*. You want to *win*."

"This isn't about winning."

"You don't even see how far you've gone. You act like you're a good guy. That you're so far above him. And then you prove time and time again that power is all you want. As long as he doesn't win, right? As long as you can prove you're better than him, nothing else matters."

"You've always been determined to see me as the bad guy," Lorcan said. His eyes narrowed. "Fine. Make me your bad guy. If that saves your life, then so be it."

And something broke inside of her at those words.

The ceremony had already begun. Her powers were depleted, and his were infinite. There was no way for her to save herself this time. She'd gotten lucky time and time again. She'd had the spear against King Louis. She'd phased to escape Jason. There was no escaping Lorcan. Not when the universe seemed to want their joining. Her approval mattered little.

There was only one way to stop this: she needed help.

But no one was going to waltz in and save her. Her friends who had always been at her side were gone. They'd been concerned about her, talking to others about her behind her back instead of bringing their concerns directly to her. They probably wanted this. Colette and Nate and Maura could do nothing to stop this. And Graves...there was no way to get to Graves.

The universe hated her enough to give her a mental connection with Lorcan and not the person that she loved. The technology that had linked them was nothing compared to this mental, emotional communion. Something she could never have with Graves.

It was truly over. She was finished. Lorcan had won.

A tear tracked down her cheek at that debilitating thought. She was a fighter at heart. She had always prided herself on her own self-reliance. On the ability to get herself out of sticky situations. But there was nothing she could do against what Lorcan was doing to her. Not when she was at her lowest. She would do anything to stop him. But what else did she have?

Her knees buckled, and she nearly collapsed as she hit peak overwhelm. Lorcan reached for her with his free hand, keeping her on her feet. He was saying something to her. Some pretentious bullshit about how this was good for her, how it would keep her mind intact. Her *magic* was what he really meant. The magic of his wife. The connection he'd lost nearly a century ago.

Lorcan wanted this. He wanted her to second-guess her friends and family. To second-guess Graves. He wanted her to have only him to turn to.

Maybe Graves was a villain, but if he was, then he was a villain of Lorcan's making.

All of that shit about Graves infiltrating her mind and breaking it was bullshit. Lies and propaganda about the enemy Lorcan had created that he really believed. It wasn't the Graves that she knew.

"No," she whispered, more to herself than anyone else.

"No?" Lorcan asked.

But she didn't elaborate. Everything was no.

She might not be able do it by herself, and she might not have anyone coming to save her—but if Graves had been in her mind, if their magic connecting during the solstice had changed his powers enough to send images into her mind, then maybe there *was* a link.

In the end, she had to decide whether love was enough. Whether love meant trust. She'd met Graves where he was in the dark and let him see her own darkness in turn. They were one and the same. A mirror.

And now she needed to use that mirror to reach him. He'd touched her mind enough over the last couple months to have left an imprint. Even if he hadn't done what Lorcan had said, she thought it was worth trying.

Her absorption was off. Her mind wide open. Anyone could have touched it and she had no defenses. It was now or never.

Graves, she cried in her mind. *Graves, please, I'm in Brooklyn. Lorcan is going to force the binding, and I can't do this alone. I can't save myself this time. I...I need you. Graves, please.*

She waited in the silence for a moment, but no answer came.

She tried again.

And again.

And again.

Crying out into her mind for just the bare hope that Graves would come and save her from this monster. But nothing changed. Nothing happened.

Their mental bond wasn't real. It was just her last-ditch hope.

And she'd failed.

"Keep doing the spell," Lorcan snapped at Niamh.

"Maybe we should wait," Niamh said in the din of the whirlwind. "This is supposed to be voluntary."

"Niamh, please," Kierse said, feeling like a broken porcelain doll. The jagged edges of her fragile exterior detonating.

"Lorcan…"

"Would you rather see *her* dead, too?" Lorcan asked.

"Of course not," Niamh said.

"More people were dragged to the ceremony than volunteered. I was lucky. I had Saoirse. But we all agreed that being bound, increasing the magic, saving the Druids and wisps, was more important than what one person wanted. In the end, yes, the ends justified the means. We were stronger. We *are* stronger. At the end of this, Kierse will understand."

Understand.

He was destroying her from the inside out, and he thought she'd just *understand*.

"I'll never understand," she told him. "You can't bring back your dead wife. All of this isn't going to make it better. I am not going to be her. And if she was here, she'd be ashamed of you."

Lorcan reeled back as if from a blow.

"She's right," Niamh said. "Saoirse wouldn't want this."

"Saoirse is dead!" Lorcan roared. "She's dead. She doesn't get to make choices. Just like Emilie doesn't get to make choices. The people I love end up dead, and I'm not going to have Kierse be one of them, too."

Niamh took a step backward. "I can't continue. I should have never listened to you."

"Niamh…"

"Look at her, Lorcan!" she yelled at him, throwing a hand at Kierse.

And Lorcan turned to face her again. Saw the tears running down her cheeks. The fear in her eyes. The pain she couldn't mask. The desperation and grief and despair at this violation. For a second, he looked uncertain. As if he might stop the ceremony.

"It'll be worth it," he promised.

Kierse deflated.

"I'm sorry, Kierse," Niamh began. "I'm so sorry. I should never have listened to him. Even if what he said was true, it never justified this." Niamh turned to Lorcan. "If you go through with this, it'll be the end of your reign."

"This is just the beginning."

The magic was up her throat, down her legs, inching toward completion.

"I declare an official challenge for the throne," Niamh spat.

"What?" Lorcan asked in shock.

"You've lost your way. You don't deserve the seat. You don't deserve the honor of the Order."

Lorcan's eyes widened. "You can't challenge me. You're my *fucking* robin."

"Then maybe I won't be anymore," she said and turned toward the throne. Each step she took against the power of the gale was like dragging through mud. The magic of the spell pushing her back toward the center and not allowing her onward. The only person who could sit on the Oak Throne was the true ruler of the Druids. Lorcan was the only one with that honor. And his queen…which would soon be Kierse. A wren on the Oak Throne. Oh, the irony.

But Niamh didn't stop. Her magic cocooned her as she pushed against the spell and headed for the throne, determined to end Lorcan's cursed reign.

Not that she was going to do it in time to save Kierse. The magic was crawling up her nostrils and heading for her eyes. She could feel it around her ankles and down into her heels. It felt like breathing. Like she could give up and wrap herself in Lorcan. Oh, how she wanted to just give up.

"You're going to lose everything."

"I'm just getting started," he told her with all the confidence of someone who never lost.

Niamh was thrown back from the throne before she reached the dais. The magic in the room held everyone suspended as the spell neared its close. It was loud enough now that she couldn't even hear the chanting. All she could see was the magic covering Lorcan's face before it threatened to close over her own head.

Then the door to the room burst open.

The wind erupted outward like a backdraft when fresh oxygen hit a fire. A boom like an explosion punched through the room. Kierse's ears rang as she turned to face the torn-off doors.

And there stood death incarnate in a black suit, holding the Spear of Lugh—Graves.

Chapter Sixty-Nine

Death was lost in Graves's thunderstorm eyes. Rage filled out the perfect suit. Nightmares in the set of his stance. And the spear at his side telling him to smite his enemies, the way it had always whispered to Kierse.

Her heart leaped at the sight of him. Had he heard her? Had their minds connected after all? She had been alone, prepared to go to the end of this ritual without help. And now he was here. He'd come. She wasn't alone. She didn't have to do any of this alone.

His eyes slid across the Druids on the perimeter of the room, Niamh struggling toward the throne, and Kierse and Lorcan at the center coated in magic, hands tied.

If fury had a face, it would be his beautiful visage.

"Graves," she gasped.

His eyes landed on her. "My wren."

He took one step through the rush of magic and into the Oak Throne room, and the chanting turning to terror. Graves cut straight through the line of magic in the Druidic room. He ignored everything—the spell whipping around the room, Niamh's fight for the throne, the Druids that tried to come for him—as he headed toward her. He was single-minded as he trod across the moss-covered floor.

Kierse felt the collapse of whatever barrier had kept her from reaching for the sacred tree. She could feel it from a distance once more. She closed her eyes and hoped to find access, to find a pool of power at her disposal. But the spell was still ongoing, and a protective ring of magic still held them in place, so when she reached, nothing happened.

Two figures appeared behind Graves. A lanky yet muscular Black man in Druid robes and a short pale redhead in an oversize T-shirt and shorts. Her vision blurred as she realized it was Ethan and Gen. Ethan, who had betrayed her. Gen, who had been injured during the heist. They were both here for her. And they were both...working with Graves?

It felt unfathomable that Ethan would do so. After going to Lorcan and Niamh about her memory work, how could he be here working with his enemy? She couldn't process the thought.

Still, Ethan dropped to his knees as soon as he was in the room and buried his hands into the soil. He tilted his head up, and Kierse felt a flutter as he drew on their sacred tree in the adjacent building. The magic flowed freely to him, and when his eyes burst open, they were blasted wide at the pupils. Gold magic wove around his hands as they surged through the earth.

Gasps rang out as one by one vines crept up the bodies of the Druids. The chanting died as they focused their own magic on severing their restraints. But Ethan had the advantage of surprise, and most were too busy with his vines to escape.

Those who did were met with Gen. Not the warrior that Ethan had become in the last six months, but her tiny, prophetic friend. These were Lorcan's strongest Druids. How could Graves bring Gen here?

Kierse screamed, "Watch out!"

But Gen lifted her hands, and suddenly she was *floating* in the air, her magic a soft glow around her body as she lifted effortlessly above the ground. She drew from their shared tree, but Kierse could almost sense a shift in her powers. As if something had amplified them since Kierse had last seen her. Without the triskel to give them the additional powers, Kierse didn't know how it was possible. But she was seeing Gen with her own two eyes as she towered over the other Druids, releasing her energy in a burst.

The first Druid to escape Ethan's vines took the brunt of her power full to the chest. He groaned and collapsed back onto the earth, knocked out. Kierse's eyes were wide with wonder as she watched Ethan shift from someone she had always had to take care of to this formidable opponent.

And then there was Graves, almost standing before them. At the last second, Declan escaped Ethan's vines, turning them to ash with his own magic and rushing for Graves.

A ball of light formed in the hands of Lorcan's second as he whispered a quick incantation. "I'll fucking kill you," he roared.

He threw it at Graves, who took up a defensive stance at Declan's approach. His own magic deflected the power. It burst into a firework over their heads. He blocked the next fireball and then a third. Stepping toward Declan each time, until he was within range. Declan's eyes widened as Graves approached. As if he truly had thought that he'd outmatch the Holly King.

"You always believed you were stronger than you were," Graves said as he whirled the spear in his hand. Then he thrust it home, stabbing Declan through the chest.

"No!" Lorcan cried.

Graves plucked the spear out of Declan's chest and pushed him backward. He collapsed to the ground, dead. Graves tutted in disgust before turning away, the dead body already forgotten.

"You're a fucking monster," Lorcan snarled.

"Yeah, I fucking am," Graves agreed.

He lifted the spear high and brought it down upon the braided threads securing Kierse and Lorcan's hands. The strands snapped into pieces as if they'd never been reinforced with god magic and filled with the power of the Oak Throne. The pieces fluttered to the ground, shining like tinsel against the moss.

The magic disappeared around them, and Kierse took her first real breath since the ceremony had started. She ripped herself backward away from Lorcan. Her wrists were raw and red from the ceremony, a visceral reminder of what had just occurred.

"You've gone too far," Graves told him. "You've fucking earned this."

Graves lifted the spear in his hand, prepared to thrust it through Lorcan's chest. Lorcan raised his hands, shining with magic. The same gold-and-blue magic that had suffused them moments ago came to him like a snap of his fingers.

Graves faltered at that.

"You're too late," Lorcan told Graves. "The ceremony is complete."

Graves's gaze shifted to Kierse in horror. "Do you have your magic?"

She reached for it. This vengeance was her own. She could tap into their sacred tree the way that Ethan and Gen had. She'd join their triskel, and she would exact revenge upon him for ever thinking he could do this to her.

But when she touched her magic, there was...nothing.

Her hand went to her chest. She could feel the thrum of her connection with Lorcan, no longer a thread but a wide open, live cable, a completed bridge. Like she could walk straight across it into his heart and soul.

Deeper into the well, there was emptiness. A long, vast stretch of desolation where her magic had once lived. She could sense that her powers were *on*—her absorption was definitely there, in a neutral on position. But she could no more switch it off and on than she could before the spell had been broken. She reached for her slow motion and found a complete block. There was no magic she could access to turn the dial on her time manipulation. She held her hand out for the tree, *her* sacred tree, and still nothing happened. Her hand went to her ears. They were pointed. Her glamour had been stripped from her at some point, and now she was fully on display. It was just gone.

"What have you done?" she whispered in horror.

"I'm protecting you," Lorcan said.

"And who is protecting her from you?" Graves asked, low and deadly.

"You fucked with her mind."

Graves looked unimpressed. "Are you actually trying to justify forcibly binding her against her will and seizing control of her magic?"

Kierse clung to her white dress as panic set in. She hadn't wanted this binding, but this was so much worse than she had ever imagined. Just when she had begun to come into her own with her powers. When she was pushing herself to her limits and coming out on the other side. Now it was like she'd never entered this world at all.

"I can't glamour," she said. "I can't hide my ears."

"You don't have to hide who you are with me," Lorcan told her.

Graves snorted. "There's no fucking way she's staying here with you."

He lunged for Lorcan. Lorcan was stronger on the solstice, his powers amplified by the longest day of the year, and he had unfettered access to *her* magic. But Graves had the spear and his rage, and Kierse didn't know who would win this time.

"Stop," she whispered as another wave of panic struck her in the heart.

She should have been able to get between them. To make them see reason. But there was no reason here. Her knees buckled, and she fell back to the moss-covered ground, shaking. She fought the binding. She fought with everything she had. Reached for the sacred tree, the Oak Throne, anything that would listen to her, but all she heard in her mind was tortured silence.

And then a voice.

Fighting me won't work, Lorcan told her.

She jolted in horror at the sound of him bridging their connection to speak directly into her mind. All that bullshit about Graves fucking with her head, and now he was speaking *into her mind*, and he didn't see the hypocrisy of it all.

Get out of my head! she screamed back down the line.

Lorcan flinched. In that moment, Graves sliced through the magic he was building and buried the spear into Lorcan's shoulder.

Lorcan tumbled backward onto the ground. Graves wrenched the spear free and raised it overhead. He was ready to finish it all, finally. She should have let him that night he'd said he was going to fix his mistake with Emilie. She should have let the showdown happen, but she'd thought she was saving him. She'd never thought Lorcan would resort to this. That was her mistake.

"If you kill me, it kills her," Lorcan told him.

Graves halted. He visibly strained at the threat. "It didn't kill you when Saoirse died."

"Our magic was connected, not entangled. Right now, *I'm* holding her magic, and if you sever it, she dies," Lorcan told him. "I'll come back after the solstice. We're connected that way. *She* won't."

For a moment, Kierse thought that Graves would do it anyway. That he was so mad at Lorcan and the fucking audacity of the situation—the horrible ordeal he was now going through a *second* time—that she thought he might just kill him and get it over with. Even if the Oak and Holly cycle would keep bringing them back, continuously. But then Graves whirled the spear and buried it into the ground between Lorcan's legs.

It was then that the solstice roared through Graves, the Holly King coming fully into his own. His arms spread wide as the surge of magic rushed up from him and blasted forward into Lorcan, reducing him from the height of his power to his weakest.

Graves fell to one knee at the end of it, drained to the bone. The Holly King had returned to his reign. A chill ran through the room. A promise of winter to come.

At the head of it all, Niamh sat down on the Oak Throne.

Chapter Seventy

Lorcan's head whipped to the front of the room. He cradled his injured shoulder in his other arm, his eyes wide with alarm at the sight of the robin on the oak throne.

"Impossible," Lorcan said.

"I am the new head of the Druidic Order," Niamh declared to the room. "You answer to me now."

No one spoke. The Druids who were still unharmed from Ethan and Gen's attack stared in apparent shock. A change in leadership, after the death of Lorcan's second, in the midst of Lorcan's ascension, had to be... terrifying.

Niamh's eyes settled on the lot of them in the center of the room. "You may leave. I have no quarrel with you."

Graves stood and then dropped to a knee before Kierse. "My wren."

"You came. I called for you, but I didn't think you could hear me," she said as tears rolled down her cheeks.

"I've always been here. I'll always be here," he reassured her, offering her his hand. She hesitated a breath of a second. His voice was soft but firm. "I'm not like him. I won't hurt you."

"I know," she said and set her hand in his.

He helped her to her feet. "Let's go home."

"And me?" Lorcan asked.

Niamh tilted her head. "You've defiled our sacred oaths. If you complete repentance, you can return to the fold."

Lorcan looked like he was going to spit at her feet as he dragged himself to his feet. But all he said was, "And if I don't?"

"Then you are in exile," Niamh said simply.

Lorcan snarled. "This isn't the end of this, Robin."

Niamh leaned forward on the throne, the power humming through her. "Looking forward to it."

Kierse left them to their new feud. She wanted no part of it. This was the last place in the entire world she wanted to remain. She couldn't even look at Lorcan as she walked to the doors. But she could still feel him burrowing down inside her.

Kierse exited the throne room, holding Graves's arm. Padded barefoot onto the hardwood floors with Gen and Ethan hurrying to keep up. They went outside into the midnight summer air. It wasn't until she slid into the back of Graves's limo, finally safe, that she felt the jagged pieces of her begin to pierce her skin. The ache and the pain and the horror of what she had experienced hit her full-on.

A sob ripped from her throat, and she buried her face in her hands. No one said a word as George pulled the limo away from the Druid headquarters. Gen slipped her arms around Kierse's body. She wanted to push her away and tell her that she couldn't accept comfort right now, but it was Gen, the one person in her life who had always been there to put the pieces back together. Gen who could heal anything. But Kierse knew she couldn't heal this.

"How are you okay?" Kierse asked through her tears.

Gen rubbed her back gently in small circles. "Cauldron."

"You got it open?"

Gen nodded. "Group effort between Walter, Laz, and Graves. They followed the instructions you laid out for yourself. They had to or else I would have died."

"I'm sorry I wasn't there."

"I don't think you had a choice about that."

No, her choice had been ripped away from her. Her eyes lifted to Ethan. The shame on his face was wide and apparent. He'd always worn his emotions on his sleeve. They were so visible that it was almost painful to witness.

"Kierse, I'm so sorry."

"Did you know what was going to happen?"

"No!" he gasped at once. He ran a hand over his dark curls. "I did tell Lorcan about your memories, but I had no idea what he would think about it until afterward. When I found out what was happening, I left."

"He came and got me," Graves said. "I was already on my way when I heard you call out."

Their eyes met. "You heard me?"

"I have no idea how, but yes, I heard you."

"I thought I was all alone."

Gen clasped her hand. "You're not alone. We're here. We love you."

Graves nodded. "We're taking you home where you belong."

"Good," she whispered.

The spear rested across Graves's lap, his hand holding it possessively as if he was afraid to let it out of his grasp. She could practically hear the things it was whispering in his ear.

"I should take that."

Graves hesitated. As if he wasn't sure that in her current condition it would be in her best interest. But the spear belonged to her. She'd stolen it. It had...claimed her. And anyway, they were far enough away from Lorcan now that she wasn't going to turn around and kill him. Maybe.

Finally, Graves passed it to her.

"Hello, old friend," it seemed to purr.

The second it was in her hands, the force of its own anger hit her. She closed her eyes against the rush. If she'd had this back in the Oak Throne, Lorcan would be dead. And she wouldn't have regretted it, even if it had killed her.

When she opened her eyes, everyone was looking at her as if she were a bomb about to go off. There was no way to dissuade them of that opinion. She felt prepared to detonate at any moment.

"I know...you won't ever forgive me," Ethan continued slowly as if uncertain if now was the time. "I wouldn't forgive me."

She looked at him. "You did the right thing in the end."

"I...did," he agreed. "But I know it doesn't make up for how I've been treating you."

"Forget it," Kierse said. "You're here now."

Gen grasped Ethan's hand and squeezed it. "You're one of us."

Ethan squeezed back, though he looked like he wanted to say more. As if he had more atoning to do to fix what he'd broken. Once an altar boy, always an altar boy.

Kierse couldn't deal with that right now. Anyone else's guilt would have to wait until she could decide how to feel about what she'd just gone through. She was connected to Lorcan, bound by ritual magic, and could no longer access her magic.

When Lorcan had said that after the ceremony she'd be safe, she hadn't thought to ask what that meant. Now she realized he meant that he would control her powers so Graves couldn't get in. Lorcan would be in her head instead of Graves. He would be in control. Just how he wanted.

And she hated him for it. Even if she could admire the absolute gall to pull it off. Bastard.

Her eyes flicked up to Graves. She could see questions swirling in his tempest eyes. The fear he kept carefully locked away behind his anger. If he was barely masking it, then she must look as bad as she felt.

They crossed over the Williamsburg Bridge, and Kierse waited for the moment when the connection with Lorcan faded and folded away, as it always had since she'd returned to New York. Except there was no dampening of the connection. She could still feel Lorcan just as strongly as if he were standing directly in front of her.

She tried to seal it away and close herself off to the flood, but it was like having a live current in her chest. She had no way of flattening the electricity as it poured into her. There was nothing she could do.

As she clawed at that space in her chest to no avail, she broke down into tears once more.

Chapter Seventy-One

The bond was still present when they made it back to the brownstone. When they deposited the spear into the vault. When she took the elevator upstairs. Ever present. All consuming. Physically nauseating.

"We could try a triskel," Ethan said as they ascended the stairs.

"Can't," Kierse said.

"Are you sure?" Gen asked.

"Yes," she said at once. "I can't touch my magic. We couldn't link."

"Maybe we could link with you."

Kierse shook her head. "Even if you *could*, you'd be linking with *him*."

"We're not doing that," Graves said at once. He slid his hands into his pockets. The tension was bleeding off of him. Gen and Ethan looked up warily.

"All right," Gen whispered. "I don't want him to have any more power, either."

"But we'll think of something," Ethan said at once.

"Genesis, would you mind showing Ethan to a spare bedroom?" Graves asked. "Kierse needs to rest."

"Sure," Gen said. She squeezed Kierse's arm. "Find me if you need me, okay?"

Kierse nodded hopelessly.

"Bed," Graves suggested, gesturing to his room. When she didn't move, he dropped his arm. "Or do you require...space tonight?"

She hesitated. If she did that, then Lorcan won.

"No, I just need to change," she said, gesturing to her dress. "And a shower."

He nodded, visibly relieved. She followed him into his room. He ran the tap on the shower for her, set out a fluffy white towel and change of clothes. She wanted to ask him to stay. She could see that he wanted to. But she...couldn't.

"Take as much time as you need," he said instead, closing the door behind her.

Her hand went to her necklace, the wren that always comforted her throughout her life. But it wasn't there. In the empty space against her chest, she found only him.

She ripped at the stupid white dress, promising to burn it. She removed the braids from her wind-tangled hair before stepping under the spray and letting the scalding water wash away the night. She lathered with soap, trying to scrub him off of her. She rinsed and did it again until her skin was pink and raw. She did her hair next and still after two washes felt that it smelled of summer sunshine and spring showers. It was infuriating.

She sank to her knees in the shower, the water cascading over her head as the reality of the situation hit her in the face all over again. A sob escaped her throat. With it came the tears again. Tears that she hated so desperately and couldn't seem to stop or control. Lorcan had done this. He'd done this *to her.*

She would cry now. She would let the tears fall. Embrace the agency that he'd stolen from her. And when she was done, she'd figure out what to do about it.

When her tears finally gave way to fury once more, she stepped out of the shower and into a towel. She slicked her dark locks into a messy bun and pulled on comfortable sweats. It was shocking that her face in the mirror could look the same as the day before and yet she felt utterly broken inside. Like Lorcan had carved out a piece of her and paved over it with his bullshit. She hated it. She hated feeling this way. Twenty years she'd been tied up by magic, and after only six months of freedom, she was back to being trapped.

Kierse stepped out of the bedroom and found Graves standing over his small collection of carved bird figurines. "Hey," she whispered.

He looked up at her. "You look refreshed."

"I feel hollowed out."

"I can only imagine," he said gently. He palmed one of the carvings in his hand.

"What's with the birds?"

"I started carving them in Ireland when I joined the Druids," he admitted. "It relaxed me then. It still does."

"They're beautiful."

Graves set a little carved raven down next to a wren. "Can you tell me what happened tonight? Where did I go wrong?"

"You? You got the cauldron and got away. You did nothing wrong."

"Kierse."

She dropped her head. "The Curator was expecting me. He kidnapped me and had me bound in iron."

"Fuck," he whispered.

She swallowed and lifted her gaze. "The Curator is Jason."

Graves's eyes widened. "Jason? Your old mentor? But you killed him."

"I thought I did, but it just paralyzed him. He's gone through a lot of therapy and uses magic so he can walk with a cane now, but it's him. He's taken on many identities. Cillian Ryan, Jason, Curator. All the same person."

"No wonder he's scrubbed his identity from the web."

"I think it's why I kept skipping through memories at the scent of the pine and lemon," she explained. "I'd think of the smell and go to Jason. It was showing me the truth all along, but I thought it was the block."

"Did you kill him?" he asked, clenching and unclenching his fists.

"He got away. And the reason for the block—the reason he completely erased my memories of that day, instead of just hiding them in the spell— was that the spell wasn't actually to hide me from the Fae Killer. That was a handy-dandy side effect to him siphoning my powers away and giving them to Jason instead. That's why I looked weak before you broke the spell."

"Fuck, I should have seen it."

"And he knows who the Fae Killer is."

Graves blinked in surprise. "He knows their identity?"

"He said he did. He suggested that I did, too, but in the memory when he kills my parents, I don't see his face." She shrugged. "And now I can't lift my absorption to look again."

"We'll find a way around that."

She doubted it.

"Had Jason done that spell on others?" he asked.

"Yeah. I bet he's done it on the people in his cult, too. He's using them as a replenishable energy source."

"You know what that means?" he asked. When she stared back at him blankly, he continued, "You might not be the only wisp."

The revelation staggered her. Tonight had been almost too much. Too much bad news. This almost didn't feel possible. The very thought that something *positive* could come out of all the shit she'd endured was too much.

"And if there are, we'll find them," Graves told her. "Together."

"Yes," she agreed.

"What I don't understand is, if you were chained with iron, how you got away. How he got away."

"I phased. That's what Lorcan called it. He said Saoirse had the ability after a hundred years. I guess I got it out of necessity," she explained. "And then Jason ran away in fear. I followed him, but he got away before I could kill him."

"These are some massive magical leaps happening to you. No wonder your magic was drained."

"Drained just enough for Lorcan to come and kidnap me."

"And he knew where you were because of the soulmate bond."

She winced. "I...called out to him when I was tied up."

"You...did," he said slowly.

She turned away from him. "I couldn't reach you. I didn't know that I even could. I only called out to you when Lorcan had me tied up for the binding because he'd suggested that you'd gotten into my mind and fucked it up."

Graves cleared his throat. "Is that right? And you believed him?"

"Yes. No," she muttered, turning back to him. His face was carefully blank. "I didn't want to believe him. But then I decided if it meant we were mentally connected, then it didn't even matter. Because nothing was worse than what Lorcan did to me." She held her wrist out where the indents of the binding ribbon were still fresh.

He took her wrist gently in his hand and pressed a kiss to the raw skin. "I should have seen what Lorcan was going to do. I should have stopped him."

"We can't go down that route. The *what ifs* lead to madness." He looked like he wanted to say more, but she continued, "Will you do something for me?"

"Anything."

"Use your powers on me."

He frowned. "But your magic..."

"Please."

"All right." His hand circled her wrist. A jolt went through her at the contact. It was both exhilarating and confusing to find that her stomach still jumped from his touch. That she still wanted him. That Lorcan hadn't been able to touch the truth of her affection for Graves. For all his bluster about how it would all be better after, he couldn't change her mind in the end.

Her choice was Graves. Would always be Graves.

"Nothing," he said on a sigh.

"Okay. He bound us to keep you out of my head. I thought maybe if you could get past my absorption, then you could change the binding."

"Ah," he said slowly. His hand was still on her wrist. He turned her palm over and traced the lines along her skin. "I'm not certain that would be safe even if it were possible."

"We wouldn't know unless we tried, but since you can't get past my absorption…"

Graves cleared his throat and glanced away from her. "Well…"

"You can't get past my absorption…right?"

"I must admit to trying."

"Like just now?" she asked, gesturing to her hand.

He shook his head. "No."

She swallowed, seeing the answer that she hadn't wanted to see in his eyes. "Tell me."

"There's sometimes a trick with my powers. Since I can get in minds, I can sometimes convince the other person's magic that I belong there. I can make it so that the magic recognizes *my* magic as the owner's magic. Then when I'm inside, it accepts my magic as not an intrusion."

Kierse's eyes widened. "What have you used that for in the past?"

Graves arched an eyebrow. "What do you think?"

The implications were endless. Not just for someone with absorption. If her magic recognized him, then he'd be able to get into her mind at any time. But if he did it to other magic, then was it possible for him to change their magic? Turn it off? Destroy it? Could he use it to thwart his enemies?

"You downplayed your powers when we first met."

Graves lifted one shoulder. "I do read people for a living."

"You manipulate minds," she said, finding herself using the words that Lorcan had thrown at her back in the Oak Throne room.

"You've always known that."

The last thing she wanted was Lorcan in her mind, his words running through her. Would she know if Graves had messed with her mind?

No. That was the easiest answer. She wouldn't know. Even if she asked him, she wouldn't know. He could tell her whatever he believed. He'd already admitted to trying to change her magic so he could get inside her mind more easily. It hadn't worked, but he'd tried. And she hadn't known.

So she wouldn't know now, either. She just had to trust him.

"It's been a long day. We should sleep."

His gaze was long and hard as he watched her break from him and pull back the sheets. "You're not upset."

"Oh, I'm furious. If you could read me right now." She clenched her hands into fists. "Trust me. I'm a volcano about to erupt."

"But you're not upset with me for…trying."

She realized that she wasn't. She knew who he was. She knew what he did for a living. She knew how he'd lived the last five hundred years of his life. She'd accepted that and decided to choose him anyway.

"You saved me," she reminded him. "You heard me and answered my call."

"Always."

"Then let me ask you a few questions."

He straightened as if anticipating a showdown.

"Did you alter the soulmate bond?"

"Of course not."

"Did you make me more loyal to you?"

He tensed at the question. "Not you."

She would look at that sidestep to the question some other time. "Did you compel me to fall in love with you?"

"No," he said darkly.

She almost laughed at how mad he looked at the line of questioning. As if the mind thief was offended at the suggestion that he would ever try to steal her affections. If he could even do that.

"I *wanted* to change your mind," Graves said after a moment. "I *wanted* to compel your loyalty as I had so many others. I wanted to force your hand to come back to me. I wanted to make you want me."

She stilled at the words. "But?"

"But I didn't. When we first met, I couldn't read you at all. It took all my effort to learn you as you were, without the shortcuts I'd learned over the years. I could only change your mind about me the hard way." His eyes were windows as he spoke. "When we started working on your memories, I wanted to do it. I could have." He clenched his fists. "I was so tempted to just let loose when you were so furious with me. And then something changed. When I *didn't* do it and I showed you how I felt, you turned to me like a flower in bloom."

Her throat closed up at the words. "I did?"

"Each earned step was more rewarding than every stolen one could have possibly been. I became determined to *not* do it. To cease using my powers. Not just on you, but on others as well."

"On others?"

"Do you not think I could have brought Ethan back to you the first day we were home?" he scoffed.

"Oh. I hadn't considered that. Did you...do it when you saw him at the engagement party?"

"I wanted to see if I could win him the way I'd won you. I...told him the truth," Graves said. "And look, he came here when you were in trouble, all on his own."

"Look at you," Kierse said, a teasing smile on her face. "If you're not careful, you're going to start looking like a hero."

"I wouldn't go that far."

"I'm almost embarrassed for you. Are you losing your nerve? You can't even compel me to love you?" she joked. "For my friends' loyalty? Are you going to be a good guy now?"

Graves snorted, a small smile appearing on his face. "Hardly. If you're expecting me to give up my work..."

"I know the monster that lurks under your skin. I'm not afraid of who you are. Jagged edges and all."

Graves's hand slid up her arm, leaving goose bumps in their wake as it came to settle on the middle of her chest where she could feel the thrum of the binding. "This doesn't change anything for me," he told her.

It did. It changed everything. But she didn't know how to say that. How to explain that having Lorcan between them made her want to run.

"We'll find a way to undo this."

It was a promise he couldn't make. A promise she couldn't even get her hopes up for.

"If not with my magic, then we'll try the cauldron," he said. "Okay?"

The cauldron. In all the chaos, she hadn't even considered the cauldron. Could the cauldron fix what Lorcan had done? It seemed impossible.

"Okay," she agreed. "We'll try it tomorrow."

Her hope flickered like a fragile butterfly in her chest. This couldn't be the end. She refused for her story to end with some man choosing her fate.

Chapter Seventy-Two

Her wrist was bruised.

She stared down at the places where braided rope had dug into her skin. Where she'd clawed against it to try to get it off. Tugged and pulled and wrenched until it tightened to a vise around her skin. Now the dark marks were a brand, a reminder of what she'd endured.

Gen offered to heal them, but Kierse refused. No one could see the internal marks that Lorcan had left behind. She didn't want to hide the physical ones.

"What the fuck happened?" Nate asked, arriving while she was still eating breakfast with Graves, Gen, and Ethan the next morning. He reached for her wrists, and she let him take them in his large hands reverently.

"Lorcan," she said solemnly.

"Fucking hell, Kierse." His eyes lifted to hers. A glint of gold in them that said he was a second away from shifting into his wolf form and going to rip out Lorcan's throat. "I'll kill him."

She pulled her hands back. "Get in line."

"If it were that simple, I would have done it last night," Graves said from his seat. A small leather book was open before him.

"Why the fuck not?"

Kierse couldn't even get the words out. The anger ripped through her anew at the lack of magic, the violation that cut to the bone.

"The binding allowed him to also take control of her magic. Usually, it's a bridge between the two. Power sharing," Graves explained. "But he's cut her off. It'd be like if someone else decided when you could and couldn't shift."

Nate's eyes widened in barely suppressed rage. "I'm all for torture," he suggested. "We tie him to a chair and fuck him up until he releases her."

"Tempting," Graves said under his breath.

"We're going to try the cauldron first," Gen said.

"Might be less violent," Ethan added.

"What *he* did was violent," Nate all but roared.

Ethan held up his hands. "I'm aware. I'm on your side. Not his."

Kierse shuddered, feeling the fresh reminder of her assault.

"I'm sorry," Nate said automatically. "I'm so sorry. We'll figure this out. I'm here for the cauldron, too. Let's go use it and see if it lives up to its name."

"Agreed," Graves said, dropping his book onto the counter. He nodded at Isolde. "Thank you for breakfast. Delicious as always."

She preened. "I'm glad you enjoyed it. If you need anything else, just let me know." Isolde's gaze fell on Kierse, and she turned away from the pity in the other woman's expression.

The five of them headed upstairs to the library with Graves at her side.

"How did things go for you last night?" Graves asked Nate.

"As planned," Nate said on a sigh. "I was nominated for the convocation alongside Amberdash."

"Who else did the Men of Valor nominate?"

"Amberdash's second, a wolf by the name of Nova Lee," he said with a wrinkle of his nose. "She's had it out for me since I helped with the Treaty. She's going to be upset when I beat her."

"We'll deal with it," Graves told him.

"Nothing I can't handle," Nate said. "Plus, I have wedding festivities that are more important. Maura's family is hosting an entire week of Indian wedding parties since the ceremony is more traditionally American. Are you still planning to come to events this week?" Nate's eyes flicked to Kierse. "Maura would understand if you had to cancel."

"I'll be there. Gen and I both," Kierse said at once. She'd rather be celebrating someone else's happiness than thinking about her own misery.

Gen smiled. "I'm all for it. I used to tattoo with henna for fun. A Mehndi would be an honor to witness."

Nate blew out a breath of relief. "Great. She'll appreciate you both there."

Kierse's hand reached for her wren necklace, remembering again too late that it wasn't there. Lorcan still had it. The last piece of her mother and it was gone. She'd kept it all those years on the streets, and somehow now it was lost. Her father's knife was on her belt. She reflexively rubbed her hand along the handle, imagining burying the thing in a Druid's chest.

Graves pushed open the door to the library, and for a second, Kierse's breath caught at the sight before her. Almost every available square space was covered with valuable collectibles that had been the showcase pieces for the Curator. Jason's thievery on display in the Holly Library.

"Whoa," she whispered.

"We did good, eh?" Nate asked, nudging her shoulder.

While Kierse and Lyra had been getting through the security for the cauldron, Nate and Edgar had cleared out the showcase room into a van. With the ballroom on lockdown thanks to Walter's warding, they'd been able to steal the entire lot of Jason's collection, not just the cauldron, without anyone the wiser.

"How did everyone take it when the doors reopened?" Kierse asked, running a finger over the crown jewels she'd noticed the day before.

"I was just as shocked as they were," Nate said with a wink.

"Lyra claimed the photograph." Graves pointed at a black-and-white picture. "If you have something in mind, you can take it. Otherwise I'll sell it all off and give everyone a cut."

"What do you think that cut will be?" Nate asked.

"I was estimating each cut at twenty-three million apiece."

Gen gaped at him. "What?"

"Too low?" Graves asked her. "It may be higher if we find the right buyer."

"That's…" Gen floundered. "That's… You're going to give me twenty-three million dollars?"

"Each." He sighed softly. "Though I may have to find new help."

Kierse shrugged. "New blood might be good for you."

"Perhaps."

Ethan's eyes widened between them. "How do I get in on this?"

Gen leaned her head on his shoulder and grinned. "Don't worry. We'll share."

"I won't," Nate said with a laugh. "And the money's great and all, but what about the cauldron?"

"Genesis," Graves said, tipping his head at her.

"Oh," she whispered. "Yeah. I mean…you want me to?"

"It chose you."

Kierse glanced between them. "What does that mean?"

"It spoke to me," Gen said with a flush to her cheeks. "Healer to healer."

She stepped up to the dark box at the center of the room. Kierse stilled in anticipation. They'd been working feverishly for weeks to get to this point. Now it was finally here. The mythical cauldron in all its glory.

Gen opened the box and removed from within a small, cast-iron cauldron with a handle and cover. So it wasn't a chalice. Just a smaller version of the large cauldron they'd all pictured when hearing the word. In fact, it didn't even look like much. Though like the spear, it didn't look its age, either. It could have come out of a Salem gift shop if it didn't radiate eternal energy.

"Traditionally, small cauldrons like this would be used to hold healing ingredients," Gen informed them. "Sometimes it was used to make black salt for a banishing, to burn petitions for magical assistance, or incense and herbs for castings. There were many uses for something like this, not just medicinal, all of them ritualistic in nature."

She cupped the cauldron in her hands, the weight of the cast iron drawing her arms down. Her eyes went wide with wonder as if the cauldron was imparting its wisdom to her.

"But *this* cauldron was used for so much more than that. Despite its small appearance, it can feed armies, heal the injured, and touch those with magic." Gen lifted the cauldron up. "When I was healed, the cauldron and I connected. It amplified my powers, drew from its depths for me. I cannot guarantee what it will do for you, but everyone is entitled to try. Who will go first?"

So Gen's magic *had* been altered by the cauldron. That was how her powers had been so much stronger last night.

"Kierse?" Nate asked.

"You go first."

Nate had a specific request—an end to the incubus curse. One he'd been anxiously waiting for. Kierse had always been wary about what the cauldron could give her. If she would have to give up her humanity. If that was even possible. She'd wanted more magic, but at what cost? Now, she had a more pressing concern. And even though she knew that Gen had gotten what she needed and more, it still made Kierse wary to hope that the cauldron could fix what had happened to her.

"All right," Nate said with a nod. He stepped forward, and Gen handed him the cauldron. He lifted it into his arms easily. For a moment, nothing happened.

A second later, a bubbling sound came from within, and Nate's eyes widened.

"Holy shit," he gasped.

He held out the cauldron for everyone else to see. It had filled with a clear liquid. Kierse's jaw dropped. She'd seen magic done so many times before, yet somehow this was still awe inspiring.

"I need a...cup or something," Nate said.

Graves stepped into the stacks for a moment and came out with a stoppered vial. Nate carefully poured the liquid into the vial, closing it shut.

He held the little thing reverently.

"If this works, then we'll be able to have a baby. I never... I was never sure it would happen."

"The cauldron said it would work?" Kierse asked.

"Yes. It said it could break an incubus curse." He cleared his throat. "I guess...I should go take this to Maura."

"You absolutely should," Gen said.

His laugh was tinged with tears of joy. He looked up to Graves when he managed to get himself together and then offered his hand. "Thank you."

Graves shook his hand. "Good luck."

Nate clapped him on the shoulder. "Still have to get chosen for the election tonight. Don't forget to show up and vote."

"I'll be there."

With that, Nate headed out of the brownstone. Kierse's hope ballooned. If it could do this, then surely it could help Kierse. If anything could fix what had happened to her, surely it was this.

"Your turn," Gen said.

Kierse chewed on her bottom lip as she walked forward on wobbly legs. Gen's smile was reassuring, but Kierse felt like spider eggs had been laid in her stomach and they were all breaking open and crawling through her body. What if it didn't work? What if she was stuck like this forever?

"Can I...even hold it?" Kierse glanced between them. "It's iron."

Graves considered. "Worth finding out."

"It's of the gods," Gen said. "I don't think it's the same thing."

Kierse nodded, searching for another reason to put it off but not finding one. She had to do this. She had to hold an iron cauldron and hope that it would fix what had happened to her. The fear that it wouldn't be able to help her with anything she needed was overwhelming.

"Kierse?" Gen said softly.

"Right. Yeah. My turn."

"Do you know what you're going to ask for?"

Kierse nodded. "Sure."

"We can do this later," Gen told her.

"No," she said on a sigh. "I just... I thought..."

She trailed off, unsure where she was even going with it. She hadn't been convinced that the cauldron could give her magic or make her wholly Fae before. She didn't know *what* it could do. Even seeing Gen's increased magic and the potion it had made for Nate, she was still a skeptic. Despite all she'd seen.

"Trust me," Gen said.

And in the end, Gen's soothing voice was all she needed. She placed the cauldron in Kierse's hands, and all the noise fell away, all the what ifs filtered out of her head, and in its place was silence.

Kierse closed her eyes, and she felt a presence. As if something was evaluating her. She didn't even have time to ask anything of the cauldron. To figure out what it was that she wanted from it. The cauldron seemed to figure out what the answer to her problem was before it was even requested.

This was done to you, a voice said in her mind.

She shivered at the sound. So like the spear, and yet...nothing like it at all. This was feminine, almost gentle, and somehow more ferocious than the spear had ever been. A duality she could hardly grasp.

And you want it gone. I can see that.

She did. She wanted the bond gone desperately.

It was done correctly. It is part of you.

No. This wasn't part of her. She didn't want it to be a part of her. She wanted it gone. It didn't matter to her if it had been done correctly. Surely there should be a way to unravel it when it had been done under those horrid circumstances.

There is another way.

Kierse held her breath. Hope still beating in her chest. She would do it. Anything to make it stop.

Anything? Are you sure?

Was she? Yes. Anything to make it stop.

Except.

Except... the voice prodded.

Her humanity. The part of her that was connected to her father. She couldn't give that up. She didn't want to be fully Fae. It was the first time that she had known. She was part wisp, part human. It was who she was. And it was who she wanted to remain.

It's agreed, then.

Agreed?

This might hurt.

Kierse only had a moment before a rush of energy hit her like a freight train. She screamed as it filled her from top to bottom. Her hands remained glued to the cauldron. She couldn't have let go if she tried. Her body convulsed, and she thought that she was going to be broken in two at the force of the working.

This wasn't healing. This was breaking. Deconstructing. Reshaping. This was tearing her down to her bones and rebuilding her from scraps.

Desolation.

Anguish.

Ruin.

She was going to die from the contact. There was no other way around it. Her body could not hold up to whatever was happening. Her insides were scooped out with a spoon. Her body raw and tender and reeling from the onslaught. Like she might at any moment unravel into thread on the floor. Except it wouldn't let her. It wouldn't let her go.

She couldn't hear her friends. She didn't know if they were trying to stop what was happening or trying to pry her hands free. If Graves was regretting his decision. If all of them were terrified for her.

All she could do was scream until she thought her vocal cords would shatter and hope for survival. Hope to come out on the other side. Hope against hope.

Then it was over. Just as quickly as it had started.

She dropped the cauldron, and it rattled noisily on the floor. Kierse sank to her knees against the plush Persian rug. Her hands dug into the carpet as she trembled uncontrollably.

"Kierse," Gen gasped, falling before her with Ethan immediately at her side. "Are you okay?"

Graves was there, pulling her into him, cradling her against his firm body. "Wren?"

She clung to Graves like he was a lifeline. Like he might pull her back from the abyss, past the point of being broken. It took several long minutes before her body solidified into a semblance of a person. Her parts all fit together again. Only her nerves tingled like she'd been electrocuted.

"What happened?" Graves asked.

She tumbled out of his arms and rose unsteadily to her feet. "I don't know."

"Did the cauldron break the binding?" Ethan asked hopefully.

Her hand went to her chest. It was still there. Humming. Lorcan just over the bridge.

"No," she said regretfully.

"Oh, Kierse, I'm sorry," Gen said.

Ethan looked confused. "What did it do instead?"

She held her hand out. She didn't feel different. Except that she had been scooped out like ice cream, beat to within an inch of her life, and then set on a cone for consumption.

"Magic," Graves said.

She frowned at that statement—and then it rushed her fingertips. The scent of Irish wildflowers. The gold-blue glow all around her. The touch of magic that lingered in her veins. She reached down deep and found her empty well was now…full again. The same as it had always been.

She laughed in wonder and reached for her glamour. The easiest spell she had to cover her ears. It fizzed and fizzled and then did nothing. Dissolving into thin air. She tried her slow motion. Nothing. She switched her absorption off. Nothing. She conjured the ability to phase. Nothing.

"I don't understand. It isn't working."

"It could just take time to get used to it," Ethan added.

Gen frowned. "Maybe it's different with the new powers."

Graves tilted his head. "What exactly did the cauldron say to you?"

"It couldn't break the binding, because it had been done properly. Even if it was done to me. It said that there was another way. I…told it that I didn't want to give up my humanity. It agreed and then said this might hurt," she told them. "Then I guess it gave me magic I can't access?"

"I don't think that's it," Graves said. "It's a loophole. You're a wisp, but you only have half the powers of a full-blooded Fae, and those powers are bound. Which means that to the cauldron, your magic was empty."

"Right?"

"If I had to guess, it gave you the other half."

"But I'm still human," she said. She knew that for a fact. She was still only half wisp. The cauldron had agreed.

"That's right. Since your magic is bound, that made it possible to give the powers to you without interfering with your humanity. We'd have to test it. But I think the cauldron got around Lorcan's binding by giving you powers he didn't bind."

Kierse's eyes widened as her magic came swiftly to her fingertips. New powers were better than no powers. New powers meant that she had a fighting chance. And the best part—Lorcan had no idea.

Chapter Seventy-Three

Over the course of the week leading up to Nate and Maura's wedding, the rest of the crew came forward and used the cauldron. Kierse still hadn't managed to figure out her magic, not even for a small glamour to hide her ears—so she'd gone with a carefully concealed hairstyle for the wedding day. She'd been curious what everyone else had received out of the cauldron, but in the end, it wasn't really her business.

Laz and Schwartz promised their treasure-hunting days weren't over—the payout was only ever half the fun. Edgar, Isolde, and George had looked insulted when Graves had promised them an early retirement. Lyra hadn't had any interest in the cauldron, after all. She only wanted her parents' photograph and called it even. She had an audition that afternoon and really needed to get back. Walter was still around day and night. He'd moved in upstairs when Graves had offered to continue his training. After Nate's nomination went through and he was officially going to the Monster Treaty convocation, he and Maura came over to thank Graves again for his help lifting the curse.

"Why haven't you used it?" Kierse finally asked Graves as she walked into his bedroom dressed in a simple pink floral dress. Graves had left it on the bed in a designer bag. She'd realized immediately why he'd picked it from the collection of wildflowers embroidered across the print.

"Used what?" he asked as he knotted his tie.

She took it out of his hands and fixed the knot. "The cauldron."

"Ah, I did."

"When?" she demanded. "I've been waiting all week."

"I used it after Gen, when we were waiting for you."

She bit her lip as she tugged the tie into place. "Can I ask what you wanted from it?"

"Magic."

She rolled her eyes. "As if you don't have enough of that. You're a fucking *ocean* of magic."

He grinned. "Careful, or I'll think you like me."

"Well, it's your lucky day," she told him, straightening the tie and stepping back. "There. All done."

He reached for her hand, and she let him take it. Things had been... tense the last week. Lorcan was no less present. Where she had once been uncomfortable with intimacy because of Jason's abuse, now she was raw all over again from a new invasion.

She wanted Graves. She wanted all of him. And yet...

"I made a mistake," he said simply.

"With what?"

"I went after the sword first," Graves explained.

"How was that a mistake?"

"The mistake was where I went to get the information on the object."

She raised an eyebrow and waited.

"I traded for the info in Nying Market."

"Oh." She frowned, seeing where this was going. "Wouldn't that have been...expensive?"

"I thought I was prepared to pay. I had objects that they wanted. I was confident that I knew what I was getting into." He paused. "I was wrong."

Was this why Graves had been so against her walking into the market alone? He had known the costs they could enact, because he had already paid them.

"What did they take?"

"My Druidic magic."

Kierse's mouth popped open. "Can they...take that?"

"They did," he said flatly. "Seventy years ago."

"Oh god," she whispered.

Suddenly, it made sense. When they had started on her memory work, she had delved into his magic. She'd felt the full depths of his power as this massive inexplicable force. And yet there had been a piece missing. She hadn't understood it at the time. Hadn't even known it was possible for magic to be missing and not be able to be rejuvenated.

He glanced away from her. "I did it to myself. That's what the cauldron said."

The cauldron had refused him. His heritage. His connection to his mother. The years of training. All gone in a blink. He likely hadn't even known how deep that connection went until it was gone. So like Kierse, now that her magic was missing, too.

Lorcan's words came back to her. That Graves wasn't going to get what he wanted from the cauldron, just as he hadn't gotten what he'd wanted from the spear, or the sword. He'd been right.

"It was a long shot anyway," Graves finally said.

"Is there a way to get it back?" she asked. Her mind went back to the time they'd been in the Dublin market. Rio had said what he'd given was in their book. Did that mean his Druidic magic was still in the market?

He considered. "What would we trade to return it? What could either of us lose that would be big enough for it?"

She didn't have that answer.

"Nothing," he said finally. "If the cauldron can't even return it, then the market will be no more generous." He reached for his suit jacket and slid it on. The conversation over. "Shall we attend your friend's wedding?"

"I'm afraid to tell you, Graves, but I think he's your friend, too."

He wrinkled his nose. "Don't remind me."

Kierse laughed, and it almost felt as light as it had a week earlier. She was still getting used to this new normal. She didn't know if it'd ever feel right again. But she was trying. She was still fighting.

They took the elevator to the limo and drove across town to the Dreadlords' headquarters, Five Points, in Chelsea. The nightclub had been shut down for the weekend to accommodate the wedding of their alpha. The festivities were on the rooftop, which was currently bursting with flowers and plants of all varieties. It was a riot of color and foliage. Wooden chairs were set up in rows on either side of a long aisle. At the end was a circular arch bedecked with flowers.

The rooftop was full to the brim with friends and family from both sides. Maura's relatives from New Jersey, in traditional saris and kurtas. Her nursing friends mingling in summer dresses. The wolves in sharp summer suits and floor-length gowns. Kierse loved and appreciated the mix of cultures.

Spending the past week with the couple as they were showered with love and attention had made her heart so happy for them. She and Gen had been there as the henna had been applied intricately to Maura's skin at her Mehndi, and through the Haldi, where a mixture of turmeric, oil, and water was applied to Maura's skin by married relatives. It had at least kept her from ruminating on her own shit and what exactly she was going to do about it all.

Gen rushed to her side and pulled her in for a hug. "You look beautiful."

Graves nodded at Gen and then began to slowly pace the length of the rooftop to give them space. He must have reined his magic in, because people weren't actively bowing away from him. Progress.

"Thank you," Kierse said with a smile. She held Gen at arm's length, admiring her shimmery blue dress. "You look amazing, too. Where's your date?"

Gen flushed and pointed inside. If Kierse angled her head, she could just see Ronan standing sentinel in a dark suit with Finn at his back. "Groomsmen haven't come out yet, but I came early to see him."

"Good," Kierse told her honestly. "I'm happy for you."

"Speaking of dates," Gen said, nodding her head in another direction.

Ethan had his fingers interlocked with Corey's across the room. Ethan's suit was a cream linen that only he could have pulled off, with a navy tie. Corey complemented him in a navy blazer with a soft blue shirt and yellow tie.

"I'm glad they seem happy."

"Not Ethan and Corey. They *are* happy. Obnoxiously so, honestly." Gen angled Kierse slightly to the right.

"Oh!" Kierse said.

Colette leaned back against the wall with a glass of brandy in her hand. She was bejeweled in a shiny, midnight-blue dress that hugged her curves. Standing next to her was none other than the Roulettes gang leader, Carmine.

A diamond glittered on her left hand. It seemed Colette was no longer reticent about declaring their relationship publicly.

"Is your mother engaged?" Kierse gasped.

"Isn't it disgusting?" Gen said, pulling a face.

Kierse laughed. "Honestly, good for her."

"She claims they're years from getting married, but it takes her off the market. Whatever that means."

"That's so Colette."

Gen made a face, but they both just laughed. Music started to play, and the partygoers were ushered to their seats. Graves reappeared at her side, taking an empty seat next to her while Gen sat on her other side. Ethan and Corey settled in behind them as Nate and the groomsmen stepped into place. Gen's eyes were completely on Ronan at Nate's side, but Kierse did a little wave for Nate, who looked stand-up in a dark suit, transfixed on the point where Maura would enter.

A moment later, she appeared in a stunning red sari with gold embellishments that she'd borrowed from her auntie. Bangles adorned her wrists, covering part of the intricate henna work that blossomed up her arms. But it was her red-lipped smile that stretched wide at the sight of her groom that made her dazzling. Her father was at her side, tears in his eyes, as he walked her down the aisle, handing her off to Nate with his blessing.

The ceremony was emotional and a little bit silly. A perfect blend for the day and these people. They exchanged vows that they'd written themselves, eliciting both tears and laughter from everyone in attendance.

Next, Nate retrieved a long, gold-and-black beaded necklace with a diamond at the end—the mangalsutra. The name translated to "auspicious thread." It was traditionally given by the groom to the bride to join their souls, like a thread wrapping them together. Though Nate had warned her about this tradition, Kierse hadn't considered what it would feel like to see it in person. As they spoke words of blessings, Nate draped the necklace around Maura's neck, binding them together.

Kierse gripped Graves's hand as the final words were spoken. Her bruises from her *own* binding were still visibly yellow and ugly. Even if this joining was blessed, it didn't make her feel any less sick about it. Like *she* was the ill-fated interloper in their midst.

She wished more than ever that she could let her absorption down and have Graves feel what she was feeling. Instead, she endured it all alone. Their connection had been shattered as swiftly as the one with Lorcan was reinforced.

"Are you going to be okay?" he whispered against the shell of her ear.

She nodded. Even though she felt sick to her stomach and wanted nothing but to walk swiftly away from this entire thing. She wouldn't.

He squeezed her hand and kept it tight in his as Nate and Maura said I dos and kissed. The crowd rose to their feet, cheering on the newlyweds, Kierse, Gen, and Ethan screaming their approval. Even Graves gave them an appropriately timed whistle. Nate continued kissing Maura, perhaps a touch longer than propriety dictated, but everyone just cheered louder.

The cheers were cut short when the doors burst open behind them and in stormed a parade of full-size trolls.

Chapter Seventy-Four

"What the fuck?" Kierse asked Graves.

He pulled her toward him. His first instinct was always to protect her. It was then that she realized that she *needed* protection—she had no idea how to use her new magic. She was a creature of stealth, and while her Fae abilities still made her physically strong and fast, without her wisp magic, she was at a severe disadvantage. She hated it.

Graves unholstered a gun from within his suit and clicked the safety off. A second later, he slid it into her hand. Well, that certainly helped.

Terror was a living, breathing thing on the rooftop as the trolls kept coming, forming a perimeter around the partygoers, blocking them in. Dreadlords shifted on the spot, surrounding their guests defensively and snarling their anger at the intrusion. Only Nate remained on two feet, holding his wife behind him. The trolls pushed in, finally forcing Nate to shift to his wolf form and jump at the first troll who came after Maura. In the interruption, the second troll got his hands on Maura, lifting her effortlessly in his arms.

"Maura!" someone screamed from the front row.

Kierse held the gun loose at her side, prepared for whatever came next. Had they all become complacent? So used to the way things had changed since the Monster Treaty, they hadn't expected an attack? What could the trolls even be after, interrupting a wedding? Or…who was controlling them?

"Men of Valor," Graves said.

Kierse noticed a small woman with black hair cropped at her chin step out onto the roof. The Dreadlords snarled as one at her entrance. She smirked, a wolf's grin if Kierse had ever seen one. A cadre of monsters of every kind lined up behind her.

Kierse lifted the gun and leveled it at the woman's head. She wanted to pull the trigger, but if she did, chaos would surely erupt. A troll had Maura. They were surrounded. Fuck.

"Who the fuck is that?" she asked.

"Nova Lee," Graves said.

"Nate's opponent for the convocation?"

"Yes."

"What's she doing here? Can I just shoot her?"

"We're about to find out," he said through gritted teeth. "If she makes another move, put a bullet between her eyes."

Gen was shaking in front of her, but Kierse could already see her magic gathering at her fingertips. Ethan was doing the same—there was enough plant life on this terrace for him to be beyond formidable.

A Dreadlord rushed at Nova. In the blink of an eye, she shifted into a small, sandy wolf. Despite her stature, she was ferocious and went straight for the throat, ripping it out of the wolf who'd attacked her.

Kierse pulled the trigger. The gun went off with a ferocious blast, but the wolf was too nimble for that, dodging the bullet with a spectacular dive.

"Damn it," Kierse spat.

A minute later, she was back in her human form, blood dripping from her chin and down onto her white shirt. "I liked this shirt," she grumbled. "Oh well…" Her eyes lifted to Nate's. "You chose the wrong side."

The room erupted into chaos. Every wolf rushed the trolls. Ethan called to the plants at his command, ripping them down toward the monsters in attendance. Gen knocked out anyone who stepped close.

"We need to know what she wants," Graves said.

"Who cares? She attacked *us*."

He pursed his lips and lifted his hands. A golden glow filled the space in between his palms, stretching like taffy. He grunted as he lifted and spread the magic into a soft, shimmering golden dome.

"It's big magic," he got out through his teeth. "Not really supposed to be used for this."

"Save the innocents. We'll take out the rest," Kierse said, directing him toward the human, non-magical partygoers, who were currently huddled in fear as monsters ripped each other apart.

Kierse lifted her gun again and trained it on Nova. The woman hadn't moved. Her trolls and the monsters were doing the work for her as she observed. She'd missed the first shot. Kierse would take another one.

But Nova's hearing must have been too advanced. She shifted fast enough to avoid the bullet, then back again just as quickly. Her gaze snapped to Kierse, and she smiled. She held up two fingers and pointed them first at her own eyes, then at Kierse, just as another scream went up from the front of the room.

Kierse whipped around to the source of the noise. Maura was being hauled away from Nate and toward the exit by a troll. It looked like they were going to kidnap his new bride. Not a chance.

"We have to get Maura."

Graves finished off the dome, snapping it into place over the unarmed guests. "That won't hold long."

"Then let's stop them."

Kierse took off with Graves and her friends at her back. The chaos was endless, but she had only one quarry. She didn't know what they were going to do with Maura, but she didn't want to wait to find out.

Graves cleared their path, pushing combatants out of the way. Ethan's magic snapped out, and a bunch of ivy wrapped itself around the troll's trunk-like neck. Gen's magic pierced through the troll's thick skin, wounding it. It struggled against Ethan and Gen's power. All Kierse would have needed to do was amplify them and they could have subdued the nearly mindless beast.

That would have been the ethical decision. But Kierse still couldn't control her new powers, and Nova had shown her hand. Kierse didn't think anyone was going to get out of here alive if she had it her way.

So Kierse lifted the gun, aimed, and fired twice into the troll's skull.

The giant monster teetered like a seesaw for a few seconds before toppling sideways. Graves's magic cocooned Maura as Ethan's vines whipped around her. Together they caught her before she could hit the ground or be crushed by the troll's body.

Nate's massive wolf was right behind them, rushing for Maura. But as he got there, Nova's sandy wolf descended on him. Nate pivoted to engage her as Nova unleashed on him. Nate was almost twice her size. This should have been an easy fight, no contest.

Then Nova sank her teeth into Nate's throat.

Kierse instinctively pushed herself into slow motion and felt for a second like it was going to work. Her magic was going to let her move into that space where she could stop time long enough to save her friend. But it sparked on her fingertips for a heartbeat before fizzling and dying.

Time didn't stand still.

Nova ripped sideways, taking Nate's throat with her.

"No!" Kierse yelled.

Maura screamed. Kierse's knees buckled. She sank to the ground in horror as she watched Nate's throat give way. He shifted back to his human form as he lay bleeding, the light flickering out of his eyes.

Maura crawled toward her husband, slipping in his blood as she reached for him. "No, Nate! Nate!" she wailed. "You can't go. You can't go!"

"Gen," Kierse gasped as she watched one of her oldest friends bleed out. Her voice broke as she asked, "Please."

"I can't." A soft sob escaped her throat. "I...I can't heal something that severe."

Nate went limp in Maura's arms. "Our baby! Nate, you have to be here for our baby! You can't leave me." The rest of her words were lost to her hysterical tears.

"Oh God," Kierse gasped. Graves fell to his knees, wrapping his arms around Kierse, holding her as she cried and the world went blurry at the edges.

Nova laughed as she shifted once more. "This is your warning," she declared to the room. "Go up against the Men of Valor again, and you're all dead."

She turned and strode from the room, taking the trolls with her.

The screams turned to moans of fear and pain and terror. Ronan held Gen to his chest as he stared in horror at his alpha, dead on the concrete floor. Corey found Ethan and held him as he cried into his boyfriend's shoulder. Kierse was numb as she watched Maura mourn. The pain was somewhere down deep, a place she had to keep hidden to survive this moment. Because she couldn't imagine a world without Nathaniel O'Connor's quick smile and jaunty personality in it. She couldn't imagine life without him.

A worse realization settled over her. This was just the beginning.

A second monster war was rising.

Interlude

Lorcan was in a safehouse in Midtown.

It was a last-resort location, one of a few he and the Druids used when they had business in the city and needed to recuperate. Sometimes the rituals and spells were draining enough that it wasn't safe to return to Brooklyn. He knew the map of every one of them in the city, and he'd sabotaged enough of the Druid's equipment and files on his way out that Niamh wouldn't be able to ferret him out here before he moved on.

He'd cleaned out his office, packed up the most important things he'd collected during his long reign as the leader of the Druids, and then taken a small force along with him as he'd left. They were now spread out around the city in some of the other safehouses. Not an army, but enough to make Niamh think before moving against him.

With Declan gone, he'd had to tap Maureen as his second. She was busy organizing the followers who had come with him, doing the work that he couldn't manage alone. She was formidable, but the loss of Declan was harsh.

"All the Druids are relocated, sir," Maureen said.

"Excellent," Lorcan said as he closed his laptop and turned to face her.

"Has there been a civil war among our kind before?"

"Yes," Lorcan said simply. "But not for a very long time."

The last schism had put him on the Oak Throne. He wasn't going to give it up this easy. Niamh had been on his side then. Now she, too, was corrupted.

His own robin.

He clenched his fist around the wren necklace in his palm. Kierse's necklace.

He needed to give it back to her. It was the last thing she had of her parents, but now it was one of the last things he had of her. The threads of their binding, and a necklace.

And the binding itself.

He could sense her presence, only blocks away from his current location. He could go to her at any moment.

He'd thought about it. Had stalked her through the Manhattan streets. Had known that she felt him drawing nearer, but still not close enough to prompt her attention. Several times he'd seen her turn in his direction as if she'd known precisely where he was standing. He'd willed her to face him.

Holding her powers had been a last resort, something that he'd been compelled to do by Graves's own audacity. He'd known he could win her in time, but he couldn't keep the bastard from killing her now. He'd done it for her own safety.

And still she was with him. Just like Emilie.

They'd been so young when they'd first met. Despite Graves's taciturn nature, Lorcan had taken to Graves instantly. Graves had been haunted by his cruel past, but in Lorcan he had found something more than friendship. He'd found family. They had relied on each other, opened to one another. They were faster than friends and closer than brothers. The sun and moon following each other into perpetuity.

He remembered a day they'd been in Wicklow, seated on the banks of Glendalough Lake. Lorcan had been sketching the mountains in the distance. Graves had strode over and taken a seat next to him. He'd stretched his long figure out, holding another one of his wooden birds in his hand.

He'd been more than pensive that day. Lorcan had instinctively known that Graves needed the time to work up to talking. He was like that.

"I'm going to ask her to marry me."

Lorcan had turned to him then. Saw the fear in Graves's expression and dashed it all aside with a wide smile. "She's going to say yes."

Graves studied him, uncertain. "You think so?"

"Yes, and then we'll be brothers in truth." Lorcan put his arms around his closest friend. "This is all I want for you, brother."

"That is all I want."

Graves looked down as if he had expected worse. Not everyone agreed with his presence among the Druids, but Lorcan had known that casting him out would only bring worse harm, to Graves and to the Druids both. He'd been right.

When Emilie had been soul-bound to Tadgh, everything had changed. The binding was sacred. Graves didn't understand. Emilie wanted to refuse. Lorcan had done all he could to explain to them, to get them to come to the other side.

Then something shifted. Over the weeks leading up to the binding ceremony, Emilie...changed. The closer they got, the further away she went. Her mind, once a lively, vibrant thing, was now slushy and unfamiliar. The light left her eyes, replaced by fear. She began to forget things—people, places, memories. And Lorcan realized too late what had happened.

When he confronted Graves, it was already over. Emilie was dead. Graves was responsible. And their entire world shattered into a million pieces.

"Is there anything else you require, sir?" Maureen asked.

"Get me everything we have on the four objects of the Tuatha de Danann."

Maureen agreed without question. "Of course." Then she disappeared to begin to research.

Because Lorcan wasn't going to sit back and wait for Graves to find a way to hurt Kierse again, as he had Emilie. He knew his brother and the risks he was willing to take to achieve his aims. Kierse wouldn't be collateral damage in his next plan.

He punched in a number to a bookstore in Dublin. Oisín answered on the third ring. "The Goblin Market bookstore."

"Oisín," Lorcan said.

"Lorcan," he said demurely. "How can I help you?"

"It's time."

"Are you certain?"

Lorcan smiled. He needed to get a step ahead of his enemy. Three of the objects were already in play: Graves had the spear and the cauldron, Lorcan had the sword locked away. That only left one, the most powerful of them all.

"Time to go after the stone."

Acknowledgments

Here we are, folks. Hard to believe that we have come to the conclusion of the second Oak & Holly Cycle book. I've had this in my head for so many years. Sometimes it felt like it was never going to happen. It was, in fact, one of the most difficult books I've ever written. There were so many threads that I had to hold onto like I had a murder board tacked up on a wall, only that wall was my brain. But as usual, the middle books of a series are always *always* my favorite. I get to blow everything up and see where it all lands. So I'm sorry, but I'm not sorry, because it was really fun, even in the pain. (Especially in the pain?) And there's another book coming to round this whole thing out.

I would be remiss to not thank all of the incredible people who helped me along the way on this incredible journey. I had no idea where *The Wren in the Holly Library* would take me, but it has brought me to you. To so many of *you!* Dear reader, you are the reason that I get to keep writing these fantastical worlds and I hope to never stop. Thank you, thank you, thank you. You make my dreams reality.

This book wouldn't be here without my great agent, Kimberly Brower. She believed in this world before almost anyone, and she has been at my side through it all. Thanks to my assistant, Devin, who keeps me sane day to day. My early readers—Becky, Rebecca, Anjee, and Polly. Y'all have been with me through thick and thin. I can't thank you enough. My friends Staci Hart and Diana Peterfreund—my ride or die girls. I legitimately wouldn't be here today without your help, forever friendship, and shoulders to lean on. I love you both!

To the team at Red Tower. Thank you for championing this book, giving it the most incredible package and marketing and finding a beautiful home for it with so many readers. Also the team at Tor UK as well as all the foreign publishers around the world who translated the books. Stephanie Németh-Parker and the team at Recorded Books for the incredible audio.

To Rebecca Yarros—I'm so thankful that we get to do this wild job together. I had the best time on the *Onyx Storm* tour and getting to run through my revisions with you, Rachel, Cassie, Ashley, and Kate. To Nana

Malone—who helped shape Imani, moderated the *Wren* tour, and told me to suck it up. I needed that reminder. To Tracy Wolff and Abigail Owen—who came on the *Wren* tour with me! To Mai Corland—who commiserated during edits. We need to meet up in NYC again soon.

To those who helped me in portions of the books that I was less familiar with. I tried to have a diverse cast that exemplified what New York is really like and I wanted to do it right. These were the people that helped me with that. If it was done wrong in any way, the fault falls to me. I can just promise to continue to learn and do my best. Meera and Kiran, who helped me plan Maura and Nate's wedding. Sarah Kates, who let me steal her last name and sensitivity read for the goblin market. Andrew Lazarus, who let me steal *both* of his names for Laz, including his Plaza secret identity. And his bestie, Schwartz, who I cannot thank enough for inspiring our little team. Fabiola, who moved back to Peru in the writing of this book and who inspired Dr. Carrión.

To my friends at Aerial Atmosphere—thank you for giving me the outlet I needed to continue to feel creative. I can't thank all of you enough for giving me a home—Belem, Bizzy, Tori, Kathryn, Megan, Michelle, Eryn, Vy, and the rest of the fam. Also Megan Allen, who I've been writing books with since we were both fourteen. I know you wanted more with Lorcan. I can only imagine the fanfic in your head right now.

To my family, who are such big supporters of my career. I love you Brittany, Shea, Mom and Dad!

To my puppy, Hippo, who passed away in the editing of this book. I love you with all of my heart and miss you every single day.

Finally, my husband Joel who is the best partner and father that I could have ever asked for me. And my son who brings me so much joy every day. This one and every one is for you two.

BEING THE SPARROW ISN'T AN HONOR.
IT'S A TRAP.

Long ago, the gods unleashed monsters upon the five kingdoms of Calandra to remind us that humans are insignificant—that we must pray to the gods for mercy throughout our fragile, fleeting lives.

I didn't need a deity to remind me I was powerless. Being a princess had never been more than a performance—twenty-three years of empty titles and hollow traditions. My sister revels in the spectacle, basking in the attention and flawlessly playing her part. I was never asked to be part of the charade.

Until the day an infamous monster hunter sailed to our shores. The day a prince walked into my father's throne room and ruined my life. The day I married a stranger, signed a magical treaty in blood, and set off across the continent to the most treacherous kingdom in all the realm.

That was the day I learned that not all myths are make-believe. That lies and legends are often the same. And that the only way to kill the monsters we fear was to *become* one…

CONNECT WITH US ONLINE

◉ @redtowerbooks

⬤ @RedTowerBooks

♪ @redtowerbooks

♥   ♥

Join the Entangled Insiders for early access
to ARCs, exclusive content, and insider news!
Scan the QR code to become part of the
ultimate reader community.

RED TOWER
BOOKS™